"I THINK YOU *DO* WANT IT . . ."

"I don't," she lied, but he wasn't listening. He was leaning closer, reminding her that she was still half naked. She could almost feel the rough texture of his jacket on her breasts, as if their bodies were touching again.

"Then put up your hand . . . That's all you have to do. I'm right here, just inches away . . . All you have to do is put your hand in front of my mouth, firmly, and push me back . . . and I'll go."

But I can't, she thought . . . and, oh, he knew it! His mouth was so near, Rachel could feel the heat of his breath on her lips. So tempting, so compelling. She could no more refuse him this one sweet kiss than she could stop the life-giving air that rushed into her lungs.

It was destiny that had brought them to that spot at that moment . . . A cruel, capricious destiny, but one that could not be denied.

JADE DAWN

by

SUSANNAH LEIGH

A TOPAZ BOOK

TOPAZ
Published by the Penguin Group
Penguin Books USA Inc., 375 Hudson Street,
New York, New York 10014, U.S.A.
Penguin Books Ltd, 27 Wrights Lane,
London W8 5TZ, England
Penguin Books Australia Ltd, Ringwood.
Victoria, Australia
Penguin Books Canada Ltd, 10 Alcorn Avenue,
Toronto, Ontario, Canada M4V 3B2
Penguin Books (N.Z.) Ltd, 182-190 Wairau Road,
Auckland 10, New Zealand

Penguin Books Ltd, Registered Offices:
Harmondsworth, MIddlesex, England

First published by Topaz, an imprint of Dutton Signet,
a division of Penguin Books USA Inc.

First Printing, November, 1993
  10 9 8 7 6 5 4 3 2 1

Topaz is a trademark of Dutton Signet,
a division of Penguin Books USA Inc.

Printed in the United State of America

AUTUMN BREEZES

Macao, October 1840

One

Ordinarily Matthew Barron liked a touch of tartness in a woman, but for this one he decided he might make an exception.

October sunlight splashed across the garden, bringing an almost springlike warmth to the autumn afternoon, and recent rains brought out a rich aroma of soil and vegetation. The foreign enclave in the small Portuguese colony of Macao, which clung to the southern coast of China, was accustomed to huddling together for companionship and security, and the fête being thrown that day by one of the larger British trading houses was no exception.

Everyone seemed to be there, garbed in the latest fashion, or what passed as the latest fashion, for it took at least two seasons for gossip and style books to make their way across the desert to the British mail at Suez, or around the Cape on sailing ships. Brilliant tropical flowers and lush green hedges were overshadowed by the scarlet and lapis and amaranth purple of the ladies' gowns, the only slightly more subdued plums and sea-pines that accented the gentlemen's tightly corseted waists and long, tapering trousers.

But even in all that bustle and color, *she* stood out, the young woman who lingered briefly alone at the end of one of the curving paths.

Perhaps, Matthew thought, running his hand unconsciously over a small, neatly trimmed beard, it was because she was dressed in white. A simple, not at all modish gown that gave her an almost childlike air of innocence and grace. Soft India muslin fell, uncorseted, as near as he could see, in flowing folds just to her instep, the only adornment, if indeed it could be called such, a lace fichu tucked into what would otherwise have been a quite intriguingly low neck.

Or perhaps it was the fact that her hair was the most stunning color he had ever seen, somewhere between red and lustrous, glowing blond. She had left it loose— no regard for fashion again—and it barely brushed her shoulders, a dramatic contrast to deep brown eyes that glanced his way just briefly, teasing Matthew with a sudden, unexpected hint of something that did not quite go with the angelic effect she created.

It startled him to realize she was not beautiful. Her face was strikingly heartshaped, the brow too wide, the cheekbones too pronounced, the little pointed chin too piquant for the trends of the time. Those large dark eyes seemed almost to belong to someone else, not at all matched to the smallish mouth with its full, surprisingly sensual lower lip.

Then she turned and called out to someone across the way and smiled, and Matthew wondered how he could ever have thought, even for a second, that she was not beautiful. Her whole face lit up, her mouth turning suddenly wide and generous. Soft, velvety eyes seemed to glow from within, dazzling and unutterably tantalizing.

"I think I'm in love," he said.

A masculine chuckle sounded in his ear. Hoarse and somewhat guttural, but not without a certain infectious charm. Even before the words came, Matthew could already hear a thick Irish brogue.

"What, again, me bucko? That'll be makin' three times since the voyage began. An' what happened, pray, to the fair Rosaline? You were keenin' your heart over her somethin' fierce."

"Four times," Matthew replied good-naturedly. He had picked Christy Gallagher up when the greatest of the Barron clippers, the *China Dawn,* had put in for repairs south of Calcutta on the long voyage from Boston to the China coast. There had already been one intense, if somewhat unsatisfying, dalliance by that time. Matthew Barron was a man who enjoyed women, and he enjoyed falling in love, albeit the resulting flirtations were notorious for not lasting very long. "That playful little chit who booked passage from Bombay was actually the second, the colonel's daughter in Calcutta the third—though she was more like a whim."

"And this one isn't?"

Matthew glanced back at the woman, standing alone again at the end of the path. Sunlight shimmered off her hair and the stark whiteness of her gown. "No," he said quietly. "I don't think she is. . . . And the lovely lady in Singapore, by the way, was Rosamond, not Rosaline. You have it all mixed up with Shakespeare. Wasn't that the silly wench poor lovesick Romeo was sighing over when he saw Juliet?"

"Shakespeare, is it now? And Romeo? Well, and why not? A fine pretty idea that is." Christy Gallagher was a broad, bluff Irishman, half a head shorter than Matthew, with a mop of curly black hair and a red, rather smashed-in face, punctuated by a good-humored grin. He had in fact some dim recollection of having heard of this fellow Shakespeare, though the names Romeo and Juliet meant nothing to him. But sensing that the allusion was associated with culture and intelligence, he saw no reason for not taking it on. "Yes, Romeo," he agreed again. "A lovesick pup, as you say. A most excellent description."

He left it deliberately ambiguous as to whom he was referring—the aforementioned Romeo or the young man beside him. Matthew, quick to catch on, laughed easily.

"And an apt one, in this case. Not only am I in love, I'm head over heels. Or, since we're referring to pups, should it be 'ears over paws'? I swear, I'm quite light-headed—and I haven't even found one of those servers circulating round with trays of hock and ale for the gentlemen."

"Well, find one, then—and quick, before you've totally lost your head. Though I must say," he added, shifting his gaze to the sunlit patch at the far end of the path. "that's a lass worth the risk of a man's head. By God and the seven saints, she's a nice one, isn't she? Have you noticed, bucko, there's not a ribbon or ruffle or glitter of a jewel about her? If you wasn't the captain o' the ship—and me a mere humble partner in one o' your lowlier ventures—I'd have a fine fair try at whiskin' her off meself.''

"You haven't a humble bone in your body, Gallagher,'' Matthew said, amused, as he glanced down at the dark head beside him. Even from the top, the little Irishman looked cocky. "And the venture is hardly lowly . . . or your part in it. We both stand to make a fortune. Shall I be a sport? A small wager— winner to approach the lady first? The toss of a coin, perhaps?''

"Your famous two-headed coin, I wonder?''' Gallagher darted him a waggish look. "Or is it two-tailed?''

"Actually, both.'' Matthew grinned. "And you're right. That's just the coin I had in mind.'' It was, in point of fact, not a coin at all, but a Chinese gaming piece, or rather two gaming pieces, carved out of wood and cleverly fitted together to appear as one. A dragon seemed to curl around it, head on one side, long twisting tail on the other—but split apart, it became apparent that each piece had the same image on both sides. Matthew had picked it up in a fan-tan parlor on his first trip to the East, three years earlier, and had come out the victor in quite a few flips of the coin since then, though to his credit, he never kept any of the spoils. Matthew Barron liked to win, but he liked to win fairly.

"Is it a coward you are, Captain Barron?''

"Ah . . . I prefer to think of myself as a prudent man. Not that I fear competition, of course . . . but you do have a way with women, God knows why. A less prepossessing face I've rarely seen, and set on a body that looks more like a barrel than a man! It must be your green eyes . . . or that glib Irish tongue. At any rate, I don't think I'm going to take any chances.''

"A different wager, then?'' The green eyes were bright with irrepressible laughter. "Fifty Yankee dollars, say, against double that amount when I get my share of our little venture?''

"Wagering what?''

"That the lady will send you on your way in less than five minutes, an' nothin' to show for all your fine foolish troubles.''

Matthew laughed. "Five minutes or five hours. The lady is too sweet and pretty to dismiss a man so rudely. And I am not a man to be dismissed. . . . Don't bother to write out a note, Gallagher. I'll take your handshake on it when I get back.''

Without waiting for a reply, he started across the garden, pausing only as a Chinese waiter passed with a tray of champagne and cups of fruit punch for the more discriminating ladies. Matthew hesitated an instant, then picked up a pair of crystal stem glasses, one in each hand. Experience had taught him that this was a time for boldness, not caution.

The girl had moved a few feet away and was standing by the low gray wall that separated the garden from a long, sloping hillside. Below, mighty tea clippers, anchored just beyond the busy harbor with its junks and sampans and European lighters ferrying officers and their families back and forth, looked like toy boats bobbing on a gently rolling sea.

"A lovely lady shouldn't be standing by herself,'' he said. "It seems a crime against nature. I hope you will not consider it too impertinent if I offer a glass of champagne. I am Captain Barron, Matt Barron—the youngest of the Barron men, though I trust you won't hold that against me.''

Her eyes seemed even deeper as she turned and took him in for a moment before speaking. She was taller than Matthew had realized, almost as tall as he, and he stood just under six feet.

"Perhaps the lady is alone because she chooses to be, Captain Barron,'' Her voice was low and cool, as velvety as her eyes and unexpectedly sensuous.

"And perhaps the intrusion is an unwelcome one?'' Matthew was aware suddenly of Gallagher's laughing green eyes, fixed on him with greedy anticipation, and he cursed himself for even thinking about it. The wager be damned! He wasn't here to win a stupid bet. He was here because this woman had drawn him with a force he felt even more intensely now that he was standing next to her and could smell the flowery fragrance of her hair.

"Perhaps," she agreed.

"And the champagne as well? You're going to leave me standing here, both hands filled, with a foolish look on my face?"

She smiled a slow, lingering smile that had absolutely nothing of the enchanting warmth he had sensed a few moments back.

"Why, no . . . as a matter of fact, I was just wishing for something of the sort. Though I would have preferred the punch. Such a rich red color. But never mind . . ." She accepted the glass, holding it up but not touching it to her lips. "The champagne will do nicely. How convenient of you to provide it for me."

"Convenient?" Matthew felt suddenly, inexplicably wary, though he couldn't for the life of him have said why. She was even lovelier than she had seemed from a distance, soft and exceptionally sweet and feminine, and yet . . . "That seems an odd way to put it."

"Not really." She turned the glass around in her hands, glancing down at it, then up again. "How is your vocabulary, Captain Barron? Have you a good command of language?"

"I have a good education, if that's what you mean," he replied, puzzled. "At least, I have a very expensive education. I expect I have as many words at my disposal as any other man."

"How about the word 'bastard'? Do you have that one at your disposal?"

Matthew felt himself stiffen. Too late, he sensed he had walked into a trap, though he had no idea what it was or why she had set it. "I have a certain familiarity with the word," he confessed. "In both its meanings."

"Good." A momentary flash of something in her eyes reminded him of the look he had caught in them before. "Then you will understand which meaning I intend when I say—you are a bastard, Captain Barron!" She raised the glass, flipping the bubbly liquid neatly in his face, then set it on the wall and turned and walked away.

Matthew was too stunned for an instant to do anything but stare after her as she swept across the garden, not so much as glancing back. Then suddenly, the cold champagne still dripping down his face onto his shirt and immaculate white satin waistcoat—thank God it *wasn't* the punch!—he threw back his head and laughed.

It seemed there was a touch of tartness in the lady after all. More than a touch! She might look sweet as sugar candy, all innocence and melting softness, but there was as sharp a tongue there as it had ever been his pleasure to spar with. A quite dazzling flash of fire that far from dampening his enthusiasm took his breath away.

He had no idea why she had called him what she had, much less why she had thrown the drink in his face, nor did he at that moment truly care. He knew only that she was not as docile and predictable as she looked.

And volatile, tempestuous, unpredictable women had always been like the flame to the moth for the youngest of the Barron men.

"What a vixen!" he said as he returned to where Gallagher was waiting, a broad Irish hand outstretched for his winnings. "Did you see what she did? One quick toss—and straight in my face! Not so much as a drop missed the mark."

"And you admirin' her aim." Gallagher shook his head with mock bewilderment. "Where, pray, is that sweet and pretty manner that would ne'er let her treat a man so rudely?"

Something in his tone made Matthew take a better look at him. Smug, yes—that was to be expected—but not at all surprised.

"You set me up."

Gallagher laughed, delighted as a boy as he curled

his fist around the wad of cash that had just been placed in it. "You didn't think I'd risk double fifty on a bet I was as like to lose as win? You might have asked, boy, if I knew who she was. You might indeed. . . . Very careless, but you was after gaping so hard, all the thoughts must 'ave flown out through your eyes."

Matthew watched him, more intrigued than annoyed. He *hadn't* been thinking of anything else since the second he laid eyes on her. "All right, Gallagher, I admit I was remiss, but I'm not remiss now. Who is she?"

"That, me bucko, is Miss Rachel Todd. I just happened to find meself on the other side o' the garden a few minutes past, an' just happenin' to notice the lady, I made a point of askin' a few discreet questions. Her father is the Reverend Gideon Todd, who runs the American Protestant Mission outside the China Gate." His lips puckered on the word "Protestant," as if he found it painful to utter. "It's a medical mission. Very moralistic, mind, but concerned as much with the bodies as the souls of the heathen Chinee."

Matthew was beginning to get the picture. "And?"

"And if there's one thing the lady hates more than an old sinner the likes o' me, it's an opium runner like you." He tucked the cash in his pocket, feeling no such fine qualms as Matthew about winning a wager with a trick. "Especially one from a fine old firm like Barron Shipping that has never filthied its hands with the foul stuff before. It seems her contempt runs too deep for words."

"Oh, she expressed herself verbally, too," Matthew replied dryly. A speculative look came over his face as he stared in the direction she had gone, trying but failing to pick her out from the crowd. "I suppose this means it's common knowledge that the *China Dawn* sailed out of India with a load of opium in her hold. No one has come right out and asked, of course—they wouldn't say anything without at least a hint from me—but they've been speculating. And they must be pretty sure, or even the fiery Miss Todd would have given me the benefit of the doubt."

"They knew in Calcutta when the first chest was lowered down from the deck," Gallagher said gruffly. "The news went off with the first ship t' be leavin' the port. An' with a relish, no doubt, especially on the part o' the British. Yankees have long been prudes about the trade—even Russell an' Company are gettin' out, or so they've been tellin'. The *China* may be the pride o' the Barron line, the fastest ever t' ply the Eastern route, but we did linger a while in Singapore . . . as you will recall."

"And let the gossip get ahead of us."

"Not gossip, boy. Gossip is lies an' half truths, nasty whispered things, an' this is all true. There *is* opium in the hold of the ship, a full load, an' we'd be after sellin' it this very minute, openly in Canton, if war had not broken out, all sudden like—and most untimely—between the British and the Chinese." Gallagher threw a sidelong glance at the younger man without appearing to do so. He had known from the moment they weighed anchor in Calcutta that this would be the dangerous time. It had been easy enough to persuade an impetuous youth to lay in a valuable, if somewhat controversial, cargo—to dazzle him with visions of the heady fortune just waiting to be grabbed. Easy enough to convince him that the old patriarch, whose own fortune, after all, was founded on piracy, would be impressed with his grandson's initiative . . . so long as no one was around to provide reminders of the Barron pride and the Barron name. And the fierce cohesiveness of the Barron clan.

"True, indeed," Matthew agreed, somewhat more wanly than Gallagher would have liked. "Not gossip then, but news. Which, unfortunately, seems to have come—and moved on—even before we arrived. I wonder how long it will take to reach Boston. Or is it there already, and retribution skimming over the waves for me?"

Gallagher took encouragement in the grim humor that had crept into the younger man's voice. "Will he be after comin' for you himself, do you think? The famous old grandfather with the wild white hair and beard? By the saints, for all that it spells trouble, I wouldn't mind havin' a peep at him.''

"I almost wish he would.'' Matthew shook his head. "He'd be furious, of course, that I dared risk the Barron 'reputation,' what with public opinion turning against the trade—but I've always been able to wheedle him into seeing things my way. Even strong-willed old tyrants have soft spots sometimes for the youngest of their grandsons. No, he'll send my older brother, Jared—who makes pretty Rachel Todd look like a sweetheart when it comes to moral standards—and maybe my cousin. And God help me if I haven't managed to convert the opium to cash by then, and shown myself more than a match for any Barron who ever set out to prove himself at sea!''

Gallagher chuckled, easier now than he had felt since they set foot in Macao. Whatever the moment, it had gone, and the boy's jaunty resolve was as firm as ever.

"It's a lucky thing then, the lady *didn't* fancy you, what with that way your thoughts have o' turnin' to mush when fine soft eyes so much as look on you. It's hard pressed enough we'll be to find a way round the stoppage of trade at Canton without worryin' our heads over that. Best to let her go.''

"That's what you think? That I'm letting her go?'' An unexpected brightness showed on the younger man's face as he turned and looked Gallagher straight in the eye. "There was a time limit on the bet, and I lost it. Not exactly fair and square, but I acknowledge I lost. But I'm not planning on losing the lady.''

"Ah, it's a bold one your are.'' A hint of admiration crept into the heavy Irish brogue. "I give you credit for heart, boy . . . though not for brains. There isn't so much as a slim chance in hell you'll get even one sweet word from that one.''

"No? Would you care to put a small wager on it? The same amount as before . . . ? No, I thought not.'' Matthew laughed. "You're a man with a taste for a sure bet, Christy Gallagher. And if there's anything sure about this, it's that I'm going to have another try at that fiery-headed little tiger who just dug her pretty claws into me. Miss Rachel Todd has not seen the last of Captain Matthew Barron.''

Two

The air was cooler at the far end of the garden, almost chilly as the afternoon latened and shadows began to spread, but Rachel Todd felt only the warmth that seemed to be rising from her breast and flooding into her cheeks. Finding a secluded spot, she sat on the wall and stared down at the harbor. The view had changed subtly. Fishermen were beginning to return from their day's work, and the sea was glassy smooth, bathed in the golden luster of a slowly lowering sun.

What on earth had prompted her to behave like that? The sound of laughter echoed disconcertingly in Rachel's ears as she relived those horrible, long seconds, gliding across the garden and trying desperately to cling to her composure. Not mocking, scornful laughter, brittle with anger and wounded pride—but light and genuinely amused! It was the one thing she had not expected, humor in this man she had been prepared to look on as a monster, and it had thrown her badly.

She half turned away from the ocean. The noises of the party were beginning to fade as people drifted off in twos, threes, and fours for dinner parties and quiet evenings at home. Whatever had she been thinking, taking on a man like that and in such a public manner? Her father would be mortified when he heard, her older brothers wild with teasing that would not end for weeks—water and, no doubt, cold tea would be tossed in her face with great roars of laughter every time she turned around! And her poor gentle mother would feel obligated to sit her down for a painful little talk about what a lady did—and did not—do if she expected people to continue considering her a lady.

No, Rachel thought uncomfortably, it was not the *one* thing she had not expected—that unsettling strain of humor in the man. Even more unexpected was the fact that she found him quite uncommonly attractive.

Her mind drifted back to the way he had looked when she saw him across the garden. A tallish man with a fashionable beard, lean and elegantly modish in a dark green, superbly tailored coat and very expensive embroidered white waistcoat. Everything Rachel ordinarily despised—but on him the fashions did not look foolish or effete.

Arrogant, she had thought, not altogether with distaste, though that was what she had tried to feel. Arrogant and utterly assured. There was not a doubt in her mind that his man knew exactly who he was, and what he was—and how the ladies would react to him.

And he had not been far wrong about her at that. Rachel grimaced unconsciously. She had pretended to look through him, but actually she had been thinking as he stood there, smiling, the glass extended all unknowing in his hand, how intriguingly his hair seemed to change colors, so fair it was almost white in the direct glare of the sun, turning golden as the shadows deepened and the light mellowed into late afternoon. And how dazzlingly, piercingly blue his eyes were.

It was not the brazenness of her recent behavior, or even the explanations she would have to give when she returned home, that deepened her blush now, and Rachel was honest enough to admit it. It was the way her body had responded, against all sense and reason, to the proximity of this man that every rational impulse warned her against. And was responding even now when he was nowhere near!

Half of her wanted to get up and run out of there as fast as her feet would carry her. The other half longed to linger a little, to see if he would seek her out . . . if he had an answer to the challenge she had thrown with the champagne into his face.

"You seem to have put your admirer in his place.

You really do amaze me sometimes, Rae. . . . I must say, he took it quite well, don't you think?''

Rachel looked up to see a pretty girl in a gold-and-lavender gown that would have looked hideous on anyone else. Her eyes were huge and violet, with long jet-black lashes and curls of the same color bobbed, short-cropped, over her head.

''He took it arrogantly . . . as one might expect. He's a disgustingly smug, puffed up, *hideous* man who doesn't even have the good sense to know when he's been insulted!''

''In other words, you find him devastatingly handsome . . . and there's a reason why you didn't *flounce* out to my carriage and *command* the coachman to carry you posthaste to the China Gate.''

''I find him nothing of the sort!'' Rachel retorted, a little too vehemently to be convincing. ''Oh, his features are pretty enough—but I never liked the sort of dandy who prances around in the latest style! You know that perfectly well, Cammie. We've argued about it often enough. And if I commandeered your carriage, how would you get home? Never mind—don't answer that. I'm sure you'd find a way.''

''And I'm sure *you're* changing the subject.'' Camilla Crale perched daintily on the edge of the wall, like a brightly colored bird flitting for a second before flying off again. She was a year and half younger than Rachel, who had just turned nineteen, but ages older when it came to worldliness and experience with men. ''It was bound to happen sooner or later, you know. You've always been *much* too serious about romance. Not like me. I can take a man or leave him—mostly both—but *you* . . . Well, I always said when you fell, you'd fall hard. And fast.''

''I haven't fallen . . .'' Rachel started to protest, then caught herself with a little laugh. Honesty was a failing sometimes as well as a virtue, it seemed to her. And she could never stop being brutally honest about herself. ''Oh, all right . . . I admit I find him attractive. There, does that make you happy? He's a very attractive man. But I haven't 'fallen' for him. And I never will. Not a man like that!"

"Haven't you? My dear, dear innocent." Camilla's smile turned unpleasantly feline and she seemed to hesitate, then her face relaxed. She had a cat's instincts. Her scratches could be sharp and cruel, but rarely for the one member of her own sex she had ever called her friend. "Well . . . be that as it may. I didn't come to discuss the merits of the youngest Captain Barron. I came with a message from poor dullwitted Steven Wu. You know, the one who clerks for those sanctimonious Bible-spouters at Zion's Corner."

Rachel smiled in spite of herself. "Zion's Corner" was Olyphant & Company, which had never handled opium—and whose directors never tired of saying so in tones that had a way of rankling. And Steven Wu was poor and dullwitted because he was one of the few young men in the colony who had been able to resist Camilla's determined advances.

"What on earth does Steven want with me?" she asked.

"Something about a donation," Camilla replied, bored now that the conversation had drifted into less stimulating channels. "Some newcomer in our midst, probably associated with the Corner since he picked Steven as his errand boy. I gather he's interested in the mission. Your work with the poor . . . helping to fight the scourge of opium, and all that. . . . It probably means a fat five dollars in your reticule!"

"Or ten, if I'm lucky." Rachel groaned. With the five or ten dollars would come a long-winded sermon to which she would be expected to listen with wide eyes and nod admiringly in the appropriate places. She was tempted for an instant to have Camilla tell Steven Wu she had already gone. But even five or ten dollars would buy sorely needed medical supplies. "Where is he, my unknown philanthropist? In the house?"

"In the library, Steven said. On the second floor, at the rear. Nice and private . . . just the place for a romantic rendezvous. It's a pity Captain Barron doesn't seem the philanthropic sort."

A pity indeed! Rachel could feel the heat rising to her cheeks again as she headed for the entrance, and she hated herself for it. There had been more than a hint of insinuation in Camilla's tone when she had spoken of the seclusion of the library, and like it or not, the image caught Rachel's fancy and was flying away with it. She couldn't help wondering what it would feel like, had things been different, to be going to that same private place for a secret meeting with the man her heart longed to know even as her brain and soul fiercely rejected him. Ridiculous, but her pulse was racing wildly, and she was actually out of breath!

I should have worn a bonnet, she thought rebelliously. She had actually had one on when the Carpenter carriage, belonging to her friend's uncle and guardian, had called for her at the China Gate. But Camilla, who never wore hats because she thought they shaded her spectacular eyes—which, in fact, they did—had convinced her to leave it behind.

She would have behaved much more sedately if she'd been wearing a bonnet! Something in the very nature of the object seemed to bring with it a demeanor of propriety. Women in bonnets didn't throw drinks in men's faces!

The upstairs hall was dark when she reached it, and almost eerily silent, the thick walls and heavy-glazed windows muting the last sounds of the party. The room was every bit as isolated as Camilla had described it. Empty, or so it appeared, and Rachel was aware of a childish twinge of disappointment, as if she had really come to meet a lover and not the pompous bore she ought to be relieved to avoid.

She had just stepped over to the window and was wondering how long she ought to wait when she heard a slight sound in the shadows behind her. Whirling, startled, she saw a slim, immaculately garbed man locking the door!

A rakish grin twisted the corners of his mouth as he slipped the key in his pocket and turned to face her.

''Hello, tiger,'' he said quietly.

Matthew Barron! Rachel's heart leaped into her

throat, and she knew suddenly that she ought to be frightened. Here she was, alone in a room with a man of questionable character, a man she had just done her best to insult—and the only exit was locked! But she couldn't repress a perverse, utterly illogical surge of elation that he had sought out and found her.

So he did have an answer to the challenge she had thrown in his face.

"Is this your idea of manners, Captain Barron?" she said, keeping her voice as cool as she could manage. "Turning the key in the lock to assure a lady that she has your full, undivided attention? Or am I to consider myself your prisoner?"

"If you wish. I would like it very much if you were to consider yourself my . . . prisoner." He let his lips play around the word, making it deliberately impudent but somehow not insulting. "I had in mind, however, something more like a chat."

"Do you always lock the door when you want to 'chat' with someone?"

"I didn't know what to expect from you. It seemed a sensible precaution. When a lady hurls her wine in a man's face—and calls him a most unladylike name— I think he has a right to ask why she went to such extremes. . . . Not an unreasonable question. I wanted to make sure it was answered."

As would anyone, Rachel had to admit. There it was again, that unwelcome prick of honesty, forcing her to see things from his point to view. She *had* doused him, quite liberally with the bubbly, even if he did deserve it.

"So you lured me here under false pretenses." She held her head high, secretly pleased that she could look him nearly straight in the eye, and hoping it disconcerted him. "You promised a donation . . . which you never intended to give. I think that makes us even."

"Not false at all." Reaching into an inside coat pocket, Matthew pulled out a sheet of white paper, which he unfolded and waved in front of her. "A draft on Barron Shipping, payable to Miss Rachel Todd.

How would a hundred dollars strike you? Any of the clerks will honor it if you call at our office.''

Rachel paled but did not back down. A hundred dollars was an exceptionally generous donation, far more than they usually received. ''I see you fancy yourself a man of honor,'' she said tartly.

''*Fancy*? Cruel, heartless creature, you cut to the core . . . or at least you're trying your damnedest! Pardon me—your darnedest. But, yes, I do have fancies, at least of a minimal honor. And—'' he held the draft up tantalizingly, then refolded it and slipped it back in his pocket. ''—the donation is yours, to do with as you choose. As soon as you answer my question. Or had you forgotten it?''

''I haven't forgotten, Captain Barron. What do you think, that women are poor flighty creatures who can't keep an idea in their heads twelve seconds at a time? I would have thought the answer was obvious. I acted as I did, and labeled you as I did—and accurately, I might add—because you are what I abhor most in the world. A leech who make obscene profits distributing opium to wretches so enslaved they would sell their children to get it!''

If he was the least bit nonplussed, it did not show. He raised one brow, just slightly, and most unfortunately, since it made him even more appealing.

''Don't you think that's a bit hypocritical?''

''*Hypocritical?*'' Rachel gaped at him. Of all the retorts she had expected, this was not among them. ''I am a nurse who sees the evil effects of opium every day of my life. I work in the mission hospital. I tend the poor emaciated victims when their bodies are so wasted their families have to carry them in on litters. I hold them in my arms when they die! How is that hypocritical?''

''You are also a very lovely young woman who enjoys a good party—even if it's given by one of the major traffickers in that drug she professes to abhor! You eat the canapés those 'obscene profits' have provided, you drink the champagne—''

''And accept donations when drafts are offered,

neatly folded in two? It's a necessity in our business. My father had taught me to be practical. Though I didn't actually *drink* the champagne," she reminded him, with a wry half smile that surprised her. "But you're right. It *is* hypocritical in a way to come here— only it's hard sometimes, being young and not having any fun. And everything is tainted in a colony that was built on opium."

A slight quaver came into her voice, embarrassing her horribly. Matthew reached out and touched her, very lightly, on the wrist, sending a shiver through her which embarrassed her even more. Especially since she knew he had to have felt it, too.

"I'm sorry, Rachel . . . Miss Todd. It was never my intention to hurt you. I just thought it a trifle unfair that you singled me out from all the others."

Reasonable again, Rachel thought uncomfortably. that was the trouble with the man. He had a way of turning reasonable at the most inconvenient times.

"It's just that the others . . . well, they've always dealt in opium," she said falteringly. "Especially the English. It was their idea in the first place—to tilt the balance of trade in their favor! I don't admire them for it, but I . . . I'm used to it. The house of Barron was always clean! I never met your brother, Jared, but my father has, and he speaks of him with great respect. *He* never touched opium, or the other one, either— Alex—or even old Gareth Barron, for all that he seems a dreadful scoundrel. Then suddenly here *you* are, and everything is changed!"

"Barron Shipping is not a 'house,' " Matthew said, stiffening as usual when he found himself compared with his older sibling and coming out on the short end. Jared was always the strong one, the capable one, the one who never did *anything* wrong. What would she say, this young woman, if he told her a good part of the reason he'd gotten into the trade in the first place was to finally and definitively best his brother at something? "It's a company, and companies are in business to make money. But company policies *can* be changed . . . perhaps with a bit of gentle persuasion?"

He was amused to note that the line had no effect. She was much too smart to be taken in by vague hints of something in the distant future. And yet he could have sworn she had reacted when he touched her just now.

"Are you a gambling woman, Miss Todd?"

"I beg your pardon?" Rachel eyed him cautiously. The question was odd, the look on his face even odder. As if he had something up his sleeve.

"Oh, I didn't mean fan-tan parlors or anything squalid like that. I know you're a missionary's daughter. But you *were* raised among the Chinese, and they have a great passion for gambling. Could you be tempted, I wonder, by a small bet? Say, the flip of a coin?"

His hand had been in his pocket. Now he drew it out, and Rachel could see a small round piece of wood resting on his palm. Not quite a coin, but something very like it. The caution was growing now: a tangible, physical sensation. Every instinct warned her not to pursue the conversation, but curiosity got the best of her.

"And what would we be betting? On this flip of a coin . . . or whatever that is?"

"It's a gaming piece, actually." Matthew turned it over on his palm so she could see it better. A mythical dragon seemed to be coiled around it; fire-breathing head showing clearly on one side, long, triangular-tipped tail on the other. "Unique, isn't it? It came into my hands a few years ago—in Macao, as a matter of fact. I always use it for my wagers. Shall we make this really interesting? The amount of the draft I promised before? Double or nothing . . . no, that wouldn't be fair. You can hardly gamble with mission money. Double the amount for you, then—if you win."

"And if you win?"

A faint smile played around his lips. "If I win . . . a kiss from a lovely lady."

Rachel heard herself gasp. "You don't seriously think—"

"Of course I do. Why not? One small kiss, on your

terms. To last as long as you want . . . to end when you want . . . what could it hurt? And surely the mission could use another hundred dollars. Wouldn't it be terribly selfish of you to refuse the risk?''

And terribly foolish to take it, Rachel thought helplessly. Her lips were already burning, treacherously, imagining the force of his mouth on them. But she couldn't help thinking how much two hundred dollars would buy for the hospital. And how pleased her father would be to get it—so long as she left out one small detail as to how it had been acquired.

"You swear you'll pay off? On your honor?"

"On my . . . honor."

There was a faint tinge of irony in his tone, but Rachel did not catch it. After all, she told herself, it was only a fifty-fifty risk. She could as easily win as lose.

And, a wicked little voice in the back of her mind teased, even if the worst happened—even if she lost— she would only be forced to submit her mouth to the very tantalizing fervency of a hard male kiss. It wouldn't even be sinful, not really, since it was in a good cause.

"All right . . . but I get to pick."

"Naturally. Ladies' choice." Matthew had been holding the gaming piece in both hands, casually, as if waiting for her decision. Now he eased them apart, thinking as he did how lucky it was that he was naturally ambidextrous and could maneuver equally well with either hand. "Well . . . heads or tails?"

Rachel took a deep breath. "Heads," she called.

Matthew slipped his right hand into his pocket. Tucking the thumb of his left under the slender wooden circlet, he flipped it deftly in the air. It landed with an almost metallic clink on a table against the wall.

"Well, what do you know?" he said softly. "It seems to have come up . . . tails."

Rachel stared at it, stunned and horrified. Suddenly the world seemed to be whirling around, and she realized for the first time what she had gotten herself into. It had all seemed so different somehow, daring

but safe—just titillating enough to be slightly scandalous—when she still thought she had half a chance to
win.

Matthew saw her eyes dart toward the door. Raising
both arms, chest high, he held them out from his sides.

"The key is in my left trousers pocket. Take it if
you want. Or do you, too, perhaps have 'fancies' of
honor that force you to pay a debt . . . even though it
is obviously distasteful?"

Only it wasn't distasteful, Rachel thought with an
inner wail of despair. She did want to kiss him, desperately—shamelessly—and for that very reason, she
was tempted to snatch the key out of his pocket and
run. But he had challenged her pride . . . and she knew
she couldn't do it. She *had* lost the bet. She was going
to have to pay.

Then his hands were on the side of her face, very
gentle, not at all what she had expected, and she knew
that it didn't matter anymore. He was going to kiss
her, and she was going to let him. Even if there hadn't
been a bet, she would have let him.

Her eyes drifted shut, a mask to hide the naked hunger she was terrified he would see in their depths.

His mouth was as gentle as his hands, infinitely
tender, surprising Rachel as much with its softness as
the suppressed passion that seemed to vibrate all through
her even from that light touch. So sweet, she thought, so
infinitely sweet . . . and so compelling. Even without
thinking, her body arched closer, touching, as their
mouths touched, lightly, tantalizingly.

Rachel had played at love before, as much as a girl
with four older and very protective brothers could. She
had kissed—and liked it—but she had never kissed a
man quite like this. She had not known how intensely,
provocatively masculine if would feel.

Her mouth was opening—she was aware, but could
not stop it—a wanton invitation he was only too quick
to take her up on. As if sensing the deep, dormant
needs she could not even understand herself, he grew
bolder. His tongue was hard, demanding suddenly, as
he thrust it forward, daring her to suck it into her

mouth. His hands slipped to her breasts, cupping, fondling . . . the flimsy fichu was sliding away, and Rachel could feel his fingers on her naked flesh.

"Oh . . ." The sound seemed to be torn out of her throat, a cry of yearning and surrender. Her body was clinging now, pliant, holding to hard male contours.

Helplessly, Rachel realized, now that it was too late to do anything about it—too late to *want* to do anything—where her stubborn pride had taken her. What a fool she had been to think she could control the fierce, overwhelming passions he evoked in her. He could draw her to the floor if he wanted—he could take her right there on the patterned Chinese carpet—and the only sounds that would come out of her mouth would be moans of excruciating pleasure.

Then, just as she was sure she was lost—just as she could almost feel the man-force of him challenging and defeating her last frail defenses—he was drawing away, slowly, inexplicably. The fichu was at her neck again, and he was tucking it in—his fingers still provocative, every touch still seemed to sear into her skin—but somehow the assault was over, and Rachel could feel herself trembling violently as he took a step back and studied her in the waning light.

"What a surprise, Miss Todd."

Laughter brimmed out of his voice, shocking her back to reality. Rachel could have wept as she felt waves of shame rolling over her, like great storm-tossed combers crashing into the shore. He thought it was funny! He had held her in his arms, provoked the most intimate responses, made her show her feelings for him with devastating plainness, and he hadn't even *wanted* her! It was just a game with him, a little jest to prove his mastery. And once proven, he was content to drop her!

He had wanted to punish her for humiliating him publicly. And heaven help her, he had—with a vengeance!

"You took advantage of me," she accused.

"I did not," he replied reasonably. "I told you the kiss would be on your terms. As long as you wanted, to stop when you wanted. Although,'' he added with an infuriatingly wicked grin, ''I did get the feeling . . . perhaps . . . you might not have wanted to stop.''

Rachel turned away, confused and angry and hurt. She knew she was not being totally rational. She had started this duel—she could hardly whine and snivel when she lost it. And at least he had had the decency not to damage her with anything more than a kiss.

The coin was still lying where it had landed, on the table, and she picked it up, more to cover her confusion than anything else. Such an innocuous-looking thing, almost pretty—the twisting dragon tail rising in sharp definition out of the wood from which it had been carved. It seemed strange to think that it was only a few moments since she had first seen it. She felt as if she had aged years since then, and lost a good part of her innocence.

It was a second before she turned it over and saw exactly the same image on the back. Shame and embarrassment crystallized into one fiery flash of rage as she realized what had happened.

''You *bastard*!'' she said, with considerably more feeling than she had uttered the word before.

The grin widened, even more maddening now. ''And you thought I had a limited vocabulary. But never mind—I like a woman who knows how to express herself.''

''You *did* take advantage of me!''

''Tell me you didn't like it,'' he challenged. ''Tell me you didn't respond when I kissed you—and hope I'd kiss you more—and I will apologize.''

But she couldn't tell him that, Rachel thought furiously. And he knew it! He had felt her mouth open, felt her trembling uncontrollably in his arms. And he was perfectly capable of throwing it in her face if she tried to deny it!

''You never intended to pay off the bet!'' she lashed out. ''It wasn't even a real bet since you knew all the time you were going to win. You never intended to donate *anything*, did you? That's just a blank sheet of paper in your pocket!''

"Ah, there you're wrong." He drew the document out again and extended it toward her. "It was a trick, I admit, but I never intended to take advantage. The kiss would have been nothing more than a peck on the lips, if that was all you had wanted. And before you judge me too harshly, you might have a look at that."

Rachel glanced down, almost automatically, certain that nothing on the paper could possibly mollify her. Then her eyes focused on a five, followed by a pair of zeroes, and the same number written out in script.

"Five hundred dollars?" In spite of herself, she was impressed. And more than a little alarmed at her own reaction. Even after everything he had done, she wanted to like and trust this man.

"You have to admit I'm a sport," he said lightly, then added in slightly more serious tones, "I knew in the garden there was a spark between us . . . and I was right. You *had* to take the bet—you could never have resisted—but I always intended you to win. Dare I hope you enjoyed the deception? Just a little? And perhaps might consider a repeat performance?"

He was laughing again, but differently now, or at least Rachel perceived it as different, and she struggled desperately to resist the emotions that threatened to catch her up. She couldn't let herself fall under his spell again. She couldn't! Not now that she knew where it led.

"I suppose you think this makes everything all right. This—this *cash* payment for my kiss! I suppose you think I'm going to fall into your arms again, and swoon with pleasure . . . and heaven knows what else you have in mind."

Matthew refrained from reminding her that if "heaven knows what else" **was** indeed what he'd had in mind, they wouldn't be *discussing* it at the moment. "I'm not planning on carrying you off to my bed, if that's what you're thinking. No, that's not exactly true. I have every intention of bedding you—and I will—but that's not what I meant."

Rachel was watching him warily, not sure if he was

playing a joke again, not even sure if she wanted him to.

"What *do* you mean?"

"I mean," Matthew said, as surprised as she at the words that came out of his mouth, but knowing they were true, "I'm going to marry you, Rachel Todd."

Three

"He wants to *marry* you?" Camilla Crale's violet eyes widened as she curled up sensuously on the silk-upholstered settee in her uncle's parlor and stared at her friend. 'He actually said that? In just those words?"

"Not exactly." Rachel grimaced wryly. "He said he was *going* to marry me, which isn't quite the same thing."

"No," the other girl agreed, appreciating—and enjoying—the difference. "He's very cocky, that one. Very sure of himself . . . and very, *very*, attractive." She laughed softly, a low throaty sound. "I think this time, sweet, innocent Rachel, you've met your match. A bawdy rogue with only bed on his mind might—mind you, I said just *might*—be resistible. *If* you summoned all your courage . . . and concentrated *fiercely* on your prayers! But a man with honorable intentions . . . ?"

"And a very dishonorable way of making his fortune," Rachel reminded her, deliberately changing the subject. Heaven help her, Camilla's insinuations were much too close for comfort. She *had* found Matthew Barron devastating attractive, and her reaction to him had been swift and frightening. Without so much as a murmur of protest, she had melted into his arms—had forgotten everything else, even honor and decency, under the sweet, sudden assault of that hard, masculine mouth. "I don't even want to *think* about a man like that!"

"But fortunes are *so* nice," Camilla protested. "Honorable or not. And a man with the Barron empire behind him can find so many lovely ways to make money. He *could* be persuaded to try something else, you know. Men are so foolish. A few words whispered in their ears at just the right moment have the most *amazing* effect.''

"So he said himself," Rachel replied. "Or insinuated. But don't you see, Cammie—I don't want a man who has to be persuaded to do the right thing! I want one who has some moral backbone to start with . . . and I don't think I'd trust that kind of promise anyway. Besides," she added, her body shivering at the mere thought of Matthew Barron, and not with the horror that should have been there, "I've no intention of getting close enough to shout, much less 'whisper in his ear.' I wouldn't dare. He has far more effect on me than I'll ever have on him. And more experience manipulating members of the opposite sex!"

Camilla raised a pair of daintily plucked eyebrows.

"Then as I see it, you have two choices. Unless, of course you think the dashing captain is going to respect that ban on closeness you're imposing. You can either marry him, as he suggests, or you can hop in his bed and have a rousing good time! Virginity is such a bore, anyhow."

"Cammie!" Rachel gasped.

Camilla giggled infectiously as she half walked, half pranced toward a low round table on which a tea service and several plates of sweets had been laid out. "*Cammie*!" she mimicked, her lips puckering around each well-chosen word. "You're such a shocking, *scandalous* creature! What outrageous things you say. But you *do* have a lot of fun! And I do sometimes . . . *secretly* . . . envy you."

Rachel tried not to laugh, but it was hard when Camilla was in one of her impish moods. And, in a way, of course, she was right. Rachel *had* been shocked three years ago when Robert Carpenter's pretty niece had appeared in the colony—and the nature of her rather obvious "flirtations" became abundantly clear! But she had been intrigued, too, and it was from Camilla that Rachel had had her first explicit lessons about men. Many an otherwise dull afternoon had ben spent listening avidly, and quite shamelessly, to the engrossing details of went on—and how and why and in what order—behind closed bedroom doors.

And surprisingly, for all her utter lack of conventional morality, young Camilla Crale had proved a loyal friend.

"Very well," Rachel confessed. "I do envy you sometimes. But I wouldn't trade places with you. You know that. Any more than you'd trade places with me."

"Wouldn't I?" Camilla poured out a cup of tea and placed it on a translucent China saucer dotted with lavender rosebuds. "Not even lukewarm, I'm afraid. Uncle Robert is out on some *tedious* business again— Lippincott and Co. is wasting no time taking advantage of the ban on British trade—and everything seems to fall apart when he's not here. Why is it there's never a servant around when you want one, but the place is absolutely *crawling* with them the instant you crave a little privacy?"

"Lippincott and all the Americans," Rachel added. Little else had been discussed in the colony for months since the Chinese, in a desperate effort to halt the flow of opium, had raided foreign warehouses in Canton and outlawed the British from trade until they came to terms. It was a futile gesture—it would only drag them into a war they couldn't win—but the reverend's daughter, with her passionate hatred of drugs, couldn't help admiring their gallant spirit. "For once, it's more profitable *not* dealing in opium. The English are paying ruinous rates to neutral Americans to ferry their teas and silks and spices thirty miles down the Pearl."

"And making my uncle and the other directors of Lippincott very happy—which is fine with me." Camilla brought over the cup and held it out. "It's the first time in *months* he's been too busy to worry about trying to marry me off! Here . . . I daresay cold tea is better than nothing. I'd offer a glass of brandy, but I suppose you'd refuse."

The way she was feeling, Rachel thought she would have accepted almost anything. But her blood was already hot enough as it was—and her heart seemed to be hammering in her ears.

"Tea will do just fine, thank you. The colder the better."

"To cool your ardent yearnings? It isn't going to work, you know. Matthew Barron is a very exciting man. *Very* exciting. All the cold tea in the world isn't going to take your mind off him."

Something in her voice caught Rachel's ear, and she looked up from her drink. "I do believe you're attracted to him yourself, Cammie. That's why you keep going on and on about him!"

"But, of course," Camilla did not look the least bit embarrassed as she sank back into the cushions on the settee and tucked her feet up under her. "I have a great weakness for *both* the Barron brothers. Have you ever seen the other one—Jared? No? He's very tall, very strong . . . with the most *incredible* shoulders. I can just *imagine* what they look like without any clothes on."

"He's never let you see them?"

"He called me a piranha." Camilla's eyes widened, as if in surprise. "I had to ask one of the naval officers what it meant. It's a kind of *fish,* it seems, from South America, or someplace like that. It eats men alive. That's what he said I do . . . Jared. I *devour* the men who adore me. Well, he didn't say 'adore' exactly, but that's the idea."

"And don't you?" Rachel asked. "Devour men?"

"I wouldn't have devoured him." She was silent for a moment, strangely far away, a look coming into her delicate features that made Rachel feel unaccountably sad. "I think, in fact, *he* might have devoured *me* . . . So, you see, it was all for the best! Saved from the *awful* fate of lifelong devotion to *one* man!" She was laughing again, the moment gone, as if only an illusion. "Then this afternoon, absolutely out of nowhere, there *he* was—another Barron brother—and it occurred to me it might be interesting to try my luck again."

"But you didn't?"

"I didn't get the chance. I would have, though, if you hadn't seen him and gotten yourself all in a dither. And I would have *succeeded* this time. So you see what a sacrifice I'm making for friendship."

Sacrifice? Rachel felt her heart stop just for an instant. Camilla *would* have tried her luck with him if things had gone just a little differently that afternoon. And she would have succeeded, Rachel had no doubt of that.

And that would have been the end of it! There would have been no question of Captain Matthew Barron and Rachel Todd. Because it would have been Matthew and Camilla Crale.

"Why don't you try now?" she said impulsively. "If you really want to. I'd consider it a favor. I . . . mean . . .". She stopped, blushing furiously as she realized what she was saying. "I haven't any right, of course . . . What am I thinking? I . . . I can't ask you to—to . . ."

"To sleep with him?" Camilla looked amused. "Go ahead, you can say it. Lightning won't come streaking out of the heavens and strike you dead! And you don't have to *ask*—I'd be delighted to offer." She paused, the tip of her tongue running unconsciously over her lips. "I've been dying to get much, *much* closer to our young captain. . . . But why on earth would you want me to?"

Rachel felt suddenly sick. She could almost see that same pointed pink tongue flicking over various parts of Matthew Barron's body, and she hated herself for the wild, irrational jealousy that flooded over her. If he had been any other sort of man, she would have been ecstatic at what had happened between them that afternoon. But he wasn't! He was an opium trader. A man who dealt in drugs and death, and she had to do anything in her power to remove herself from temptation.

"Don't you see?" she blurted out. "That would solve everything! If he were involved with you, my closest friend—if he were having an affair with you—

I couldn't have anything to do with him. And he couldn't ask me to!''

"But he doesn't know you're my friend," Camilla reminded her.

"Oh . . . I'm sure, if we put our heads together, we can think of a way to enlighten him. Then it would be *over*, Cammie! Truly over. And even if I wanted to change my mind, I couldn't.''

She had grown so pale, the other girl was alarmed. Camilla's hand came down on hers, uncharacteristically gentle. Her eyes were sensitive and probing as she said, softly:

"Are you sure, Rachel? Very, very sure? You aren't going to be sorry about this?''

Rachel smiled wanly. "Are you sure *you* aren't going to be sorry?''

The mirth was back in Camilla's mouth, a distinctly feline expression.

"Oh, yes . . . I'm sure. I am not going to be sorry about *anything* tonight.''

Matthew Barron was no less shaken than Rachel by that afternoon's unexpected occurrences, if for somewhat different reasons. Though being a man, he was less willing to admit it to himself. Night had fallen swiftly, and darkness seemed to envelop the small front salon of the modest house the Barron men maintained for their use when they were in Macao. The glow of a pair of table lamps formed an island of warmth, beyond which shadows deepened and melted away. The only other light spilled through the open doorway from sconces in the hall.

Rachel Todd. Even the name had a romantic ring to it. He liked the way it sounded: simple but strong, flowing off the tongue.

Just for an instant he saw her again, as he had seen her first in the garden, sunlight shimmering on reddish-golden hair. Saw that unexpected flicker of brightness in her eyes as she smiled and raised her glass. Saw those same dark eyes turn soft and misty, with something halfway between wonder and fear, as he placed one hand, gently, on each side of her face.

Then she was in his arms again, in memory. Matthew could feel the quivering warmth of her, the sweet feminine acquiescence that called out to everything that was strong and male in him, and his body responded, as before, sharply and excruciatingly, reminding him of needs left unfulfilled.

Rachel Todd . . . or Rachel Barron?

His hand was shaking as he reached for a decanter and poured himself a good stiff dose of whiskey. There was an even more melodic sound to that particular combination of syllables. Incredible, that he should see a woman across a crowded, sun-splashed garden—that he should hold her once in his embrace, touch his mouth just once to hers—and suddenly life seemed insupportable if he couldn't share it with her.

Only that morning, he had thought he was years away from marriage. That very afternoon! It wasn't until the words slipped out of his lips—unexpectedly and utterly unbidden—that he realized they were true. He did want her. He wanted her with every fiber of his being. And he wanted her as his wife.

He shouldn't have let her go.

The whiskey had a bitter bite as he raised it to his mouth and took a sip. He had been foolish to take the chance. The room was secluded; he had chosen it for that reason. The door had been locked, she unresisting . . . He had enough experience with women to be sure she was a virgin. And ruined virginity had little choice but to accept the man who offered honorable amends.

But, dammit, he didn't want her that way! Matthew slammed the glass down, sloshing liquid over the polished mahogany table. He wanted her to come to him, not because she had to—not because one moment of reckless passion had taken away her options—but because she loved him, and enjoyed him . . . and longed to be with him always.

And that, he thought grimly, was one thing she was not likely to feel for a man who traded in opium!

''You're deep in thought, Captain Barron. Pining for

lost loves? Or are you thinking perhaps of a beautiful lady with jet-black curls you saw at the rather silly gala this afternoon . . . and wishing you had gotten to know her better?''

Matthew turned and saw standing in the doorway the very same lady who had just given an accurate, if not particularly modest, description of herself. She had changed from the garish gown she had been wearing earlier to something deep purple and very clingy, which he couldn't help noticing, even in his distracted state, accented more than it concealed.

Beside her, an agitated manservant was trying very hard to hold her back without actually reaching out and touching her.

''So solly, masser. Lady, she no listen. I tell her Ah Sing come first. I tell her Ah Sing ask Masser is all right or no. But lady, she no—''

''It's all right, Ah Sing. It's not your fault. And the lady, of course, is most welcome. Won't you come in, Miss Crale?''

''You know who I am?'' Camilla started past him, turning as if on impulse, when she was just inches away. It was a favorite trick, and it always worked. ''You *did* notice my jet-black curls then . . . and were interested enough to make an inquiry or two.''

''Actually, I noticed your eyes. They're quite a stunning color in the sunlight, though they seem almost black now.'' He took a step toward the table where he had left his drink, then hesitated as he spotted the manservant still hovering in the doorway. ''It really *is* all right, Ah Sing. You don't have to stay and protect me.''

''A pity,'' Camilla said, ignoring the servant as he vanished into the shadows of the hallway. ''They're my most devastating feature. My eyes. Perhaps you should have a closer look . . . in the lamplight. And you might just offer a glass of sherry. That would be only hospitable, wouldn't it?''

''No doubt,'' Matthew replied drily. He noticed that his guest had settled herself on a low burgundy velvet divan, her legs tucked coyly under her, one slim white ankle sticking out just far enough to draw his attention. She was an uncommonly sensual little thing, and Matthew was reminded suddenly how much he liked petite women. They seemed to fit into the curves of his body.

But then he liked tall, leggy women, too, and the image of Rachel Todd came back, abruptly and quite devastatingly for his composure. He could taste her mouth again, feel that body heat they had shared, and he imagined himself on that same burgundy velvet with her, long legs twining possessively around him.

"Uh . . . here you go." He concentrated on holding his hand steady as he walked over to the divan and extended the glass. "The hospitality you requested, madam. And in return, perhaps you'll be good enough to tell me the reason for this unexpected visit."

Camilla glanced up through very dark, teasing lashes.

"And here I thought you looked so clever," she chided coyly. "You did admit to inquiring about me. You *must* have learned *something*."

"I learned that you're the niece—and ward—of Robert Carpenter, one of the directors of Lippincott and Company," Matthew said cautiously. "And that he has his hands full keeping you in line."

She smiled: the peculiarly predatory smile for which she was renowned. "Then surely you can guess why I'm here."

"I might prefer to have it spelled out."

"Very well, then." She raised her lashes, giving him the full impact of her eyes, steamy and unmistakably bold. "I have come . . . naturally . . . to allow you to seduce me."

Matthew was uncomfortably aware, as he knew she intended, of the nearness of her breasts, rising and falling with each breath she took. He had the feeling she had come with nothing underneath her gown. The sheer silk left little to the imagination—her nipples were large, he noticed, and very hard—and he found himself wondering what it would be like to take them in his mouth.

"It didn't occur to you, I suppose," he said, keeping his voice as even as he could manage, "that a man might like to choose the time and place of a seduction himself. And the woman."

"I don't please you?" She had placed the glass down, slowly, very deliberately, holding his eyes on her all the while. Now she touched his wrist, catching him lightly, but somehow compellingly, and Matthew felt himself being drawn down on the divan beside her.

Blast that little minx! She knew exactly the effect she was having on him. "You please me very much . . . You're a very beautiful woman. But every time isn't the right time. Or every place . . . And a man isn't always inclined to play the seducer."

"Then *I* will have to *seduce* you." Her voice dropped deep in her throat, so low he had to lean closer to hear. "It's more fun that way, anyhow. Or perhaps . . . you're afraid?"

She was smiling again, her lips slightly parted, teasing, challenging—making Matthew intensely conscious of his own vulnerability. He was more than ready for love; his body had been aching all evening, every muscle and nerve ending throbbed with the denial he had imposed on himself. It would be so easy to surrender. So easy to move those few scant inches and give himself up to the pleasures of the moment.

But if he did, he could kiss his chances with Rachel Todd goodbye. He knew enough about women to know that this deliciously bold creature was not one to keep her conquests a secret. And enough about life in a small community to realize that it would take about twenty minutes for the news to reach the mission behind the China Gate.

"I'm not afraid . . . and I'm hardly disinterested, as I suspect you're well aware. But the time *isn't* right. Yesterday, I would have been enchanted if you'd come here like this, but today. . . . Today there's another lovely lady, and she has won my heart."

"And you're planning on being *faithful* to her?" The look she gave him was more than a little disconcerting. "How very . . . *quaint*. Really, you do surprise me, Captain Barron."

In fact, Matthew was surprising himself. He felt stuffy and somehow old-fashioned as he extricated himself awkwardly and went over to where his whiskey rested, still barely touched, on the table. Her assessment had been nearer the mark than his. He hadn't resisted merely—or even mostly—because he was afraid Rachel would learn of that trifling assignation. He had done so because he couldn't bring himself to be untrue to her.

Ridiculous. He raised his drink and downed it in one steadying gulp. She had no claims on him. He'd made no promises to her, or she to him—but there it was. He loved her, and it would feel like the worst kind of betrayal if he were to lie with another woman.

Camilla had risen while he was looking away. He turned to find her halfway between the divan and the place where he was standing. There was an expression on those distinctly feline features that should have warned him, but his brain was dulled with desire, and he was startled when she raised her hands to some fastening he couldn't see that seemed to hold her bodice together. A second later, it was coming loose, the sheer fabric sliding off her shoulders, to her waist.

Matthew heard his breath come out in a long, low gasp. She *was* wearing nothing underneath! Her breasts were exquisite in the lamplight—round and very heavy, but firm—teasing his mouth and teeth and tongue—and he felt his body leap to the inevitable response. God help him, it would be *so* easy. . . .

"Are you sure you wouldn't like to change your mind, Captain?" Her gaze dropped wickedly to the unmistakable bulge in his groin. "Fidelity is such a silly thing. . . . And you aren't even married yet."

"I *would* like to." Matthew could hear his own voice as if from far away. "I would love to change my mind. I'm *dying* to change my mind. . . . But I'm not going to."

There was a quiet finality in his tone. Camilla did not fail to hear it or misunderstand what it meant. She realized as his hands came up what he was going to do, and she regretted it deeply.

He held the flimsy silk for a fraction of a second, then surprised her by kissing, very lightly, first one engorged nipple, then the other, before drawing it up and fastening it quite expertly.

And with that tender, singularly nonprovocative gesture, Camilla knew suddenly that she wanted this man more than she had ever wanted anything in her life. Just as she knew that she was never going to have him.

Then those same hands were on her shoulders, turning her around, pushing her gently, but firmly through the door, and she found herself alone in the flickering light of the hall.

There she stood for several minutes, regaining her composure—and intensely grateful that he had had the tact and good taste not to hang around and watch! The conflicting feelings that swept over her now were not at all what she had expected. She had just been rejected, very definitely—and very throughly—by another Barron man. But her body was glowing, still warm, as if from his caresses, and she felt somehow strangely cherished. Not with love perhaps, but kindness.

And at least, she thought, as she headed back toward the carriage she had had the good sense to keep waiting, he hadn't called her a piranha!

"He's a very nice man." Camilla Crale's smile was uncharacteristically soft in the early morning mist. She leaned forward in the open carriage, her words addressed to the young woman who had just come over to greet her. "I know that's not what you want to hear, but he really is very, *very* nice. And quite devoted to his lady love."

"Lady love, indeed!" Rachel had to work to keep the disdain in her voice. There had been very little alarm mingled with the relief she had felt when she looked up a moment earlier and saw the Carpenter carriage rolling through the China Gate with the last

pink streaks of dawn. Camilla never rose before noon
without a reason—and if the reason had been the suc-
cessful seduction of the youngest Captain Barron, she
wouldn't have been on the other side of the colony
now. "I just spoke to the man for a few minutes. The
word 'love' is absurd! And I'm surprised to hear you
call him *nice*. It looks like he threw you out."

"With both hands!" Camilla was laughing, but not
bitterly, as if she didn't mind that the joke was on her.
"By my shoulders. Right out into the hall! But he
didn't make fun of me, Rae. He could have . . . and
he didn't. He made me feel somehow that he really
liked me . . . that he was . . . well, *flattered*, you
know, and hated to say no. I've never been treated so
gallantly in my life. And that, whether you like it or
not, *is* nice."

"I know it is," Rachel admitted. "And I know *he*
is . . . in a way. I'm glad he treated you decently."
She hesitated, a little guiltily. Camilla always seemed
so sure of herself—it was easy to forget sometimes that
she had feelings, too—but there had been a peculiarly
haunting expression, just for a second, in those unusually insouciant violet eyes when the carriage had appeared at the gate. "I'd have hated it if he'd hurt you.
Honestly I would. It was stupid of me to ask you to
go there, but just because he's 'nice' doesn't make
everything all right."

"Oh . . . the opium again. Matthew Barron has
dared to bring a shipload of the vile stuff into an area
which is already rife with it—so naturally he can never,
never *presume* to look on you! For pity's sake, Rachel,
don't you think you're going a little overboard with
this? I mean, *everyone* dabbles in opium, at least a
little—except those pious bores at Zion's Corner. And
even you get a little tired of their preaching sometimes."

"But that still doesn't make it right!" Rachel insisted indignantly. "You can't just say, 'Everyone's
doing it, so I'll do it, too, and who cares if a few more
lives are ruined in the bargain?' "

"No-o-o, but it does make it . . . well, *common*.

Sort of casually accepted, if you know what I mean. I don't suppose Captain Barron even thought twice about it when he went into the trade. Everyone doesn't agonize over every little thing, you know, the way you do. It probably just seemed like a good way to make money. He's not the sort who would *deliberately* set out to ruin lives.''

"I didn't say he was," Rachel replied stiffly. "But deliberately or not, he is ruining them; and the fact that he didn't think twice about it doesn't make it any better! A quick way to pick up some cash—and why stop to worry about the consequences? That doesn't show a lot of character.''

"Character!'' Camilla sniffed. "You know, sometimes you can be incredibly rigid. I suppose that comes from having missionaries for parents! This passion for 'character' is going to lead to an empty bed . . . and an empty life, if you're not careful. You're a fool, Rachel Todd, if you sit around waiting for a *perfect* man with *perfect* moral standards. And double the fool if you let this one get away! It's not every man who's nice without being frightfully boring.''

A fool? Rachel wandered away from the carriage toward the gate with its view of Macao in the distance. A fool with silly, unrealistic expectations . . . and an empty bed in her future. Matthew Barron *was* nice. Even that innocuous word sounded pleasant when applied to him. He could clearly be kind when he chose, and thoughtful. And generous of spirit.

That was what made it so hard. She bit down on her lower lip, unconsciously, not even feeling the pain. There were so many things that were so very likeable about him. It was a sore temptation to dismiss the others, to compromise just a little . . . to pretend that the values she had always fought for weren't quite so important when they got in the way of her heart.

And that would make her truly a fool!

She sighed as she turned back toward the interior of China and thought, as always, how beautiful the hills looked in the first light of morning. A pretty line with the ladies and a way of making them feel good about themselves wasn't enough. She could never respect a man who wouldn't "think twice" about turning evil loose in the name of profit.

She could love him. The thought came abruptly, and not altogether by surprise, and she who had always been brutally honest forced herself to face it. It seemed, after all, the word was not quite so absurd. She had met a man under the most impossible, outrageous circumstances, and with no reason she could fathom, she had fallen hopelessly and instantly in love.

But she couldn't respect him—and, heaven help her, she could never commit her life to a man she didn't respect. The light was brighter on the hills, clear now, with no tinges of pink. Her heart would ache for him always, she would regret the chances not taken—and yes, her bed would be empty—but she knew what she had to do.

So . . . she *did* care for him.

Matthew Barron looked down at the paper in his hand. It was already well into the afternoon, and the sun was slanting through the window, shafting an elongated rectangle of light on the patterned Oriental carpet. He leaned back into the cushions of the same burgundy velvet divan that had very nearly been his Waterloo the night before, propped his feet on the table in front of him, and allowed himself the luxury of a distinctly relieved laugh.

No question about it. She cared! Matthew had shown what he considered admirable restraint, remaining behind an hour or so ago while his carriage rumbled toward the China Gate overflowing with a profusion of colorful tropical blossoms. He had had more than a twinge of anxiety when it had returned, empty. If Rachel had been able to accept the extravagantly romantic gesture with a cool note of thanks, he would have known that their passion had been, for her, a brief indiscretion. A purely physical sensation which had caught her by surprise, and now that she had had time to think about it, she had regained her composure.

But the reply on the piece of paper Matthew was

holding now had been in the Reverend Gideon Todd's
boldly distinctive hand. Rachel had gone off, he said,
quite suddenly, to help at another mission somewhere
vaguely "inland." But flowers were always welcome
at the services in their modest chapel. And Mrs. Todd
would enjoy one of the larger bouquets in the house.

She had run away!

Matthew jumped up restlessly and went over to the
window. Even the narrow sidestreet was bustling with
color and activity. Slender Chinese in dark pants and
loose white tunics threaded their way between black-
robed Jesuits and scarlet-coated Marines, and stout
Portuguese housewives juggled huge straw baskets,
vivid with mangoes and sweet, juicy melons, Macao
oranges, cabbages, potatoes, and peaches, gaudy yellow bananas from Canton. Children seemed to be everywhere, running back and forth with messages or
squabbling over stalks of sugar cane clutched in dirty
hands. No room for carriages here, but sedan chairs
pushed through the crowds, their silk-curtained windows screening perhaps a minor mandarin, late for
some delicate negotiation—or perhaps a British trader,
leaving work behind to begin a somewhat early evening in one of the houses where gambling and drinking were combined with pleasures of a more exotic
nature.

The window was open, and the smells of the Orient
drifted in: tea and dust, cinnamon and warm salt
breezes and the sweat of many bodies crowded together. She was afraid of her feelings! She cared, much
too deeply—her emotions were out of control, and she
didn't trust herself to see him again. She had run away,
not from him, but from the yearnings of her own heart.

And in doing so had played right into his hands.

Going over to a small writing desk in the corner, he
pulled out a sheet of paper, and without bothering to
sit down, scribbled a few hasty words. The only thing
he had lacked was time, and Rachel had just handed
that to him, most generously, on the proverbial silver
platter. What, after all, was the one thing she objected
to? The opium in the hold of the *China Dawn*.

But given an appropriate amount of time, the opium would be gone!

Contrition could come later. Matthew folded the paper deftly and sealed it with a dab of red wax. He could throw himself on her mercy, swear that he had seen the error of his ways. The opium would be gone, of course. Too late to do anything about that, but he could vow most solemnly—and quite truthfully, for he was already beginning to regret the trouble the stuff was causing—that he would never foul his hands with it again. She would forgive him. If she cared, she would have to forgive. Especially if he donated the money he had made to her father's mission.

"Ah Sing!" He headed for the door, calling out again, "*Ah Sing!*"

Yes, that was a nice touch, giving the proceeds to the mission! More than one problem solved with a single bold stroke. As long as he showed a sizable profit, Matthew knew he could get around his grandfather. The old tyrant would be secretly impressed, in spite of himself. And donating the money to charity would remove whatever taint might have soiled the Barron name. Even brother Jared, for all his damned stiff-necked way of looking at things, wouldn't have an argument left after that!

Now, all he had to do was get rid of the stuff. . . .

"Ah Sing!" Where was that boy? "Ah—there you are. I want you to take this letter to Steven Wu. At Olyphant. You know where to find him? Then go to Mr. Gallagher—he and the Indian lady have taken rooms around the corner from the English Club. Tell him I want them on board the *China Dawn* by midnight. We sail with first light in the morning."

Four

The fog came abruptly, rolling and rising with the wind until the anchorage at Lintin seemed to be enveloped in a silent gray shroud. Only seconds before, Matthew had been able to count more than a dozen vessels silhouetted against the high, brush-covered hill on the far end of the small island. Now the tall masts, stripped of their sails, had drifted into the mist, and it was as if the *China Dawn* were alone in the world.

"I suppose you'll be lettin' me in on what we're doin' here. In your own time, o' course." Gallagher's Irish brogue was rich with sarcasm. "When you're ready."

Matthew turned with an easy grin. Fog had settled in little droplets on his hair and beard, giving him an almost luminous look in the waning midday light.

"I should have thought you'd already figured that out. A fine clever rogue like you. We're here—naturally—to get rid of the opium."

"Easier said than done, me bucko. Every man on every one o' those great ships out there is after tryin' the same thing, an' not a one o' them havin' a bit o' luck. What with the Chinese gettin' their hackles up and bannin' the trade—an' with it every trader who's ever dealt in the stuff—there hasn't been so much as a chest o' opium settlin' onto the shore. The smugglin' crabs go out, and back they come, near in the blink of an eye, with tales o' fire an' fury from the big ugly junks with fierce eyes painted on their hulls. I'm thinkin', like them, all we can do is sit back an' wait."

"And risk losing everything?" Matthew drew his

hand impatiently through his hair, brushing it back where the wind had blown it in his eyes. "The hostilities between the British and the Chinese are just beginning. They'll lead to war, and the war will be over quickly, but it might not be quick enough for us. You forget, my brother may already be on his way, breathing more fire and fury than the red-sailed junks. Jared was always good at that. He could be here in as little as three months—with my grandfather's authorization to do whatever he wants! I damn well better be sure the opium is converted into cash by then."

He did not mention that the timeframe had tightened considerably since he met Rachel Todd, but he was thinking it. And wondering how long he dared wait before falling on his knees—figuratively, of course— and vowing contrition for what was over and done with and couldn't be helped anymore. Gallagher had a tendency to get testy when the subject of the missionary's daughter came up, and no wonder. His profits as well as Matthew's would be forfeit if she forced him to choose between her and the evil cargo in his hold.

"You're regrettin' perhaps that you took the stuff on in the first place?" Gallagher had an uncanny way sometimes of seeming to read his mind. "You'll be askin' yourself, if a man had the chance t' go back and do things again, would he do the same as before?"

"That depends," Matthew said grimly. "I'll regret it like hell if it blows up in my face! But I still think we can pull it off, though I admit I'd ponder a while longer before I took you up on that tempting scheme you dangled in front of me. It's a fine glib tongue you have, Christy Gallagher"—his voice caught the lilt of the other man's accent with droll accuracy—"an' me takin' it all in, without so much as a thought for the consequences."

"It's a gift of the Irish," Gallagher agreed, unruffled. "But I'm thinkin', it was not so hard as it might o' been t' persuade you t' see the light."

No, Matthew thought, strolling over to the gunwale and leaning out into the void, he had put up very little resistance. The metal bar on top of the railing felt like ice beneath his hands. It had sounded like a good idea at the time. Gallagher, being—reluctantly—British, had access to the higher quality Patna opium in Calcutta, a zealously guarded monopoly that had always been rigidly closed to outsiders. Matthew had the money and a swift, well-armed clipper to carry it to market. It had seemed a natural partnership, and the Irishman's one-third share a small price for such enormous potential.

It would have worked, too—if the Chinese had not decided suddenly, and quite irrationally, to close down the trade. With more courage than common sense, they had seized all the supplies of opium in the foreign factories or *hongs* at Canton and, splitting open each brown, hard-crushed ball, had mixed the drug with lye and sluiced it out to sea. The British were screaming for blood and reparations, but in the meantime, they were barred from their teas and silks and spices. The only way they could get them down the Pearl River and onto their ships was by paying exorbitant sums to Yankee traders, who could move in and out freely since they were not involved in the trade.

Which, Matthew thought glumly, made his own situation doubly precarious.

He scanned the sea, looking for a hint of light or motion, but nothing was visible in that vast gray void. All he needed now was for the Chinese to find out what the newest and fleetest of the Barron ships was carrying, and ban them from Canton, too. Not only would they lose the considerable sums they were getting from the British, but they, like their rivals, would have to pay to have their own goods ferried out!

"Well, then . . . we'll just have to hurry it off," he said, more to himself than the man who had remained somewhere in the mist behind him. If Jared Barron arrived to find that his younger brother had not only tarnished the precious family name but lost legitimate profits as well, his rage—and contempt—would be devastating. Matthew could almost feel himself reduced to a small boy again, the runt of the tall Barron clan, failing once more, as he had always failed.

It seemed to him that he had never measured up to his brother. The wind was biting now, stinging his eyes as he stared out into the emptiness. Nothing he did was ever quite enough. He could make Jared laugh. He had learned at an early age the value of whimsy— he could lighten sometimes even the direst situation— but he had never won his respect, and he ached for it now, at the moment he sensed he was in imminent danger of losing it forever.

The fog seemed to come and go, thickening occasionally, then swirling away, though never clearing quite enough to see ships that were barely a hundred yards off. He had been to Lintin only once before— his last voyage to the Orient, and the last on which he had ridden as mate—but he remembered it distinctly.

Less a harbor than a city on water. He could almost see the great floating warehouses around which the smuggling trade had long centered. The *Governor Findlay* of Jardien, Matheson, the *Samarang,* shared by Magniac and Dent, the Spaniard's *General Quiroga*—homes as well as factories, with potted plants and children playing on the decks. Laughter floated across the water at night, and music sometimes; bands played, quadrilles were danced under the stars, and life went on, much as it did on shore.

There was a small nucleus of ships in permanent residence, except during the southwest monsoons of late spring and summer when the traders were forced to take shelter at Dam-sing-moon, north of Macao. Other vessels came and went, staying a few days, or a week or a month, before sailing off again. Much of the trade centered now in Canton—Lintin was not what it once had been—but fast crabs or scrambling dragons, as the smuggling boats were called, continued to make profitable runs up the coast.

Matthew could still remember being amazed and fascinated the first time he walked across the decks of the *Samarang* and saw huge chests of Patna and Benares being lifted off the clumsy teak wallahs from India, and inferior Malwa, packed not in balls, to his vague surprise, but large, loose cakes. Every one had to be carefully examined—sniffed and probed before the traders made their selections—and nearly as many, it looked to him, were turned down as accepted. Silver seemed to be everywhere, here in bags, there spilling over dirty, rough decking, not holystoned to the meticulous Barron standards.

Some of the silver was in coin, some in sycee, which looked to Matthew like small pigs of lead, though brighter in color, catching the glint of the sun. *Shroffs* or money-changers could be seen moving among the sacks and piles, much as they did on the back streets of Macao or in the vaulted factories in Canton. A constant clicking sound accompanied them as they weighed and counted each glittering piece.

The war junks in the distance had presented little threat then. They were always there, lying just off the shore, a vivid reminder of the disapproval of the Chinese, but even their few forays closer were primarily symbolic. One had occurred on the last afternoon of Matthew's stay with his hosts at Dent & Company. A quite astonishing armada of junks had floated past, brilliant banners streaming out in the wind, gongs beating wildly, and the most hair-raising shouts adding to what was obviously intended as a ferocious cacophony. Everyone had been greatly amused, and there had been much laughter as they drifted inside to brandy and dinner.

No one was laughing now. The junks were armed, with ancient cannons, perhaps, and primitive fire bombs, but they were a definite threat. Gallagher had been exaggerating, as usual, when he said that all the fast crabs were being beaten back by the Chinese. But operations had grown considerably more difficult. And more dangerous. A man who ventured into those waters now stood to lose everything. Unless . . .

A sail loomed suddenly out of the mist, startling Matthew even though he had been watching for it. A darkish gray mass, straight on one side, slightly rounded on the other, turning red-brown as it grew nearer.

A chuckle sounded in his ear. Gallagher had come to stand at the rail beside him.

"A junk, is it now? And an oculus painted on the hull, I'll warrant, lookin' down for fish in the water. So that's your idea, boy. . . . No, two junks. I'm seeing another behind it. One for you then, an' one for me . . . an' two loads o' opium ashore, so slick not a soul 'll see 'em comin'."

"The eyes are looking forward," Matthew corrected. "Not fishermen, but war junks, and Chinese crews on deck. If anyone spots them—though with all this fog, I doubt they will—they'll think its the Emperor's finest, out looking for red-headed devils skimming their fast crabs over the waves. And actually there are three—Romack will take the other one—and three separate rendezvous. Negotiate well, my friend, and you should see a tidy return on your one-third share."

"An' Romack with a tidy piece o' *your* two-thirds in his pocket—an' not a tickle o' conscience, I'll wager. That second mate o' yours is an out-an'-out thief. He'll be after comin' back with some half-cocked tale about how the payment wasn't what was expected. An' him weighted down with a fine bit o' change for himself."

"But not as much as I'd have given outright—if he'd been an honest man." Matthew laughed at his companion's reaction. Not being devious himself, he had never been particularly threatened to discover the trait in others. "For the risk involved, the pay is fair—if not fairly taken. He's quick-witted, that one, and fast on his feet—better, I think, than the first mate for the job. Besides, I need Varnay to watch over the ship while I'm gone. There's no one else but a Barron I'd trust with the *China Dawn*."

Gallagher threw him a quick look out of the corner of his eye. There was something in that Yankee profile: pride bordering almost on arrogance as he spoke of the flagship of the Barron fleet. Not just the largest, swiftest clipper ever built, but young Matthew Barron's first command—and the sudden spark of possessiveness Gallagher had noted before might have been

troubling if he had given himself time to think about
it. But the third ship was gliding into view, and he
found himself staring at the misty trio, running over
in his mind possibilities that were becoming pleasanter with each passing moment.

"If I were a curious man—an' we Irish have our
share o' that human failing—I might be wonderin' now
where you found Chinese pilots t' guide those things
in."

"And too polite, naturally, to ask. Let's just say it
pays to have friends in high places. Or more accurately, in rather low places. Steven Wu is a clerk at
Olyphant and Company, but he's well connected on
the mainland."

"The comely lad o' mixed blood? I've noticed him
. . . or rather I've noticed the girls takin' considerable
note o' him. But surely, with all that prayin' an'
gnashin' o' teeth at Zion's Corner, a little caper like
this 'd put a terrible strain on his conscience."

"I don't think the Chinese have consciences. They're
too practical. And being of 'mixed blood,' as you so
quaintly express it, puts Steven in a peculiar position.
It seems there's a lady who's taken his eye."

"An' you'd be knowin' about that."

"I would," Matthew admitted. "But this lady, unfortunately, is his father's race, not his mother's. That
is to say, white. And a bit on the expensive side, which
put him in need of some ready cash. Her uncle is a
director at Russell. She's here on a visit, apparently,
from one of the southern states, though I rather suspect her family packed her off to get some breathing
space."

Gallagher glanced back at him. "Not the little trollop
with the eyes?"

"Camilla Crale? Old Carpenter's ward, at Lippincott? No, though I suspect poor Steven would be better off if it were. To give the lady her due, extravagant
gifts don't seem to be on Camilla's list of require-
ments. If she likes a man, I daresay she likes him—he
could be poor as dirt and she'd probably enjoy the
novelty. This one, now, is going to cost a pretty penny.

The foolish wretch thinks he's buying himself something permanent.''

''But he isn't.'' It was not a question.

Matthew shook his head distractedly, his mind and eyes returning to the junks. They were lined up in a row now, being secured with stout cords to the larger vessel. ''Exotic romances with handsome Eurasians make an amusing diversion, provided they don't go too far—which I'm betting this one won't. She'll go back to her own kind in the end. They always do.''

Gallagher followed the other man's gaze, Steven Wu's ultimate disappointment and the reason for the junks dramatic appearance already forgotten. The fact was, they were there, and things were definitely looking up. He had to give the boy credit, he surely did. He would not have thought his brain was so bold.

''It just might work,'' he ventured.

''It *will* work . . . and the weather couldn't be better. Look around, man! You can't see the hills on the island. If the fog holds, we should be able to make three, maybe four, trips before anyone stumbles on to what we're doing. After that, we'll have to move up the coast, sailing ahead of the news—taking more risks. But it can be done, my friend. It can be done.''

Gallagher whistled softly through his teeth. ''It would be a chancy thing . . .''

''Nothing on this earth is certain. Except the fact that we will leave it, though not the when or how of it.'' He turned from the railing for a moment to watch the older man. The wind gusted full in Gallagher's face, slicking dark hair out behind him, and his eyes glistened green in the fine sea spray. ''You had occasion to taunt me with cowardice recently . . . over a certain young lady. Should I return the compliment now?''

''No man has ever called Christy Gallagher a coward—and lived!''

''Or been right?'' Matthew laughed, realizing the bargain had been struck. Not that there had been any doubt. Gallagher was a man who thrived on challenge, who would reach for it always in preference to the easier, surer way—even, he suspected, if the easy way offered more reward. The daring of the mission appealed: the very risks that would have turned another man aside.

A scent of jasmine mingled with the salt and moisture, warning Matthew that they were not alone. He looked back, but for a second could see nothing. Then a slender, dark-skinned form materialized, clad in a graceful golden sari that seemed to glow out of the dismal mist.

"Ah . . . there you are, Gallagher," a feminine voice said. The words were flawless, only her inflection betraying the land of her origin. "Your tea is waiting. It grows cold soon. I have made it for you with my own hands. And you, Captain Matthew? You will join us, of course?"

"Not this time, Shanti," Matthew replied with a faint half smile. It was a little game they played. She always asked, and he, knowing they cherished their privacy, always refused. "I have much to do, and damned little—*precious* little—time to do it."

Shanti laughed, a light, bell-like sound. "I have heard the word 'damned' before, Captain. And do you also need him—this man of mine—since there is so much to be done? Or can I steal a little time with him for myself?"

"I think I can spare him for an hour or two. It will take a while to load the junks. Send him back to me at six bells—three o'clock. We should be ready to pull out then."

He was startled by an uncharacteristic stab of envy as he watched them move away, Gallagher protectively close but not quite touching his woman. Shanti had come as a complete surprise when the bawdy Irishman brought her on board in Calcutta. Not because she was beautiful—Matthew would have expected no less of the man—or even because she seemed so young, barely more than a child, though he caught an ageless look in her eyes sometimes. That, too, might have been expected. But there was a gentleness, a kind of sweet

acceptance, about her that almost made her seem unreal. And that was most definitely unexpected.

It was not that he envied Gallagher the woman herself. Matthew turned back to the sea, knowing that he
had to get to the hold to supervise the loading, but
unable for the moment to make himself move. Shanti
was lovely and gentle and serene . . . but gentle serenity in a woman had never made his pulse beat faster.
He envied Gallagher because he was part of a couple.
Because there was someone there for him, and he for
her, and the afternoons and evenings would only be
lonely if he chose them to be.

Rachel, he thought, and remembered again the way
she had felt, soft and trembling in his arms.

"Damn you, Matt Barron, you're a fool!"

He said the words aloud, grimacing as the wind
seemed to catch them and buffet them back in his face.
One thing and one thing only was keeping him from
the woman who seemed to want him as much as he
wanted her. And that one thing was not worth anywhere
near what it was starting to cost!

He watched the wind swirl the fog around the graceful lugsails of the trio of junks. In truth, he had already begun to have qualms about the cargo he was
carrying, even before he had met Rachel Todd, and
not altogether for the reasons he was willing to admit.

Stocking up in Calcutta had been one thing. He had
felt like such a clever rogue, outsmarting the other
Americans, getting his hands on superior goods. And,
really, he had told himself, what difference was there
between opium and the barrels of rum that were reg-
ularly carried in the holds of every Barron vessel on
eastern Atlantic crossings?

But it had been something else to sail into Macao
and watch the speculative looks in the eyes of men he
respected . . . and feel the first nagging doubts in the
back of his mind.

There was, after all, more of the Barron heritage in
him than he realized. The same strong New England
background that had shaped the others had molded
him, the same granite homeland that showed in the

features of all the Barron men, himself included, even cousin Alex, for all the southern softness that had come from his mother's family.

Like it or not, somewhere deep inside, he had been bred with a kind of rigid inflexibility when it came to right and wrong. And he was beginning to have a sneaking suspicion that what he was doing now just might be wrong.

"Damn!" he said again. He would be glad when they got the final load on shore—all the problems and doubts behind him at last—and he could get on with his life.

"There is danger in this thing you are going to do? With the young Captain Matthew?"

A faint rustle of silk accompanied Shanti's movements as she poured out a cup of tea in the flickering golden lamplight. Fog shrouded the windows, giving the large passenger stateroom with its green-upholstered benches and dark, wood-paneled walls the shadowy illusion of night.

"Some," Gallagher admitted, admiring her grace and almost convincing self-control. Her hand was steady as she finished filling the cup and held it out to him, nothing in her voice or beautiful dark features betraying more than idle curiosity. But he knew her well, this woman who had been part of his life for nearly a year, and he knew she was afraid. "Nothing I can't be handlin'—an' that with two hands tied behind me back! So don't go worryin' your head about me."

"But I do worry Gallagher. I must. And for the most selfish reasons. You are all of my life. I have nothing else. What will happen to me if you do not return this day?"

"You'll be taken care of, girl," he said gruffly, and set the cup untouched on the table beside him. What he craved now was something a mite more potent than tea. "I've promised you that, and I'm a man o' me word. There's money enough set aside. Young Matthew will see you settled someplace safe. One of us is

sure to get back. . . . There, there, I'm teasin', girl—
now take that look out o' your eyes! I'm a fine strap-
pin' man. Have you ever known a man so strong?''

"No, Gallagher." She took a sip from her own cup,
attempting a smile as she did. "Never so strong."

"Then trust me to be comin' back, an' I will. An'
young Matt, too." His mouth twisted wryly. "He has
reason enough to take care o' his life, now that his
heart's found its lovely desire."

Shanti threw him a quizzical look. She missed very
little when it came to this man. "You don't like her?
The woman the captain has found? She sounds very
pretty."

"And very pure." He was coaxing the cup out of
her hand, drawing her down on his lap, enjoying the
yielding warmth of her supple young body. The memory of Matthew Barron's expression came back suddenly, the way he had looked when he refrained from
mentioning Rachel before. The naked longing in his
eyes. "It's not that I don't like the lady," he said
thoughtfully. "I don't like the hold she has on him,
and that's a fact. He's a different man somehow, just
lettin' his mind rest on her." His mouth was searching
for her neck, nuzzling, still playfully, awaiting the response he knew would follow. "Besides . . . what kind
o' man looks for a woman who's pure? An' a missionary's daughter! God save the poor fool."

"We had a missionary in the village I come from,"
Shanti said softly, her voice changing subtly with the
beginnings of desire. "A black-robed priest. From
someplace called London. He taught me to speak your
language. And write a little, too."

"Ah . . . that's why you talk with an English accent."

"I do not. I speak like an Indian." The saffron-hued
sari had slipped from her head. She shrugged if off her
shoulders, languidly, as if unaware that their time together was limited by the sounding of the ship's bells,
then reached for the fastenings of the small shirt beneath it. He liked to see her breasts, naked and glowing in the lamplight, and she liked to give him what

he wanted. "He was a kind man. The priest. He was the only person in our village who treated me like a human being. I forgot when I was with him that I am an untouchable. As I forget when I am with you. Perhaps that is because you are both British."

"I am *not* British, blast it, girl!" The force of the exclamation was muted somewhat by the appearance of very round breasts, whose fullness never ceased to surprise and delight him anew. And the fact that the sari was falling completely to the floor. "How many times do I have to be tellin' you? I'm Irish, and proud of it!"

"It is the same thing. You are very alike, you and the black robe. He spoke quietly—I never heard him raise his voice, and you are always blustering—but you are kind, too. And very good in your heart."

Her hand was on the top button of his shirt, working it loose, moving slowly downward. She was very aware of the intensified beating of that same good heart, thumping almost audibly against the wall of his chest. It amazed her, as always, the power that love gave a woman over a man. She had discovered right from the beginning the way he liked her to be bold, even when he pretended to protest.

"Here, girl, what are you doing?" he had bellowed the first time she had started to remove his shirt. "Where's your respect for me masculine pride? It's I should be undressin' you!"

"I am not a girl," she had reminded him firmly. "I am a woman, and I want to please you. . . . I want you to teach me the things that you like."

He had not stopped calling her "girl," which in truth she enjoyed as a kind of special endearment, but she noticed he did not protest anymore when she did her share of the disrobing.

She had finished with the buttons and was pulling his shirt open, not bothering to remove it entirely. She loved the look and feel of his chest, smooth and almost hairless beneath her probing fingertips. She had thought all Europeans were covered with hair—certainly the mop of his head had led her to expect it—

and she had been secretly pleased to learn she was wrong. She loved him enough so she would have accepted him any way he was, but she had always been a little repulsed by fur on men. Besides, it would have obscured the strong, hard muscles her eyes could never get enough of.

Half kneeling, still half sitting on his lap, she dropped her hand boldly to that other very hard part of him.

"Ah, Shanti, love . . ." he moaned. "You are a marvel."

A convulsion ran through his body. His hands were behind her suddenly, enveloping her buttocks, thrusting her sharply forward and down. The sheer force of the motion took her breath away, the rock-hardness of him filling and exciting her, and she was surprised again, as she had been when it first happened, at the all-consuming hunger that surged through her.

She needed and wanted him as much as he needed and wanted her—no, *more!*—and it was a new miracle every time their bodies joined together. She could feel him struggling to hold back, feel the sweat that was pouring from his body onto hers as he resisted the primitive urge to surrender. And she was resisting with him, gasping, fighting, clinging to the power and exhilaration of the moment.

Then the pleasure was too intense, and there was no resisting any longer. Shanti felt the small explosions in her own body at almost the same instant that his was wracked with a long, intense shudder, and she knew they had lost again. Lost and won both, and he was withdrawing abruptly, spurting the warm wetness of his masculine passion onto her belly.

They lay for a long time in each other's arms, silent and utterly satisfied, content with a relationship that had grown comfortable without losing any of its rapture. His shirt was on the floor, discarded somewhere in their lovemaking without either of them having noticed, and his pants were kicked half off, gathered in a clump around one of his ankles.

"Look, girl, what you've made of me," he said with a gruffness that would not have fooled a stranger. "All twisted up like a sailor's knot, an' tangled in me own trousers. A man could lose his dignity with a snippet like you."

"You always leave me too soon," Shanti complained gently. "I want to feel all of your love. Inside me . . . the way it is meant to be."

His mouth turned soft as he kissed her long dark hair, which had come loose and was spilling over them both. "I am not a man for stayin', love. There's nothin' in this life can be counted on, an' no one should count on me. When I leave—an' I will be leavin'—I'll not be sayin' goodbye to you with a child at the breast. I may be a rogue, but I'm not such a monster as that."

"I know you will leave, Gallagher. I have always known, and I have no regrets. Nor would I regret the child that was a part of you."

She snuggled closer into his arms, knowing there was no point arguing further as he picked her up and carried her, naked, over to bed. Nor any need, she thought as she felt the first warm rekindling of desire. The child she longed for would be hers in time.

He made love to her slowly this time, very gently, matching the rhythm of his aching need with hers, and Shanti sighed as she felt the skill that drew her out of herself and closer to him. There would be no carelessness this afternoon, no chance for miscalculations as he drew her with superb control toward the peak that was already beginning to make her forget everything else.

But there would be other times, other afternoons and other nights with the taste of him in her mouth and the smell in her nostrils. He was right. He *would* come back from whatever venture he had set himself on—she sensed that even through her fear—and they would be lovers again and yet again. She would have her chance. She had made him forget before, though it had not yet had the desired end. She would make him forget again. Perhaps in the middle of the night when he was drowsy and so besotted with passion he would not think what he was doing.

She would lose the man she loved. She had always been realistic about that. But she would have a part of him to keep and cherish forever.

The bells sounded all too soon. Shanti had been counting unconsciously, even at the height of their lovemaking, and at last she came to the number she had been dreading.

"Five bells," she said, needlessly, for the clamor echoed through the ship and Gallagher had been counting, too. "In half an hour there will be six. You had best get dressed. What a pity. The tea is cold. Now you will have to make do with whiskey."

Gallagher watched appreciatively as she slipped across the room and poured out a glass of the dark amber liquid she knew he had wanted all along. She was not shy in front of him, but she had draped the saffron-golden sari around her again, carelessly, because she knew he enjoyed the sensuous way it clung and swayed as she moved. He thought how beautiful she was, and was reminded once again with an unwelcome jolt of the look on Matthew Barron's face when he had been longing for Rachel.

It was a powerful thing, the desire of a man for a woman. And young Matthew's passion was as compelling as any he had ever seen. It could lead almost anywhere.

The lady was out of the picture now. Gallagher rolled out of bed and pulled on his pants abruptly, tightening the belt with a rough tug. Perhaps she would stay that way—but he didn't like the feeling that came into his bones when he thought about her.

He took half the glass in one gulp, but did not relish as usual the warmth as it spread through his belly. Gallagher was Irish through and through, no drop of anything foreign to taint *his* blood. And no Irishman worth the name ever ignored a feeling in his bones.

Rachel Todd was trouble. He didn't know how or why—or particularly, when—but he had the distinct feeling that she was trouble. A man would a fool if he

saw trouble looming ahead and he didn't make himself
a plan or two.

And if there was one thing Christy Gallagher had
never been called, it was a fool.

Five

"I can't see a damn thing!"
      The boy's voice floated through the fog. He was a scant five feet away, flat on his belly on the other side of the junk's prow, but the wind carried the words off, making it sound as if he were some distance away.

"That's good, " Matthew replied tersely. Like the boy, he was on his stomach, stretching forward, head well over the edge, and he was wishing himself that he could catch more than an occasional glimmer from the pair of lanterns dangling off the hull. "As long as you don't see anything, we're doing just fine. It's when you *do* see something—say, a rock jutting out of the water—that we need to worry."

"Yeah . . . well, a heck of a lot of good it's going to do then. If I spot something, it'll be too late to maneuver out of the way."

"Not if you keep both eyes where they belong," Matthew cautioned, "and concentrate like crazy. The fog drifts in and out—it seems to clear a bit every few minutes. We ought to be able to see far enough ahead to anticipate problems . . . if there are any."

"And you think there won't be?" The boy's tone was sharp enough to prompt Matthew to turn and peer into the fog. He could barely see a vague profile staring, as ordered, straight ahead.

Cursing under his breath, Matthew forced his gaze back to the water. It seemed he was the one who needed the reminder!

The faint yellow glow that barely suffused the mist had an eerie feel to it, and a smell of salt and dampness clung to his nostrils. He was already having second thoughts about the boy. Young Peter Swayde had just turned seventeen—or, as he liked to put it, was "almost eighteen"—and had been clerking in the firm of an elder cousin who did considerable business with Barron Shipping, and who had been instrumental in acquiring the three junks. Peter had been beside himself with excitement when he heard of the plan, and Matthew, recalling his own thirst for adventure at a similar age, had allowed himself, somewhat reluctantly, to be persuaded to bring him along.

After all, he had told himself then, another pair of eyes might come in handy. Now, it was occurring to him that the danger the youth was facing might be more than he had bargained for.

"Sorry you signed on?" he said quietly.

"Not on your life!" the boy shot back with a bravado he probably felt. For all his qualms, Matthew allowed himself a smile.

"That's a good lad, Petey. Keep your backbone stiff, and don't let anybody scare you off. You'll grow to be a fine man one of these days."

He could almost feel the stifled indignation on the other side of the prow, and it was all he could do to keep the smile from escalating into a chuckle. He had hated it, his first voyage out—as mate because he had convinced a doting grandfather that anything else was beneath his dignity!—and old Angus Dougal, with a canny way of knowing just how to get under his skin, had referred to him bluffly as "Mattie lad."

And he had taken it, Matthew thought with a grin, because he had wanted desperately to play with the big boys—and he knew the game was played by their rules or not at all.

The wind picked up. Hints of winter coming already, and Matthew turned the collar of his jacket up, keeping his eyes all the while on the undulating grayness in front of the junk. He had been first mate and Dougal second—by virtue of birth, not ability—but there had never been any doubt where the authority lay. And Matthew had revered and respected the older man for it.

As, he suspected, young Peter revered and respected him now, though perhaps not with quite the same justification.

"Shouldn't we be getting there soon?"

The question startled Matthew, echoing as it did his own thoughts. He nodded brusquely; then, realizing that Peter couldn't see him, he added aloud:

"We should have been there an hour ago by my calculations. We've been moving steadily, and at a pretty fair speed. Of course, we might have drifted in the fog—where the devil is that Chinese pilot, anyway? He's been gone a blasted long time."

"Back checking on the compass, I'll wager. Probably trying to figure out where he went wrong!"

"Maybe," Matthew admitted, though he didn't like the way things were looking. He couldn't put a finger on it, but every instinct warned him something was wrong. His hand slipped unconsciously to the gun at his belt, resting on the cold metal even as his thoughts were elsewhere.

They *should* have been there by now. Matthew had studied the charts before they left, memorized them thoroughly, and he had a good sense of how much distance they had covered. He had only been at sea three times, this his first stint as captain, but he had a feel for it. It was in his blood, the Barron legacy again, and he was sure of himself and his judgment.

He stretched out, every muscle feeling stiff and cramped, but didn't dare move from his post. It almost seemed as if they had been going around in circles. . . . And, in truth, they might have. Even the most skilled pilot could get lost in the fog, and he had only Steven Wu's word for it that this man was the best. Still . . .

Damn, he should have insisted on holding onto the compass himself. He might not know these shores, but he knew the sea and he knew charts, and he'd feel a blasted sight better trusting himself than some stranger he had never laid eyes on before. He *would* have insisted, but the man spoke only a few words of barely comprehensible pidgin, and Matthew, though he'd never had any difficulty with European languages, wasn't up to tonal Chinese. Communication had been mostly by signs, and it had been daunting, to say the least, to try and tell his pilot with hand signals and waving arms that he didn't want him to use a compass!

He was beginning to think now that it might have been worth the effort to try a little harder.

A faint whisper of movement told him that the wayward pilot was back. He wondered why the thought somehow made him even more uneasy. Peter, finding himself displaced, had come over to squat beside him. Matthew glanced up.

The mists were closing in again. He could just make out a nice-looking young man, about his own height and build, also blond, through somewhat darker. He had a beard that was about as scrawny as Matthew's when he first started it.

Matthew grinned. And he was undoubtedly growing it for the same reason—because he thought it made him look older! It didn't, but by the time he realized that, it wouldn't matter any more. He'd probably shave it off, as Matthew himself was considering doing, now that it had served its illusory purpose.

"Here, take my place," he said, sliding back along the hull and pressing Peter forward. "I want to have a look around, see what's going on. Probably nothing, but it doesn't hurt to be safe."

He started away, soundlessly, not sure why but not wanting the pilot to know what he was doing. As an afterthought, he crept back and hissed:

"Keep one eye on the water—but keep the other on him!" He jerked his thumb toward the pilot. "Don't let him out of your sight."

Peter nodded, and Matthew knew he had been thinking the same thing. A smart one, that lad. He would go far. If not in his cousin's firm, then perhaps with Barron Shipping.

The deck was slippery as Matthew inched across it, feeling his way with his feet. The large central sail loomed ahead, and it occurred to him that the top of the mast would offer the best lookout when the fog let up again. Moisture formed in shallow pools, as if it had been raining, and it took all his concentration to keep from sliding as the junk swayed and rocked.

He managed to reach the mast without making any noise and was congratulating himself on not having bumped into anyone, though most of the half dozen hands were probably huddled in the stern, trying to keep warm. The climb was an easy one; the bamboo battens that held the lugsail taut provided footholds, and even with everything dripping wet, he got to the top without incident.

He paused to catch his breath, feet braced firmly, hands gripping the ropes that secured the mast to the hull. Without expecting to see anything, he turned his head in the direction that instinct told him was land.

There were no surprises. The fog seemed to be clearing, not just here and there, but great empty patches with tendrils of mist trailing through them. Still, Matthew could see nothing that hinted at hills or shores in the distance. He was startled to realize that details on the deck were coming into focus. He pulled back abruptly, afraid someone would notice.

But there was no place to hide on the open mast. And even if one of the men did look up, what was unusual about a sea captain climbing a mast to get a better view?

His anxiety was turning him paranoid. Matthew grinned inwardly. And playing havoc with what little common sense he seemed to have left! Several minutes had passed, uneventfully; more were passing now, and he had the distinct feeling he was going to have to creep back to where young Peter was waiting and admit he had been wrong.

They *had* been lost, after all. Nothing more sinister than that. Now that the fog was easing, they would have a look at the compass together, he and the incompetent pilot, and find a way to their rendezvous.

He had just repositioned his hands to slide back down, a trickier prospect than climbing up, what with the wet shrouds and battens, when he caught a glimpse of something in the distance.

A light? At first he thought it was one of their own lanterns, reflecting off the water. Then he realized it was farther away and blinking strangely. As if being blown behind some solid object by the wind . . . or perhaps sending a signal.

They had arrived! A little late, but that was hardly unreasonable . . . and clearly they were expected. Relief flooded through him, and a sense of foolishness at the unfounded fears that had been stirred up by the fog. The party on shore was already waiting and flashing signals to bring them in!

Time to get down and spread the news, he thought, hesitating an instant as his eyes picked out a second light beside the first. Continuous now—had he only imagined the blinking? Then slowly, unexpectedly, the twin lights started to move, drifting away from each other . . . closing in again.

Matthew did not for an instant imagine that the rolling of the junk had created the illusion. He knew ships and water well enough to recognize the difference, and his blood ran as cold as the mist that was beading up on his forehead. Not lanterns on the *shore* but on small boats, and there were three now—no, four. Hardly a group of harmless fishermen out in weather like this.

They had been set up!

Thoughts of the pilot's peculiar behavior rushed into his mind, crystallizing now, making sense where they had been only vaguely disquieting before. The shiftiness in his eyes as he had cooly surveyed everything on deck. The slight reaction when he caught sight of Peter, a last minute addition and totally unexpected, as if he hadn't liked having an extra man on board. The obtuse way he had ignored Matthew's obvious protests and insisted on keeping the compass himself.

They had seemed to be going around in circles because they were! The fog had prompted them to leave early, and the man had been stalling to give his cohorts time to get to whatever place had been set up for the ambush.

How right he had been, thinking before that they

were expected. Though not quite in the way he had anticipated.

Matthew did not have time to form even the most rudimentary plan. The fog was denser than he had realized, making the boats seem farther away than they were, and it was barely a second before he felt the first jolt as they butted alongside and began tying on. Matthew counted four in the confusion—small, squat outlines like Chinese sampans—but there might have been more. Each seemed to be carrying three or four men. They were swinging up onto the deck, swarming everywhere at once.

Young Peter in the prow was caught by surprise. The boats had approached from the windward side, and all he could do was jump up, gamely standing his ground. As Matthew watched, sick with horror, one of the attackers headed toward him. The boy had just enough time—and foresight—to whirl around, grabbing the pilot by one arm and flipping him neatly over the rail.

A surprised yowl punctuated the splash Matthew heard as the man landed in the water.

Good lad, he thought. Good lad, *good* lad! Judging from the tumult, it seemed that some of the crew were not involved in the piracy. Three, it looked like, were resisting fiercely. That left two, and the pilot, who would take some time to swim back into the fray.

And the pilot was the only one who knew that Matthew Barron was suppose to be in the prow and might have an inkling where he had gone! That left him a little time at least to try and come up with something.

They could have the opium and welcome to it! He'd had his fill of the damned stuff. All he wanted was to see young Peter safe, and the devil take the profits that were pricking his conscience, anyway!

He pulled the gun out of his belt, clinging to the mast with his other hand, and took tentative aim. But the junk was jostling too erratically, the men seemed to be all over Peter now, five or six at least, massing into a human tangle, and he didn't dare risk a shot.

Helplessness and anger mingled as he remained frozen at his post, trying desperately to come up with something—*anything*—to rescue the boy. The men had him by the arms now, and Matthew was startled to see them bring out a rope and tie him stoutly to the forward mast. Whatever they had in mind, apparently it didn't include violence. Not at the moment, anyway.

He lowered the revolver, still keeping it ready, but deciding for the time being to hold his fire. Better not to provoke a confrontation if none was intended.

At least they didn't seem to be looking for *him.* Matthew shifted his position, bracing his feet more steadily against the batten. And why should they? If this attack was as well planned as it appeared, they would have been told to expect a slender, tallish man with blond hair and a beard. And they would think they had found him!

Some of the men had entered the large cabin under the poop deck, others were in the hold, and chests of opium were being dragged out onto the deck. They knew what they were after, all right! No question that this raid was an unfortunate coincidence. They weren't even bothering to open the chests as they lowered them on ropes to the waiting sampans, which were already becoming dangerously overloaded.

It would serve them right if they sank and drowned!

Matthew felt his gorge rise as he clung uselessly to the mast and watched a passel of pirates boldly and thoroughly loot his boat. They were all dressed the same, in black pants and baggy black jackets which made them so alike it would be next to impossible to identify them later. No wonder they felt safe, just tying Peter to the mast and leaving him there! Casting a quick glance back, he saw the the other three men who put up a fight had gotten similar treatment and were bound in the stern.

The fog was dispersing quickly now. Everything on deck had become alarmingly clear, though Matthew still could not make out any traces of land in the distance. The men could have seen him if they had glanced up, but they were too busy with their blasted thieving to notice anything else!

One stood out from the others, catching Matthew's

eye. Apparently their leader, for his cronies seemed to look to him for guidance. He was garbed in the same nondescript black, but his hair, instead of dangling in a pigtail down his back, had been cropped short, Western style. Like some of the clerks in the bigger trading houses.

Steven Wu?

Matthew's hand tightened around the gun. He wondered why it surprised him, that the young man should prove so treacherous. He had taken generous wages with one hand from Olyphant and Company—who were nothing if not vehement in their opposition to the opium trade—while with the other, behind their backs, he had been perfectly willing to accept a share of the profits for smuggling that very commodity.

It was a natural next step to take the entire profit for himself.

Then the man turned, and Matthew saw that it was not Steven Wu after all, though he still sensed the clerk's fine hand in this. The junk acquired from Peter Swayde's cousin had been legitimate, and the three men who came as his crew, but the pilot and the two others who had been picked up with him were clearly part of the conspiracy. Only one person could have set that up, and that person was the man he had trusted to arrange things for him.

He had not only been taken, he had been played for a damned fool!

He swept his eyes toward the prow again. Peter was still bound, but struggling manfully, and it looked like he might manage to work himself free. Matthew didn't know if he wanted him to or not. Renewed fighting might turn a bad situation brutally ugly—but, God, it was hard to stand by and do nothing!

The boy was aching for a fight, and Matthew was aching with him!

He looked back to see that the sampans were fully loaded now. Not another chest could be piled on—they were alarmingly low in the water—and he wondered fleetingly what the pirates were going to do next. Ferry the stuff to shore and come back for more? But to his surprise, they began prying the remaining chests open, spilling hard-crusted balls of opium out on the deck.

The idiots, he thought. Didn't they know they could ruin the stuff? One good wave might wash it overboard!

Then, as he watched, too stunned for an instant even to react, they started in with what appeared to be axes and large mauls, and he realized that that was just what they had in mind. Arms were coming down again and again, smashing the balls open, and with little regard for the decking in the process! Hands were busy sweeping it into buckets and hurling it overboard.

They weren't pirates at all. Not in the conventional sense. They probably considered themselves *patriots*. Their cause was moral—and highly personal! The influx of opium was ruining their country, and they were going to stop it by any means they could!

Ironically, instead of soothing, the thought made Matthew even angrier. Twice he had misjudged Steven Wu, and each time he came out looking a little stupider. He was damned if he was going to cling to the top of the mast, cringing and hiding like a coward! The opium was his, right or wrong—moral or not— and he wasn't going to stand by and watch a bunch of ruffians steal it from him!

Without stopping to think, he aimed the gun above their heads and pulled the trigger. No sooner had the deafening blast roared in his ears than he regretted it. If these fire-breathing fanatics hadn't been inclined toward violence before, this could set them off!

Bit it was too late now; the die was cast, and Matthew pointed the revolver at little lower and shot again. Fragments of wood splintered out of the hull and spattered over the startled faces of those who were standing closest.

The effect was dramatic. Everyone was looking around suddenly, dropping what they were doing, panicking as they tried to figure out where the attack had come from. Matthew's heart stopped as he watched . . . and prayed that they would be too confused to look up! He wished fervently that he hadn't left the extra ammunition safe and dry in the cabin. He had fired two shots; that meant there were three left.

After that, it would be bare hands, and one man against about fifteen! Or two men, if Peter Swayde somehow got loose.

Then suddenly, they all seemed to be moving at once. A sea of black was surging toward the rail, men jostling and scrambling as they leaped into the sampans, practically falling over each other in their desperation to get away.

Matthew could have shouted with exhilaration. It had been a foolish gamble, but it had worked. They hadn't expected resistance. They had been so sure everyone was accounted for, they were utterly demoralized by a couple of gunshots.

He spotted the man he had noticed before—the leader?—sprinting toward the stern, and suddenly he had an overwhelming urge to stop him and drag him back. With that haircut, he would be certain to speak a little English or French, or one of the other languages Matthew was comfortable with. And there were a few questions that needed answering!

He half climbed, half slid down the mast, taking only a few seconds to reach the bottom, but even that was too much. The man was gone, and with him most of the others. Only two sampans remained, one just pulling away, the other untied but still hugging the side of the boat.

Waiting for—what?

Matthew turned, curious and somewhat apprehensive. Had he been a fool to hurl himself down on the deck? But there was only one of the raiders left: a slim fellow, quite tall, and definitely cheeky. He seemed utterly oblivious to everything else as he worked with single-minded frenzy, hellbent on destroying the last ball left in the chest.

Something snapped inside Matthew. Anger intensified into a burst of fury. This rickety junk was his. Not the *China Dawn* maybe, but his vessel, nonetheless. *His* command, and they had violated it! He strode forward, closing in on the black-clad figure. At least he was going to bring one of those devils back with him.

He might not be able to speak the man's language, but there were those in Macao who could. He was going to see that he was interrogated, and very thoroughly. With any kind of luck, they'd find a link to Steven Wu and expose him for the two-faced liar he was!

He must have made a noise, for his quarry turned, alarm flashing out of jet-dark eyes, and started toward the rail. Matthew lunged at him, but the deck was treacherous, and his feet slid all over the place. All he managed to grab was a long black pigtail, wet and strangely tacky from the mist.

The man's head jerked back, and he let out a cry, shrill and high-pitched like so many Chinese tones. Almost girlish, Matthew thought with contempt. The men on the last sampan had seen what was happening; there were two of them, and they were climbing back over the rail, but the fellow gestured them off, calling out something Matthew couldn't understand. Whatever it was, it had its effect, for they turned back reluctantly and shoved away from the side.

"Good, you little bastard!" Matthew growled. He knew the words would have no effect, but they were more for himself than the other man, anyway. He'd had about as much as he could take for one day. "Let's see how you enjoy yourself now that your pals are gone! A little greedy, weren't you there? Well, it's going to cost you. Plenty."

He tugged on the slimy pigtail, intending to bring the fellow close enough to get a better grip. But to his amazement, the thing snapped off in his hand. A fake! With a particularly pungent curse, he tossed it aside.

Another short-haired Chinaman. The place seemed to be swarming with them! Well, at least that meant they'd have a basis for communication. The man tried to get away, but it was a small deck and there was nowhere to go. Matthew caught him again, this time by the back of his jacket, and pulled him, struggling and squirming, toward the cabin.

"All right, buddy. You and I are going to have a little chat. . . . And I don't think you'll like what's going to happen if you don't tell me the truth."

Someone had lit a couple of lanterns in the cabin, no doubt so they could see better to complete their plundering. A soft yellow glow spilled over furnishings that probably once had been quite luxurious but had grown somewhat seedy with time. A large raised platform dominated one side, mattressed and canopied in red, like a Chinese marriage bed. The fellow's eyes flicked toward it, wide and suddenly terrified, and he gave a startled gasp.

Matthew was surprised enough to relax his hold. The man, sensing the change, hurled himself at the door, very nearly getting away. With a bellow of rage, Matthew pulled him back so roughly the jacket, like the pigtail before, completely ripped off, and he was left with it dangling in his hand.

Reacting quickly, he stepped around putting himself between his captive and the door, ready to grab him again. But he came to an abrupt stop as the lantern-light played on a pair of small, but perfectly rounded, very nicely shaped breasts.

A woman?

Matthew gaped, too stunned for an instant to move or speak. The possibility had never even occurred to him. She was tall, even for a Chinese male, and she had been playing what was very much a man's game.

But most clearly, she was a woman, or perhaps a girl, for there was something very young—and touchingly vulnerable—about the half-nude body in front of him.

Matthew found himself reaching out, not knowing what he intended to do, just responding, more from instinct than reason. His hands were on her shoulders suddenly. God, he thought—how soft her skin was.

He felt her shiver, but not with revulsion—not even with the fear that would have been natural—and suddenly he *did* know. As he sensed she had known when she saw the bed and gave that odd little gasp.

He jerked her toward him, roughly, hungering for

the warm, feminine feel of this unexpected rebel against his chest and thighs and throbbing manhood. She was trembling, almost violently now, but not struggling, not resisting. Indeed, her body seemed to melt into his, as impatient for what was to come as he.

One hand slid down her body, through the loose waistband of her trousers, onto the roundness of firm young buttocks. The answering shudder that ran from her body into his removed whatever last doubts Matthew might have had that she was an unwilling participant in this affair. Or that he was going to pull back himself.

The mating was as inevitable as it was urgent, and he was going to have her.

Matthew had no idea what was happening to him. He had never so completely lost control of his senses before, or his body. He pressed her against him, hard, his free hand tilting her chin up, longing for one kiss to make the thing more personal before he pulled her to the floor and possessed her right there. It was as if everything had culminated suddenly in this excruciating physical need. All the anger and horror of the afternoon, the confusion that had come before . . . the unexpected love that burst upon him and turned his life upside down.

His body had gone unsatisfied too long. He had demanded too much of it. First with Rachel, when things came so wonderfully close to getting out of hand; then Camilla, who had been a sore temptation, the little minx. It was not going to go unsatisfied now.

Her mouth was opening, freely, still unresisting, and he took it harshly, as he would take her in a moment. The heat excited him, the fervency, and he probed her lips eagerly, finding them soft and impudent . . . and quite unexpectedly familiar.

Damn! He would recognize those lips anywhere.

Matthew drew back, staring at her in mounting comprehension. Even before he dragged her over to the lantern, he knew what he was going to see. And he knew what his body had been trying to tell him with its insatiable urges before.

Her eyes no longer looked black. In the light they had turned a soft, velvety brown. And the tips of her hair, where the stain had not quite taken hold, showed flashes of reddish gold.

"Well, tiger," he said. "What a surprise."

Six

Rachel stood in the flickering light and stared helplessly back at the man whose sudden assault had
left her so weak she could hardly breathe. Her whole
body seemed to be trembling; she was excruciatingly
conscious of her bare breasts in the chill draught of
the room, but she could not make herself move or even
turn away.

The last thing she had expected was to find *him* here.
She had come knowing only that there was a trader
trying to smuggle opium into the country. That the
trader might be Matthew Barron had never even occurred to her. Indeed, a good part of her own personal
mission that afternoon had been to forget, for a while
at least, the turmoil he had stirred in her heart and her
body.

And then she had spun around to find him advancing
on her!

Sweet heaven, it was the same thing that had happened before! Every muscle, every nerve ending still
throbbed with the remembered closeness of him, that
savage masculine pressure so hard against her own frail
femininity, it had seemed as if they were one single
being. He a part of her and she of him, their desires
mingling and fusing.

No, not the same, Rachel though with a gasp of
anguished despair. A thousand times worse—for that
first time he had caught her by surprise. The emotions
had come so quickly; they had been so new and confusing, she had not had a moment to make out what
was happening. This time her body knew and under-

stood him and had responded with a primitive, utterly terrifying intensity.

It was as if she had no will of her own! She had wanted him, beyond all sense and reason. And, heaven help her, she wanted him still! If he tightened his hold, if he drew her toward him, she would go, like a puppet on a string—and eagerly, joyously. Her mouth would welcome his kisses, her body whatever else he had in mind.

Summoning the last remnants of her strength, she managed somehow to jerk her arm free and took a step back.

"What . . . what are you going to do with me?"

His expression changed subtly, little crinkly lines forming in the flesh around his eyes, more unsettling than the passion that had blazed out of them before.

"What should I do? You come like a thief in the fog, destroying what is mine. Should I tie you up and throw you overboard as you deserve? Or should I toss you on that bed over there and show you what happens to little girls who kiss men like you did just now?"

"I am not a *little* girl!" Rachel tossed her head back, defiance waving like a banner with the black-stained hair that flipped around her face. But it was a false defiance, for the teasing tempted almost as much as the touching, and little thrills were shivering through her. "I'm quite unusually tall. But I *am* only a woman. I'm not as strong as you. You can do what you like with me—on the bed or elsewhere. There's no way I can stop you."

"But I would not do what *I* like," he said quietly. "I would only do it if you liked it, too . . . and you know that, Rachel Todd, so stop pretending that that kiss was merely a kiss . . . and our bodies only 'flirting.' The longing was yours as much as mine. But then, that can hardly have come as a surprise. That was what you expected, wasn't it . . . when you came here to find me?"

"To find *you*?" Rachel gaped at him, genuinely shocked—and grateful for the diversion. This was one thing she didn't find appealing in him, or any other

man, for that matter. The supreme arrogance that made
them all think the world somehow revolved around
them! "I didn't come to find you. I didn't even know
you were here. I came to find a load of opium, which
I fully intended to pitch into the ocean. And at least I
got part of it!"

"It didn't occur to you that that opium just might
happen to belong to me?" he taunted maddeningly.
"And that I just might happen to have come along
with it?"

"No. Why should it? I didn't see your fancy ship
anywhere. Just a tired old junk, and it wasn't exactly
flying the red-and-white Barron colors with pride! We'd
just heard from—from someone that there was a smuggling operation and it was set to begin tonight."

Matthew let the allusion to "someone" pass. Now
that he'd had time to cool off, he wasn't angry with
Steven Wu anymore, and he admired her for her loyalty.

"So you decided you'd see if you could thwart us?"

"We had to try! We couldn't let all that opium get
to shore. There were supposed to be three junks,
heading in separate directions. We figured if we split
into three groups, at least one of us would succeed. I
hope the others managed better than I did!"

"So do I . . . if it means that much to you." Matthew caught the startled look on her face and smiled,
gently, but with little hope that she would believe him.
"I must say I'm surprised at your father, letting you
get involved in this. I can understand a pastorly zeal
for reforming the world, but pirate raids can be dangerous, especially for a woman. And I don't mean the
bullets that aren't always aimed in the air! You might
have paid dearly for your impudence . . . if I hadn't
recognized those sensuous lips just in time."

"My father doesn't know where I am, or my
mother." Rachel could feel herself squirming, and not
merely in reaction to the unavoidable lie she had told
her parents. She couldn't help thinking of what would
indeed have happened if he hadn't stopped just short
of what her traitorous body was still half hoping for.

"Or my three oldest brothers. I told them I was going to be helping friends at an inland mission. My youngest brother, Sam, is with one of the other groups. He can pass for Chinese, too. Carter and Gideon John are much too tall—and Joshua's shoulders are about the size of the stern of your junk!"

Her eyes seemed to glow as she spoke of her family. A faint smile played unconsciously with the corners of her mouth, and Matthew was touched. He had almost forgotten with the intensity of his desire for this woman that he also loved and adored her.

"It must have been a surprise finding me here."

"More than a surprise." Rachel struggled to block out the affection in his tone. She had had a moment of panic when she had spotted the blond, bearded youth in the prow, but she had realized instantly it wasn't him, and she had been sure—*so* sure—that she would have a few hours at least without conflicting thoughts of Matthew Barron. "It was a shock. And not a pleasant one!"

"But not altogether *un*pleasant." He was laughing, softly, coaxing her in spite of herself to look at him. Why were his eyes so blue? She had never seen eyes quite that color. They made her feel as if she were drowning in them.

"Maybe not," she blurted out, honesty getting in the way again before she had time to choke it back. "But it was certainly . . . confusing."

"It was confusing for me, too," Matthew admitted. "Though I think we might be able to work through that. I am going to kiss you again Rachel. On that lovely, remarkable mouth." He had taken hold of her chin with his fingers and was tilting it gently upward. "I won't do it if you don't want me to. All you have to do is put up your hand and hold me back. But I think you *do* want it. . . ."

"I don't," she lied, but he wasn't listening. He was leaning closer, reminding her that she was still half-naked. She could almost feel the rough texture of his jacket on her breasts, as if their bodies were touching again.

"Then put up your hand. . . . That's all you have to do. I'm right here, just inches away. . . . All you have to do is put your hand in front of my mouth, firmly, and push me back . . . and I'll go."

But I can't, she thought . . . and, oh, he knew it! His mouth was so near, Rachel could feel the heat of his breath on her lips. So tempting, so compelling. She could no more refuse him this one sweet kiss than she could stop the life-giving air that rushed into her lungs.

It was destiny that had brought them to that spot at that moment. A cruel, capricious destiny, but one that would not be denied.

His mouth felt unexpectedly gentle on hers; a kiss that was more like a sigh, echoing her own helpless surrender, aching and tender . . . and utterly undemanding. As if he were caressing her, reassuring, telling her not to be frightened, and Rachel understood without words what he was saying.

He was not going to push her before she was ready, not going to use the urges of her own body against her. He was just going to drink in the honey of her lips, and offer his to her, and wait with infinite patience until the yearnings came by themselves, natural and unforced.

He pulled away slowly. His fingers barely brushed her cheeks, an infinitely enticing gesture.

"I love you, Rachel Todd," he said softly. "Not just today, or for what might happen in that bed . . . but for always, I love you."

"And I *hate* you!" she replied with feeling. It wasn't fair the way he kept changing, doing something unpredictable the minute she thought she had him figured out. If this were any other man . . . *any* other man . . .

"Yes," he agreed. "But not quite as much as you want to." He was smiling again, teasingly and, unfortunately, very disarmingly.

"I'll work on it," she snapped.

"I'm sure you will." He kissed her one more time, lightly, just on the edge of her mouth, and went over to where the shabby black jacket had been dropped in the awkward haste of their passionate embrace. "This looks mendable," he said, all brusqueness and business suddenly. "There's a crew's quarters of sorts in the stern. I daresay I'll be able to rustle up a needle and some thread. In the meantime, you might want to check out those chests against the wall. The chap who had this tub before departed rather, uh . . . hurriedly. He might have left something useful behind."

Rachel crossed her arms instinctively over her chest, feeling self-conscious somehow, and strangely bereft by this abrupt change in his manner.

"I don't suppose there's a . . . blanket, or something like that."

"Here." He took off his own jacket and tossed it at her, his head half-turned, as if to spare her further embarrassment. "There are probably plenty on the bed, but I wouldn't trust either one of us anywhere near it at the moment." He was grinning rakishly as he looked back. "That barrel has water in it, and you should find a tin bowl and some soap over there. Not that you don't look fetching with that exotic black hair, but I think I prefer you as a redhead."

"My hair's not red. It's blond—with a trace of ginger."

"Really? I could have sworn the red predominated. Maybe because of all that fiery temper. It will be interesting to see which one of us is right. . . . I should be back in an hour or two. Try not to miss me too much, tiger."

"You're . . . going somewhere?" Rachel heard the quaver in her voice, and she could have kicked herself for it. Wasn't that what she wanted? For him to leave her alone? Why on earth was she acting like a perverse little ninny, feeling suddenly betrayed because he could bear to be separated from her?

"I do have a few things to tend to on deck, you know," he reminded her. "You and your buddies wreaked quite a considerable amount of havoc with my vessel."

"Oh—the *opium* again!" Rachel spat it out, despising herself for the softness that had made her long for one treacherous instant to believe in him. All the gentle kisses and protestations of love in the world couldn't erase the fact that she was less important to him than salvaging what he could of his disgusting cargo! "That's all you care about! The opium and the money you're going to make from it. Nothing else really matters, does it? I wish I had gotten it all! Every last bit of it!"

"I don't give a damn about the opium," he retorted with surprising heat. "If you haven't figured that out yet, you don't know the first thing about me. But you did leave four men tied up out there . . . or have you forgotten that little fact? I trust you won't consider it too crass of me to make sure they're all right. And see that no irreparable damage has been done to the boat."

Rachel could only be thankful that he didn't turn back to see the flood of crimson that rose to her cheeks as he stomped rather noisily out of the cabin. She *had* forgotten. She had been so wrapped up in herself, she hadn't given one thought to the discomfort the boy must be suffering. Or the three Chinese crewmen in the stern.

She waited until his footsteps died away, then found a large metal basin and began filling it with water from the barrel. The last thing she had wanted was for anyone to be hurt. It had always been a condition, right from the beginning, that there was to be no violence or killing. If it hadn't been for her strict ban on weapons, he would never have been able to rout them so quickly!

But then someone would almost certainly have been hurt. And Rachel realized uneasily that the sharp little pang in the pit of her stomach was more at the thought that it might have been Matthew than for any of the others.

Slipping off the jacket and baggy Chinese trousers, she knelt naked over the basin and began to wash her hair, very thoroughly, scrubbing out all the bootblack that had become sticky and stubborn in the mist. There *were* blankets on the bed, thick and surprisingly plush.

Rachel dried her hair with one and selected another to wrap herself in when she finished bathing.

There was no place to throw the used water, but fortunately the cabin came equipped with another basin. She filled it and took the bar of soap, sloshing it around until it frothed into a rich, bubbly lather.

Such sweet-smelling soap, she thought, forgetting everything else for an instant as she enjoyed the scent . . . and so soft it foamed easily. She began very slowly, with no conscious thought that Matthew might be back at any moment, to cleanse away the dust and perspiration and feverish heat that still seemed to sear wherever he had touched.

Bathing had always seemed a sensual act to Rachel. It was even more so now with the strange and bewildering new feelings that flooded over her with the sleek, soothing caress of the water.

It was as if her body had memories of its own. Her breasts could feel again the coarse fabric of his jacket; the soft skin of her buttocks burned, not from the slight pressure of her own soapy fingers, but the provocative impudence of his; her belly arched hungrily toward the hard mass jutting into it, which she had not been naive enough to miss—or mistake. And her lips sighed anew with the dazzling gentleness of a kiss that made her want to forget everything but the man and the sweet love he promised.

It was the gentleness that frightened her most. She swathed herself in the blanket and sat on the edge of the bed, shivering, but not altogether from the cold. Passion she might somehow learn to control, or avoid if she couldn't trust herself with him again. But the gentleness was different, reminding her of the many things about Matthew Barron she did truly like and admire. It made her long to be more forgiving, to understand and accept him as he was—a man with all his flaws and virtues, like any other man.

What was so terrible, that gentleness seemed to whisper insidiously, with a little imperfection? What was so wrong with accepting a man on his own terms? Cherishing him . . . and letting him cherish you?

What on earth was she thinking?

Rachel got up restlessly, throwing off the blanket again, longing for the brittle evening air that had chilled her before. This was exactly what she had *not* planned to make of her life!

She wanted a man secure in his knowledge of the world and wordly things. She was not looking for some fragile flower of the field. But she wanted a man who was strong in his faith, like her father and brothers, and righteous and decent. She wanted a man who would find something like opium so inherently repugnant he could not bring himself to touch it!

She began to fling the chests open as he had suggested, finding some small distraction in riffling through the contents. Whoever possessed the junk before had been a man of peculiarly sybaritic tastes— everything was red and silk and decadently sumptuous—and Rachel found herself wondering who he was and what had caused him to leave so "hurriedly." A panderer, probably. And judging by the cut of the garments, he had not catered to men who fancied young *girls*.

She selected a particularly vivid pair of crimson trousers, so immaculate they looked new, and slipped them on. They were a little short, but otherwise fit perfectly, as did the matching shirt which she secured with a silken sash at her waist. Her hair was almost dry, and she fluffed it out with her fingers, not having a comb—and not being exactly eager to search for one, since she had no idea who had used it before.

The silk felt almost incredibly sensuous as she sat back down on the bed, a lingering softness teasing her skin. Like Matthew's last kiss, she thought, and the way his hand brushed her cheek . . . and she knew suddenly that all the pondering and questioning and agonizing in the world wasn't going to make the least bit of difference.

He *was* going to kiss her like that again. And she knew what would happen when he did.

As I see it, you have two choices. You can either

*marry him, as he suggests . . . or you can hop in his
bed and have a rousing good time!*

Wise little Camilla. She seemed such a flibbertigib-
bet sometimes, but she knew what she was talking
about when it came to men.

She couldn't marry Matthew Barron, of course. That
was for sure! But she could have an affair with him,
and she would—so she might as well do it willingly.
It was going to happen anyway. It would just make it
that much more humiliating if she struggled against
him and lost.

At least this way she would retain a part of her pride.

The silk felt sleek and cool against her skin, making
her body seem even warmer as she wrestled one last
moment with her doubts and gave in to the inevitable.
He would still win, in a way. He would still have her
in his arms and his bed. But she would be there because she wanted to, because she had made a deliberate, conscious choice. Not because his superior male
will had broken her down!

The greater triumph would be hers. Rachel felt a
moment of almost calm serenity as she realized all the
agonizing was over and she had already let go of her
inhibitions. This was the man she wanted; there was
no changing that, but she could control the conditions
under which she came to him.

Only the innocence of her body would belong to him
tonight. He would never, *never* touch the purity of her
spirit and her soul.

It did not surprise Rachel when Matthew Barron re-
appeared in a new and quite stylish outfit. Looking
good was something he obviously took pride in—he
had been quite dapper even in rough sailor's garb—
and she had to admit he did it well.

Apparently, he had stashed a fair amount of luggage
in the ''crew's quarters of a sort,'' for the fawn-colored
trousers that hugged his long, lean legs were tailored
to fit like a second skin, and flowing sleeves on a loose
white shirt had been fastened at the cuffs with red-
stoned links. Hardly the sort of clothing most men

would pack for a jaunt like this! The neck was open, showing wisps of hair as fair as the soft curls that spilled casually onto his forehead.

Rachel felt a lump come to her throat as he lingered just inside the doorway, the light catching and accenting his features and dramatic coloring. How handsome he looked. . . . It was going to be harder than she had thought, setting conditions on this love of theirs, when all she really wanted was to feel his arms around her . . . his mouth on hers . . . making her forget everything else.

"The men are all right?" She was surprised to hear how husky her voice sounded, settling somewhere deep in her throat.

"Nice of you to ask," he replied with barely a trace of sarcasm. "Yes, they're fine. They managed to work themselves loose before I got there, and showed quite a bit of initiative at that! They went after one of the sampans in a dinghy I wouldn't have thought would hold water."

"They didn't *catch* it?"

"Easily. There were four men on board, but they were no match for my three—and the boy, who was so mad he was spewing lava! . . . Don't look so alarmed. I told them I already had one captive, and that was sufficient. *More* than sufficient, though I didn't think it would be quite appropriate to explain why." He had moved over to the bed and was staring down at her with an expression that sent little shivers of anticipation down Rachel's spine. "They're dropping your pals off on shore, then they have orders to find out what happened to Gallagher and Romack—the men with the other two junks. So it looks like it's just the two of us . . . here. Alone."

"I see." Rachel tried very hard to be glad that her friends had gotten away, but it was impossible to concentrate when he was looking at her like that. She was surprised to feel that her palms were sticky, almost as if she were frightened. "Well, you did warn me . . . before. When I asked what you were going to do with me."

"Did I?" He sat on the edge of the bed, reluctantly, giving Rachel the strangest feeling that he, like she, was being drawn by forces over which he had no control. "I think I was right," he said quietly. "There *is* more red in your hair . . . though maybe it's that, uh . . . garment. Scarlet becomes you."

"I'm glad you like it." Her throat was so dry suddenly, it was hard to talk. "It's better that way, if . . . if you're going to . . . You know—it's better if you're pleased with how I look."

"If I'm going to *what*?"

"If you're going to . . ." She took a deep breath, struggling with the conflicting feelings that were making her dizzy and confused again. This was what she wanted—wasn't it? This was what she had decided to do. Why, then, was her heart pounding so violently is seemed to be drumming in her ears? "If you're going to *hurl* me on the bed and show me what happens to women who kiss men the way I dared to kiss you!"

"Not hurl. Throw."

"Toss," she corrected, and was disconcerted to hear him laugh.

"You *were* paying attention . . . I thought you might be." He was stretching out his hand, almost without realizing it. His fingers were on her cheek again, unutterably gentle, as before. "You aren't afraid of me, Rachel? I told you—you have nothing to fear from me. I won't do anything you don't want."

"That's just it," she replied with a disarming honesty that caught him off guard. "I'm afraid I'll want it too much."

Her face had turned meltingly soft in the pale yellow light, vulnerable, yet expectant somehow, and Matthew felt his breath catch in his chest. He had vowed when he came back into the cabin that he wasn't going to touch her; he was just going to sit and talk with her, teach her slowly to trust him. This wasn't some trollop he had picked up for a night's amusement—this was the woman he wanted to love and take care of for the rest of his life.

But she looked so ravishing. In spite of himself, he

felt his resolve weakening. So devastatingly desirable in that absurd silk outfit. The filmy fabric lay like a whisper over fragile young breasts which he longed to see and touch again. His body had already begun, man-obstinate, to harden for her; his hands were defying him, finding and tugging on the silken sash.

"So clever, the Chinese. . . . I think they invented this stuff because it slides away so easily. See, love . . . it's already gone. Anyhow, your skin is burning hot. I don't think you need that shirt right now."

"Matthew . . ." It was barely a sigh, so soft he could hardly hear it. It occurred to him that this was the first time she had called him by his name.

"It's all right, I just want to see you. . . . You're so lovely. . . . But I give you my word—the same promise as before. All you have to do is say no, push me back, tell me I've gone too far. Even if you don't, I'm not going to let things get out of hand this time."

He was easing the silk off her shoulders as he spoke, enjoying the sensuous luxury of it, as he enjoyed the warmth and quivering of her flesh beneath. He had never felt like this before, never wanted to possess and protect a woman so much at the same time . . . even if what he was protecting her from was himself.

And he would protect her, he vowed. He *could*. It would be enough—this time—to see her. To touch her just a little. He hadn't understood before the intensity of his hunger for this woman, and it had gotten hold of him before he knew what was happening. All he had to do was be more careful.

But, oh, God . . . she was beautiful. The night was pitch black now; the windows and even the walls receded into the void, and her skin picked up the gold of the light until it seemed to glow from within. Her breasts were so small, they would fit into his hand—his fingers ached to fondle them—but high and temptingly firm, with dark pink nipples, engorged as if to test his will.

Then he *was* fondling them, and she was sinking into his arms, making soft little sounds that were halfway between whimpers and sighs. She felt so right in

his embrace, so perfect . . . as no woman had felt
before. He wanted her, he ached for her; every fiber
of his being cried for him to let up his resistance.

At least for a moment. . . . He could still keep his
control. But he needed all of her now, for his eyes and
his hands, if not his sorely throbbing manhood. He
was laying her back on the bed, stretching out full
length beside her, slowly, gently, coaxing off the scarlet silk trousers.

He *had* been right. He smiled, even through the passion that was making it increasingly difficult to think.
The soft downy patch between her legs was darker
than her hair, but of a distinctly reddish hue. And glistening, as if with desire.

His fingers could resist no longer. He touched her
lightly, tentatively, not daring yet to caress, and was
surprised to feel how warm and wet she was. Surely
she could not be ready for him. . . . Not yet . . .

Rachel felt the sudden, soft pressure of his hand,
barely brushing the inside of her thighs, and a soft cry
slipped out of her lips. Not because she was startled
by this abrupt invasion of her privacy, but because it
was so exactly what she wanted. And he seemed to
know exactly *when* she longed to feel it.

As if she were already a part of him, as if their
bodies had merged these many times past, and he knew
and anticipated her every desire. Rachel let herself
move closer, her body curving instinctively against
him, reveling in the strength and hardness of his masculinity. She had never understood before what passion was. She had thought she did, and she had sensed
that it would be important to her, but she had had no
idea how compelling and consuming it would be.

It was funny—she had been so frightened a moment
ago, turning timid all of a sudden when she realized
they were actually on the bed and *it* was really going
to happen. But there was no fear now. Not a breath of
hesitation. Only the tantalizing knowledge of how vir-
ile and exciting this man was . . . and how much her
body loved what he was doing and longed for him not
to stop.

He seemed to sense the completeness of her surrender. His hands grew bolder, caressing, though not in
that same place she had thrilled to feel him before.
But they seemed to be everywhere else—on her hips,
running down her thighs, cupping and fondling her
breasts. Not cautiously now, seeking and waiting for
permission, but with the ravishing certainty of a man
who knew his advances were welcome.

Rachel could feel his mouth searching for hers, and
she was pressing closer, eager to respond, their kiss
mutually satisfying as never before, for this time it was
as much hers as his, shared and equal. This was what
she had always wanted. She was surprised at how clear
everything suddenly seemed. This was what she had
dreamed of, all those sweet, dark nights alone in her
bed.

This was the man for her. The only man her body
could ever truly accept. Right or wrong, good or evil—
fair and honorable or weak and treacherous—he was
hers, and she his, and that was simply the way it was.

His mouth left hers, blazing a trail of hungry kisses
down her throat, to the throbbing pulse at the base of
her neck, across her aching breasts. Rachel was intensely conscious of the provocative tingle of his beard
against the satin-smoothness of her skin.

How could his hands be hard and soft at the same
time? Demanding and yet coaxing? She could have
wept as she felt him tease the soft inner surface of her
thighs, then retreat again. His tongue was an agony,
licking and tormenting her nipples until she wanted to
scream with the bittersweet pain.

Then suddenly his leg was between her thighs, rough
and impudent and welcome—oh, sweet heaven, how
welcome—and she was opening instinctively, willing
him to come to her. This was not the triumph she had
expected: the cool, sure victory of her will over his—
just so much given, and nothing more, a part of her
held back forever.

In the morning, she would withdraw into herself
again and decide just how much of her spirit and soul

were left. But tonight she would be utterly and unreservedly his.

She waited, breathless and quivering, but the bold invasion she expected did not come. She could feel the longing vibrating through his body, and the heat—the sense of it was an urgent, tangible presence—but there was restraint, too, taut and unyielding.

Had she done something wrong? Bewildered, Rachel cursed herself for not having listened closer to Camilla's coaching. His hand was right *there,* at the center of all her desires—her legs were wide and inviting—but still he made no move to possess her.

Then she remembered the promises he had uttered earlier. He would do nothing she didn't want. Was he expecting some sign from her?

"It's all right, Matthew," she murmured. "I don't mind . . . really, I don't."

"You don't *mind*?" His voice was hoarse with repressed desire. "Minding has nothing to do with it. This isn't something a woman gives because she doesn't want to hurt a fellow's feelings."

Rachel felt him draw back, arching his body up on the bed to gaze down at her, but she couldn't bring herself to meet his eyes, Embarrassment seemed to be flushing through her; she was sure she must be pink all the way to her toes! It was unfair—she was so inexperienced. Was he really going to make her say the words?

"I . . . I didn't mean 'mind' . . . exactly." She kept her eyes closed so she wouldn't see if he smiled at her clumsiness. "I meant that I want this. I . . . I *want* you to make love to me."

"Oh, God."

His body went rigid. He seemed to be bending over her, peering closely, but still she couldn't look. She could only lie there, waiting, until he spoke again:

"Tell me the truth, tiger. Have you ever done this with a man before?"

Rachel gasped. Shame and humiliation flooded over her, sweeping all the sweet desire away. Did he really think she was so wickedly depraved? But after the way she had just behaved, what did she expect?

"No . . ." she whispered miserably, and was startled to hear a muffled, but very distinct, *"Damn!"*

That brought her eyes open. His face was as red as every inch of her body. Not with embarrassment, but what appeared to be tautly leashed-in longing.

"You . . . you *want* me to have done this before? With somebody else?"

"At the moment," he said with telling emphasis, "you bet I do!" Then catching her confusion, and struggling with the almost irresistible urge to take her in his arms again and kiss it away, he added, softly: "No, of course not. I'm arrogant enough to want you all for myself. No sharing . . . no tender memories of other men. But if you *had* done it, there'd be no reason to stop. Our bodies would be together—no space between us—and I'd be inside you right now."

Rachel could almost hear the heavy silence in the room as the meaning of his words slowly sank in. This wasn't the way things were supposed to turn out. She had planned it all so carefully. She had been so sure, once she made up her mind. It was going to be the ultimate concession, the gift of herself—even though he didn't deserve it.

And he was rejecting her.

"Blast it, Rachel!" he burst out, leaping up from the bed, "I want more than this for you. This shabby cabin on an old tub that's seen God-knows-what debaucheries in the past! A woman's first experience with love should be sweet and magical. Something she'll remember the rest of her life. Innocence is too precious to be discarded lightly, like an old garment that's outlived its usefulness. I want you to have a wedding night, beautiful, beautiful Rachel, with all that that implies. I want *us* to have a wedding night to share."

Rachel blinked back the tears that rose to her eyes. He *was* rejecting her. He was making it sound very nice, but he was rejecting her because what he wanted was the one thing she could never give.

"Then you're going to wait a little longer than forever. Because we're not going to *have* a wedding night!''

''We will if I show a little restraint . . . which I seem to have a great deal of trouble doing with you.''

''Restraint isn't the point!'' she retorted. ''You can't have a wedding night without a wedding. And weddings require the consent of the bride!''

''Ah . . . and you're not going to consent?'' He was looking unsettlingly smug, not the least bit put off.

''Did you really think I would?'' she said sarcastically.

''I had hopes. . . . I still do.''

One brow had gone up, irony that was echoed in his lips as he turned and sauntered maddeningly toward the door. It occurred to Rachel for the first time that he was fully clothed and she naked, and she had not even noticed before. It also occurred to her how nicely those clothes molded themselves to his body, and she found herself wishing irrationally that he were just a bit more of a scoundrel.

He turned one last moment in the doorway.

''I love you, Rachel Todd . . . and you love me, though you won't admit it. People who love each other should be making commitments, not bouncing around for a few hours pleasure on a bed somewhere.''

Then he was leaving, and she couldn't stop him. Rachel knew it, and she hated him for it! The triumph was his, after all, and in exactly the way she had vowed would never happen. He had not gotten the body she was willing to give—but a part of her heart was going out the door with him.

''I am *not* going to marry you,'' she insisted.

''I know. . . . Because I am foul and evil and have filthied my hands with opium.''

''No,'' she snapped illogically. ''Because you have a beard! I've always hated beards. I would never, *never* marry a man with hair all over his face!''

Seven

Stupid, Rachel thought the next morning when she woke almost lazily in the surprisingly comfortable bed. Such a stupid thing to say . . . and so utterly pointless. No doubt there was a razor and mirror in the ''crew's quarters of a sort.'' The next time she saw Matthew Barron, she had the distinct feeling he was going to be clean-shaven.

And with an infuriating grin spreading across those naked features, which she was compelled to admit she probably deserved!

The beard *wasn't* the problem. The problem was indeed the opium he had taunted her with, and his greed for a profit that was so important he was willing to risk even the love he had declared for her!

The sun was streaming through narrow slits that ran along the tops of the walls on both sides of the cabin. The fog had lifted, it seemed, and Rachel was startled to realize it was well into the morning. She got up and refilled the basin which had somehow gotten itself emptied and wiped clean again. Matthew tiptoeing in in the darkness? She rarely slept this late, but she had been up most of the night destroying the rest of the opium, which had been left out on deck. Carelessly, perhaps? Or perhaps as a magnanimous gesture, since so little remained anyway?

At least she had managed to wear herself out. The vessel seemed steady as Rachel splashed water on her face—barely swaying, so the wind must have calmed. She had been so exhausted when she finally tumbled into bed that no memories of Matthew Barron and the humiliating rejection she suffered at his hands had come to trouble her dreams.

She finished dressing and found her own jacket, neatly folded on a chest against the wall. Not with a needle and thread, as she might have imagined, but quite serviceably mended, and she was a little surprised to be reminded that he was, after all, a seaman. Apparently, he wasn't quite as useless as his wealth and insouciance seemed to imply.

Slipping the jacket on, Rachel went up on deck.

There were no surprises here. Matthew was standing high on the prow, one hand resting on the forward mast, staring off at something just beyond the range of her vision. And his face was as smooth as that of a newborn babe!

He seemed to be miles away, his eyes thoughtful as they scanned the craggy coast of the small inlet where the junk now at lay at anchor—so that was why it felt so steady—and Rachel had a moment to study his profile before he realized she was there.

It was a strong profile, and almost defiantly proud. As if he recognized, but refused to acknowledge the inherent power that came with his birth and his breeding. Rachel has always thought that men who grew beards did so because they had weak chins, but there was nothing weak about any of these features. Every bone seemed to be sharply chiseled: his nose slightly aquiline without the softening effect of his beard; his cheekbones and brow, where the breeze blew the hair back from his face, looking as if they had been carved out of the sheer pale rocks that rose behind him.

She remembered suddenly everything she had heard about the arrogance of the Barron clan, and she knew, for all his laughter and lightness, that this man was one of them.

"You've been busy, I see," she said, and waited as he turned with exactly the grin she had expected. Smug and deliberately infuriating—but if he thought she was going to rise to the bait, he would be sorely disappointed! "We were some distance out, last time I took note. It's fortunate you know how to handle the sails alone.''

"I've had some experience with ships," he reminded her, nothing in his expression showing that he was the least bit nonplussed by her snub. "And developed a few instincts, which stood me in good stead since that rascal of a pilot took my compass when he went for a swim! I've just been trying to figure out where we are. I expected we'd be well into the estuary of the Pearl River, toward the first bar, somewhere near Whampoa."

"You passed it in the fog," Rachel informed him. "We're actually on the other side of Canton, a little beyond the Macao Passage. In territory that's strictly forbidden to foreigners, incidentally. You're lucky the river traffic doesn't use this inlet often. You make an inviting target up there, with all that yellow hair gleaming in the sun."

"Damn!" Matthew muttered as he leaped down, then started to apologize. Rachel cut him off.

"Every minister's daughter isn't a prude. I heard a 'damn' or two out of those lips last night and didn't melt away." At least, not because of that, she thought, and hastily decided to change the subject before it got too embarrassing. "We can't afford to stay here very long. Someone's bound to come by, and they're going to be curious when they see a junk anchored in these waters."

"I daresay," Matthew muttered. His gaze drifted back the way they had come the night before, unknowing in the fog. "We'll never slip this tub past Canton—unless we wait for dark, and that would be risky. But it would be even riskier trying to make our way on foot. What we need is a small boat. Something that can maneuver the water passages to Macao."

"I think I know where we might pick up a sampan," Rachel told him, "with a little rounded roof that would shadow the occupants. Assuming, of course, you're really ready to walk away from the junk. It *is* an investment . . .''

"A very small one. Junks are cheap. This one, especially. It was purchased with an eye toward being left behind at some point. Now, that sampan you have in mind . . .''

"Is one of the ones used in the raid," Rachel said, finishing the sentence for him. "They're supposed to leave it for me, the others—I told them what to do when they sailed off." She hesitated. "Unless, of course, those were the men your crew captured. You did let them go, didn't you . . . like you said?''

Matthew nodded distractedly, and she was relieved to realize he was telling the truth. If he hadn't been, he would have made more of an effort to convince her.

"What else did you say?" he asked curiously. "When you signaled them back? They didn't want to go, but they did. How did you persuade them?''

"I told them you wouldn't hurt me when you found out who I was. A white woman and a missionary—can you imagine the scandal if one hair of my *blond* head was ruffled? They, on the other hand, would be whipped within an inch of their lives. And you *didn't* hurt me, so it seems I was right. . . .''

"Didn't I, tiger?" he said, very quietly. "And *feathers* are ruffled, not gorgeous red hair.''

"I also told them," Rachel hastened to add, deliberately avoiding the tender concern in his gaze, "to find my brother and head him off with a story about running into acquaintances and going back with them. Sam is barely a year older than I, and a good three inches shorter—and skinny as a bamboo stick—but he can be ferocious when he gets his temper up. You wouldn't want him coming after you.''

"I wouldn't indeed," Matthew agreed. Not that he was afraid of skinny, ferocious Sam Todd, but he would have hated to have to hurt Rachel's brother. And he had the feeling she'd never have forgiven him for it, either! "But we're wasting time. We'd better get some things together. Soap and blankets, whatever grub I can lay my hand on, clothes . . . I'm afraid I don't have much to offer you except those red silk things.''

"That's all right. My wardrobe—such as it is—is on the sampan. I don't pack quite as extensively as you."

"Ah, well, we can't all be fashion plates." He started back toward what Rachel assumed was the crew's quarters, then spun around with a devilish look. "By the way, you missed a couple of chests. In the hold. I finished them off this morning while you were still sleeping. It's funny-smelling stuff, isn't it? Opium?"

Rachel stood absolutely motionless for a moment. "Then you *did* leave it out on purpose. For me to dump overboard if I wanted."

"Not *if* . . . when," he said softly. "And yes, of course I did. I run a very tidy ship. You can call it an early wedding present."

A present for a wedding that would never be! Suddenly, Rachel felt unutterably sad. Life had always seemed so simple before, everything neatly fitted into its appointed place. Good was easy to recognize, and bad instinctively repugnant . . . and it had never occurred to her that evil could come with such sweetness it would tear her heart apart.

"I didn't really mind," she said. "About the beard."

"I know . . . but *I* did. I was getting tired of it, anyway."

In spite of herself, Rachel started to laugh. It was hard being serious when he didn't want her to. And she got the distinct impression that solemnity was far from the most important thing in Matthew Barron's world.

"You are a very unsettling man," she said.

"I intend to be," he replied, the grin coming back, but not quite so infuriating as before. "I intend to be."

The series of waterways that connected Canton and Macao were twisting and complex, dotted with numerous islands, some no larger than sandbars, but Rachel knew the area well and automatically took over handling the small sampan. She had half expected that

Matthew would try to take charge and was surprised when he didn't offer so much as a murmur of protest.

His pride, it seemed, was secure enough not to need to be in command every second, or to have her prove with false frailty over and over that he was a man, and she found herself admiring him grudgingly for it.

They traveled mostly under cover of darkness. Without her bootblack and false queue, Rachel could no longer blend in with the landscape, though a sailor's bandanna wrapped around her head gave her a degree of anonymity at night. All she needed, Matthew teased, was a gold ring in her ear, and she'd look like one of the pirates who were notorious for prowling those waters. He himself managed fairly well in a sea jacket, dark-dyed canvas trousers, and a watch cap pulled down over his hair. But only as long as there was nothing brighter than moonlight, and only as long as they were careful not to drift too close to shore.

In the daytime, they would tie up in some secluded cove and catch a few hours of sleep, together, for the small open sampan offered no privacy. At first modesty prompted them to doze fully dressed, but the weather had turned unseasonably warm, and the shadowy space under the arched roof was close and almost unbearably stifling. Matthew finally resorted to taking off his shirt and stretching out bare-chested, and Rachel would sleep in one or another of the red silk outfits she had impulsively brought along.

The long, hot hours were excruciating for both of them. The more Rachel tried to steel herself against him, the more her body betrayed her, burning and aching for the way he had touched her before, making her pray that he would forget his resolve. And Matthew, lying beside her, listening to the even pattern of her breathing, was constantly aware that the choice had always been his.

All he had to do was let down his guard for an instant. It would be so easy, when the warm breezes blew and her body curled instinctively against him, soft and uninhibited in sleep. It almost did happen sometimes, on lazy, languid afternoons when the flies woke him up and he was still drowsy . . . and it felt like she had been made to fit into his arms.

"It really *is* all right, Matthew," she whispered one day, when his hand had slipped much too intimately where he vowed it would never go again. "I can't marry you. I will never be your wife . . . but I can be your woman. And I want to. . . . For a time."

"But I can't be your fancy man, love," he replied. "Only your husband. So, you see, you will have to make an honest man of me."

Only she *couldn't,* Rachel thought as she felt the strength of his arms tighten around her and longed for the intimacy he seemed so determined to deny them both. Loving him would be enough of a compromise— and, heaven help her, a sin. If she married him, she would be doomed forever to the bitter knowledge that she had forsaken all her values and principles.

But, oh, it was tempting sometimes. What was it Camilla had said? *You're a fool, Rachel Todd. You're going to end up with an empty bed. . . . And an empty life.*

And was it so absolutely unforgivable, once—just *once*—to have made a terrible mistake? Maybe, if she showed him the error of his ways, he would change. Maybe the love of a good woman *could* reform a man.

It was a dilemma, she thought, and was grateful when dusk came at last and put her out of her misery, at least in part, for they were no longer touching. Gliding through the night water, alert for rocks and logs and trying not to make any noise took all her concentration.

At that pace, the journey lasted several days. Most of the time they remained on board, but in some of the smaller villages or isolated rural areas, Rachel deemed it safe to venture out at dawn or dusk, she in the single dark violet dress she had brought along, a hand-me-down from Cammie, altered to fit her height and somewhat less garish taste; Matthew looking quite dashing in fawn or bottle-green breeches, with a clean white shirt every time and the same cuff links she had noticed before.

Now that she had a closer look, Rachel saw that the red stones were half-round rubies, set in some light metal she supposed was white gold. A clever miniature of the semicircular dawn sun on the famous Barron flag.

"I suppose you have an evening coat in your bag, too," she said with a wry shake of her head. "And an embroidered white waistcoat?"

"Of course. You never know when you're going to be invited to dinner. One wouldn't want to be embarrassed.

"Of course," she echoed, not knowing whether to believe him or not. The drollness of his teasing, as always, kept her just a little off guard. Probably the waistcoat was a bit much—though she wasn't at all sure about the evening jacket.

Ordinarily, as she explained to Matthew the first time they visited a local market to pick up rice and fresh vegetables, they would have been able to wander about freely. She was well known in these parts, as were her parents and brothers. The people here were open and kind-hearted; they would have welcomed her warmly, and Matthew, too, for they would have assumed that any man with her was another reverend or doctor.

But with the pending war, the atmosphere had darkened, like the shadows that were now lengthening into dusk at the end of the long sunny afternoons. Fear seemed to be everywhere, and suspicion, fanned by rumors that spread with lightning speed from village to small village. The "redheaded devils"—the British—where coming with their armies and their great, fire-spitting gunboats, and hatred was flaring in places into open violence.

"And to the Chinese," Rachel said, "anyone with white skin and a foreign accent is a redheaded devil right now."

Matthew enjoyed listened to Rachel talk about the land she so clearly loved, and the people who had been a part of her life almost as long as she could remember. She knew the name of every flower and every tree, and stories about them sometimes, and the most amazing details that he would have found hard to believe if he hadn't known her to be scrupulously honest. Those were the last of the summer peonies, those prettily colored blossoms—as late as forty or fifty years ago the English had still been using their roots and flowers and seeds in medications. And that tree over there was a banyan, centuries old, predating the time that Christ had walked the earth, but there was a written record of when it had been planted and why and by whom.

They might pause at the base of a shallow hill, beneath a small rural temple, and Rachel would regret that the uncertainties of the time did not allow them to go up and see it. Like everything else, every house and shop and burial site in China, its exact placement had been a matter of *feng shui,* wind and water. Only after the geomancer had gone through his elaborate divinations—and been well paid for his trouble—could the actual building begin. Ignoring *feng shui* would have created a very real danger that the temple might be situated on a dragon's neck—or worse, his head! And everyone knew that disturbing a dragon's sleep released evil spirits and brought terrible joss, or luck.

Another time they stopped along one of the earthen dikes that separated rice paddies into a flooded patchwork of oddly irregular geometric shapes. The dying sun shimmered on the water, turning it into a silver-red mirror, but Rachel knew the fields and she knew the seasons, and she did not need her eyes to see what lay beneath. She knew when the seeds had just been coated with mud, so the little rice birds that dipped and flitted through the twilight couldn't fatten themselves too easily. And when the tender sprouts were about to peek their heads through the water. And where the weeds were growing between them, fighting for the limited nourishment of the soil.

"It's the women's job to pull them," she told Matthew. "They roll up their trousers and bend down from the waist and tug out first one weed, and then another . . . and the another, until their backs are so stiff they feel like they can't go on. And then they bend down and reach for the next.''

Matthew heard the passion in her voice and sensed the deep empathy she felt for these people. "It's a hard life," he agreed.

"It's unbearable sometimes. And those are the lucky ones! At least they have fields to cultivate and weeds to pull! There's so much poverty here. So much despair! It breaks my heart and I can't do anything about it! You see that house over there? I knew the woman who used to live in it. She was quite well off, by local standards. But her husband was an opium fiend. He sold everything—literally *everything*! And in the end, even that wasn't enough.''

She paused. Waiting for an answer, Matthew knew. And he knew what he said would be important, but he was blasted if he had any idea what it ought to be.

Should he remind her that rum ruined lives, too, and nobody blamed the poor innkeeper who was simply supplying a service? But somehow he didn't think that argument would make much of an impression on her. And, in fact, he was getting less and less impressed with it himself.

He was relieved when an old man appeared at the end of the road, and catching sight of Rachel, hobbled toward them with a big, toothless grin. A distraction, at least for the moment. As he drew near, he called out in something Matthew assumed was Cantonese, which Rachel answered volubly in kind.

It fascinated him, as always, the skill she had in this alien tonal language. It seemed to flow so easily out of her pretty pink lips, and in more than one dialect apparently, for even Matthew's untutored ear could make out differences in the various greetings she offered. The singsong rising and falling of the syllables was still beyond him, but he had begun to pick up some of the sounds.

When he tried to compliment her on it, however, after the old man was gone and they had begun to drift down the road again, she only threw him a look of rather patronizing amusement.

"You don't speak any languages yourself, I suppose. That's so typically American. I'd probably be the same if my family had remained in Connecticut."

"I speak French and Italian fluently," Matthew protested. "Without an accent! And I manage to bumble along quite adequately in several others."

"And modestly, too, no doubt." Rachel laughed. "I'll have to ask a Frenchman or an Italian for *his* opinion. I must admit, though, I am impressed."

"I did tell you, you know, that I had an expensive education. Something was bound to rub off. I also know Latin and ancient Greek . . . so if we run into a Roman or an ancient Greek, you can ask his opinion, too."

They were laughing easily as they strolled along the bank toward the boat. It was later than usual. The sun had gone down some time ago, but it was going to be a full moon, and briar and wild myrtle and old lychee trees that no longer bore fruit stood out sharply in the eerie pale blue light.

Matthew found himself looking over at this woman beside him and wondering what would happen if he took her hand. She didn't balk at the most startling intimacies, but tenderness seemed to frighten her.

"That was where you were born?" he asked, suddenly curious to know more about her. "Back in Connecticut, where your family comes from?"

"My mother's family," she corrected. "My father is actually from Ohio. She began corresponding with him because they both wanted to be missionaries. It was a bond between them, you see—their faith and dedication. They decided to get married even before he came to Connecticut to meet her. . . . And no, I wasn't born there. My brothers and I were all born in Hawaii, which you probably know as the Sandwich Islands."

"I'm familiar with either name," Matthew replied, his heart sinking as he thought of the mother who had agreed to marry a man she'd never seen out of religious zeal and "dedication." If that was the ideal of marriage Rachel had in her head, how the devil was he supposed to convince her that the thing could also involve passion and affection—and plain, old-fashioned fun? "Uh . . . I've only been to Hawaii once, and then briefly, but I found it very beautiful. You must have liked living there. I'm surprised your parents could bring themselves to leave. I suppose they were ordered by the church."

"No." Rachel was smiling gently, as much with her eyes as her lips. "They were strictly volunteers. I think life was too easy for them in Hawaii. There were too many missionaries. They needed new challenges . . . and they found them. Here."

Matthew caught the softness that came into her voice. "You care very much for this country, don't you?"

"I love it with all my heart," she said simply. "I cannot even imagine living anyplace else. And I could never commit my life to someone who didn't understand—and share—my feelings."

He was aware of dark eyes searching his face in the moonlight, asking questions he knew ran deeper than mere words.

"I am not an unfeeling man, Rachel," he said.

She was still looking at him, as if pondering something in her mind, deciding. Matthew had the idiotic feeling that he had just been put to a test, and he didn't know if he had passed or failed.

Then, unexpectedly, she said:

"She had a daughter . . . the woman in the house I showed you. The Chinese don't always keep girl-children—they are not highly looked upon here—but the woman was rich and could afford to indulge herself. Then her husband started smoking opium, and they needed money. The jewels were sold first, and then the furnishings, and then the cooking pots . . . and after a while everything was gone."

Silence lingered in the air, heavy and expectant. Memory flashed back, disturbing. That naively ardent exaggeration about wretches so enslaved they sold their own—

"Good God, surely you don't mean . . . But that's monstrous! He didn't actually *sell* the child?"

"We managed to get her back. The woman had many friends, and the mission helped. We searched all night. We asked people in the streets, and finally we found her. In a terribly, foul-smelling house with so many little girls with gaunt, hungry faces. She was very happy—the woman. She loved the child very much, even if it was only a girl, and she was glad to have her back."

She paused again, a hint that Matthew did not fail to catch.

"But . . ." he prompted.

"But he sold her again. Of course. And that time we could not get her back."

They did not speak of the woman and her child again until the next morning.

It had been a long night, with the sound of water splashing against the boat, and the pungent, marshy odor of rice paddies drifting across the river. Rachel had been handling the sampan, and Matthew, though he kept his eyes and ears open for trouble, had had more than enough time to think about what she had said, and why she had said it to him.

"What happened to her?" he asked, when they had finally secured the boat in a small clump of reeds and were settling down for another uncomfortably steamy day. "The child? Was she sold into, uh . . ."

"Prostitution?" Rachel had prepared a plate of rice and vegetables, which looked bland and unappetizing, especially in the heat. "You do have trouble speaking plainly in front of women. Or is it because I was raised so 'purely'?" She put the plate down on the straw mat covering the rough decking and lowered herself beside him. Matthew noticed that she had changed into a particularly flimsy wisp of silk, in a rather starling pinkish color that clashed quite intriguingly with her hair.

"Prostitution, then," he agreed. "But was she?"

"I don't know," Rachel admitted. She could have

been. That's not uncommon. But there are the Mui Tsai, too . . . and the child was well raised.''

''Mui Tsai?'' The term sounded vaguely familiar, though Matthew wasn't sure what it meant.

''Slaves, you might say. Girls from about seven on are frequently sold into domestic service by families that can't afford to feed them, or just don't want them anymore. They might, of course, be used in the manner you suggested, especially if they're pretty. But a concubine is often the same thing as a wife in the Chinese culture. . . . It's not quite as cruel as it sounds. At least it provides a future for girl children. And at any rate, it's better than the alternative.''

Matthew decided not to ask what the ''alternative'' was. He picked at the food on the shallow, shared dish, but only managed a little. The beautiful Rachel was proving to have many surprising talents, but clearly cooking wasn't among them.

''It *is* distressing,'' he admitted. ''But you can't blame opium for all the ills of Chinese society. Or even for what happened in this particular case. It wasn't the drug itself that created the problem but the man who misused it.''

''Ah, yes . . . now you're going to give me the favorite trader's argument. People misuse demon rum, too, but you don't see the Chinese or the British—or the Americans—fighting wars to keep it out of their countries! We all have our little weaknesses, after all, and is it fair to take away a man's free choice?''

''Well, is it?'' Matthew replied. He hadn't, in fact, been planning on using the argument at all, but she had backed him into a corner. ''A sip of rum—or hock or champagne—doesn't lead most of us down the path to wildly wasted lives. The most we suffer is a fuzzy head in the morning. Or are you going to tell me now that I have to take *that* out of the holds of every Barron clipper, too?''

''Oh, I don't know . . . I've been known to find an occasional use myself for a glass of champagne.'' She smiled, but fleetingly. ''Opium isn't like alcohol, Matthew. There are no pleasant social uses for it—and I've never yet known a man who could control his cravings. It takes over. You think at first—you're so *sure*—you're going to be the master. But it always takes over. The body first, then the spirit . . . until there's nothing left but an empty shell.''

Matthew was tempted to suggest that she might be exaggerating, just a little, but then he remembered that she had not been exaggerating before. Besides, he was tired of defending a drug he didn't even believe in himself.

''I have no intention of spending a lifetime at this, Rachel,'' he said. ''I never did, even before I met you. It was just—a lark. A stupid boyish prank from someone who ought to have been old enough to know better. I'm sure as hell—how's that for not protecting your dainty ears?—not going to bring the stuff onboard again.''

''But you *are* going to sell what you already have,'' Rachel said sadly. ''The money means more to you than the damage you will cause.''

And more than the chance to marry me, she longed to add, but she couldn't let herself say it. If he was going to change—*if*—it had to come from inside, and not because he thought he was going to get something for it.

''The money doesn't mean a blasted thing. I wasn't planning on keeping it anyway.'' A lopsided grin twisted one side of his face up, giving him an unexpectedly sheepish look that tugged at Rachel's heart. ''I was going to donate it to your father—for the mission. I thought I'd have time to get everything settled before you came back from wherever you'd gone. Then I was going to prostrate myself on the floor in front of you and beg for your gentle mercy!''

Rachel watched him warily, longing but not quite daring to believe.

''If you don't care for the money anymore,'' she said hesitantly, ''if you just were going to give it away . . .''

''It was never the money. It was the chance to prove myself, love. Money isn't important when you've always had plenty of it. Have you ever met my brother, Jared? No? Well, he's about four inches taller than I am, and several years older, and he's always been better at everything. I'm my grandfather's favorite, in a way. I look like my father, who died when I was a baby, and the old man doted on him. But it's always Jared he calls in when the talk turns serious.''

"And Jared he's looking to more and more as he gets older and is thinking about turning over the reins of his business?'' Rachel ventured.

"I can't imagine Gareth Barron turning over anything. But, yes, Jared's the heir apparent all right. My Uncle Garth is extremely competent, but he's much too conservative—Grandfather made his fortune in piracy!—and Alex, his son, is very like him. I, of course, am always a few years too young. I remember following my brother around when I was a little boy. He seemed almost godlike then, so strong and confident, and I prayed that, just once, he would look down and take me seriously. But all I ever could do was make him laugh. He liked me—I think he liked me—but I could never make him *love* me. And I wanted that more than anything in the world.''

"But I thought the Barrons had vowed never to handle opium. It seems a strange way to win your brother's love—and respect—taking on a cargo he had condemned.''

"Maybe, but it'll sure as heck get his attention!'' Matthew laughed shortly. "One of the reasons my grandfather decided against opium in the first place was the East India Company's monopoly in Calcutta. Probably the main reason! As long as we couldn't get our hands on superior goods, we couldn't compete. Finding a way around that—and picking up a tidy profit in the bargain—is going to make him proud enough to forget everything else. Grandfather is very fond of profits.''

"And that's so important to you?'' Rachel asked softly. "Winning you grandfather's approval?''

"Ethics never counted as far as you can spit with the old tyrant. But initiative does. And success. . . .

If I can pull this off, for the first time, I'll be on an equal footing with my brother.''

He got up and wandered over to the edge of the deck, staring across the tops of the reeds at fields and rice paddies, yellow-bright in the hot morning sun. It was careless, exposing himself like that, and he knew that Rachel behind him had to be thinking the same thing. But she seemed to sense his need to draw into himself, for she did not say anything.

It was the first time he had put it into words, though he had thought it out in bits and fragments before. He was still competing with his brother, still the little boy who always came in second. He had done all this just to try to beat Jared!

He was a damned fool, and he knew it, but he still couldn't let go. He still needed to stand up to his brother, to look him square in the eye—just once—and say that he had succeeded. That he had come out on top, even if it was at something Jared wildly disapproved of.

Maybe, he thought wryly, *especially* at something Jared disapproved of.

He felt the light touch of a hand on his arm. "Try and get some rest, Matthew," Rachel said. "It's been a long night, and it looks like the heat is going to be beastly.''

Matthew let her draw him back to the straw matting, over which she had thrown tattered quilts to form a makeshift bed. His body ached with the longing that never quite went away as he felt her curl up against him, temptingly in his arms. His shirt was off already, and he was easing hers open, as had become their habit in the long sultry mornings and shaded afternoons. He was excruciatingly conscious of the softness of her skin, the little rounded peaks of her breasts pressing into his chest, and all he could think was how desperately he longed to possess this woman.

Not because she was beautiful and aroused his senses, though God knows, she did that. But because she was caring, and knew how to be quiet when quiet was called for . . . and for one brief moment had seemed to understand him better than he understood himself. He did not just want her, he needed her, with a compulsive urgency that was like a cry of pain from deep within, and he longed to ease himself on top of her and finish what had already, very thoroughly and provocatively, been begun.

This is crazy, he thought as he struggled against the desire that threatened like never before to engulf him. It wasn't suppose to be like this. He was the man! He was supposed to be wheedling and coaxing, pulling out every trick to break down her resistance, trying manfully to seduce this lovely creature into submission. And she was the one who was supposed to be holding out for commitments and an encounter at the alter!

By everything that was rational and normal, he ought to be surrendering now to his baser instincts and giving them both what they so fervently longed for!

But if he did, he had the terrible feeling that she would slip through his fingers, and he would lose her forever.

Rachel sighed as she felt him fall asleep in her arms. His head had slipped down, cradling instinctively on her breast, and he seemed in that sweet moment very innocent and quite surprisingly vulnerable.

She *had* understood, and with the understanding had come the first glimmer of hope since she had seen him across a sun-splashed garden and realized to her horror that she was extremely attracted to this man who had seemed the devil incarnate.

It was not money he cared about, after all! He had not sold his soul for a fortune in gold. The effect was the same—the drug would still be as devastating when it was released—but the motive was not, and Rachel's heart was pure enough to realize that motives and actions were sometimes very different. It was not greed that had driven Matthew Barron, but a fierce hunger for love and acceptance.

And love was something that could be forgiven.

Perhaps there was some way she could show him how horrible even one shipment of opium would be.

If she could just bring it home graphically enough, he might be as eager as she to toss his evil profits into the ocean.

He might lose his grandfather's respect, but he would gain hers, and perhaps that was more important.

At least, she thought with a sleepy smile, for the air was turning sultry and even the flies were too lazy to stir, she would know . . . one way or the other. She let her lips rest lightly on his forehead, gently kissing, so as not to wake him.

Now . . . if only she could come up with something.

Eight

"**H**ow much farther is this place, anyhow?"

"Just a short way yet." Rachel was conscious of Matthew behind her, staying close to the light of the lantern she was carrying. The fog had come back, and the night-darkened streets seemed to close in around them, silent and lost in the mist. "I think I recognize this corner. Yes, here . . . down this alleyway. Be careful, it's barely wide enough to walk through."

"You don't have to tell me," grumbled Matthew, who could feel the walls brushing against his shoulders in places. In the moisture of the fog, they seemed spongy and coated with slime, and the mysterious errand she had brought him on was looking less and less appealing with each passing minute. "What the devil are we going to find when we get there?"

"I told you—something I want you to see."

Rachel paused, raising the lantern in front of her to get her bearings. With the fog had come the wind, brittle and wintry, and she tried not to shiver noticeably. Matthew would be comfortable enough in the rough seamen's garb she had told him to wear, but she had only the thin Chinese jacket over her violet cotton dress. Her hair was concealed again, under the bandanna, though there was little need for stealth here. The small village was only a few hours out of Macao, and the streets and alleys frequently saw Westerners searching for the seamier pleasures they would not care to be caught indulging in at home.

There might be a war blowing on the winds of change that were sweeping China, but money was money, and even a redheaded devil was welcome as long as he brought cash.

"Ah, there it is! Just ahead."

"It looks charming," Matthew said drily. "But hardly the place for a lady."

"This lady knows how to take care of herself. And don't worry. I've been here before."

They had reached the doorway, or rather the opening, for no door was visible, just a black pit that seemed to sink into a deep recess in the wall. Matthew held back for a second as Rachel started inside. Dampness seemed to soak even through the thick wool of his jacket, and the smell of dirt and defecation was permeated by another, vaguely unpleasant odor. Sweetish and almost cloying . . . and then he realized what it was.

"Opium? You've brought me to an *opium den*?"

"Why not?" She turned, and the light of the lantern picked up her face beneath the dark kerchief, making it float as if disembodied in the night. "Are you surprised that I would know where an opium den is? Or are you thinking perhaps that it's not a suitable place for a *gentleman*? But you deal in the drug, Captain Barron. Surely, if you're going to sell it, you ought to know what it is."

"I do know," he protested. "And I know its effects can be ruinous. You'll get no more arguments out of me about that. I've already admitted it. What good would it do me to go in and gape at the poor wretches, as you call them, sucking on their pipes and turning into 'empty shells'? I concede the point."

"But I didn't bring you here as a *spectator*," she replied, very softly. "I said you ought to know what opium is. You can't get to know something by standing back and looking at it."

"You mean . . . you expect me to smoke a pipe myself?" Matthew was aghast. Even for Rachel, whom he had already learned would go to nearly any length to get her will, this was too much.

"Or two, or three. You're looking very pale, Matthew. . . . Don't tell me you're afraid?" She leaned forward, blowing out the lantern, then started into the inky blackness of the recess. "Didn't you say that opium was no different from a glass of rum or champagne? Surely you weren't this apprehensive when you had your first taste of rum. Or is it so long ago you've forgotten?"

Matthew had no choice but to follow. As his eyes adjusted, he realized there was a faint light ahead, as if at the end of a long hallway. He had *not* forgotten; if anything, it almost seemed like yesterday. It had not been rum, but whiskey, and he had been in his grandfather's house, about eight or nine years old, and very conscious that everyone was watching as he tried manfully to take the glass in a single gulp. And choked and sputtered with the inevitable humiliation!

They had roared with laughter, his grandfather and all his grandfather's friends, even his uncle. Only Jared had stood up for him. "He's just a boy," he had said, and surprisingly the laughter had stopped. "What did you think, that he was going to have the sense to tell you he'd never tried it before and take a sip to test the way?"

"They did the same thing to me," he had said then, turning to Matthew with a rare comradely smile. "And I hated it as much as you do."

"Did you sputter, too?" Matthew had asked.

"Yes," he had said. "Even worse than you." But Matthew had known he was lying. Jared would never have sputtered, no matter how much the stuff burned and stung. Jared always did everything right.

The hallway ended in a small, dingy room, the only light trickling through the blackened shade of a lantern dangling from the ceiling. Muffled shouts and bursts of laughter accented by the sharp clatter of gaming pieces drifted in from a fan-tan parlor that must have been somewhere around another twist of the corridor. The smell was stronger now, nearly choking, the air thick with smoke from tobacco and what Matthew supposed was the opium. His eyes were watering, and he could barely make out the dim figure of a man seated beside a table with tins and what appeared to be a crude scale on it.

The man was rising, coming toward him, and Matthew felt a sudden, irrational burst of panic. Ridiculous, of course—he had known plenty of men who had tried opium and boasted of it. And in point of fact, it *was* no worse than rum, the first time or two, at least. But the place was filthy and sordid, and he longed for nothing so much at the moment as to get out of there.

"I remember my first taste of alcohol very well," he hissed in Rachel's ear as the man approached. "And it was not in surroundings like this!"

"Well, we can't all be rich, can we? And I'd be willing to wager you've patronized a tavern or two worse than this."

Matthew could not deny it. There was a place in particular in Calcutta, which Gallagher had introduced him to—but a tavern was still a tavern, and a drink just a drink, even in a grimy glass! Now that the man was nearer, Matthew could see that his skin was brittle, like old, crinkly parchment, so thin the veins in his temples showed through.

He was greeting Rachel, speaking in Chinese, so he must have recognized her. His mouth showed only a few rotting teeth as he grinned, looking exceptionally amused. But then, why shouldn't he? Matthew thought irritably. It couldn't be every day that the missionary's daughter who hated opium brought him a client.

His face must have lost all its color again, for he felt Rachel lay her hand on his arm, as if in reassurance. The rhythmic *click-click-click* of the fan-tan parlor intruded on his consciousness, the hoarse cries that accompanied each victory and loss. Familiar, comfortable sounds—it was in such a place that he had gotten the two-headed gaming piece which began this unexpected odyssey of love—but there was nothing familiar or comfortable about what he doing now.

"It's all right to be alarmed," Rachel was saying. "I know how you feel. I was frightened myself."

"You . . . ?" Matthew's eyes narrowed as he turned to look at her in the dim half-light. "Are you telling

JADE DAWN 123

me you went to an opium den and actually smoked a
pipe yourself?''

''Not *a* den. This one. You can't fight something
you don't understand, Matthew. How could I go to
someone and condemn his craving if I didn't even
know what it was? My brother had experimented with
opium the year before. Sam. He's the real adventurer
of the family. Naturally, when I found out, I insisted
he help me try it, too.''

''Naturally.'' Matthew felt his blood run cold as he
watched the man tip some small black pellets about
the size of a pea onto the scale and weigh them. ''And
naturally, he agreed.''

''Well, 'agreed' might not be quite the word. Sam
was just getting involved with one of the *tongs,* a group
of rebels headed by—by a friend of ours, and they
were beginning to plan raids like the one on your junk.
Of course, with the potential for danger, my parents
would never have allowed it, if they had known.''

''So you blackmailed him?''

''Let's say I *persuaded* him. I can be very persuasive, you know. I had to learn whatever I could about
the drug. Don't you see? It would be an extremely
foolish general who didn't study his enemy, upside
down and inside out, before going into battle. And I
am a general—or, more likely, merely a humble foot-
soldier—in the war against opium.''

''And what does that make me?'' Matthew asked,
somewhat sarcastically. ''A new recruit? I feel like
cannon fodder.''

''Hardly that. It's just a pipe of opium, after all. No
more nor less than your first glass of rum—albeit in
rather inelegant surroundings.'' The man had finished
weighing the opium. Rachel took several coins out of
a handkerchief knotted at her waist and handed them
to him. He seemed to be enjoying his own wit, for he
chirped and twittered as he exchanged them for the
pellets, but beyond one curt nod, she paid him no
heed. ''I must admit, I didn't find the place very ap-
petizing myself. I was quite appalled at Sam's taste!

But then, perhaps, if you're not as brave as I am . . . we *could* go back. . . .''

It was a challenge he could not resist, and she knew it.

"You seem to have survived—quite nicely. I expect I can manage as well."

Matthew allowed his jacket to be taken from him and hung on a peg on the wall. On Rachel's prompting, he slipped off his boots and padded down another, shorter hallway after her. She seemed, disconcertingly, to know the way rather well.

The hall ended in a large, eerily nightmarish room. Deep, slatted benches, almost like shelves, ran along three of the sides, one stacked above the other, and an open grating near the ceiling provided a meager breath of air. The odor was almost overpowering here, rank with sweat and opium and rancid, burning oil. Little tongues of flame, leaping from the tops of small glass lamps, provided enough illumination so that Matthew could make out recumbent forms on the benches, barely moving, if at all. The only sound, beyond an occasional low murmur, was the hissing and bubbling of the pipes.

He half-expected Rachel to lead him to one of the benches, and his stomach turned at the thought. But she headed instead for a series of small cubicles he had not noticed before along the far wall. Apparently, even here, wealth had it privileges.

The room was cramped and disgustingly filthy, with rough partitions and flooring, but at least it offered a modicum of privacy. A shallow bench had been padded to resemble a couch or bed with a scarred wooden headrest as a pillow, and Matthew was reminded abruptly of a brothel he had been taken to once as an adolescent by older friends.

No doubt to test his mettle—and, Lord, it had! He could still remember the dirt and the smell; it had clung to his skin and his clothes. And the woman they had brought him! So thin, her ribs had been sticking out, and almost no breasts at all. He had hated it then, as he was hating this now, but he had been too proud to admit it in front of the others.

Then Jared had come after him. . . . Jared again. Roaring with rage when he found out where his brother had been taken. "I have nothing against working women, boy," he had told him, not unkindly, "but a place like this, you'll find only squalor and disease." And Matthew had been extremely relieved to allow himself to be dragged, loudly and indignantly protesting, out of there.

An attendant came in, carrying a low table with paraphernalia of some sort—a lamp like the ones he had noticed outside, a clay-bowled pipe, a knife, a sponge—which he set beside the couch. Matthew readjusted the headrest and stretched out, feeling strangely self-conscious.

As he had in the brothel all those years ago, he thought wryly. Only this time, there was no big brother to come and rescue him.

He stared, fascinated in spite of himself, as the man began arranging the articles on the table. His hands were almost skeletal, loose skin hanging off the bones, and a peculiar deep yellowish color, though perhaps that was the effect of the lamp.

"That will be all," Rachel said, repeating the instructions in Chinese, though the man seemed to understand well enough, for he was already backing toward the door. "We will not require you any longer. I can cook the opium myself."

"*Cook?*" Matthew felt the first twinges of curiosity, which he did nothing to resist. He was still apprehensive, but if he was going to go through with this, he might as well learn something in the process. "Good God, if your opium cooking is anything like what you do with rice and vegetables, I might as well give up right now. I'm dead!"

"Mercifully, cooking the opium is much easier." She smiled faintly, but with little mirth, as she took the pellets out of the handkerchief in which she had placed them and lined them up on a small tray on the table. "And just wait till we get to the mission tomorrow. . . . *If* we get to the mission. You'll be grateful enough for *my* cooking then."

She turned up the lamp, and while Matthew watched, frankly intrigued by now, she held the tip of the pipe stem for a moment in the flame, then wiped it off with the handkerchief. A gesture he appreciated, considering how many mouths had sucked on it in the past. He might be willing to risk the evil effects of opium, but he was damned if he was going to die of typhus or plague in the bargain!

"This is the *yen tsiang,*" Rachel explained as she squatted down beside the table. "The opium pistol. The bowl is clay, for burning the opium, but the stems are made of bamboo or cane or sometimes orangewood. Most of them are plain, but I requested one with a brass tip for obvious reasons—which, of course, the proprietor found very funny. They're the color of straw when they're new. Black ones like this have seen considerable service."

"I daresay," Matthew replied, eyeing the thing warily. It looked almost charred from more use than he cared to imagine. "He seems to have a rare sense of humor, your proprietor. He was laughing all the time you were negotiating with him."

"I told him you were an opium trader . . . and I was going to reform you. Then you'd help me stop the flow of opium into the country, and between the two of us, we'd put him out of business."

"He didn't look too worried."

"He wasn't. He figured one pipe of opium, and not only would he still be in business, he'd have a new customer." She had picked up a long needle and was securing one of the sticky, gum-like pellets to the tip of it. "But I told him you were stronger than that. There was no danger of the craving taking hold of you in a single night."

She lowered the needle and looked at him for a long, thoughtful moment.

"Are you, Matthew? Strong? If you have any doubts, tell me now, and I won't torment you any

longer. Opium can be very enticing, even in the beginning.''

He shook his head. ''You don't need to worry. I
didn't like this when I came in here—I won't lie about
that—but now that you've got me going, I'm curious.
And yes, I am sure of my strength.''

''And your arrogance?'' she said softly. She had
raised the needle again, the *yen hauck,* as she called
it, and was holding it over the flame of the lamp. The
dab of opium bubbled in the heat and swelled to several times its size, changing color as it did. Subtly at
first, losing its blackness, then mellowing into a rich,
deep butterscotch brown.

Rachel took it off the flame, and with a twirling
motion began to roll it over the smooth surface of the
pipe bowl. Every once in a while she would put it back
on the fire. Using the tip of the *yen hauck,* she caught
at first one edge, then another, drawing it out like thin
strings of taffy so it would cook thoroughly.

''This,'' she told Matthew, ''is known as *chying* the
opium. It's a little trickier than I implied before. Timing is critical. A poor cook will end up with it either
underdone or overdone, so it's too sticky or crisp to
smoke well. Fortunately, I'm a little better with this
than vegetables.''

In fact, she seemed quite skilled for someone what
had tried it only once, Matthew thought, but he said
nothing as she finished the *chying* process and rolled
the opium once more across the hard clay bowl. The
color was still the same golden brown, and he noticed
that the odor, while fresh and warm, was almost
creamy and not at all distasteful.

When she had finished, Rachel plunged the needle
down into the congealed mass and forced it through
the hole in the pipe.

''Here,'' she said. ''Lean forward a little—over the
lamp. That's it.'' Taking his hand, she showed him
how to grasp the bowl and tip it just enough so the
flame caught the drug. Matthew felt a pang of nervousness again, a tightening in his chest, and saliva

rose to his mouth, but he could not bring himself to admit his fears to her.

He hesitated an instant, then forced himself to inhale, deeply and steadily, taking the smoke into his lungs.

It was stronger than he had expected, hotter, and his first impression was of a burning sensation that made him afraid he was going to cough and sputter as he had with his first try at whiskey. But he managed to maintain more control this time, and the smoke came out evenly through his nostrils. Thick and white, and not, after that first sharpness, as unpleasant as Matthew had expected.

His second impression was one of vague disappointment. Three good puffs had completely depleted the small brown pellet, and he felt nothing. Not even a faint dizziness or disorientation.

"Either this stuff is overrated," he said, almost giddily, now that he knew there was nothing to it, "or else I'm immune."

"I think," Rachel replied, "you don't know what you're talking about." She had removed the pipe from his hand, and rolling a new mass of opium neatly around the bowl again, she cooked it to the proper consistency and handed it back to him.

Matthew leaned a little smugly over the lamp, feeling almost comfortable with the procedure now. It gave him considerable satisfaction to realize that he was indeed strong enough to deal with the surprisingly mild effects of this drug which had defeated so many other men. Perhaps he simply had a hardier constitution. Or perhaps there was a natural weakness in the Chinese.

He finished his third pipe, then a fourth, inhaling deeply, each new effort confirming his earlier conclusion. Whatever the problem with opium, obviously it didn't affect him. He was already on his fifth and about to say something again, when he felt an unexpected wave of nausea. The room seemed to blur suddenly, as if he couldn't focus his eyes, and Matthew was aware of a strange drumming in his ears, a low throbbing sound that seemed to be getting louder.

He tried to remember what he had been about to
say, but he couldn't, which was probably just as well.
His tongue seemed to be swelling in his mouth, and
he wasn't at all sure he could have formed the words.

Rachel was handing him another pipe. He didn't
want it; he tried to say so, but he found his hand cupping around it anyway. It was as if there was no will
left in him. His pulse seemed to be racing, and his
body and face were flushed. Sweat was pouring off
him; he could feel it soaking into the cushions beneath, but every movement was an agonizing exertion.
He could barely lean forward to tilt the bowl over the
flame.

He was on perhaps his seventh or eighth pipe, perhaps more—he had lost count—when an almost uncanny sense of peace swept over him. A kind of quiet,
easy, very languid contentment. *So this is it,* he
thought—and wondered what the fuss was all about. It
was pleasant enough, but it seemed relatively benign.

He had the strangest feeling that Rachel was watching him. She seemed to have stopped refilling the
pipe—or perhaps he was mistaken—and was standing
over him, staring down. At least, he thought it was
Rachel, but there were lights floating all around, and
it was hard to make her out. So bright they hurt his
eyes, shimmering and iridescent, great swirling shapes
melting into and through each other, like the colors
on changeable silk.

Then suddenly the pipe was in his hand again. So
she hadn't stopped filling it, after all. Matthew could
feel his heart beating faster as he put it to his mouth
and sucked in the smoke again. The mildly euphoric
sensation was gone. He could hardly remember it now.
He hadn't even noted its passing . . . or perhaps he
had only imagined it.

Every nerve was tense and surprisingly jittery. *Had*
he imagined that moment of contentment? He longed
to get up and pace the room, but he couldn't make
himself move. The nausea was worse now, twisting
and churning in his stomach, but the heat seemed to
have evaporated. His skin felt clammy and cold, and

he was itching all over, violently, his nose, his back, his armpits, his groin.

He wanted to reach out to Rachel—he *tried* to reach out—but he couldn't find her anymore. She was lost in the lights and the shadows.

Then he turned head to the side and vomited.

"I did tell you, you know," Rachel said softly, "that you didn't know what you were talking about."

Matthew groaned. It was several hours later, and he was back on the sampan, having been brought there by litter, or so Rachel had told him. He himself had no recollection of anything before waking a few minutes ago and feeling nauseated and utterly drained.

"You did—and next time, I'll believe you," he replied with as much fervor as he could muster. "Or better yet, next time I'll stay away from the stuff altogether. You win, tiger. I acknowledge that opium is an abomination on the face of the earth, and I'll never have anything to do with it again. In my body or the cargo hold of my ship. Is that what you wanted to hear?"

Rachel came over and knelt beside him. It was not yet daylight, but the fog was holding, and she had turned up the lantern so she could see his face. He was alarmingly ashen, but tinges of color were beginning to return to his cheeks, rather sooner than she had expected.

"In part, yes." She tucked the quilts tighter around his shoulders and under his chin. "I wanted you to understand, though I'm not sure yet that you do."

"I understand that I've never been so sick in my life. Damn, does the itching *ever* stop? I've had a bit too much rum once or twice, but I never felt like this in the morning. And at least I had a some fun the night before! There was a pleasurable moment or two, but hardly that exciting—and, Lord, what came after! Or was my reaction unusual?"

"Quite the contrary. The itching does stop, by the way, after a day or two, though you'll be smelling opium for quite a while. It's very *usual* for a novice to react exactly like that. Especially if he takes a few pipes too many."

"Which, of course, you made sure I did?" Matthew was beginning to catch on.

Rachel smiled softly. "I wanted you to have the experience of the drug, but I didn't want it to be *too* pleasurable. That would have been foolish and irresponsible. Just a hint to let you know what it was like . . . but not enough to tempt you to try again. Even if you are as strong as you claimed."

"I don't feel very strong right now," he admitted ruefully. "I feel like a mop some swabbie's wrung out and flung back on the deck. But if you're right—if what happened to me is typical—then why in God's name does anyone go back? You'd think they'd try it once and learn their lesson like I did, and that foul den really would go out of business."

"Curiosity, sometimes. The stories are so incredible." Rachel slipped off his jacket, which she had draped over her shoulders, and tried to add it to the quilts. But he saw that she was shivering and made her take it back. "Or desperation. the Chinese are good people, and remarkably patient, but their lives are oppressively hard. Every day is a bitter new struggle— you can't blame them for being tempted. They think if they can just make it through the initial discomfort, a beautiful world of opium dreams will open up and carry them away from all the weariness and deprivation."

"And does it?" Matthew asked quietly. "Even without the unpleasant side effects, it seems to me that the fabled euphoria is awfully mild."

"You really *don't* know what you're talking about, you know." Rachel drew back slightly, pulling her knees up and wrapping her arms around them. "The dreams come later. Very wonderful, compelling dreams. Not just the whirling colors and flashing lights you see the first time, but a whole beautiful, magical paradise, enveloping you . . . and sweeping you up in visions and sensations you can't even imagine. A paradise so enticing you almost feel it's worth giving your life for.''

Something in her voice made Matthew uneasy. He managed to raise himself up on one elbow. "You sound as if you'd been there. To that 'magical paradise.' Good lord, you didn't try it again! After it made you so sick?''

"I wasn't quite as sick as you. I had a kinder teacher. My brother.'' Her face took on a faraway look, softening in the mist. "But, yes . . . I smoked again. Several times. And, yes, I journeyed to that unearthly paradise . . . and it frightened me more than anything in my life. Because it was so beautiful, you see. So very beautiful, and I longed to go back . . . just *one* more time. . . .''

"But you didn't," he reminded her.

"No, but I wanted to, and that's what was so frightening. Because I knew if I went back once, I would be trapped forever.''

Matthew sat up with an effort and drew the quilts around him for warmth.

"Perhaps,'' he said gently, "if it's really that beautiful—and there are really people so desperate and sad—it's not so unremittingly awful to allow them the respite they have chosen.''

"Perhaps,'' she said, though he sensed she didn't mean it, "if it weren't for the little girl who was sold. And if the beauty continued. But it doesn't. After a few months, a year at most, the wonder fades, and the opium smoker becomes an opium fiend, taking more and more pipes, not from pleasure any longer but because of the terrible suffering that wracks his body if he tries to withdraw. And then he's a thousand times more wretched than ever.''

"I see,'' Matthew said, and for the first time he did. "That's why you brought me to that place tonight. That's what you wanted me to understand.''

"I hoped,'' she admitted quietly. "I wasn't sure . . . I'm not sure now . . . but I *hoped.*''

Matthew watched her in the diffused half light and thought how much he loved and admired this woman, and what a constant surprise she was. He wanted her enough so that he would have given in anyway. There had never been any question, really, who would hold out the longest. But he knew now she was right.

There was a moral issue here, and he could no longer evade it. He had sensed tonight, however fleetingly, the agonies that came with the use of the opium. It would be a shabby man indeed who allowed himself, in however small a way, to spread and perpetuate it.

"All right, tiger, you *do* win. You can have the opium in the hold of the *China Dawn*. Or rather, the sea can have it, since I assume that's what you've got in mind."

Rachel's heart was in her eyes as she studied him in the softly flickering mist. She had wanted this so desperately when they set out that night. It had been hard, giving up so much of what she believed in. She still wished he had never handled the drug. But if at least he understood—and was willing to make amends . . .

"You mean that? Even if you have to give up the chance to prove yourself to you grandfather?"

"And my brother. Yes, I mean it."

"All of it?" she persisted. "Every bit you brought from India?"

"Well . . . all that's mine to give. Part of it belongs to Gallagher, naturally. My partner. I gave him a one-third share for his help in procuring it. That's not mine anymore, but everything else—"

"But you brought it here," Rachel interrupted, feeling suddenly betrayed, as much by her own foolish hopes as by the half-hearted commitment she ought to have expected. "Your partner's share along with your own. You're the one whose money purchased it, and you're the one who had it loaded onto his ship. It's your responsibility. And it's still in your possession."

Oh, Lord! Matthew stared at her helplessly. So much for the fond picture of her falling into his arms, sobbing in gratitude for his magnanimous generosity! She was beautiful, she was exciting, and no matter how irrational she might be, he would always adore her—

but there was only so much a man could give! Surely
even she understood that?

"I gave my word of honor, Rachel. I can't go back
on that."

"Even after what happened tonight? After everything you've seen and experienced? This one-third
share you so cavalierly dismiss is going to destroy
lives. More children are going to be sold. Where is
the honor in that?"

"I'm sorry, but my word is still my word. The opium
is Gallagher's."

"I'm sorry, too," Rachel said softly. She felt the
tears in her eyes and turned away so he wouldn't see
them. It was her own fault, really—she should have
trusted her first instinct. They came from different
worlds, she and this man who had made such a place
for himself in her heart. They would never agree on
the things that mattered. "I'm afraid I put you through
all this for nothing. It was very unfair . . . I expected
too much. I'm sure you understand there's no possibility I can ever marry you now."

Matthew sank back on the rough matting, feeling
confused and hopelessly feeble as he watched her drift
away toward the stern of the small sampan. In his
weakened state, he was having trouble taking in her
abrupt, absolutely unexpected response to what he had
thought was his abject surrender.

He liked unpredictable women, but this was carrying it too far. His love for her against his honor as a
gentleman? *Unfair* was hardly the word. She was being utterly impossible! He had given as much as he
could. He had met her halfway—no, *more* than halfway! But she hadn't been able to yield an inch. It was
all or nothing with her. She didn't know the meaning
of the word compromise.

She was the most exasperating, infuriating woman
he had ever known! If he had any sense, he would drop
her off at the mission tomorrow and go on to Macao
and forget he had ever laid eyes on her!

But even at his angriest, he still wanted her, as he
knew he always would. Matthew watched her through

the swirling fog—her soft, loose hair blowing back from her face, the dark violet skirt swaying against her legs—and tried to imagine what his life would be like without her, and found that he couldn't.

Oh, Lord, he thought again, and was almost grateful for the debilitating weakness that still made it difficult even to move. She had denied him only marriage; she had said nothing about the other feelings between them, and he sensed that she would not resist, or not for long, if he took her into his arms and kissed her again.

It was lucky they would be reaching their destination the next day. He didn't think he could lie beside her one more time with his strength restored and not make love to her.

Nine

It was well after dark when they arrived at the mission. Although it was barely an hour's walk from the place they had left the sampan, Rachel, worrying about the lingering effects of the drug, had insisted that Matthew rest first. He also had the distinct impression that she was beginning to wonder how her family would react when they saw him, and wanted to cut short the time before she could reasonably suggest they offer him a warm tub and a bed.

Matthew spent an uncomfortable night alone in a spartan room off the men's ward of the small hospital, set aside, he supposed, for the private care of more difficult cases. Rachel had hurried him off after only a few minutes with a wildly far-fetched tale about being threatened by bandits and having to abandon the boat miles and *miles* away. Poor Captain Barron had had to trudge all that distance with the luggage—most of which was his—and was naturally *exhausted*.

Poor Captain Barron had listened wide-eyed. For a woman who put such emphasis on right and wrong, she had the most amazing ability to stretch the truth!

Sleep defied him most of the night, and he lay awake, his mind going over and over those last hours they had spent together. He hated the way things had been left so badly between them. He couldn't simply get up in the morning, murmur a few polite words of thanks, and leave without straightening things out. But what kind of excuse would he find to stay when his own, considerably more comfortable, home was barely a carriage ride away?

He was still mulling the problem over, and coming

up with no ideas, when he rose and went out to find
the sun already streaming down from high in the sky.
He was a little embarrassed as he poked his head
through the door of the separate structure that served
as a kitchen and dining hall both. He could just imagine the questions Rachel had parried the night before.
"We thought you were with acquaintances—plural.
Surely you weren't with this one man alone?" "You
mean you traveled with him for a *week*? On a little
sampan?" "Doesn't he have a . . . well, you know—
a rather *colorful* reputation?"

Whatever her answers, they seem to have been sat-
isfactory, or at least to have allayed suspicions somewhat, for when Rachel's mother caught sight of him in
the doorway, she greeted him warmly and settled him
down with a bowl of rice she had kept heated for his
breakfast. A generous dollop of butter and brown sugar
on top reminded him pungently of the porridges of his
childhood.

Matthew resisted a grin as he poured on some heavy
cream and attacked it with gusto, his appetite having
returned full measure. It was simple fare, and the rice
was overcooked and rather mushy, but big chunks of
mango and slices of Canton banana made it quite tasty.
It didn't look like he was going to pine for Rachel's
cooking, after all, if he managed to stay.

He had not yet come up with a way to broach the
subject, but as it turned out, it wasn't necessary. The
conversation drifted naturally to food, and he heard
Rachel's mother apologizing for the fact that they had
just lost their cook. It was hectic working at the mission—the hospital was overflowing sometimes, and
people were always stopping by. It was impossible to
keep help more than a few weeks. She hoped Matthew
would not mind humble meals.

Mind? He was ecstatic, especially after Rachel's father came in and, pulling up a chair to join them for a
few minutes, casually mentioned an outing their guest
might be interested in the next day, or perhaps later in
the week. Apparently, the subject had already been

discussed, and they had come to the conclusion that he was going to be staying with them.

Matthew wondered, just for an instant, if Rachel had said something. But she was still angry and unreasonably hurt because he had refused to give up Gallagher's share of the opium along with his own. She would never have suggested to her parents that she actually wanted him to stay.

More likely, he thought wryly, he looked like a cross between a sheep in heat and a lovesick moose every time he gazed at their daughter. They had probably assumed they had a young man come courting—of whom there had, no doubt, been many in the past—and decided to make the most of it.

He had ample opportunity during the remainder of the morning to explore the small mission, and everywhere he turned, he seemed to find a new surprise. Even the buildings were not at all what he had imagined. He had known that money was tight, and he certainly had not expected grandeur, but being accustomed to the churches of his native New England, he had thought the chapel at least would be modestly imposing. Not elegant, perhaps, but strong and austere, with a spire pointing like praying hands toward the heavens and a somber, polished interior that inclined one to contemplate the frailties of the world and pray for one's sins.

Instead, it was the humblest of the structures, off to one side and dwarfed by the sturdier hospital. The walls were not brick or even rough-hewn siding, but woven rattan bound to a flimsy board-and-bamboo scaffolding which no doubt was blown away periodically by the devil winds, or typhoons, that swept the area. High, open windows on both sides sent splashes of sunlight through the surprisingly inviting room.

Not at all what he had been taught a church ought to be, and yet, in some unaccountable way, Matthew found himself liking it. Garlands of flowers, wilting and forgotten, twined frivolously among the rafters from some service now past, and the spaces between the windows were adorned with huge red papers on which Chinese characters had been scrawled in gold. Like the scrolls in ancestor shrines on backstreets and rural hillsides, though presumably these contained the Lord's Prayer or uplifting sayings from the Bible.

It was not just the place itself that surprised him, but the people who had created and nurtured it. It was not hard to think of the Reverend Gideon Todd as a minister. He was a big, handsome man, about as tall as Matthew, though wider in the shoulders, and hair nearly the color of Rachel's, touched at the temples with gray, waved back from a noble brow. With his broad, square jaw and keenly piercing hazel eyes, he would have been the darling of every ladies' aid group in Boston or Connecticut. But it was next to impossible to imagine him toiling his life away as a humble missionary in a poor outpost on the fringes of China.

Abby Todd at least fit the image better. Matthew paused to watch as Rachel's mother hurried out of the barn with a basket of eggs and headed toward the house. She was big, like her husband, but what he suspected had once been angularity was now solidly padded into a matronly form. Dark hair, tidy but unstyled, still more pepper than salt, had been bound in a utilitarian bun at the nape of her neck.

As a girl, she must have been what the ladies of the family would have described in their charitable tone as "plain," though time and hard work had etched lines that were not at all unpleasant on her brow and around the corners of her mouth. Matthew could easily visualize her corresponding with an earnest young divinity student and agreeing to marriage sight unseen as a way of dedicating her life, not to him, but to God.

It was a bleak picture, though, in truth he had to admit it didn't seem to have turned out badly, and it made him feel somehow sad—until Gideon Todd happened around the opposite corner of the house and laid a broad hand with an extremely familiar pat on his wife's ample derrier.

Abby spun around, laughing as she slapped the offending hand away with mock indignation. A hearty, very earthy laugh that carried all the way to where he was standing, and Matthew found his entire picture of Rachel and her family background undergoing rapid revision.

"They do that all the time!" Rachel's third brother, Joshua, shifted a heavy water bucket on his shoulder as he paused good-naturedly beside him. "Used to humiliate us—horribly—when we were children, the way they carried on. Really embarrassing, you know. They ought to have been beyond that sort of thing at their age! Now I've got a woman of my own, and I hope she's as lively when *her* children are growing up."

Matthew watched as Joshua headed back to his chores, moving with surprising grace down the gentle slope. In a way, Rachel's brothers had proved the greatest surprise. They were very different, in looks and in spirit. Carter, the oldest, the only true redhead in the family, could be almost solemn sometimes, his hazel eyes alert and thoughtful. Gideon John, the image of his father, if somewhat more facile in rhetoric, seemed destined inevitably for the pulpit. Joshua was big and brown haired and brawny, and always full of laughter.

But they were alike in one thing: the way they regarded their only sister. Matthew could feel them watching him sometimes, with oddly speculative looks and he realized uncomfortably that they all thought he was *sleeping* with her. Only instead of the vengeful wrath he would have expected—would indeed have indulged in himself if this were his sister!—they seemed to be holding off, reserving judgment.

There was an intense practicality in this family, which ran counter to everything he had ever heard about missionaries. What's happened has happened, they seemed to be saying. There's no turning back and changing it now. We'll just wait and see if he's going to be honorable and make things right.

If they only knew, Matthew thought—if they *only* knew!

His sole confrontation, if it could be called that, came with Sam, the youngest of the brothers, and the

one who was most like Rachel. Not in appearance perhaps, for he was short, no more than five or six inches
over five feet, and dark hair spilled onto his brow. But
his eyes were the same: a deep, clear brown, flashing
with fire and impatience.

Matthew was reminded, as he came around a corner
and found the young man blocking his path, of Rachel's
warning that he didn't want to tangle with her brother.
It may have been a little premature, he decided, dis-
missing him so lightly. Sam might be small, but he was
wiry and fast, and looked as if he could be mean in a
fight.

"Rachel is not only my sister," he said bluntly.
"She's my best friend. I am very fond of her. I would
not take it lightly if any man were to hurt her."

"Nor would I," Matthew replied. "I'm very fond
of her, too."

Sam regarded him for a moment, as if thinking it
over. "Just so there are no misunderstandings—later,"
he said. "We are clear on this?"

Matthew thought about telling him that what he suspected was wrong, that his sister's innocence was still
remarkably intact, but he settled on what seemed a
more believable reply.

"My intentions are honorable, Sam. I give you my
word on it. And my hand, if you'll take it."

It seemed to be the right thing to say, for Sam
reached out, and they shook, almost amiably. He
would still be watching, like the others, but like them,
he was apparently willing to give Matthew the benefit
of the doubt.

"I think your brothers like me," he said later, when
Rachel had finished her work at the hospital and appeared on the lanai in front of the house. She was
wearing a simple, dark gray dress with a large white
apron, and a gauzy cap covered hair that had been
piled in a jumbled heap on top of her head. Little curls
spilled onto her forehead, and Matthew thought how
strange it was that he who had always adored fashion-
ably attired women should be so taken with the way
she looked now.

"You're full of confidence, aren't you?" she replied tartly, but not without humor, and he sensed that at least some of her anger had dissipated. "What makes you so cocksure of yourself?"

"The fact that they haven't beaten me to a bloody pulp, and they think I've been taking advantage of you. Except for Sam, they haven't even threatened me obliquely. . . . Do you have any idea how pretty you are, standing there in the sunlight? That filmy white thing looks like a halo around your head."

"Sam has always been overprotective," she said, pointedly ignoring the compliment. "You'd do well to watch out for him. As for the others, they don't *dis*like you—yet. They're waiting to see what happens with us."

"And I suppose you're going to let them go on believing I've been an unspeakable cad—and tear me limb from limb if you decide not to marry me!"

She hesitated in the doorway, her lips twisting into the subtlest hint of a smile.

"*If* I decide . . . ?" she said, and disappeared into the house.

Rachel was not quite as displeased as she ought to have been to discover that her parents had virtually invited young Captain Barron to remain with them in their home. The rift that had marred their last night alone had distressed her as much as it had Matthew, and she found herself grateful for the chance, if not to repair their relationship, which she still firmly believed was impossible, at least to part as friends.

The days at the mission proved to be good for both of them. The passion that had dominated their feelings to that point had been so blinding they had not been able to get beyond it. Now, under the watchful eyes of Rachel's father and mother—to say nothing of four very obtrusive brothers, who were obviously determined that not so much as one more kiss was going to be stolen without the proper contracts negotiated and sealed!—there was little else they could do but talk and get to know each other.

Rachel was finding to her surprise that Matthew was far from the spoiled dandy she had originally assumed. He still looked good in his clothes, even when he had to wear the same shirt more than once, but there was nothing effete or foppish about him as he pitched in and helped with the chores. He went to the river without complaining every morning with her brothers and brought back barrels of water in an old creaking wagon; he split and stacked huge piles of wood for the fireplaces in the hospital and the house; he gathered eggs for Abby, and learned with much laughter and only a little ineptitude how to milk the cow. He even listened attentively to Gideon's sermons, though the good reverend had a tendency to ramble sometimes, and even his wife had been caught nodding more than once.

But it was in the hospital that he was especially helpful. He took off his fancy cufflinks, slipped them in his pocket, rolled his sleeves up over his elbows, and plunged into whatever needed doing, without having to be asked or directed.

Even Rachel had to admit she was impressed as she paused at the end of an especially long day and looked into the small room that separated the men's and women's wards. Matthew had set a young boy's badly broken leg, quite expertly, gone on to assist her father in a particularly unpleasant surgery without once turning green or looking like he was going to relieve himself of his lunch, and now he was calmly scrubbing the table and closing up, as if it were all in a day's work.

"I'm afraid I owe you an apology. I thought you were as useless as you looked."

"Then you owe me double apologies," he replied as he finished the table and rolled down his sleeves. "I do not look useless. Just handsome and debonair— which is hardly the same thing."

Rachel was too tired to rise to the teasing. "You set that boy's leg very well. It was a nasty fracture, but he won't suffer any permanent effects, I think. And my father said he's never had a better assistant. You knew just what to hand him when, and you didn't waste

time asking pointless questions. One might almost
suspect you'd had medical training.''

"In a way, I have," Matthew reminded her. The
sleeves were down now, and he was taking his cufflinks out of his pocket. "I'm a ship's captain, as you
will recall. We're used to handling emergencies. And,
if fact, I've actually had some formal training. Five
months at a hospital in Boston. I thought it might be
a good idea since none of the *Dawns* carries a sur-
geon.''

He did not mention that it had also been a good
excuse to keep from shipping out until he was too old
to go as anything but an officer. He didn't want to
dispel the good impression he had apparently created.
It was not that he was afraid of hard work. But as the
baby of the family, he had become exceedingly weary
of always taking orders from everyone else.

"Why are the Barron ships always called *Dawn*?"
Rachel asked curiously. A wisp of hair had tumbled
over her eyes, and she brushed it back with her hand.
"I know it's a tradition on some lines, like the chil-
dren in a Chinese family, to always have one word in
common in their names. Precious Jade and Prosperity
Jade and Listening-to-the-Orioles-in-the-Morning
Jade. But why 'Dawn'?''

"Ah . . . that's an old family story." Matthew did
up his cuffs and looked around, making sure everything was tidily put away. "Dawn was my grandfather's first love—and my grandmother, incidentally,
though by the sheerest of coincidences. She jilted him
for someone else, and years later, her daughter and
my father fell in love. It's commonly believed that he
named his ships after her in a fit of romantic nostalgia,
but personally I think he did it out of spite. So every
time she looked out in the harbor and saw the half-
round red of the dawn sun on the mighty Barron flag,
she'd think about all that wealth she threw away.
There's nothing romantic about my grandfather.''

Rachel laughed in spite of herself. "You make him
sound so diabolical, though from what I've heard of
old Gareth Barron, you might very well be right. . . .

I think that's everything, Matthew. You've cleaned up even to my father's exacting standards. And he's *very* exacting when it comes to his surgery.''

''I've noticed,'' Matthew replied with a wry grimace. ''I tossed a soiled towel on the counter the first day, and he fairly took the roof off! He seems to have a fetish for cleanliness. Though,'' he added, not wanting to offend her as they closed the door behind them and started up the narrow dirt path to the house, ''I have heard very sound physicians argue that unclean conditions can actually *cause* infection, and perhaps even spread certain diseases.'' Lord knows, the hospitals in Boston had been disgusting enough to turn his stomach, with the stench of blood and pus everywhere, and flies settling in droves in the summer on instruments that were given only the most cursory cleaning between uses. ''But your father carries it to extremes. I've never known anyone who insisted on boiling every drop of water that was used for anything, even mopping up!''

''Father believes,'' Rachel explained earnestly, ''that if water isn't pure enough for your stomach, it isn't pure enough for anything that might touch an open wound. And, of course, boiling water before drinking it is an old Chinese custom. That's where tea comes from, you know.''

She caught the startled look on his face and smiled.

''Officially, tea was a gift of the Bodhidharma, who came from India to China many years ago. He had vowed never to sleep, passing all his time in prayer and meditation, but one day he dozed off. He was so angry with himself for his weakness, he cut off his eyelids and cast them on the ground, and the Buddha caused them to grow in the form of tea shrubs. The leaves look like eyelids—well, pushing the point—and the beverage that's brewed from them inhibits sleep.''

Matthew laughed obligingly. ''But actually—?''

''Actually, the Chinese have long recognized the hazard of impure water. They're centuries ahead of us sometimes! They've been boiling it for ages, and one day someone discovered that floating these funny little leaves on top gave it a pleasant taste. I wonder, would he have been so pleased with his discovery if he could have seen what it would bring all these years later?''

She was about to add it was the British passion for Chinese tea, and the resulting drain on His Majesty's treasury, that had caused the introduction of opium into the country in the first place. But the air was crisp and cool; autumn was latening into winter with re-freshing breezes that wafted away the heat and stag-nant smells, and she could not bear the thought of quarreling again.

Matthew seemed to sense what she was thinking, for he was as anxious as she to change the subject.

''Your father has made quite a success of the hos-pital, though I don't see many people in the chapel, except at Sunday service. I thought missionaries were supposed to dedicate their lives to spreading the word of God and christening little pagan children. Where are all the prayer meetings and the Bible classes?''

''We're a medical mission. We believe in souls, too—my father, especially, poor man, but he's so busy tending to the body, he never seems to have time even to prepare a decent sermon for the soul. He used to be a very powerful preacher when we lived in Hawaii, or so they say. I was too young to remember.''

Matthew was not hypocritical enough to suggest that Gideon Todd was still good at preaching. ''At least he's a good and caring doctor, which will probably win more souls in the end. Though I've noticed that it's just the men who come to him. You and your mother care for the women. Is that part of the natural pattern of subservience in the Chinese culture? Only the men are good enough to be tended to by trained physicians? Nurses and midwives for the women, and damned lucky to get them?''

''No.'' Rachel shook her head. ''At least I don't think so. It's more a matter of modesty. A woman couldn't allow herself to be touched by my father or a male Chinese physician. In drastic cases, she might stick her arm out from behind a curtain or screen so her pulse could be taken, but generally, symptoms are described by pointing at the appropriate places on a little ivory female doll.''

''Are you serious?''

''Unfortunately, yes. At least my mother and I can get close enough to examine them. Not that we always know what we're doing. But we report back to Father, and he tells us what comes next. Hardly an efficient system, but it's the best we can manage. What we really need are *women* doctors,'' she added so fervently that Matthew shuddered. He loved her spirit, but he could just imagine the world if all the fiesty women were allowed into fields like medicine!

''They must come to you, then, for childbirth,'' he hastened to say. ''Particularly if it looks like a difficult confinement. Or do they cling to their own midwives?''

Rachel hesitated. She was tempted to skim over the subject with an easy, conventional answer. But she had already held back too much in an effort to keep things smooth and pleasant between them.

''We do a rousing business in babies, but only with the foreign enclave in Macao. Because of my father's 'fetish for cleanliness,' as you put it, we have a much lower incidence of childbed fever. Even the Portuguese Catholics send their wives to us when the time comes—Father refuses to leave his duties to rush off and hover over them. But we've never been popular with the Chinese, either here or in their homes. . . . We won't bring the bucket of water, you see.''

''Bucket of—water?'' They had reached the lanai, and Matthew stopped to throw her a puzzled look before going back to his own small room to clean up for dinner. ''But, surely even the humblest peasants have a source of water themselves. And some sort of facility for boiling it, if you consider that necessary.''

''I don't mean that kind of water,'' Rachel replied softly. ''I mean the bucket of water to set beside the bed if the baby is a girl. I told you, Matthew—these people are very poor. They can't afford to feed another mouth if that mouth is attached to someone who's not going to be productive. It's as humane as possible, I

suppose—the distance between the birthbed and the
grave but a short span, and with little pain—but, naturally, we cannot be a part of it.''

She could see that he was shocked, for once too
much even to speak. Thinking about it later, after he
had gone, Rachel realized that she had touched him.
Deeply. She sat down on a wooden bench and leaned
back wearily against the wall.

But she had touched him before, she thought. She
had forced him to see the sorrow and pain of this country she loved, and it hadn't made any difference. He
still clung stubbornly to his masculine ideal of
''honor.''

As if honor were only a matter of keeping one's
word! And if that conflicted with accepting responsibility for one's own actions . . . well, a man's word
was his word, after all.

She let her eyes close briefly. She was too tired for
her usual show of spirit, and in that unguarded moment, a sneaking little thought came into her mind that
maybe, just *maybe,* she wasn't being totally fair to
him. The more she got to know Matthew Barron, the
more she liked and honestly respected him. He was
decent and fair and good-hearted; he would never willingly hurt her or anyone else; and except for that one
trick with the gaming piece—which she had not exactly found objectionable—he had always been scrupulously honest with her.

And a man's word, or a woman's, wasn't something
to be lightly dismissed.

''He really *is* a nice man,'' Camilla Crale had told
her again that morning when she had appeared suddenly with an armful of autumn anemones and eyes
brimming with laughter and curiosity. ''I did warn you,
you know. I expect you're busy—you always are—I'm
not going to stay, but I thought these might come in
handy. In case there's going to be a wedding. Or . . .
for the boudoir?''

''A wedding, indeed!'' Rachel had taken the flowers
brusquely and handed them to a Chinese girl to be

delivered to her mother. "They'll come in handy for Sunday service in the chapel, if they last that long."

"But you *are* sharing your boudoir with him?" Camilla had persisted. "You *have* to tell me . . . I've come all this way to hear! It's really so mysterious. You disappeared for *weeks*, and he disappeared . . . and now here you are, together! Surely you haven't resisted his advances *all* that time?"

"*One* week," Rachel had started to protest, then gave up, half smiling in spite of herself. Camilla always wormed things out of her anyway, and it had felt good to have someone to talk to. "I didn't resist at all. I didn't even try, but he did. It's marriage or nothing with Matthew Barron, so I'm as pure as when I started out—well, almost as pure. He says I have to make an 'honest man' of him."

"Ah . . . ?" Camilla had laughed knowingly. "He's cleverer than I thought, your handsome captain. I think he loves you . . . more than you deserve. You're a very lucky lady. *Very* lucky . . . and so foolish you don't even know it."

Was she being foolish?

Rachel let her eyes drift open as she remembered Camilla's words again and realized there was more than a little truth in them. She wanted perfection, but perfection wasn't possible in love—and Matthew had been more than willing to accept the imperfections in her. Should she allow him to work through the conflicts that honor imposed on him now, and accept whatever conclusion he came to, knowing it had been made in good conscience?

She had thought she had already gone as far as she could. She turned her head, staring off into the hills as she often did when she was trying to work things out in her mind. Tolerating the mere existence of the opium seemed concession enough. Now it occurred to her that perhaps she might be able to give more.

They had one more visitor that evening. Steven Wu slipped in long after dark, meeting Rachel by prearrangement in the quiet chapel on the far side of the hospital. She had been feeling badly left out—that week away seemed an eternity in more ways than one—and she was so full of questions, and so engrossed in Steven's answers, that she didn't notice anything amiss until a tense, closed look came over his features.

She was almost as nervous herself when she turned and saw Matthew in the doorway. But he only laughed.

"It's all right, Steven. I don't hold any grudges. In fact, I gave the rest of the stuff to Rachel after your boys botched the raid. I suppose you got my other two junks."

The comment seemed oddly offhanded, and Rachel realized a little belatedly that he hadn't even asked about them before, though he had to have known Sam would keep her informed. It was almost as if he didn't care.

"One of them," Steven said cautiously. "That mate of yours, Romack, is very stupid. It was easy sneaking up on him . . . almost as easy as it was with you. But the other one, Gallagher, got rid of our pilot and took on his own. He had already arranged for a separate rendezvous. The *Co-hong,* the merchants in Canton are as greedy, some of them, as the British—and even more evil, for it is their people who suffer. It is said that representatives of Howqua himself met the junk on the shore."

Matthew smiled wanly. It was the powerful merchant Howqua's representatives he had thought *he* was going to meet. "Gallagher has more experience with deviousness than I. He might have warned me, but then, credit where credit is due. He's a sly dog, and it has served him well. I daresay he negotiated a very decent profit."

"But not as much as you will make in the end," Steven reminded him perceptively. "You lost only a small amount in the raid. You have a shipload left."

"Not I. I presented the lot of it to Rachel." He saw the startled expression on her face and grinned. "It's still yours, tiger—whatever happens between us. I gave it to you outright, no strings attached. My word of honor . . . and you know I *always* keep my word."

"That's good," Steven ventured with a strangely bold look. "That will save us some considerable trouble."

"You mean . . . ?" Matthew turned to look at the young Eurasian, realization dawning slowly that the foray against the three junks was far from the end of what he had in mind. "Surely you weren't planning on attacking the *China Dawn* itself! At the anchorage in Lintin? But, good God, man—that's more than foolhardy. It's suicidal! Even if you managed to slip some sampans through the fog unseen, one good blast from the cannon would bring a dozen other armed vessels."

"But the *China Dawn* isn't at Lintin." The boldness in his eyes turned to a kind of passion Matthew couldn't define. "Your friend Gallagher is taking his operations up the coast. He and his smuggling boat will meet with a nasty surprise this time. Little sampans approaching from the front, and while he's swatting at them like gnats, a pair of war junks bearing down on his rear. But he'll try again."

"And the *China*?"

"He had it moved to a more convenient location. A small cove at the mouth of the Pearl River."

"What the devil—?" Matthew broke off in disbelief. Tactically, the thing made sense. If he'd still been set on moving the opium, he might have done the same himself. But it left the flagship of the Barron line extremely vulnerable. "My first mate would never agree to something like that. Nobody moves the *China* but me. It's my command—and my decision! Varnay knows better than to listen to the likes of Gallagher."

"But there's always a way to persuade even the shrewdest man, if you're not too scrupulous about how you do it," Rachel said softly. "A note, perhaps, forged to look like your handwriting. Or simply swearing that the order came from you. And *this* is the man to whom you are determined to keep your word, no matter what the cost? Are you still sure it's a matter of honor?"

No, Matthew thought later, he wasn't sure, though he hadn't been ready to acknowledge it to her at the time. He had left shortly after that, while Rachel was still with Steven Wu, and wandered down the path to the edge of the mission. It was very dark, and without a lantern, he could just make out the dim outline of trees against a rocky mass of hills in the distance.

In fact, he was becoming more and more sure that honor had nothing to do with dealings with Christy Gallagher. The man was as sly with him as he had been with Wu and his rebels, and Matthew knew if he turned his back too long, he would like as not feel a blade protruding from it. He did owe Gallagher something—the bargain had been struck—but it could be settled as well with cash as a one-third share of a shipment of opium.

Gallagher might not like it. He would miss the thrill and adventure that smuggling promised, but it would be a fair offer—fairer than he would have given himself—and he would take it.

It was not that Rachel was wrong, Matthew thought uneasily. He had been coming more and more to understand that she was very right. He *had* brought the opium here. The responsibility for it was his, and he ought to clean up the mess he had caused. But she went about telling him so blasted emphatically! Setting conditions for this and conditions for that, not letting him make up his own mind. Didn't she know a man had his pride?

And yet . . .

His mouth softened into an unconscious smile as he thought of her. It was the very fire in Rachel Todd that made him adore her so much. She had wounded only his pride, after all—or, more accurately, his vanity. And vanity seemed a very stupid reason for losing the woman he loved.

The Reverend Gideon Todd had one passion in his life besides his pulpit and his hospital and his family, and that was his garden. It was a passion that brought at least as much frustration as joy, for even when he had time to tend it properly, he wasn't much of a gardener.

With flowers he managed passably well, perhaps because he loved them so much. The first crocus peeping out of the snow in the spring had always been like a song in his heart, and he could be moved nearly to tears by a drop of dew glistening on a perfect yellow rose in the summer sunlight. But years as a minister in a poor country had left him with an inherently guilty sense that time spent on pure pleasure was time wasted, and he struggled instead with the food plants that would forever defy him.

It was inching on toward sunset, the day after Steven Wu's visit, and he was working his way, or trying to, through a tangle of squash vine, which had come all the way from Connecticut—and been tended, no doubt with considerable amusement, by some ship's crew or other. It was not only thriving for a change, it had taken over the garden. He could have sworn there was a patch of tender young carrots over there, just waiting to be pulled, but he could not make out a trace of it now. And even the hardy Chinese cabbage looked as if it were about to give up the fight for existence.

"Let that be a lesson to you, my boy," he said to Matthew, who was standing beside him, trying very hard not to laugh. "Women are like plants. Vegetable plants, by heaven! Don't ever let anyone tell you they're life's delicate flowers, born to please and be succored. Plant a rose, water it in the drought, prune it back to shape it properly, and you know what you have. But plant a vegetable, and it rambles all over the garden— willy-nilly, here and there, doing whatever it pleases— and all you can do is stand back and shake your head."

Matthew allowed himself a faint smile. He had not known what to expect when the good reverend had spotted him on the path beneath the terraced garden and signaled him to come up. Certainly not a lecture on women as vegetable life.

"There speaks a man with a willful daughter," he ventured.

"Hmmm. Well, yes . . . I suppose I *have* spoiled Rachel." He picked up a hoe and attacked a particularly dense growth of vine, but being too tenderhearted to uproot it entirely, he accomplished little. "I daresay it's my fault. Abby would have been stricter. But she was such a pretty little thing—and so clever— and we'd waited so long for a girl. It was hard to say no."

"I can imagine," Matthew agreed. He could picture Rachel as a toddler, red-gold curls and big brown eyes, already learning to twist the men in her life around her little finger. "It's still hard to stand up to her when she wants her own way."

"Indeed, indeed," the reverend agreed, chuckling. "You'll have your hands full with that one. Takes after her mother, she does. Abby is the kindest woman on earth, and the soul of patience most of the time, but when she gets her back up about something, there's no moving her. . . . Here, hand me that blade over there, will you? Maybe if I cut it back—about here. What do you think?"

"Uh . . . I don't know." Matthew watched as the older man stooped and began whacking with more determination than skill at trailing tendrils of vine. The comment had been thrown in so subtly, it had almost slipped past him. He wasn't quite sure he had heard right even now. "I'm afraid I don't know much about vegetables."

"You'll learn, my boy . . . you'll learn. Yes, that does it. That should save the cabbages, at least for a time." He glanced up unexpectedly, his gaze disarmingly keen. "Rachel loves this country, you know. She took to it right away, more than any of us, the moment we arrived. Her heart is at home here. She would find it very hard to leave."

"I wouldn't ask her to," Matthew replied quietly. There was no mistaking now the very pointed questions, no matter how gently asked. "I haven't really thought it out, but there are plenty of opportunities for a young man here. The war won't go on forever. When it's over, trade is bound to pick up. Barron Shipping will need someone to head their operations in the East." Assuming, that is, he thought wryly, he was still part of Barron Shipping—and the Barron family—after this fiasco with the opium. "Or perhaps I'll go out on my own. Either way, I should do well enough."

"Good . . . well, I'm happy to hear that. I daresay it would have been all right anyway. Flowers don't transplant very well, you know, but vegetables . . . That squash over there came all the way from New England. Yes, I daresay it would have worked out well enough. But all the same, I'm glad."

Matthew had the uncanny sense that somehow, without the words actually being spoken, things had just been settled between them. But he was still uncomfortably conscious of the one subject that had not been touched on.

"You do know about the opium, sir?" he said stiffly.

The other man straightened up and leaned on the hoe. "I do, and I won't insult you by pretending it hasn't troubled me. But I was young once myself, though you might not know it to look at me now. We all make mistakes . . . and the Lord knows, I've had more than my share. You're a good man, Matthew. Your heart is in the right place. And your conscience. I have confidence in you to do the right thing."

"I'm not sure Rachel would agree with you."

"Aren't you, my boy? Well, as I said, I was young once myself. Just be kind to her, that's all I ask. Love her and be kind and make her happy. She has been the joy of my life, as now she will be yours."

He was chuckling softly under his breath as he watched Matthew make his way in a somewhat bewildered state down the hill. He had carried that off quite nicely, if he did say so himself! He had always hated those little chats between fathers and the men who wanted to marry their daughters. Do you have enough income to support my girl properly? Will she be living someplace her family considers suitable? Do you meet all of our exacting qualifications, which might not have anything to do with the needs of her heart?

He had been dreading the day Rachel finally set her sights on a man and he had to go through the ordeal himself. But really, he thought, he had slipped the thing past quite painlessly.

He *had* been young once. Gideon Todd leaned on his hoe again and thought how strange it was that the years passed so quickly, and what had been only yesterday was now a long-ago memory. Unexpectedly, his mind drifted back to another afternoon in another garden, when he had looked across the late spring roses and seen Abigail Carter smiling at him.

He had not intended to marry her when they began their unlikely correspondence. He hadn't even intended, honestly, to enter the ministry. Life had been good, lively and raucous, and if he got into a few scrapes too many, he always managed somehow to get himself out again. He had expressed interest in the Lord's work only to cozy up to a devout and well-heeled grandmother, and it had been she who suggested that he correspond with a young lady of suitable piety.

It had begun as a lark, but Abby's first letter, far from being priggish and riddled with homilies, was gentle and unaffected and surprisingly rich in humor. Gideon had written eagerly the next time, and the next, and by the third reply, he already knew that he had found his heart's desire. The next day, he had enrolled in divinity school in earnest.

It had taken three years of study, including some rudiments of medicine, but they had continued to correspond, and long before the end, they had been sure enough to pledge themselves to each other. When Gideon finally made the long trip to Connecticut, it was to claim Abby Carter as his wife.

She had told him she was plain, and in the view of the world, he had no doubt she was right. But Gideon had looked into dark brown eyes and seen the inner beauty shining out of them, and he had loved her from that first moment with a deep and passionate intensity that had grown every day of their lives.

He allowed himself another chuckle as he thought of that other garden. They had raised no objection, Abby's very proper family, when he had suggested an unchaperoned stroll. She was homely, after all, and he a man of God, though alarmingly good looking. Their relationship would be on a more ethereal plane.

He had taken her into a small summerhouse and kissed her, just to show her that what he had in mind was not all *that* ethereal. And she had kissed him back, and the marriage they had waited three long years for had been consummated a little before the ceremony with the warmth of the sun spilling through the windows and the smell of earth and roses in their nostrils.

They had walked in the garden every day after that, and while Abby's relations sat in the parlor, congratulating themselves on finally finding a husband for her, and such a *good* man, he had been out in the summerhouse showing her things that would have shocked them to the core. The official ceremony had taken place a month later, and almost immediately, they had set sail on the arduous voyage around the Horn with a group of other missionaries to the lush, tropical isle that would be their home for the first years of their marriage.

They had not even had time to be seasick. The sun was sinking rapidly, and Gideon began belatedly gathering together his tools. They had been too busy getting to know each other in that pious atmosphere which ought not to have been conducive to physical love.

Only one other couple had been as interested in each other, and they had seemed surprised, almost shocked, by the lust that swept over them. He and Abby had lain in their bunk, listening to the sounds the poor souls were trying so hard not to make, and they had giggled softly at the thought that they were not alone, after all. But then they had turned to each other, and everyone else had vanished for them, and they *had* been alone again.

Their oldest boy, Carter, had been born a month too soon. A big baby, robust and powerful of lung—no pretending he was premature. They had talked it over for a while and considered altering the date of their marriage. But the lie didn't sit well with either of them, and they had decided in the end they didn't care.

It had become a family joke. Dates were constantly mentioned, fingers counted on, and eyebrows raised in mock astonishment. The boys were awful as adolescents, as boys always are. They had figured out what nine months meant, and they took great glee in calculating back to just when and where each of them had been started. And poor Carter, though he was quite good humored about it, always found himself with the summer roses in Connecticut.

That was the kind of bawdy atmosphere Rachel had grown up in. She had thrived on it, as the squash plant sucked nourishment from the soil, and she had grown up with much too earthy a view of life. It had made Gideon exceedingly nervous as she had matured, and the inevitable stream of boys had come up from Macao with minute scratches that suddenly needed bandaging. But she had always been sensible, and sensible girls with four hawk-eyed brothers had a better chance than most.

He had been a little worried when she had appeared suddenly with her Yankee captain, and about forty implausible stories of how they had spent their week together. It worried him still, but he had been watching young Barron, and he sensed that his intentions were decent and that he had stuck by them. Though he was not quite so sure about his daughter.

Well, never mind. Gideon picked up his hoe and his blade and his shovel, and started slowly down the hill. Rachel loved the man, and he worshiped her—that was plain to see. Whatever had happened between them, whatever would happen in the future, he would make her happy, and that was all that mattered.

She was a willful wench, but her heart was kind. And young Matthew Barron had a strength he was just beginning to understand himself. They were well suited.

It made him sad, losing his little girl. A part of him would miss her forever. But he was not sad at the choice she had made for her life.

"I think I just asked your father for your hand." Matthew had an odd look on his face as he stopped

Rachel in the deepening shadows that stretched almost to the woods behind the small chapel. "I'm not quite sure . . . the conversation seemed to drift along in the oddest way, but I got the distinct impression he's given his blessing."

"Conversations with Father can be like that." Rachel smiled, an unexpected lightness coming over her, though she was so tired after another long day she could hardly hold her head up. "He can be rather vague when it suits his purpose. But if that's the impression you got, you're probably right. Father does have a way of getting his point across."

"He knows about the opium," Matthew said quietly. "I asked him about that most directly."

Rachel could feel her breath catching in her throat. This was the moment she both longed for and dreaded. They had to come to terms, at last, with this thing between them, and if one of them was not going to be able to give . . .

"What did he say?"

"He said he was young once himself, and we all make mistakes. He said he knew I was going to do the right thing."

"And are you?" she asked. The silence that followed was so intense, she could almost hear her own heart beating.

"By my standards or yours?" he said finally. "No, never mind—that wasn't fair. I came to surrender, tiger. The opium is yours. Gallagher's share, too. I'll buy him off somehow. It'll leave me a little strapped for cash. I won't be able to give you the palace you deserve, but I have a feeling you don't want a palace anyway."

Rachel shook her head, trying to take in what he had just said. Could it really be over, as simply as that? "A cottage would be nice."

"A cottage, it is. . . . And anything else your heart desires. The victory is yours, love. Completely. If I were a general, this would be the moment to hand you my sword."

Rachel held back, one last moment, searching his face, unable to find what she needed. The shadows were so deep now, she couldn't see his eyes.

"Are you sure, Matthew? This is what you really want? It isn't any good if you're doing it just to please me. I was very unfair, asking you to compromise your honor for what *I* believe in. I realize that now. If you are going to do this, it has to be because it's what *you* believe.

"I probably would have done it a long time ago, if you hadn't put my defenses up," he replied gently. "You're not the only one who can be stubborn, Rachel Todd."

"Then it really *is* mine? All of it? Every last chest you brought from Calcutta?"

"Everything except the chests that were already sold."

"Yes, but they're still in Canton," she said, suddenly forgetting the weariness that had hung over her before. It really *was* working out, and just the way she had hoped. "Steven was telling me about them. They were unloaded from Gallagher's junk and stored in a *hong* on Hog Lane. Not far from the foreign factories."

An alarming light had come into her eyes. Matthew realized a second too late that the negotiations with this beautiful, impetuous woman were not quite over.

"You aren't thinking . . . Rachel, that would be madness! It's much too dangerous, pulling a stunt like that. Do you think the *Co-hong* don't have guards on their warehouses?"

"I wasn't talking about breaking in! Steven has a plan, about bribing some of the clerks or something. There'll be a great deal of confusion once the war starts. He swears it isn't going to be dangerous."

"Oh, Lord!" Matthew felt a chill come over him as he realized that she had surprised him once again, and just when his resistance was at its lowest. "Rachel—"

"Someone is going to get that opium, Matthew, and I want it to be me. I want it to be *us*! If only we can destroy every last part of it ourselves . . . ! Don't you see? I want us to start out with a clean slate.''

Matthew did see, and he knew there was nothing he was going to be able to do about it. He wanted to start out with a clean slate himself. Though perhaps not quite as clean as all that.

"Tomorrow," he said firmly.

"You want to go after it tomorrow?" Rachel was startled. "But Steven said—"

"Not the opium. I want to be married tomorrow. I've waited long enough as it is. Marry me then, and I'll take on the opium whenever you say. I give you my word. And as you know, love—except for poor Gallagher, who no doubt deserves it—I'm a man of my word.''

"I'm not sure we can arrange everything—" she started to protest, but half-heartedly, and was not at all surprised when he cut her off.

"Tomorrow. And now that I've conceded everything you want, I have one demand of my own.''

He was standing so close Rachel could almost feel the strength and the hardness of him, and she was reminded suddenly of long sunlit afternoons on the small sampan with her body curving against his.

"And that is . . . ?"

"I haven't had so much as a kiss since we've been here. Do you suppose we could elude the watchful eyes of those brothers of yours?"

"Oh . . ." She was in his arms now, enjoying the welcome embrace she had denied herself—foolishly— much too long. "I think that might be arranged." Her lips were tilting up to his. "If Father spoke to you, then he's spoken to them, too. I think we can count on a few minutes alone."

Ten

They were married the next day in a quiet service in the little chapel, with flowers hastily festooned again through the rafters and sun spilling rich and warm on the gold-and-red Chinese silk banners on the walls.

It was a simple ceremony, with only the Todds in attendance, and a handful of friends who had managed to rush up from town at the last minute, but neither bride nor groom missed the splendor of a more elaborate affair. Rachel was wearing the same plain white gown she had worn the first time Matthew saw her, and he thought again as he looked at her how breathtakingly lovely she was and how frighteningly close he had come to letting himself lose her.

And Rachel looked at him, in his expensively tailored pearl-gray trousers and dark jacket, his ruffled white shirt with the whimsical miniatures of the Barron flag at the cuffs, and thought how strange it was that he was so very handsome, and how little it really mattered. For she had seen the goodness of his heart and the valiant generosity of his spirit, and she knew at that moment without any doubt that this was the man she would love every day for the rest of her life. Her hand did not even tremble slightly as she felt him slip the hastily procured ring on her finger.

"You were right, my love," she said later as she snuggled a little closer in the open carriage that was bringing them through the China Gate and into the shadowy lanes and seaside esplanades of town. "And I was wrong . . . and very foolish."

"What? *You* wrong? Can my ears be deceiving

me?'' His arm was closing around her, drawing her
hard against him, with no regard for the scandalized
eyes that had to be watching their passage. ''And I
was right? About what, pray tell?''

''About the wedding night you wanted for me—for
us—and how much better our love would be if we truly
belonged to each other. I'm glad we waited, Matthew.
I'm glad you *made* me wait.''

Rachel felt his lips on her forehead, just grazing the
place where her hair curled back from her temples.
Hot and moist, and not quite as gentle as she suspected he had intended. ''So am I, tiger . . . but I'm
not sure I'm going to have the forbearance I thought.
Night is still a long time away. Would you settle for a
wedding late-afternoon?''

Her body arched nearer, instinctively seeking the
tantalizing warmth of his, helped along by the jolting
of the carriage that constantly seemed to be throwing
them against each other.

''I would be yours here . . . right now, if you wanted . . .'' she whispered, letting her lips brush the soft
flesh of his earlobe. She was only half teasing, for now
that they could touch and hold each other again, every
part of her body seemed to be tingling and aching,
and she wasn't at all sure she didn't want him to throw
her on the floor of the carriage and take her right there!
''Though it is awfully public. Poor father, as a man
of God, would have much to answer for my upbring-
ing. And imagine my mother when she heard . . . !''

''Then, for their sake, I'll restrain myself.'' But he
was dropping his mouth to the side of her neck as he
spoke, nuzzling shamelessly, not at all setting actions
to words. His hand slipped up from her waist, just
hidden by the raised wall of the carriage, stroking and
taunting the underside of her breasts through the thin
cotton and the silk chemise beneath. ''But I warn you,
love, when we get home, I'm not going to restrain
myself any longer.''

''When we get home,'' she murmured huskily. ''I
won't want you to.''

When we get *home*, she thought. What a lovely word

that was. Home. A place where they could close the
door and draw the curtains and be alone at last. When
we get home, I'll want you to take me in your arms,
Matthew Barron, and teach me what it is to love a
man. And, oh, my dear . . . I am so glad you were
wiser than I. . . .

The house was silent when they reached it. Rachel
barely had time to form the briefest impressions. A
narrow white facade, surprisingly modest, but then the
Barrons were sure of their power and their wealth and
had no need to flaunt it. A well-proportioned but
sparsely furnished hall, understated elegance again.
Shadows in the rear, leading to rooms she could guess
at but not see. A polished mahogany rail on the stair-
case.

If there were servants, they were discreet, and she
sensed no peering eyes as Matthew lifted her in his
arms and carried her up the stairs.

"I'll show you the rest of the house later, love. Right
now, the only room I want you to see is in the back,
looking down on a quiet garden."

Rachel could feel the urgency shivering through his
body, barely leashed in, all the harder to control now
that fulfillment was so near. She buried her head in
the curve of his shoulder, excited by the feel of him
against her cheeks, the smell of his neck and hair in
her nostrils.

She was hardly more conscious of the bedroom than
the rest of the house. Burgundy velvet draperies had
been drawn over the windows, leaving an almost twilight hush, and bureaus and a massive oak armoire
were dark and almost severely plain. A masculine
room; one that had not seen a woman's touch, except
perhaps temporarily.

Her eyes drifted toward the large, canopied bed that
seemed to fill up one side of the room, and she was
unnerved by a sudden image of Matthew cavorting
cheerfully and quite passionately under the gauzy
mosquito netting with some platinum blonde or tawny-
skinned, bold-eyed brunette!

She must have stiffened, for he set her down, very gently.

"Am I going too fast for you, Rae? Should I take you downstairs, give you a glass of sherry—call out the cook and the houseboy and introduce them to their new mistress? I forget sometimes how innocent you are. You mustn't let me push you before you're ready."

"No that's not it. It's just that I . . . I saw the bed, and I couldn't help thinking about all the women who—well, you know—slept there before."

"Legions, no doubt." Matthew smiled indulgently. "But none with me. The Barron men are a lusty lot. Jared, who's stayed here many times, always has four or five women on the string. And Alex may be quieter, but he's no monk. I daresay this room would have a story or two to tell if it could speak. Come on, angel, sit over here. Next to me."

He was drawing her toward a settee on the far wall, easing her down, and Rachel was suddenly embarrassed by the irrational way she seemed to be trembling all over. This was the man she loved, the man for whom she had thought sometimes she would *die* if she couldn't have.

"I'm sorry, that was such a silly thing to say. It just slipped out."

"Listen to me, tiger." He took her hands very tenderly, and clasped them in his own. "I'm not as innocent as you are. I never pretended to be . . . I never thought you wanted me to be. There have been other women in my life—too many, perhaps—but not in his room. I would never defile you, or begin our love so shabbily, by asking you to spend your wedding night in a bed where I had lain with someone else."

There was so much love and sweet, undisguised longing in his voice that Rachel felt her resistance ebbing away. Other times and other women didn't matter. The past was over. He was here with her; he had married *her* and she was his future. She was even more aware now of the bed that loomed ever larger in the corners of her eyes. But it was a very different awareness . . . not at all unpleasant.

"What do we do now? Do you take off all my clothes, and carry me . . . over there? Do I lie very still, keeping my eyes tightly shut—only peeking a little—while you undress and climb under the covers beside me?"

"*Peeking*? Woman, where is your modesty?"

"Gone off with a sly rogue, who has taken all sorts of liberties with my body! Or do you kiss me again, like you did that night in the cabin on the junk, and toss me on the bed and show me what happens to little girls who dare to let their mouths kiss back?"

"Which would you prefer?" He had slipped off his jacket, almost unconsciously; Rachel could feel the steamy heat of his chest and arms as he moved closer, his tongue flicking pointedly over his lips, and she suspected that it was the latter course he had in mind.

"It all sounds good to me. Except that part about shutting my eyes. I want my eyes open every second of the time. I want to experience *everything* tonight."

But even as the words came out, those same eyes were already betraying her, closing instinctively as his mouth came down on hers. Rachel felt as if she were drowning into the inky blackness that seemed to envelop her. His arms were an iron-hard enclosure, his hands exploring, impudent, slipping up from her waist to her breast again, not holding back this time, but cupping, fondling. His mouth was a familiar pressure, the taste of him, the darting audacity of his tongue taunting hers. But there was a newness, too, an almost overpowering sense of wonder that came with the knowledge that this man with his mouth and his tongue and his searing, brazen hands was truly hers, and she his.

He seemed to understand the fierce need that surged excruciatingly into every corner of her being. His lips still fastened hard on hers, he plunged those same impudent hands boldly into the rounded neck of her dress. Rachel gasped as skillful fingers sought and manipulated one pliant nipple until it erupted in a sharp peak of the most exquisite pain she had ever known.

The dress was coming down, sliding off her shoul-

ders in one easy shrug. Rachel was not even aware
that he had found and undone the fastenings. She knew
only that it was a burden suddenly, that she wanted to
feel the air against her naked breasts again, wanted
him to look at her, touch her, make her quiver uncontrollably, as he had before.

Only this time she knew the yearnings he roused
would not go unsatiated.

He was lifting her in his arms again. . . . Had she
asked him to, or only willed it? The bed felt soft and
welcoming as her back sank deeply into it. Her dress
had come completely off; she was not sure exactly
when, and the chemise and single petticoat she had
been wearing was in a rumpled heap on the floor. Beside it lay a ruffled shirt, no longer immaculate, and
one fancy cufflink, the other kicked aside, she knew
not where.

Now, Rachel thought, it's going to happen *now,* and
she could feel her breath coming faster, in funny little
sounds that would have embarrassed her if she not been
so caught up in her love and aching need for him. The
hair on his chest looked incredibly soft, every pectoral
muscle beneath delineated with an awareness she had
never felt before.

Then his hands were at his belt, and suddenly her
breath had stopped, and she was waiting.

"I think, love," he said gently, "this *is* the time to
shut your eyes."

Just for a moment, Rachel didn't understand. Then,
softly, she began to laugh. After everything that had
happened between them, he was still trying to protect
her sensibilities!

"I have seen that part of a man before. I *am* a nurse."

"You tend to the women."

"And the men sometimes in the wards, when no
one else is available. And I do have four brothers!"
Her hand was playing with his chest hair now, enjoying the texture and slight moisture of it, the way it
narrowed into a thin line as it ran down his belly toward the place where his trousers were already unfas-
tened. "You promised me a wedding night . . . or late

afternoon. I'm not going to let you cheat me out of any part of it.''

''Even if it alarms you?'' he asked, knowing that glimpses of men on hospital beds or bathing in a stream was hardly the same thing as a close look at full male arousal.

Rachel could feel the restraint that held him back, even as she felt the longing that merged with and intensified her own. ''I won't be alarmed,'' she said, and willed her eyes to be bolder as he slid his pants off and stretched out beside her.

But she was, of course, just briefly, as she saw what he already knew, that his swollen member was indeed much larger than she had expected, and ramrod stiff, jutting arrogantly against the soft skin of her thighs. Rachel could almost feel it, ripping into her, tearing her delicate flesh. But with the fear came a warmth that seemed to ignite somewhere deep in her belly, diffusing outward and downward until she sensed that that ultimate intrusion would be as much a release as an agony.

He was kissing her again, all the savage urgency renewed and intensified. The warmth seemed to be spreading. Every part of her felt as if it were on fire—her lips under the bruising pressure of his relentless kisses, her cheeks, her arms, the small hollow in her back where his hand was sliding down, the smooth inner skin of her thighs. Then his fingers were there, suddenly, where she needed to feel them, sending little jolts of pleasure through her. At the same time, his mouth was claiming one small creamy white breast, sucking it greedily in, flicking his tongue over her nipple, and Rachel heard herself moan with longing.

''I do love you, Matthew . . . so very much. I want to be with you . . . *that way*. . . . ''

''I'm going to hurt you . . . I'm sorry.'' His voice was muffled and husky.

''I know. It's all right. I just want you to do it and get it over with. . . . Then I won't have to think about anything except how good it feels to have you inside me.''

"Oh, God . . . Rachel. I meant to be gentler. . . ."

But the need was too great; they had denied themselves too long, he as well as she, and the urges of his body took over. Matthew's mouth was greedy on hers again as he let his weight sink down. One finger probed and parted those secret inner lips, deftly manipulating, until she was writhing on the soft mattress, her legs instinctively trying to twine around him, to draw him closer.

He slid his hands under her, grasping her buttocks to facilitate his entry. But it was not necessary, for she was already arching up as he thrust downward, and he felt the slight resistance of her innocence give way.

She gasped, but only for an instant as he penetrated her. The pain was sharp and tearing, but not as bad as she had expected. And mingling with it almost immediately came another, sweeter agony that swelled inside her body, drawing her up and closer, as if there were no separation between them. As if his hard, throbbing assault and her hunger to enclose and devour were in that perfect moment a single entity.

He had stopped, just briefly, holding himself rigidly motionless to give her time to recover. Now sensing the renewal of her desire, he plunged into her again and then again, deeply and very satisfyingly, and almost immediately Rachel felt a jolt of pure pleasure that intensified for one breathless moment, then seemed to explode, leaving her quivering and clinging, desperate to hold on to him. The sharp little cry of surprise and delight that slipped out of her lips was nearly lost in Matthew's deep shuddering moan as his own body surrendered, and he felt his manhood spilling into her.

"I didn't know," Rachel murmured, after the passion was spent and they lay in each other's arms, their limbs so entwined it was hard to tell in the deepening shadows where one left off and the other began. "I didn't *know*." It had been so unexpected, the sheer intensity of that sweet moment of release, the waves and waves of tenderness that spilled over her afterwards. The most incredible tenderness she had ever known, and an overwhelming sense of love and contentment, seemed to fill her now, as the hardness of his masculinity had filled her body before.

"Neither did I, love," he replied, his voice so muffled she could barely make it out. "Neither did I."

"Are you laughing at me, Matthew?" Rachel pulled a little away to try and look at him, but the darkness was growing heavier, and they had neglected in the eagerness of their unslaked passion to light a lamp.

"Not I, my angel. You are so beautiful in the shadows—did you know that?" He was tracing the outline of her lips with one gentle fingertip. "So very soft. I didn't know how complete a man could feel with a woman . . . because I have never truly loved a woman before. . . . Did I tell you I wanted a wedding night for *you*? It seems the magic worked for me as well. I have never known with anyone else, lovely, lovely Rachel, what you have given tonight. And I suppose now I never will."

"Well, I hope not!" Rachel tried to look scandalized, but even in the shadows, she could see he was smiling. "It *was* good . . . wasn't it? I never thought anything could feel like that. Of course," she added impishly, "it might have been just as good if we'd done it before."

He moved his finger so it lay very lightly across her lips. "Shhh, love. It would have been extremely pleasurable—you wouldn't have heard any complaints out of me—but it wouldn't have been this same sweet perfection. You weren't yet ready to commit your heart. And only the body is satisfied if only the body is involved."

"Oh . . . I don't know." Rachel felt flushed again, but it was an easy warmth this time, satiated and content. She couldn't help remembering that night she had tried to go to him, and how she had been so sure she would be able to hold her heart back. But even then she had known it belonged to him. "I think I loved you from the beginning. But I am glad we waited . . . for tonight. I think every woman should have a wedding night like this."

Matthew leaned closer, kissing her tenderly, comfortably, and it occurred to Rachel that this was the first time their lips had ever met without any agony of desire. She was finding that she rather liked it.

"Mmmm, your mouth tastes sweet," he said. "And salty . . . and just a little tart. Funny, I never noticed before."

"You were too busy trying to have your way with me."

It was too dark to see one brow popping up, but she knew it was. "I beg your pardon? Who, pray tell, who was trying to make a fancy man out of *me*? And damned near succeeding—it was all I could do to hold onto my virtue! Now tell me, love . . ." He was half sitting up, half bending over her, and Rachel was very aware of the smell of his naked skin, the soft hair on his chest that had teased her fingers before. "Shall we lie in the dark . . . in each other's arms . . . until pretty soon the desire comes back and we make love again? Or shall we light the lamp, and sit and talk for a while, until pretty soon the desire comes back . . . ? Or shall we ring for the houseboy, who will bring a tray discreetly to the door, and nibble on noodles and lychees and an occasional earlobe, until pretty soon . . . ?"

Rachel laughed. "I think all your choices are the same. Are you really going to be ready again . . . soon? Cammie says there are men who can do it over and over all night long. She says it can be *very* tiring."

Matthew found it hard to imagine brazen little Camilla Crale ever tiring first. "And would you like it?" he said. "If I were to do it over and over? All night long?"

"I think," she replied softly, "tonight . . . I would."

"Then tonight—if you are a very good girl—you might just have what you want."

He got up and, going over to a small table, struck a light which cast an eerie flicker of yellow-gold into the darkened shadows.

"Since you didn't make a choice, I will . . . and I opt for the lamp." He hesitated, holding the light in his fingers briefly. "Or would you prefer that I put on my trousers for a while? We're still new to each other— you might turn shy again. You did before."

"I did not," Rachel protested. "Not much. And anyway, how could I be shy with you now? A woman can't be shy with a man after she's felt him inside her."

And yet strangely she was. He seemed to sense it, for Rachel noticed that he busied himself with the lamp longer than necessary. It had been less shocking some-how, the first time she had glimpsed him shirtless, or seen that unmistakable bulge at the front of tight pants which left very little to the imagination. Desire and curiosity had sustained her then. Now she was almost painfully conscious of his nudity, this man who had just become her husband and lover, and the dull ache between her legs reminded her what she was going to see when he turned around.

He waited just long enough for the sudden fit of shyness to leave, and her eyes were no longer afraid to play with the lean, hard contours that her body al-ready knew so intimately. It surprised her a little, as he turned, how very different he seemed. Perhaps a woman never truly saw a man until they had made love and he was standing naked before her.

She loved the clean lines of his face; she always had, but now that wide, generous mouth was all the more precious for the intimate part if had played in so many new, provocative sensations. She loved the leanness of his body, the way his shoulders were pro-portioned to the rest, not overpowering, but strong and masculine. She loved the light froth of hair that just covered his chest, only partially obscuring the muscles underneath, the little round nipples which it occurred to her might be fun to tease with her tongue and lips. She loved his slim hips, his hard, compact buttocks . . .

She let her eyes drop impudently to that soft pink part of him, looking so benign and harmless in its nest of dark blond hair. It had not looked so harmless before. It had looked bold and arrogant and hungry to claim her.

"You're staring at me very intently, tiger," he said, a hint of huskiness beneath the laughter in his tone. "Hasn't anyone ever taught you it's rude to stare?"

"You stared at me the first time you saw me without any clothes on. You can hardly complain if I do the same. And besides—you're staring again."

"I am . . . and I like what I see."

His eyes were raking her, very frankly, making no effort to be subtle. Rachel half sat, half lay on the bed, arching her body back instinctively, all self-consciousness gone now as she reveled the searing intensity of his gaze. It was almost as if he were actually touching her. Everywhere those insolent eyes lingered, he seemed to be branding his passion into her flesh. The soft skin of her breasts . . . her smooth, flat belly . . . that place between her legs where he had touched her with such devastating effect before. And then she was burning there, too, the desire returning, suddenly, abruptly, and she was welcoming it.

Her eyes dipped again to that corresponding part of him and found that he did not look quite as he had before.

"It's lucky we decided not to ring for the houseboy," she said.

He was laughing as he came over and sat beside her on the bed. An aching, almost heart-wrenching tenderness swelled with his mounting desire, and he drew her very gently down against him on the soft, yielding mattress—slowly, almost languidly, letting his hands explore her again, coaxing her hands to grow bolder— to dare to touch and fondle, too.

This time, there would be no hurrying, none of the urgency that had marked their hasty coupling before. This time he would tease her, and kiss and nuzzle playfully—all the little things a woman needed and deserved from the man who shared her body. This time they would allow themselves the luxury of getting to know each other and the secret yearnings of their bodies . . . this time and all the other long lamplit evenings and sweet dark nights of their life.

"I do so love it, Matthew," she murmured, "lying here like this with you. I didn't know I would love it so much."

"Silly girl. I could have told you." He let his hand run down her side, her hip, onto her thigh, a lingering, loving caress. "I hope we're going to have a little time before you force me to make good on that promise I was foolish enough to let you coerce out of me. Every bride has a right to her wedding night . . . but no groom should be cheated out of a honeymoon."

"Will a month do? Or two?" Her eyes were glowing as she looked back at him; there was a faint flush in her cheeks that made her extremely enticing, and Matthew was beginning to suspect he might have underestimated the insistence of his rapidly recurring desire. "The war is already beginning—the Chinese have appointed a new High Commissioner, Ch'i Shan, to 'soothe' the barbarians—but I don't think the overt hostilities will start for several weeks. We can't do anything until then."

"Honest answer, tiger," he said, watching her in the soft light. "Did I *have* to promise the last of the chests in Canton . . . or would you have let me off the hook?"

Rachel smiled. "I would have. The opium in Canton, and Gallagher's share too. I wanted you that much. But you did promise. And you *are* a man of your word."

"Rae . . . this isn't a lark. . . ."

"It won't be dangerous. Not like the raid on the boat. I swear we won't be running any risks. But I need to see this through, Matthew. It's important to me. And besides," she added impishly, "you did promise."

Matthew groaned. His body was already beginning to burn and throb for her again. He'd been a damn fool, thinking there would be any less urgency now, and he had a sudden picture of what life was going to be like with this beautiful, headstrong woman. She would always want something more from him—something impossible!—and, God help him, he would always give it to her. Because the most important thing in the world was that beautiful smile. And he couldn't even imagine how he was going to survive her first tears.

"Nothing dangerous," he insisted, holding onto the last shred of control.

"Nothing dangerous," she promised, and suddenly they were kissing again—clinging, caressing, arousing, her hands as hungry as his to touch every part of that sinewy male form, to feel his reactions, learn what he liked, as he knew what pleased and excited her. Lamplight played warm and illusively soft on their torsos and limbs, the ivory pallor of her skin, the more golden tones of his blending and merging, as their bodies would soon blend and merge into each other.

There were no doubts now, none of the brief hesitances that had threatened to mar their earlier mating. Rachel understood what her body wanted, and she knew that he could give it to her. When his mouth came for hers, she was there, meeting it ravenously, opening to the hard, primitive invasion of his tongue. When that same tormenting tongue sank lower, flicking like little darts of flame over her breasts, she writhed and twisted until her own tongue found his hair and his ear, and she was kissing, licking, nibbling—savoring the man-taste of him in her mouth.

And when his hand finally slipped into the warm, moist place between her legs, she was ready and quivering for the touch she had already anticipated. His finger seemed to remember what she needed, or perhaps it had known all along, and it was finding that secret spot where all the heat and passion in her body seemed to be centered—stroking, cajoling, insinuating itself inside, preparing her very skillfully for what was to come.

He entered her slowly this time, savoring the mo-

ment and allowing Rachel to savor it, too. The hardness of him was achingly familiar now, the sliding motion of that long, deep penetration into her.

Rachel felt as if all the breath were coming out of
her body in one long, tremulous sigh. She wasn't sure
what she was supposed to do; she didn't know what
he expected of her, but it didn't seem to matter. It was
as if her instincts knew, and her body, and she could
feel her hips begin to move with his, following the
rhythm he had set—up and down, up and down again,
faster and then faster, until she seemed to be soaring,
feather-light and powerless, on winds she could not
see or control.

She recognized it this time, the last sweet pain before surrendering, and suddenly she was falling, helplessly, dizzily, plummeting into some dark, nameless
pit without time or bottom. And he was falling with
her, and the room was gone and the bed and the soft
yellow lamplight, and they were lost in a fleeting eternity of love and pure physical sensation.

This time it was he who lay awake, long after she
had fallen asleep in his arms, and wondered at this
strange, unexpected miracle that had happened between them. He had thought he understood about love,
certainly the physical aspects of an act he had enjoyed
many times. He had thought there was nothing that
went on between a man and a woman he didn't know
about—but he had been wrong.

He hadn't realized it at the time, but he had come
to this encounter in many ways as innocent as she. He
laughed to himself, but silently, thinking what a fool
he had been. He had looked at her at the wedding and
thanked his lucky stars that he hadn't let her get away
. . . and he hadn't understood even then.

This was his wife, his heart—the best and purest of
everything in his life, and he would be nothing if he
lost her.

You'll have your hands full with that one, her father
had said; the Lord knows, he was right. But the re-
wards would be enormous, the challenges exciting. She

would stretch him, bend him, force him to reach beyond himself, and it occurred to Matthew as he drifted off beside her that, in the end, he just might be a better man for it.

BRITTLE
WINTER WINDS
Canton, January 1841

Eleven

Rachel stood at the rail of the small English frigate and stared into the quiet cove where the *China Dawn* lay at anchor. The morning was still early, but a winter sun glistened warm on the water, though the wind had a biting edge, and she wrapped the Chinese shawl that had been a gift from Matthew tighter around her. It was hard to believe that nearly two months had passed since their marriage; Christmas had gone and the Western New Year, and it was already the seventh day of January.

It was a day that would go down in the history books, she thought bitterly. She turned to cast a speculative look at the islands in the distance, where the mouth of the Pearl began to narrow. Even now, British naval vessels loaded with seamen and marines were moving up the river to begin their assault on the Bogue forts that protected the entrance to Canton. Or perhaps it had already begun, and the humiliating defeat the Chinese were sure to suffer was at hand.

Rachel let her eyes drift back toward the *China Dawn*. In spite of herself, she almost smiled. There was so much pride in Matthew's voice whenever he spoke of his first command. She was the newest, largest, fleetest clipper ever to sail these waters, he told her—and the clippers were the aristocrats of the China trade. Lean and sleek, with their sharp bows and raked masts, they had a kind of natural arrogance that drew all eyes to them as they skimmed past lesser vessels. Rachel herself, though she knew next to nothing about ships, had often paused on the esplanade to watch as one of the great clippers appeared on the horizon, a

vast cumulus of white sail, gallants and royals and top
gallants swelling and billowing in the wind.

Even at rest, her canvas furled, her lines secured,
the *China* was an impressive sight. Power showed in
her massive size, half again as long as any other clipper Rachel had ever seen, and there was grace in her
superbly designed hull. Full-rigged, a "three-piecey
bamboo" as the Chinese would call her, each of her tall
masts—the fore, the main, and the mizzen—carried square
sails, not the usual five, but six, a skyscraper or moon-
raker fluttering boldly from the top.

Watching her across the water, Rachel understood
suddenly Matthew's fierce pride and possessiveness.
He loved the sea and ships the way she loved the land
in which she had been raised, and she realized with a
bittersweet pang what a sacrifice it had been for him
to give them up.

"Mrs. Barron, ma'am—"

Rachel turned to see a young naval officer standing
apologetically at her elbow. He was probably two or
three years older than she, but round pink cheeks and
baby-soft lashes made him look like a boy.

"That's all right, Lieutenant. I was just admiring
the *China Dawn*. She's a beauty, isn't she? Did you
want something?"

"The captain sent me to tell you, ma'am, that we
can't wait much longer. The *Nemesis* and the gunboats
were supposed to be in place by first light. They'll be
hammering the forts with their cannons now." A feverish look had come into his eyes, and Rachel tried
not to be sickened as she saw how excited he was. "It
will be nigh unto noon before we get there as it is.
We're only a wee frigate, but we're ready to do our
part! If your husband isn't back from his own ship
soon, we'll have to leave without him."

"Don't worry . . . he only needs a few minutes, as
he assured your captain. You'll see the cutter coming
back with him any time now." She managed a wan
smile. "It isn't going to be all over by the time you
get there. There'll still be plenty of war left to see."

And to tell your grandchildren about, she thought

as she turned back to the clipper and looked in vain
for signs of Matthew. About how the mighty men-of-
war and one wee frigate had soared up the river, ram-
ming—artillery pounding, rifles blazing—through
barricades of gaudily decorated, banner-waving junks.
About how hundreds and hundreds of sailors and sepoys and marines had swarmed out on the shore. And
how valiantly they had defeated the heathen Chinese
who fought so fiercely with their ancient rusty cannons
and medieval swords and fire bombs that could be cat-
apulted several yards across the water.

It was indeed going to be a noble day for the British.

Matthew looked across the deck of his ship with a
practiced eye. Smooth and clean; the daily holystoning
had not been allowed to slide—that was good. Brass
fittings gleamed brightly in the sun, and ropes were
neatly coiled and out of the way. He *had* noticed a few
new crewmen, but that was to be expected, he supposed, with any layover this long.

Otherwise everything seemed trim and as it should
be. Varnay had done well. He was a good man, trustworthy usually, and perhaps not quite deserving of the
sharp tongue-lashing he had just received from his
captain.

He had taken it well, Matthew had to admit. Damian
Varnay had never been one to whine or grovel, or try
and weasel out from under his mistakes.

"I did worry some, sir," was as close to an excuse
as he had come, "when Mr. Gallagher brought me to
the orders. But he swore up and down they came from
you. And this did seem a likely place to anchor a
ship."

It did indeed, Matthew thought, taking an instant to
look around again. He had to give Gallagher credit.
Obviously, he'd gone to pains to protect his investment. The cove was narrow and virtually inaccessible
by land, with sheer rock walls rising high out of the
water. No one would attack from that direction. And
any ship, even an armada of junks, approaching by the

sea would be open to the devastating force of the *China*'s cannons.

"Don't let it happen again, Varnay," was all he had said to the chastised mate. "Next time Mr. Gallagher—or anyone—relays orders, you make damned sure he's got something to back them up!"

He had said it a little louder than necessary, to make sure his voice carried across the deck. Varnay was still the first mate. He would still be in charge while Matthew was gone, and no one better for the job. But a first mate was more likely to be on his toes if the men knew what was going on and were watching over his shoulder.

A blast of wind gusted in his face, reminding Matthew that he had dressed much too lightly, and he jammed his hands into his pants pockets as he headed aft toward the passenger suite. Something cold and sharp-cornered met his fingers, and he grinned as he drew it out and recognized his cufflink.

So that was where it had gone. He had looked everywhere that first night he had spent with Rachel, though not quite as diligently as he might, since there had been ample distractions. It must somehow have gotten shoved into his pocket. He had, as he recalled, been wearing those same pearl-gray trousers.

"Is it Christy Gallagher you'll be lookin' for, me bucko?" a hearty voice boomed out. "An' with fire in your eye, if what I'm hearin' is right."

Matthew spun around, thrusting the cufflink hastily back at his pocket. "A little more than fire, Gallagher. What the devil is my ship doing here?"

"Now is that any way t' be greetin' an old friend? No 'Hello, Gallagher. Are you well, Gallagher? An' that fine beautiful lady o' yours?' What better place for your precious ship? No threat comin' from any side, an' two days saved on the way up the coast. You should be pattin' me on the back an' thankin' me for settin' things up so tidy."

Matthew didn't bother to mention the fact that he had lied blatantly to the first mate. Little niceties like that were a mere nuisance to Gallagher.

"I hear you had an interesting trip upcoast yourself," he remarked drily.

"Ah, well . . . a man can't be winnin' all the time. There was a party waitin', that was for sure, an' a bold clever passel this time. Not the likes o' the others. I was after losin' the cargo, I was, an' one o' your last two junks. But I do seem t' recall your mentionin' yourself as t' how they were expendable."

"I'm not worried about the junks—but I don't want any more forays up the coast. We'll get a better price in Canton. This blasted war is going to be over, some say in a week or two. They'll be hungry for the stuff after being cut off so long. That's where I'm headed now, as a matter of fact. I persuaded one of the Navy captains to carry me as far as Whampoa."

"Are you now, boy?" Gallagher was watching him speculatively. "An' so soon, with the war just startin'? You're thinkin' perhaps you've found a way to make a deal before any o' the others?"

Matthew looked into those shrewd green eyes and wished he were as good a liar as Rachel.

"Let's just say I'm on to something that looks, uh—promising. If it works, I should have everything I want."

"Then you'll be leaving the *China* here? With me?"

Matthew hesitated. He threw a quick look at the bank of cliffs behind him, the narrow opening to the sea in front. He'd feel a damned sight better if the ship were safely at anchor in Lintin. But with the war going on, it would probably be more dangerous to move it.

"I'll leave her here. With *Varnay*! He has strict orders not to do anything without my explicit permission. I don't think you'll pull the wool over his eyes again."

At least, he hoped he wouldn't. Matthew plunged his hands into his pockets again as he sat in the prow of the small cutter a few minutes later and watched the naval frigate loom closer. There was no reason for him even to try. Gallagher was a scoundrel—he'd stir up trouble as like as not just for the fun of it—but he was a man who enjoyed the sound of cash jingling in his pockets. And he knew that the profits would be enormous if he waited for the Canton market to open up.

They had almost reached the British vessel when Matthew realized with a start that the cufflink was no longer in his pocket. He must have dropped in on deck when he thought he was shoving it back in. No time to retrieve it now. Fortunately, it was a distinctive piece. One of the men was sure to recognize it and turn it in to the mate.

Then they were pulling alongside the frigate, and Matthew looked up and saw Rachel waiting at the rail, and everything else went out of his mind.

Christy Gallagher stood on the deck of the *China Dawn,* a mariner's glass at his eye as he watched Matthew's cutter ease up to the naval frigate. It was too far to make out distinct details, but he caught a graceful swirl of something that looked like wind-blown skirt. And the flash of fine-looking red hair in the rising morning sun.

So . . . the missionary's daughter had gotten him after all. And he had something "promising," did he, to take care of in Canton?

Well, that was only to be expected. Gallagher lowered the glass and continued to stare at the small smudge that was the ship sailing off into the distance. He had thought from the beginning that the girl was trouble, and now he knew. Time for a little hasty revising of his plans.

He slipped his hand deep into the pocket of the rough sea jacket he had hastily thrown on when he first spotted the cutter approaching. Pulling it out, he opened it and looked down with amused satisfaction at a small innocuous square on his palm.

White gold with a half-circle of ruby in the center.

Yes, he thought again, time to be revising his plans. And it looked like lady luck was playing into his hands.

But then, Christy Gallagher had always been a lucky man.

* * *

The estuary of the Pearl River, or Chu Kiang as it was referred to by the people who lived along its banks, was always bustling with traffic. The more maneuverable sampans, their snug cabins fashioned out of woven rattan mats stretched over bamboo hoops, would dart like little rice birds in and out of the heavier chop boats and plain-varnished upcountry tea boats. Lorchas with Western hulls and high Chinese sterns lumbered past at perhaps two or three knots, trailing the scent of hemp and rotting fish on the salt breezes behind them; and exquisitely decorated mandarin boats, delicate as dragonflies, provided bursts of color, overshadowed only by the "flower boats" that coasted first alongside one large vessel, then another, the brightly clad ladies who leaned over the sides and called out explicitly raucous greetings leaving little doubt as to their purpose.

Against this vibrant Oriental backdrop, the proud clippers and East Indiamen would glide past with their hired Chinese pilots, heading for the tollhouses of the Bogue, and the ten-mile fortified stretch that led to Whampoa. It had long been a sore point with the traders. The captains of their vessels distrusted the native pilots and bristled at turning over their wheels, but a foreigner wishing to do business in Canton had little choice.

There were no Chinese pilots today, and no cargo-laden traders' vessels. The river seemed almost ominously quiet as the small frigate left Lankit and Boat Island to port, and the entrance to the Bogue drifted into view. Rachel gasped as she saw the extent of the British force that had been amassed to assault the Chinese stronghold: corvettes and brigs seemed to be everywhere, first-class frigates and massive 74-gun ships-of-the-line. Here and there smaller boats could be glimpsed carrying officers and messages between them.

All those ships, she thought helplessly. All those gunners and mercenaries and marines! It wasn't going to be a victory—it was going to be a debacle. She had always known the Chinese would lose, and badly. But she hadn't understood until that moment how truly devastating it would be.

Matthew seemed to understand, too, and sense what she was thinking, for he put an arm around her waist.

"At least it will be over quickly. With as little injury as possible. The traders are out for blood, God knows, but the officers aren't. Their men aren't animals."

Rachel, remembering the stories that had gone around after the invasion of Chou Shan Island several months earlier, was not so sure. The troops had gotten into a stock of *samshun,* it was rumored, a potent rice wine flavored with garlic and aniseed, and the resulting rampage hadn't stopped until there was nothing left to plunder or destroy.

But those were only rumors, after all, and rumors had a way of getting out of hand.

"I hope you're right," she said quietly. "I'd like to believe you, but with all those men and guns . . ."

"Let's go inside, love. It's too cold for you here, with just that flimsy shawl. I swore to the captain I'd keep you out of the way. I had the devil's own time persuading him to take on a woman in the first place. It pays sometimes to be the scion of one of the biggest trading houses in America."

"I can't Matthew . . . I *need* to be here. It's awful, but I can't just run and hide. Besides, I think the fighting is already over. Or nearly, anyway." She thought of the young lieutenant and the eagerness in his eyes, and realized that she had been a bit rash in her promises of action still to come. "We'd be able to hear the cannons from here, or see the smoke from the fire junks. I don't think any unpleasant missiles are going to come splatting down on the deck."

"I'm not worried about cannons and firebombs. But fighting has a way of getting out of hand. All we need is some hotheaded sailor brandishing a pistol and looking for trouble where there isn't any. I really think it would be better . . ."

Matthew's voice trailed off as he saw the look on her face, and turning, he followed her gaze. They were just approaching the twin promontories that stood like a pair of mute dragons on either side of the glittering stretch of water, guarding the entrance to the Bogue. On the left, to port, was the massive presence of Taikoktow, on the right the headland of Chuenpi, whose fort had long been the Chinese first line of defense.

Now, waving in the wind above it, in place of the usual yellow banner, was the red, white, and blue of the Union Jack.

"I remember coming here when I was a little girl," Rachel said softly. "It seemed so magnificent then. I just stood and stared . . . and hardly dared to breathe. The hills seemed to brush the sky, and the forts looked invincible—very, very strong. I thought the country beyond them must be the grandest place on earth."

There was nothing grand or invincible now. With Matthew strong and silent beside her, Rachel sailed once again between the hills she had first glimpsed as a child. The battle *was* over, the powerful ships' cannons had done their work with brutal efficiency. The fort of Taikoktow was an abandoned shell, gouged like a deep scar into the earth, its seaward wall battered to rubble in places by the broadsides that must have come at point-blank range. Where were the fierce fire junks that were supposed at least to pester the British into keeping their distance? On the far side, the outlines of Fort Chuenpi were hard to make out, but even at that distance, it seemed to Rachel ominously still. No masses of prisoners being marched out in long lines, no frightened imperial footsoldiers scrambling like insects over rocky slopes in a desperate effort to flee.

A boat had pulled alongside about the time they drew even with the forts, and an officer had come aboard to confer with the captain. Now, he drifted over to greet Matthew soberly. He was an older man, his face lined and leathery from years in the sun, and he looked grave and disturbed as he filled them in briefly on what had happened.

The area, it seemed, had been well defended, in numbers if not superior weapons, and the Chinese had apparently been confident that they would repel the redheaded barbarians with ease. And why not? Rachel thought as she listened. Three thousand of the Emperor's finest firmly entrenched, their flanks protected by artillery, the forts in the hills and a huge iron chain drawn across the river, fire boats and war junks and their gong-beating, ferociously shrieking crews massed in Anson's Bay, just beyond the twin promontories. How could the forces of the Son of Heaven possibly suffer defeat?

They were to find out quickly enough. By nine o'clock, the British already had their vessels in place. The *Larne* and the *Hyacinth* took up positions opposite Chuenpi, backed by the *Queen,* towing the 26-gun frigate *Calliope,* and the *Druid, Samarang, Modeste,* and *Columbine* closed in on Taikoktow.

"The poor bastards—beggin' your pardon, ma'am—never had a chance. Some of them cannons were left over from John Weddell's bombardment in sixteen hundred and—what? More than two centuries old, and so foul and rusted, it'd take a braver man than me to light the powder. All fixed in concrete, too, or lashed to massive blocks of wood. They couldn't lower or elevate 'em—or turn to take aim. Not that it would have mattered much. Their powder was so inferior, they'd have been lucky just to hit the water."

Matthew nodded grimly. "Taikoktow seems pretty well leveled. I take it there was a land battle at Chuenpi?"

"If you can call it that. The *Hyacinth* opened fire about nine-thirty, and there was no opposition taking the beach. The troops ran into some wood-and-earth barricades in the valley, but all they had to defend themselves against were a few outdated muskets and jingals."

Even the Tartars, the elite of the Manchu dynasty, had been more show than substance, the officer told them, jumping out of their trenches and waving banners and beating gongs, as if the mere sight of them would be enough to drive the barbarians back. In fact, the only thing that even slowed them down was the thick mud through which they had to drag their field pieces.

The fort had been taken easily from the rear. Designed like so much in China for appearance, only the long, straight side fronting the water had been fortified. The curved wall that butted into hills behind was completely without moats, bulwarks, or embrasures. All an attacking party had to do was place its scaling ladders.

"They fought to the last man," the officer said. "They didn't even *try* to surrender. Some of them made a run for the hills, but they had the bad luck to bump into a company of marines; others stumbled into the water and were cut down in the crossfire. Inside, the place looks like a charnel house—blood and bodies everywhere, horribly burned and disfigured. They would carry their powder in their belts, God save their souls." He paused to look back across the water at the fort, grim and still now on the hill. His face seemed to have lost all its color beneath his deep tan. "God save *our* souls," he muttered under his breath.

Rachel turned away, unable to listen any longer as Matthew continued speaking with the officer. It seemed so stupid . . . so incredibly senseless! She stared at that same quiet spot on the hill and imagined the carnage which had just been described. The opposing forces had been hopelessly mismatched. The British had nothing to fear from ancient jingals and waving banners! They could have afforded to be generous in victory. They didn't have to *annihilate* their enemy!

She was still seething with horror and rage when a commotion a short distance away alerted her to the fact that a prisoner had been brought in. At least one man had survived that savage slaughter! The captain and several officers were trying vainly to question him in a combination of pidgin and very bad Chinese.

He was a Tartar apparently, for Rachel saw as she moved closer a distinctly Slavic slant to his features, and he tried to spit in his captors' faces with fierce defiance. But sheer terror blazed out of his eyes, and she sensed what he had just seen.

Modern warfare, with all its brutality and grim efficiency—like nothing he had ever experienced or imagined. He must have felt as if he stepped off the edge of the earth into Hell!

"Let me try," she said, breaking into the small circle of men. "At least I know more than a few words of mispronounced Chinese, though I doubt he'll talk to me. He's a Tartar, and he must hate us very much."

It took the better part of an hour, but her command of the Mandarin dialect seemed to arouse his curiosity, and Rachel finally managed to convince him that she was indeed a missionary and no part of the forces that had come to pound them into submission. He didn't like the missionaries, but he wasn't afraid of them. And being a man, he could not allow himself to be intimidated by a woman.

Even then, she only managed to get one thing out of him, but it was the one the others seemed most interested in learning. Why, even when it was clear that their cause was hopeless, had they made no attempt to surrender?

"Because they heard that the British took no prisoners," Rachel said in a small strained voice. "The foreign devils with their greed and their hunger for war have come to eradicate China and everything Chinese. They were gong to die anyway. They would rather die fighting than be lined up and shot. . . . Or worse."

There was a stunned silence. Then one of the younger officers spoke up.

"But couldn't you convince him, ma'am? You speak his language. Surely, if you told him . . ."

"No." Rachel shook her head. "He wouldn't believe me. Why should he? Would you in his place? Besides, what would be the use? They're all dead anyway, aren't they?"

She left the men and returned to the rail. They had slipped through the high sandstone hills while she had been unaware and were now drifting into Anson's Bay, with North and South Wangton Islands just ahead, Tiger Island beyond. Rachel remembered suddenly that Matthew always called her "tiger," and she wanted to weep. The endearment seemed so cruelly out of place in that bleak setting.

She was still standing at the rail, still trying to come to terms with what she had heard and seen and felt, when she became aware of an odd, extremely ugly vessel cutting across their path.

In spite of herself, Rachel turned and gaped at it. She had never seen anything quite like it. The squat black hull could not have been two hundred feet long, but it had a strangely heavy appearance, as if crafted of metal, though it seemed almost to skim on top of the waves. The thing was barquentine-rigged but carried no canvas, moving instead by force of a large wheel that had been fitted out with what looked like paddles of some sort and was revolving slowly through the water. Great puffs of black smoke belched out of a funnel into the air.

She could just make out the name on the hull as it chugged past: the *Nemesis*.

"What on earth is that?" she asked Matthew, who had come to stand beside her. He was staring almost as hard as she, with an expression she could not fathom on his face.

"The future," he said quietly. "Though some of us don't care to admit it. That's what they call a steamer. It runs on coal shoveled into a furnace in it bowels . . . God, how Jared would hate it if he were here."

"A steamer?" Rachel looked after it. "I heard that there were some steam-powered vessels carrying the mails, but I've never actually seen one. Why would your brother hate it?"

"It's going to push the great sailing ships out of the seas one day. Back into the past, like the Roman galleys with crews of slaves at the oars—or the ancient war junks that were so badly defeated today. Jared has salt running with the blood through his veins. He couldn't even imagine standing on the deck of a ship and not hearing the thunder of canvas slapping in the wind above him, or the singing and whistling of the rigging.'' He was chuckling softly under his breath. ''Yes, Jared would hate it. Alex, too. Alex was always partial to grace and beauty.''

''And you?'' Rachel asked. ''Do you hate it?''

He seemed to ponder the question. ''No . . . I think I'm curious. Grandfather would be curious, too. I said it was the future, and I wasn't exaggerating. There are seven separate watertight compartments in its hull. It can strike a rock and not go down—and it's designed to draw no more than six feet of water, fully loaded. Someday, cumbersome boxes like that are going to be all over the rivers and seas. Not in my lifetime, perhaps, but someday . . . *that* is going to be the future of Barron Shipping.''

Rachel watched as the strange vessel moved steadily away. It had only been a few minutes, there was almost no wind at all, yet it was already some distance off. Her heart felt heavy suddenly, and everything that had happened came rushing back, centering on that one ugly object. With such awesome equipment, how could anyone ever hope to defeat the British Navy?

''It isn't fair, Matthew. The Chinese didn't ask for this. They're good, kind, gentle people. They aren't warlike and filled with hatred. All they want is to be free of us and our abominable drugs! Is it right to slaughter them like beasts?''

Matthew, recalling the bucket at the side of the bed in case the baby was a girl, was not sure ''good, kind, and gentle'' were quite the words to apply to the Chinese. ''They were slaughtered because they lost, tiger, not because we thought they were warlike. And they *did* send junks to meet the British vessels, and armed their soldiers with what they thought were viable weapons. They were prepared to do some considerable killing themselves.''

''Yes, but they were defending their country! They didn't sail into Macao or London or Boston with their war junks and old jingals! What would you have them do? Stand by and let the British go through?''

"Not I. I'm a war-hungry American, remember? But don't you think—just perhaps—the reason they were so ready to believe that the British gave no quarter was because that was what they were planning on doing themselves? I think maybe you expect too much of the Chinese. If you're going to love them, shouldn't you love without conditions? They're people, just like us, good and bad—and sometimes they can even be excited, the men at least, by the prospect of war."

No, Rachel thought, sad and very tired suddenly as she turned away—they couldn't. Tears were stinging her eyes and she was afraid he would see. He didn't understand. No one could understand who hadn't lived and worked among the Chinese as many years as she had. They *were* good: generous with their hearts and spirits as well as their possessions, quick to laugh and boast and haggle, and live life to the fullest. Quarrelsome, yes—they could quarrel fiercely and fight for what was theirs. But they did not kill for the sheer love of killing.

She had read their poetry and studied their philosophy; she knew their history and their art and their music, and nowhere was war exalted as it was in the literature and history books of the Western world. She had watched them take their birds for walks in elaborate bamboo cages through the streets of Macao, and marveled at the fireworks that exploded for entertainment only across the black night sky. She had sat in ancestor shrines on the hillsides. Not sacrileges to her, but a way of honoring the continuity of life, and felt the quiet and serenity that came no doubt from not resting on the neck of a dragon.

Matthew was wrong. She leaned wearily against the rail, not seeing anymore as she stared into the distance. These were people who awarded scholars the highest place in their society and put soldiers at the bottom. No general-heroes, no Wellingtons or Washingtons here. These were people who respected beauty and order and the proper place of things in the world.

There was no instinct in them for violence and hate. She knew that as surely as she knew her own gentle yearnings for a better, more peaceful world. They couldn't even defend themselves properly, and her heart bled for the pain and humiliation they had suffered.

Twelve

They did not reach Canton until late the next evening. The night between had been passed in Whampoa, where they had managed to find a berth of sorts on a filthy lorcha, its cramped cabin permeated sickeningly with the stench of fish, stale sesame oil, and decaying wood.

It occurred to Matthew as he lay with Rachel sleeping fitfully in his arms that this was the first night since their marriage they had not made love, and all he could think about was whether the exorbitant sum he had paid the boatman and his greasy-haired wife would be enough to keep them from being slaughtered in their bunk! Having no such faith as Rachel in the essential goodness and lack of hostility in the Chinese heart, he spent most of the long, dark hours forming vivid images of bands of vengeful marauders roving the riverbanks, looking for someone on whom to take out their rage and frustration.

Fortunately, the Pearl was used to foreigners and their cash, and he woke after dozing intermittently to find the sun clear and brittle, and barely a whisper of wind. In this clumsy vessel, he thought glumly, we'll be lucky to reach Canton by nightfall!

It was, for Matthew, a strange feeling to pass through Whampoa so quietly. Usually, during the trading season, there were as many as fifty or sixty ships at anchor, the red-and-white of the Barron flag fluttering among the others to add splashes of color to the drab, flat village on the river's edge. Voices would be raised, men coming and going, greeting each other as they paid for the ''chops,'' or *hong* merchants' stamps which enabled them to trade in Canton, and grumbling constantly about the fact that their vessels were prohibited by law from going any closer to the city.

Now, it was almost ominously still, and Matthew was glad to leave the village and its nine-story pagoda behind and take to the river. Despite the foul odor in the cabin, he opted for caution and remained inside, peering out through chinks in the walls.

The river traffic seemed normal. The water was crowded with the usual vessels—the great seagoing junks and hundreds and hundreds of small sampans, flower boats and mandarin boats and duckboats with sloping planks so the ducks could waddle in the water—so heavy in places it reminded him of the cargo wagons and carriages that converged on the Boston waterfront after one of the great ships pulled into dock. Matthew was relieved to see that Rachel had curled up on one of the bunks and seemed to be sleeping soundly. She had had an exhausting day, both physically and emotionally, and he cursed himself for allowing her to go through it.

He had made her a promise, and he intended to keep it. But he could have stalled a few days, at least until he was sure the worst of the hostilities were over. He honestly hadn't thought it would go that far—nor obviously had the captain, who allowed two civilians passage on his navy vessel! A few shots, a show of gong-beating and banner-waving, and surely that would be it.

But he should have been more cautious, he reminded himself guiltily. He shouldn't have made assumptions. Rachel had been hurt, and badly; and he sensed she would be hurt again in the days to come. His heart ached for her, and his pride suffered not an inconsiderable wound that he wasn't able to protect her.

Dusk was already thickening into darkness when they finally reached the short stretch of waterfront along which the ''factories'' or warehouses of the foreign community were located.

The large square in front of the long row of buildings was lively, as always. The vendors were out in
full force. Torches and glass-shaded ships' lanterns
spilled light on heaps of cheap canvas shoes and inferior jade, on cabbages and melon seeds, raw pork
black with flies, dried sea horses, snake glands for the
eyes, and powdered rhinoceros horn, which promised
long nights of incredible ecstasy; and braziers with
sausages and roast duck and large bowls of hot noodles sent sparks and spicy aromas into the air. The
shrill cries of the hawkers—the soothsayer's sly wheedling, the letterwriter proclaiming his skill—mingled
with the buzz of conversation and the whining of the
beggars, the whimpering of mongrel dogs foraging for
dinner.

There were a few Chinese clerks, Matthew noticed,
chatting with the pleasure-boat girls, but for the most
part no one from any of the great trading houses was
visible. The Westerners were all inside, behind their
curtained windows, waiting as he had waited the night
before to see if the violence was going to spread.

Camilla's uncle had kindly arranged for them to stay
in the comfortable quarters his company had taken in
the American factory, and Matthew steered Rachel
there now, up the steps and through the gate to a long
arched passage that led all the way back to a court in
the rear. Barron Shipping maintained only a small office, shared with several traders, in one of the other
factories; Matthew had been meaning to speak to his
grandfather about it after his last trip, though the way
things were looking now, he was just as glad he hadn't.
Doors opened off the passageway at intervals: Number 1,
Number 2, and finally Number 3, Lippincott & Company,
about in the center of the structure.

Ordinarily Robert Carpenter or one of the other directors would have been in residence, but the fighting
seemed to have deterred them, for when Rachel and
Matthew passed through the godowns and service area
on the first floor, the offices on the second, they arrived to find they had the third floor living quarters to
themselves.

Foreigners were not allowed by the rigid dictates of
the Eight Regulations to have local servants, but the
rule was persistently ignored, and a coal fire was
burning on the brazier, taking the chill off the night
air, when they were greeted by the houseboy. The
message announcing their arrival had apparently gotten through, for the cook was already in the kitchen
putting the finishing touches on their dinner.

They sat down a short time later to a hearty meal.
Although the Chinese had never been able to understand the foreign devils' eating habits—they liked their
food so gross and greasy!—they had learned how to
cook for them, and a large saddle of mutton was accompanied by boiled vegetables and brown bread dripping with fresh, sweet butter.

Rachel, who found the typical American diet somewhat greasy herself, noticed that Matthew seemed to
be enjoying it, and she was tactful enough not to say
anything. At least the ale from Calcutta was tasty and
refreshing, and she was feeling a little light-headed by
the time she had consumed nearly an entire bottle herself.

Matthew, watching her pick at her food and noting
the dull weariness that had come into her eyes, was
beginning to think this might be their second night
without passion. But after they finished the excellent
plum duff—or rather, he finished it, for she had taken
barely a bite or two—she came to him and, snuggling
on his lap, gave him a tender but unmistakably warm
kiss.

"I need you very much tonight, Matthew," she told
him. "I need you to kiss me and hold me and drive
the ugliness away."

It was the first time she had initiated their lovemaking. Always before, it had been he who approached
her, he who kissed her first, though she had a thousand
little ways of letting him know his affection would be
ardently received.

"I might be persuaded. . . ." he said, enjoying the
new development.

"You don't think I'm too aggressive? A wife is supposed to wait for her husband to show a little interest.''

"I think you are very beautiful, and I love you. . . . And I think a wife should feel cherished enough not to have to ask silly questions.''

Rachel shivered as he buried his face in her neck, wasting no time with the preliminaries he sensed she did not need or want. Taking the pins out of her hair with one hand, kissing her hard and hungrily, his tongue ravaging her mouth, he worked her skirt up roughly, finding the places where she liked to be touched, arousing her quickly and thoroughly. Then he was carrying her down the dark, narrow passage to the bedroom at the end.

He did not fail her. The force of his entry was a wound and a healing both, abrupt and intense, filling her with his strength and his love. This time, it was all for her, every motion of his body calculated to provoke the groaning, whimpering, writhing responses that made the rest of the world disappear. Restraint when it was needed—swift, savage thrusts at the moment she was ready—and he was lifting her up, drawing her out of herself, soothing away the horrors of that terrible river voyage. All the pain and the anguish and the grief was gone, and there was just Matthew and the sweet, perfect comfort only he could give.

In the morning, Rachel felt surprisingly refreshed. Or perhaps not so surprising, she thought with a little smile, for Matthew had awakened her twice during the night—or had she awakened him?—and she was beginning to discover that there were things far more restorative than sleep. The houseboy had apparently been there, or perhaps Matthew had gone down to the kitchen, for a red-lacquered tray sat on the table with a pot of strong black coffee, fresh cream from the cowyard at the end of the settlement, and a bowl of rock candy ground into a powder.

"I can get some tea if you prefer," he said. "The coffee was already made. The staff is used to American men.''

"Coffee will be lovely . . . it smells wonderful. Lots of cream, please, and sugar," she said as Matthew started pouring it out. There were also a pair of mandarin oranges on the tray, and her mouth was already watering as she picked one up and began to peel it. "My appetite seems to be back. I think I don't care for mutton very much."

"I think you don't." Matthew smiled. "I asked the cook to roast a chicken for dinner. A fair compromise, don't you agree? And I told her not to boil the vegetables, but cook them Chinese-style in a wok. At least I think I did. 'Werry-werry good-good vegetable wok cook can?' doesn't always cut it. You might want to check."

"I might." Rachel popped a plump orange section into her mouth and licked the juice off her fingers. "I think I'm going to enjoy it here—with you. I'm awfully glad you're one of those men Cammie told me about."

Matthew looked puzzled for a moment. Then his mind drifted back to the long pleasurable night that had just passed, and he got a twinkle in his eye.

"You'd better be careful, tiger. . . . You might tempt me to try my strength again."

"Would that be so terrible?"

"It would this morning. I have a different sort of distraction planned. I talked to one of the Chinese clerks, and he told me that everything's been quiet. It should be safe enough to walk around in the daytime. Of course, you'll have to dress up." He was grinning as he handed her a pair of fawn-colored britches and a clean white ruffled shirt. "I suspect these will look better on you than me."

Rachel laughed as she caught on. The Eight Regulations were very specific about the rights of the evil barbarians, the *fan-quai,* in Canton: they could come only during the trading season from September through March, they were allowed only in the five-acre area set aside for them, they could not have Chinese servants—though, in fact, many of them did—and they could not under any circumstances bring their barbar-

ian families with them. Women, especially, were
strictly forbidden.

Camilla had slipped in twice, her uncle harboring
some illusion that he might be able to control her better if she were under his watchful eye. But when she
hadn't been quite as bored as she should, being con-
fined to the buildings enclosed in the American factory, he had become suspicious. Rightly in the case of
a handsome Eurasian clerk in one of the other companies; wrongly, as it turned out, about an older, married man. Even Cammie had her own, quite surprising
standards. Married men did not come under her definition of "fun."

The only other woman to try it, as far as Rachel
knew, had been much too flagrant, and the resulting
scandal had discouraged everyone else.

"Heaven forbid the Chinese should have their sensibilities offended by the sight of big-footed Western
women," she quipped. "And their dresses are cut so
low, one can look right into their bosoms!"

"Three cheers for Western women," Matthew said.
"But you forgot to mention that men who don't have
their ladies with them aren't likely to stay any longer
than they have to. Or set down the kind of roots that
lead to nasty colonizing."

They were holding hands as they started down the
stairs, and it occurred to Rachel that they must make
a very peculiar sight. She was in pants and a shirt, her
hair tied boyishly at the nape of her neck—he exuded
masculinity from every pore.

"I don't think you ought to hold my hand on the
street," she teased.

"I'll try to restrain myself."

"Or anything *else,* Matthew!"

"Darn," he said. "I was afraid you'd think of that."

The sun was bright when they got outside. Daylight
made the area seem completely different, and Rachel
was surprised at how impressive and even attractive
the factories appeared. There were thirteen of them,
but they had been built in four massive blocks, from
Creek Factory on the east, so-named for the muddy

trickle of water beside it, to the Danish Factory and the cowyard at the other end. Colonnaded terraces ran all along the front, and the white-painted brick-and-granite walls and green shutters provided a pleasant contrast to the confusion and squalor of the square.

The north of the "settlement," as it was known, was bounded by Thirteen Factory Street, the south by the square and river. Between, separating the blocks of buildings, were Old and New China Streets, with shops catering to the traders, and a dark, narrow, very dirty alley called Hog Lane, which appealed to somewhat different tastes.

They spent a good part of the morning exploring first Old China Street, between the American and Chungho Factories, then New China Street. Everything seemed to be available in the small shops that were lined up on both sides. Cheap jingly earrings and exquisite jade bracelets and belt buckles, polished drum tables, fragrant jasmine tea, even a grotesque set of rice paintings depicting the six stages of opium addiction in a shameless imitation of Hogarth.

Matthew enjoyed indulging his wife, as he had always previously enjoyed indulging himself. When her eyes sparkled at the sight of a shimmering bolt of silk, as deep and green as an emerald, he bought it for her. When she let her gaze linger a moment too long on an antique porcelain plate with a pretty scene of willows by a stream, that, too, was being packed up for delivery to the factory. He even got her a carved ivory chess set, though he knew he would live to regret it. He had already learned that Rachel could beat him easily at the game unless he made a serious effort to concentrate. Then she beat him with difficulty.

"You're spending much too much money, Matthew," Rachel protested as they paused in a particularly appealing shop. They had just finished purchasing an intricately carved ivory fan she knew her mother would adore, and he was pressing a set of beautiful black-and-gold lacquerware on her. "I don't need all these things. It seems so . . . so *decadent* somehow."

Matthew laughed. "That's what money is for, love.

To enjoy. You wouldn't have me be a miser, would you—or this poor fellow here lose a sale? Besides," he teased, "what's wrong with a little decadence?"

In the end, she gave in, though he noticed she bargained fiercely for the goods, getting them for about one-tenth the price he would have expected to pay. It seemed he had found himself a frugal wife!

He hadn't planned on showing her the last street, Hog Lane, but to his surprise, she seemed intrigued by it. Perhaps because she was used to the ivory and jade and beautiful porcelains of the Orient, though she had never been able to buy them before. But he'd be willing to bet her father and brothers hadn't escorted her to the places frequented by sailors. And he had the uncomfortable feeling they wouldn't approve if they knew her husband was taking her there now.

But, as always, Rachel was impossible to resist, and they found themselves a few minutes later standing at the end of a dingy alley, foul-smelling and littered with trash and excrement. Ordinarily, even in mid-morning, there would have been soldiers and seamen pouring in and out of the stalls and doorways that crowded along one side. Brawls would have been erupting everywhere, fists flailing, drunken men falling on their faces in the mud and offal, and having to be carried back to their ships.

Now it was almost unnaturally quiet. A few people were moving around, coolies labored under a sedan chair, heading toward Thirteen Factory Street at the far end, and a dog with festering sores was rooting in the gutter. They wandered only a short distance in; no need to go farther, for it would be the same all the way. Cheap painted fans and shawls with lurid patterns were displayed outside the various establishments, and joss sticks and pathetic canaries in dirty little cages, come-ons to lure men in to the food and drink.

Signs here were often in English. Bold, awkward lettering, misspelled for the most part. FLY EGGS was not as foul as it seemed, but a reference to the nasty American habit of cooking their eggs in a panful of grease. And RUM was hardly likely to be rum.

''Probably *samshun.*'' Rachel grinned as she pointed to it.

''A horrid potable if ever there was one,'' he agreed. ''They say it's made with arsenic and tobacco. Guaranteed to rot your stomach out—if it doesn't kill you first.''

''Maybe that's the Chinese revenge for opium?''

''Maybe.'' Matthew threw her a fond look. She wasn't usually so light-hearted on the subject of the vile drug. ''I wouldn't know. I've never had any—and, *no,* I have no intention of trying it!''

They spent the next several days quite happily, exploring the town, or the small part of it that was open to them. Rumors abounded, each contradicting the last—the navy was on its way, peace had been declared, fighting had broken out south of Canton, the Emperor had capitulated—but everything remained quiet, and Matthew dared to hope that that one brutal confrontation had ended the war. Whatever mass confusion Steven Wu had led Rachel to expect wouldn't materialize then, and he could take her home after what would have proved just a brief, pleasant interlude.

Legitimate information was a rare commodity during those days, and Matthew, hungry for facts, took to spending an occasional hour visiting with the other traders, while Rachel dropped in at Zion's Corner, where she was known and respected. It was from them that she learned what had actually happened.

The battle for the Bogue forts had not quite been over when they left. There had still been one last little group of junks, about fifteen, moored harmlessly in a shallow stretch of water behind a sandbar. But they were still the enemy, and the *Nemesis* had moved in, firing a Congreve rocket, its first, from a tub on the deck. Purely by chance, it had struck the powder magazine of one of the junks, and flames and debris had shot into the air and scattered in all directions.

The terrified Chinese had cut their cables and tried to run. Some had made it, but most of the junks had been abandoned by their crews, and the British burned them later. The next day, Admiral Kuan had sent a white flag to Captain Charles Elliot at the British command.

Even the kind-hearted traders of Zion's Corner were laughing when they told her. The English, apparently, had been every bit as astonished as the Chinese! It seemed a rousing good joke, and they were enjoying it enormously.

Rachel's heart was heavy as she went back down the narrow passage to wait for Matthew to return from Creek Factory, where Innes and Jardine, Matheson was located. Everyone, even the traders who weren't directly involved, was looking at things from the British point of view. She supposed it was natural, but no one seemed to think about what the poor Chinese had suffered: the mothers who had lost their sons, the wives whose children would be fatherless. She couldn't even imagine the terror they must be feeling now at the thought of the smoke-spewing *Nemesis* coming back up the river, or the degradation and soul-crushing burden of having to watch foreigners invade and occupy their proud, ancient land.

"I just wish sometimes that *someone* understood," Rachel accused pointedly as Matthew came in through the door. Her spirit was back, the private moment of anguish over, and her eyes were flashing with challenge.

"I do, tiger," he said. "In a way. I will never agree that the Chinese are noble and spiritual, and we vicious to the core. But I do deplore the way this thing has been handled, though it appears that the savagery at the Bogue won't be repeated. Elliot met the new commissioner, Ch'i Shan, at Lotus Flower Wall with a fife-and-drum band. It looks like he's managed to iron out a treaty."

"Which makes the Chinese grovel in perpetuity, I suppose?"

"Actually," Matthew replied calmly, "considering how severely they were defeated, the Chinese were given very generous terms. They'll have to pay reparations, of course, and the English are going to insist on direct official communication, no more going

through the *hong* merchants for everything. But Elliot
has agreed to return Chou Shan Island and keep an
infertile little rock called Hong Kong instead. It has
an excellent harbor, but nothing else. And no settle-
ments, except for a small pirate village on the far side.
Now that, you have to admit, *is* a fair treaty.''

It was fair, and Rachel was feeling a little better as
she dressed again in Matthew's trousers and the ruffled
white shirt that disguised her small bosom and made
her look almost like a boy. They had taken to strolling
evenings in the walled garden in front of the New English Factory, and she sensed Matthew would be disappointed if they didn't go that night. Nothing could
erase the horrors the Chinese had suffered—and she
deplored the fact that opium was going to be allowed
freely into the country again—but at least the peace
would be an honorable one. The Chinese would be
allowed to keep their dignity. And who, after all,
would make a fuss about one small island that nobody
wanted to live on anyway?

The English garden was the only place in the settlement where the traders could take a little air without
being pestered by hawkers and begging children
clutching at their sleeves, or mangy mongrels nipping
their heels. It was a beautiful evening, almost spring-
like, and for a change the small garden was empty.
Rachel made no objection as Matthew slipped an arm
around her waist and they looked up at a circle of
incredibly pure blue-white light just lifting over the
horizon.

Another full moon, she thought, and remembered
an earlier evening, on the banks of a river, darkness
falling and the whisper of the current in their ears. She
had spoken then of the Chinese woman, and of the
child that had been lost. And she had sensed for the
first time that he understood.

''I made you see that opium was evil,'' she said
softly. The moonlight gave his face a strange bluish
cast, strengthening and softening at the same time. ''I
can make you see how wonderfully different China is,
too. And its people. They're not like us, Matthew.

They have a . . . oh, I don't know—a purity of spirit, a thirst for beauty and harmony that goes back deep into their history. To the very beginnings of their culture.''

"Ah? You can, can you?" Matthew felt a surge of tenderness as he drew her slowly closer. She had been describing herself, not the Chinese. That was what she wanted the world to be like—what she *believed* it could be. It was one of the things he loved most about her, her naive faith in goodness and beauty. But she was asking for bitter disillusionment.

"I can—and I will!" Her eyes seemed to sparkle out of the shadows, her lips looked suddenly full and very kissable, and Matthew decided that now was not the time to press the point.

"Perhaps . . . but in the meantime, let's hope no one is peeking over the wall, or I'm afraid we're going to corrupt some of those pure spirits."

"Oh . . ." Her lips were teasing, almost but not quite touching his. She shivered as she felt his hands run very surely down her back. "The Chinese have never been pure about *that*."

"No," Matthew agreed. "But if they *are* looking over the wall, they're going to think you're a young man . . . and if what I'm about to do now doesn't give them something to think about, nothing will."

Rachel smiled, but only for a minute; then their mouths were joining, and she allowed herself the scandalous luxury of a very passionate kiss, right out in the open—where anyone could see. And imagine the most debauched things!

Thirteen

The peace that had been so well and painstakingly negotiated at Flower Lotus Wall did not last. Ironically, it was neither one side nor the other that rejected it, but both. The English, when they heard, were not the least bit impressed with Captain Charles Elliot's conscientious efforts on their behalf. Chou Shan Island had been fairly taken; to exchange it for a worthless rock nobody wanted was the height of idiocy! If not Chou Shan, then they wanted some other well-situated island in the mouth of the Yangtze. And why hadn't Elliot insisted that the opium trade be made legal once and for all, and new ports opened up?

The Son of Heaven, for his part, was even more appalled. It was said that he flew into a terrible fury when told of the insolence of the barbarians. He may not have wanted Hong Kong himself, but it was a part of China. No foreign flag would ever be tolerated over Chinese soil! And how dare they demand to speak directly with the mandarins? That was an impertinence too outrageous to contemplate. The foreign devils must be brought to their knees, and Elliot dragged to Peking in chains!

On the twentieth of January, nearly two weeks after the brutal taking of the Bogue forts, word reached the Chinese commissioner, Ch'i Shan, that thousands of fighting men were on their way. Six days later, agreement or no, the British took formal possession of Hong Kong, and whatever hopes Matthew had had of getting Rachel out of Canton after a pleasant interlude were dashed. But what was for her merely an annoyance was devastating to her.

Rachel had no such illusions as the Manchu emperor. She knew that the men he was sending were not fighters on a level with the English and their mercenaries. They were brave and loyal, but poorly trained and carrying weapons that belonged in another century. And bravery and loyalty without well-positioned cannons, decent powder and firearms did not win modern wars.

She had seen with horror the effects of that last brief confrontation, and she knew what the English were capable of if they put their minds and hearts into it. The *Nemesis* would come up the river again, farther this time, its ungainly wheels churning through the water, the artillery mounted on its gunwales pummeling the shores, marines and sepoys massed on deck.

They would reach the gates of Canton this time, perhaps penetrate into the city itself. There was even talk of marching on Peking!

"It's so awful, Matthew," she said, shocked and sick with despair. "Can't anyone stop this madness? There'll be nothing left after the troops come through! The country will be devastated."

"We don't have to stay and watch," he reminded her gently. "We can leave. Now, if you want. I'll take you back to Macao."

"I don't know. . . ." Rachel hesitated. "It feels so cowardly, turning tail and running away."

"Sometimes running is just common sense, tiger."

"Yes, but . . . isn't this is what we were waiting for? I mean, with all the confusion, we'll finally be able to get at the opium. Steven's plan can work now."

"Whatever his plan is," Matthew started to say, then backed off. Young Steven Wu had been very close-mouthed. Rachel seemed to know next to nothing about this mysterious "plan," though she trusted him implicitly. But Matthew was beginning to have serious doubts. "Whatever it is, surely it can take place without you."

"Maybe . . . but Steven was very insistent. He said it was important for me to be there."

"Why? Are you such a skillful fighter they can't do without you?"

In spite of herself, Rachel smiled. "Probably just the opposite. I seem to be the only one who can set down rules about guns and fighting and make them stick. *My* men were unarmed the night of the raid." Even Sam, she had later learned, much to her dismay, had knuckled under and let his men carry weapons. Not that it had done them any good—the wily Gallagher had easily outwitted them. "Steven is half Chinese. He looks at life in a different, purer way. He hates the cruel things opium is doing to his countrymen, naturally. But he knows it would be even crueller to turn them into killers to eradicate it. And men with guns in their belts are likely to panic and use them."

Matthew, recalling the passion that had burned in the young zealot's eyes that night in the chapel, did not find it at all difficult to imagine Steven Wu killing. With pleasure. Though it did seem unlikely he would want Rachel along if that were what he had in mind.

"At least think about it, love," he urged. "If it's only a matter of bribing some clerks—if it really isn't going to be dangerous, as Steven promised—then they don't need you. It's getting too late to do anything today, but we could leave first thing in the morning."

"I don't know," she said again. "Perhaps. . . . Perhaps." And Matthew dared to let himself hope again.

But in the morning, it was too late. They awoke to find the house cold and strangely empty. Orders had been issued for all Chinese servants to stay away from the foreign settlement, and this time the prohibition had stuck. There was no houseboy chattering cheerfully as he brought the morning coffee, no cook bustling over their breakfast in the kitchen, no laundry amah and silly, giggling maids. The devil barbarians were being effectively cut off. An angry mob had gathered in the square, milling along the waterfront, and a dull, vibrating drone, punctuated intermittently by the unnerving clangor of gongs, penetrated even as far as Number 3 in the middle of the factory.

Matthew stood beside Rachel a short time later at the second-floor window of Zion's Corner in the front and assessed the none-too-promising situation. Hog Lane and New China Street had been closed during the night, and a guard of coolies in loose trousers, jackets, and twisted grass sandals was patrolling the square. They looked almost comical with their rattan shields and pointed rattan hats, pikes, and heavy staves across their shoulders as they drilled self-importantly like little boys in mock training, but Matthew was not inclined to laugh. Old China Street, he noticed, was still open, but soldiers had been stationed at the end, and only those with wooden permits attached on red strings around their waists were allowed to go through.

Even had Rachel agreed to leave, it would have been impossible. Some of the traders were bold enough to venture outside, going nose-to-nose with the curious coolies; come nightfall, there would no doubt be those who would slip through to the waterfront, and probably they would succeed in getting a boat. Matthew might have tried it himself if he had been alone. He was a little nervous about leaving the *China Dawn* so long, and there was no telling when he would get back now. But with Rachel, he dared not take the risk.

Instead, like the others who chose to remain, he and his bride barricaded themselves in the factory, feeling in those first frightening hours a little like knights and ladies of the Middle Ages must have felt in a castle under siege. Doors were stoutly bolted, windows on the ground floor kept shuttered, even in the daytime. And all the windows were shuttered at night.

Matthew took to carrying a gun with him from room to room, setting it on a table wherever he went, always within reach. Rachel hated it—the color drained out of her face every time she saw it—but she said nothing, and he was relieved to realize that she understood the gravity of their situation. He even considered, briefly, teaching her to shoot, but he knew she would refuse, and it didn't seem worth the quarrel to try and persuade her.

She probably wouldn't use it anyhow. She would see

a man with yellow skin and hate-crazed eyes coming toward her, and she would think of that pure Chinese heart and how hard his life had been—and she wouldn't even be able to shoot him in the leg!

The tension eased somewhat after the first few days, as it became clear that no immediate threat was intended to the devil barbarians' safety. The gongs continued with sleep-shattering regularity throughout the long nights, joined by a spine-tingling wail of conch shells, but mornings brought a semblance of normalcy, and the coolie-guards, their need to prove their ferocity assuaged, cheerfully winked at the rules they had been mustered to enforce.

The traders were moving freely enough between the factories by that time, though always with guns at their belts, Matthew noticed, and the offices of Olyphant & Company became a popular gathering place for the view from the second-floor window. The barbarians were to be cut off from fresh meat and vegetables and limited to two buckets of spring water a day, they were informed—let them live off their jams and their beers, and salt beef and pickles and wine! But, in fact, the lure of sycee and barter continued as potent as ever, and soon the coolies were spending more time running a very profitable smuggling operation than guarding the square.

Indeed, Matthew decided, after the initial alarm was over and he was beginning to feel more secure, the main thing he had to worry about was Rachel's cooking. She had plunged in gamely with the kitchen chores at first, and because he hadn't wanted to hurt her feelings, he had let her. But after a few sodden, very bad meals, it occurred to him it was time to take over. Like any seaman who liked to eat, he had long since learned his way around a brazier and oven.

"I don't come from a family of cooks," Rachel admitted as she handed over a rather greasy-looking pork roast and the last of the potatoes from the larder.

Matthew laughed. After that first, quite tasty breakfast at the mission, Abby Todd's cooking had lived up to everything her daughter claimed for it.

"Fortunately," he said, "I do."

The resulting laughter ended up in the bedroom, and they did not, after all, enjoy Matthew's first attempt at dinner. The roast was burned, and the potatoes didn't quite come out the way he expected in sesame oil instead of lard. But they hardly felt the lack as they sat on a blanket in the middle of the parlor, sipping hock and nibbling fresh fruit and giggling like little children who had stolen away for a forbidden picnic.

Neither one of them had ever had the luxury of being alone before, with no one on that side of the bolted doors who could possibly come in and intrude. The servants in Macao had been the soul of discretion, but they had been there all the same, and certain proprieties had had to be observed.

Now there was no one, and it gave Rachel a heady sense of freedom to know they could do anything they wanted. They could kiss and touch any time—any place. They could make love right there on the blanket if they felt like it, and they did. They could lie next to each other afterwards in the lamplight and marvel at the way their bodies seemed to be joined, even after the dictates of nature had forced Matthew's reluctant retreat.

It fascinated Rachel how creamy pale her skin looked next to the tawnier hues of his. And she loved watching as he went down to the kitchen—with absolutely nothing on!—and thinking how hard and taut his buttocks were, and almost startlingly white where the sun never touched them.

Matthew kept coals burning continually in the braziers. The rooms were always warm, and Rachel, feeling quite deliciously wanton, started wearing the red silk pants and shirts she had brought to tantalize him in the privacy of their bedroom. Or more likely just the shirts, for Matthew, as he murmured provocatively in her ear one day when they were especially savoring their solitude, didn't like "all those clothes in the way when I want you, love."

He was not exaggerating, as Rachel found to her delight. There was no telling what he was going to do.

Or when. He might catch her by the arm as she brushed past him and Rachel would feel her back suddenly against the wall; then he would be touching her, without preliminaries, so abruptly she hardly knew what was happening, sending jolts of excitement through her until she thought she would die if he waited another second. Sometimes he wouldn't even remove his trousers, just rip them open. Taking her there, still pressed against the wall, the urgency of his desire thrusting deep into the core of her own throbbing need.

"Are you sure we're supposed to be doing this?" she said on a particularly steamy afternoon when they found themselves half on, half off the low divan, in a position she had not thought the human body could occupy. Her tongue, enticed by the proximity of an adjacent ear, flitted over it with little licking motions, the way he did sometimes to her. "I mean, we've been married more than two months now. Aren't we supposed to be settling down?"

"Marriage doesn't *have* to mark the end of passion."

"I know, . . ." She let her fingers dart to that part of him which been hard for her a moment before. "Won't it fall off if we keep carrying on like this?"

"I don't think so. . . . We'll have to see, won't we?" Playful fingers fondled one breast through the sleek fabric of the shirt she was still wearing, though it had come open, showing the smooth white flesh of her belly and the reddish curls between her legs. "I love you in silk. Do you know, I can see the outline of your nipples through it—as if you're always ready for me. It drives me mad."

"I think it *will* fall off," she persisted, enjoying the laughter and teasing that came after their lovemaking almost as much as the tameless passion before.

"I shall be sorry if it does," he said with mock solemnity. "I shall be *very* sorry . . . but I can't think of a nicer way to lose it. Give me an hour or two, and we'll put it to the test."

In fact, it was more like four hours later, and then he took her into his arms slowly, gently, with none of the savage abruptness that had excited them both so much before, reminding Rachel how many ways a man and woman could share their bodies and how beautiful they all could be.

It did not, after all, fall off. Rachel smiled secretly to herself afterwards as she let her lips slide down to kiss him there. It surprised her a little, sometimes, how bold she had grown these last days together, daring to do anything to him that he had done to her. She was finding that love in the daytime was every bit as pleasurable as being awakened in the middle of the night. Perhaps even more so, for long mornings and afternoons of passion had a shameless, forbidden feel to them.

The night clamor went on unabated, the gongs and the conch shells and the din of the crowd, especially just after dusk, and coolies were still guarding the square; but inside the thick walls of the factory, the initial tension had eased, and everything was warm and invitingly cozy. Even the noise seemed more like a rhythmic background to moments of passion and tender teasing. They were still on their honeymoon, for all that the world threatened, and if the gun remained on the table by the door, at least Matthew did not jump for it at the slightest creak or snap.

Rachel was surprised at how wonderfully content she felt, and she realized, incredible as it seemed, she loved this man even more now than she had on the day they stood before her father and uttered the words that had committed them to each other forever.

"I do adore you, Matthew," she said as he came up from the kitchen with a heavily laden tray. He had taken to cooking as the Chinese did, in a wok, and a pungent aroma of anise and ginger and pepper followed him into the room. "Do you have any idea how much I love you?"

"Because I'm such a good cook?"

"No. You're an adequate cook. Better, I admit, when you don't try to fry potatoes in sesame oil. But your rice is almost as soggy as mine—"

"Nobody's rice is as soggy as yours."

"Except my mother's. And you leave such a horrible mess, it takes me hours to clean up! . . . I love you because you make me feel comfortable and secure. And very, very happy."

"Ah . . . and here I thought you loved me for the part of me that didn't fall off."

"That, too," she admitted. "But there's more than passion to a marriage. There's laughter and understanding and mutual respect. Your mother must have raised you right. You know how to treat a woman."

A strange look came into his face, and Rachel realized she had said something wrong. She knew so little about his early life; only the vaguest hints had slipped out sometimes; the father who had been killed in a riding accident when he was a baby, the grandfather and his tyrannical need to control, the older brother . . .

"My mother died when I was seven, tiger," he said. The moment had passed, and his features were gentle again. "In the flesh, at least. Jared always used to say she died inside the day they buried my father, and I expect he was right. She was a sad, pale ghost of my childhood. . . . Don't look so pained, sweetheart. I had an aunt, my cousin Alex's mother, and his sisters, who fawned over the poor motherless boy. I never lacked for feminine softness—or guidance when it came to how to behave toward a lady! And, of course, there were the uncles."

Rachel caught the sparkle in his eye. "The uncles?"

"I used to be taken sometimes with Alex and the girls to visit his mother's family in Virginia. There were a couple of bachelor uncles. Sly old dogs, but Lord how I did love them! They taught me everything they knew about the fairer sex . . . which was considerable."

"And brought you to your first whorehouse?"

"Good God, woman! What do you know about places like that?" Matthew pretended to be shocked. "No, actually that was my grandfather. And stayed and watched to make sure I didn't let down the Barron honor! Now *that* was an ordeal. . . . But I didn't mean the physical stuff. I picked that up pretty well on my own.''

"What, then?" Rachel asked, curious.

"To care . . . and be caring. Never lie to a woman, Uncle George used to say. Never hurt her if you can help it, and never tell her you love her unless you do . . . just a little. I suspect old George was an expert on 'just a little.' Never rob a woman of her innocence— he didn't use vulgar terms like 'virginity'—unless you're sure she's going to give it away anyhow. And never, *never* let her believe you're going to marry her if you're not.''

"He sounds like a kind man.''

"And practical. As Uncle Eddie put it—Eddie was more of a rogue than George—you don't get a daddy at the door with a shotgun if you don't let these little misunderstandings rise up in the first place.''

He smiled, his face warm and strong, and incredibly tender, and it occurred to Rachel that this was the face she was going to see every day for the rest of her life.

"I *do* love you, Matthew," she said.

"And I love you, tiger—and I'll thank you not to forget it!''

Several of the traders had managed to make it down the river without serious difficulties. Now, as January eased into February and February moved on toward March, some even returned, chafing at the delay that was ruining the trading season, and bringing with them much-longed-for news. The island of Hong Kong was already a British colony; buildings were going up at a rapid pace, people were beginning to move in to some place they called Happy Valley, and Elliot was preparing another show of force. At the Bogue forts again, as usual. Only this time, as one of the traders related with a vitriolic jubilation that made Rachel's blood run cold, it was not going to stop there. Within a few weeks, Canton itself would be on its knees to the devil barbarians!

Robert Carpenter made one brief trip upriver, confirming what they had heard. He arrived at dawn, just after the banging and wailing had died down in the square, and was planning on leaving at the same time the next morning.

"I wanted to make sure everything was all right," he said that evening as they sat in the parlor after an excellent joint of beef Matthew had managed to prepare without danger of burning this time. He was a smallish, pleasant-looking man with thinning gray hair and deep lines in the skin around his mouth and eyes. "You have no idea the rumors we've been hearing. I half-expected to find our godowns raided and all the merchandise looted or destroyed. It was an agreeable surprise, seeing everything so relatively calm. But there are some ledgers that are going back with me all the same. Just in case . . ."

"Uh, a brandy, sir?" Matthew opened the cupboard where Lippincott & Company kept a generous supply of various libations. Things *did* seem calm at the moment, but he didn't want Rachel unduly alarmed. "I believe I noticed an excellent cognac. Ah, yes, here we are. Or is it crass of me, offering you your own liquor?"

"Not mine, my boy—the company's." He chuckled, a surprising touch of humor showing in thin lips as he caught Matthew's hint. "Yes, yes—I daresay I'm being an alarmist. One does become foolish when one gets to my age. Oh, by the way, my dear," he said, turning to Rachel and deftly changing the subject, "Camilla said to make sure I told you she sends her love. She would like to have sent the latest gossip, but she was afraid it would singe my elderly ears."

Rachel laughed obligingly. "I expect it would. Cammie always seems to pick up the most amazing information."

"She does indeed. I can't think what the world is coming to, the things you young people find to talk about nowadays. Most improper, it seems to me. But then, if it were proper, I expect Camilla would find it 'utterly boring.' "

Affection sparked his voice as he spoke of his niece, and Rachel was startled to realize that he was fond of her. She had always assumed, the few times she met him, that he was kind, but detached, and found his guardianship a burden.

"I imagine Camilla can be very trying sometimes," she ventured.

"Ah, well, she does the best she can, poor child. She hasn't had an easy life . . . but, yes, she can be *very* trying."

"You said you think Elliot will be moving soon," Matthew cut in. "A sherry for you, my dear? No?" He picked up the pair of brandy snifters and handed one to the other man. He had caught something, just for a second, in Robert Carpenter's expression, but he was talking fast so Rachel wouldn't pick up on it. "A couple of weeks, would you guess? Around the middle of March?"

"Or sooner." Carpenter swirled the glass in his hand and took an appreciative sip. "They want to salvage what they can of the trading season, and there's precious little time left. Even the Yankee clippers aren't anchoring at Whampoa now."

"All those teas and silks sitting in the warehouses, and no getting them out. Business as usual—is that it? And blast the hell out of the heathens if they get in the way?"

There was an edge of bitterness to the words that made Robert Carpenter look up. "You can't really blame them," he said reasonably. "Fortunes are made or broken in a single season in the China trade. If it were the Americans who'd been cut out—and the English were lining their pockets with a good chunk of *our* profits for ferrying those teas and silks—wouldn't we do the same thing?"

"I suppose so," Matthew admitted. "Still, it does seem unnecessarily brutal, savaging the Bogue all over again. It's a pity the treaty didn't take."

"How could it? No one is satisfied, as near as I can tell. Oh, a few of the traders think it may work out, but . . . Hong Kong in exchange for Chou Shan? A nasty, unhealthy little island, all granite and marshes. Wait till the steam rises in the summer—that will drive all the wives and children out of those fancy new houses in Happy Valley and back to the cooling breezes they're used to. You mark my words. Hong Kong will never replace Macao. Have you ever been there?''

''Once. One of our captains, a fellow named Rawlings, took me on my first trip East. Or rather an early storm took us both. It has a superb natural anchorage, deep enough for the largest vessel and well-sheltered in a typhoon. Everything will be in one place for a change. No more setting up offices in Macao, keeping your ships in Lintin, and worrying about moving them every summer to Dam-sing-moon.''

''Well, you'll never convince me,'' Carpenter argued amiably. ''Of course, you're the sea captain, but it does seem there ought to be a better justification than merely finding a place to dock one's boats. If Hong Kong had anything at all to recommend it, surely *someone* would be living there, other than a handful of fishermen and pirates in a filthy little village on the southern side.''

''All the more reason to claim it. What more can you ask? An excellent location, good access to Canton, a year-round harbor, and no indigenous population with deep and passionate ties to the soil. The Chinese there will be Chinese who have come of their own volition, because they *want* to be with the foreign devils and find a way to relieve us of our cash.''

''An interesting argument.'' Carpenter allowed himself the faintest hint of a smile as he sipped the last of his cognac. ''I hadn't thought of it like that before. There's more to you than meets the eye. Though perhaps I should have assumed it, since Rachel here has chosen you. She's not a woman to be taken in by a pretty face. You'll do the House of Barron proud, I think.''

''That remains to be seen,'' Matthew replied drily as he took the other man's glass and went over to the cupboard again. Rachel laughed, enjoying the banter between the two men for a few minutes longer, then excused herself to go down and see if she could find some tinned biscuits and cheese.

"I think I might be able to manage a pot of coffee, though Matthew is strictly in charge when it comes to serious cooking. As you said, there's more to him than a pretty face.''

She was still laughing as she disappeared through the door and down the stairs. It made Matthew somewhat nervous, allowing her to move about freely by herself, but as there had been no overt threats, he could hardly order her to stay in his sight every second of the time. And breaking through the bolted doors would require so much time and noise, he'd easily be able to reach her.

"A fine woman.'' Carpenter's voice came from behind. Matthew set himself to pouring out their drinks, a generous one for the other man, considerably less for himself. Everything appeared be calm, but he wanted to stay alert. "A woman of character, one might say. Beauty doesn't last, but character does. You've done well for yourself, my boy. Very well.''

"I think so,'' Matthew agreed. "Though, unlike my wife, I don't find anything objectionable about an *extremely* pretty face. Here you are, sir. You'll be leaving early, I assume. That commotion in the square usually dies down three or four hours after midnight.''

"A little before first light, I thought. I want to be out of the congestion of the harbor by daybreak and ready for a run on Whampoa.'' He turned the glass in his fingers for a moment, then looked up thoughtfully. "You might consider coming with me. There's been very little trouble on the river. Oh, here and there— but mostly with some of the younger hotheads. Out looking for a challenge, if you ask me. And, of course, Rachel does speak Chinese.''

Matthew shook his head slowly. The idea had occurred to him, and it was tempting. He was becoming more and more concerned about the *China Dawn*. Not that there was any reason; the anchorage was secure enough, and Gallagher would hardly be likely to pull anything with the Canton market promising to open as soon as the latest round of hostilities was over. But he'd have felt better if he could have been there himself.

"It would still be dangerous," he said reluctantly. "Especially for a woman. And I don't want to be on the river, God help us, when Elliot makes his move. It was devastating for Rachel last time. She loves these people, you know."

"She's too attached," Carpenter agreed. "I don't think anything will happen this soon, but perhaps you're right. And it wouldn't do to get caught in the crossfire. We have to take care of our women, don't we?"

Matthew was reminded suddenly of the look he had seen on the older man's face a short time earlier. "You mentioned something before, sir," he said impulsively. "About Camilla. You said she hadn't had an easy life. I'm probably being much too forward—tell me if it's none of my business—but she is Rae's best friend. If there's something I ought to know . . ."

"Hmmm?" Pale gray eyes studied him for what seemed a very long moment. "Yes . . . perhaps you're right. It's hard to tell, but as you said, she and Rachel are very close. . . . They're so different, those two. yet they seem to understand each other."

"Look here," Matthew put in, beginning to feel uncomfortable and wondering why he had brought the subject up, "I *am* being too forward."

"No, actually I think you were being rather kind. At least, I hope you were. Camilla is my sister's daughter." He raised the brandy to his lips again, but barely seemed to taste it. "A very much younger sister. I'm afraid I didn't know her well. She fell in love, when Camilla was ten or eleven, with a man somewhat her junior. There was no attempt to divorce the husband, mind . . . not that he would have been likely to permit it. But he died soon after, so she was able to keep the child."

"I see," Matthew said, feeling even more awkward now, and wishing fervently he hadn't started all this.

"No, I don't think you do. When Camilla was

twelve, I found out that the man was mistreating her. Most abominably."

"You don't mean . . ." Matthew felt something unpleasant run down his spine ". . . he beat her?"

"I wish I did. He used her in the most degrading way a man can use a woman, much less a young girl. My sister knew. That was what made it so terribly unspeakable. She *knew,* but she couldn't bear to blame him, so she blamed the child."

"Good Lord," Matthew said quietly. He thought he had reached a stage in his life where nothing could shock him, but he had been wrong.

"I took her away, of course, as soon as I learned. I've tried to make it up to her, but damage like that can never be undone. She manages fairly well, I think, but . . . I am not a young man anymore. It would be different if there were a husband on the horizon. Not that I blame her for being less than excited with the suitors I've found, though there *have* been one or two. . . . But I shudder to think what will happen if I die without having made provision for her."

Matthew had the uncomfortable feeling that he had just been asked to accept the lifelong guardianship of his wife's very troublesome friend. And knowing Rachel, she wouldn't let him refuse.

"You strike me as a hardy sort, sir," he said with considerable feeling. "As long as you take care on that trip downriver tomorrow, I expect you'll outlive us all."

He was still shocked a few minutes later when Robert Carpenter took his leave, sending apologies to Rachel for the biscuits and cheese, and retired to a couch in the office downstairs. He was tired, he said, and would be rising very early. No need to see him off; in fact, he'd prefer it if they didn't. He wouldn't like to inconvenience Rachel. And, of course, there was no point distressing her by mentioning their little conversation tonight.

Matthew had no intention whatsoever of distressing Rachel with that appalling revelation, but he couldn't stop thinking about it as he set the glasses on a side-table and put the cognac back in the cabinet. He had heard of such things, naturally. They were discussed among men occasionally when the ladies were safely out of earshot. But they had always happened to someone else; they were always another man's problems to resolve or requite. It had never occurred to him that he might actually *know* one of the victims himself.

He remembered suddenly the night that Camilla had come to him. The teasing challenge in those dazzling violet eyes, the little pink tongue darting, catlike, over her lips. Her breasts, full and bold in the lamplight when she dropped her bodice and stood naked before him.

Foolish, frivolous, gallant little Camilla. She had been used, but she had not been broken. She had simply learned how to use back. Now she took advantage of men before they had a chance to take advantage of her.

She does the best she can, Robert Carpenter had said—and, by God, she did! He poured another drink and, raising the glass, downed it in a single gulp. If she were a man, everyone wold be clapping her on the back, winking, and congratulating her for her conquests. Who had the right to regard her with any less respect because she took her pleasures—and perhaps her revenge—as a woman?

He thought of Rachel: his warm, sensual, passionate Rachel. He loved her fire and her boldness, the way she had learned to come to his arms as an equal, demanding as much from him as he from her. With just a change of circumstance and fortune, it could have been Rachel! He couldn't even imagine that beautiful, proud spirit so horribly wounded, struggling to survive. If any man had ever done anything like that to her—if anyone even *tried*—he would kill him!

He caught her up in his arms as she came into the room, and putting the tray with the biscuits and coffee down, he held her hard and close for a very long time.

She looked a little surprised when he finally released her.

"What was all that for?"

What was it for? "Because I love you, tiger, and I want to take care of you and keep you safe . . . and you make it so blasted hard!"

Matthew was to remember those words the next evening, shortly after dusk. They were alone in the front room of Zion's Corner, looking down through the window at the night-darkened square below. The crowds seemed thicker; torches glowed everywhere, sputtering and tossing sparks into the wind, and a sense of anticipation rippled through the air. The others had just left, summoned by one of the junior clerks to the godowns on the ground floor, an emergency of some sort apparently, when Steven Wu suddenly appeared.

"Tomorrow," he said, his black eyes seeming to flicker and shine in the faint moonlight that drifted through the window. "Listen carefully. I haven't much time. Meet me tomorrow—at midnight, exactly. Just past the cowyard, near the little alley by the Danish factory. I've arranged for the guards to let us through."

"You bribed them?" Rachel asked, "But what—"

"I can't explain now," Steven cut in. "I don't want anyone to see me here. Tomorrow. Midnight. And dress like the daughter of a missionary this time."

And then, before she even could try to question him again, he had slipped through the door and was gone. It did not occur to Rachel until he was no longer there that he had not been his usual fastidious self, but almost disreputable looking, in black pants and a rumpled black jacket, with grass sandals like the coolies in the square. His hair was longer and unkempt, as if being grown to plait in a queue down his back.

"Doesn't it seem odd," Matthew said softly behind her, "that Steven Wu who clerks for Olyphant and Company doesn't want to be seen in their office?"

"Maybe he's not supposed to be here," Rachel replied. But she had been thinking the same thing, and she was worried, too. "He might have been told to stay in Canton."

"And he couldn't think of any excuse to get away? An urgent message which needed delivering, perhaps—like whatever that little emergency was that got everyone out of here just long enough for him to contact us? I didn't see much that looked 'good' and 'kind' and 'gentle' in your Chinese friend tonight."

No, Rachel thought as she stepped over to the window, standing just far enough back in the shadows so she wouldn't be seen as she tried to pick out Steven Wu in the anonymous snarl of figures below. He had not seemed gentle at all. He had seemed angry and excited at the same time, and the sheer force of the hatred emanating from him had almost seemed to reach out and strike her physically.

She had spent so much time reminding herself that Steven was half Chinese, she had forgotten that he was half his father's race, too. And if the Chinese in him grieved for the terrible rape of his country, the part that was European screamed out for blood and vengeance.

"He did seem half-crazed," she admitted. "And it does alarm me a little that he still won't tell us anything about his plan. But, Matt—he *knows* how I feel. If he were going to do something bad, I'm the last person on earth he'd want anywhere around!"

"I've been thinking about that, tiger," Matthew said slowly, "and I'm not so sure."

Rachel turned her head to look at him. Something in his voice made her nervous.

"What do you mean?"

"I mean, if you aren't needed tomorrow for any specific task—and I don't think you are—then there must be some other reason for your presence. And if Steven Wu wants you to dress as the daughter of a missionary, then mightn't that be it?"

"I don't understand," Rachel said, but of course she did, and it made her feel ill inside.

"I think . . . I'm afraid . . . what he's planning on doing is a little more than bad. I'm afraid it's evil.

And he believes the missionary's daughter will bring
with her an aura of sanctity that will somehow make
it more acceptable.''

Evil?

Rachel shivered as she turned back to the window.
Such an extreme word. She tried to believe it wasn't
possible—she had called this man her friend!—but she
remembered the look on his face, and she knew it was.
She didn't have any idea what it might be. She couldn't
even imagine a scheme to dispose of the opium that
would be that extreme, and she sensed Matthew
couldn't either.

But Steven Wu could. She knew that, and she knew
he was planning on involving her.

The night had grown almost pitch-dark. Rachel's
eyes drifted from one yellow-orange pinpoint of light
to the next. There had been a moon only minutes before, so clouds must have floated in on the wind, turning the night scene even eerier and somehow more
frightening. The peasants and laborers and boatmen
seemed especially restless. Did they know something,
she wondered, that had not yet reached the traders
behind the bolted doors of their warehouse-fortresses?

She thought for a second that she caught sight of
Steven. She could not make out his features; she only
sensed it from the furtive way he seemed to glide from
shadow to shadow. Then he was joined by four or five
others, heading toward the alley near the Danish factory, and she was sure she was right.

She had not lost her faith in the basic nobility of the
Chinese people, and she vowed now that she never
would, though she did not mention the fact to Matthew, who she knew would not agree. There truly was
no meanness of spirit in the Chinese. Even the dreaded
tongs, the societies of rebels and fighters, were there
to protect the rights of the people and keep them from
being oppressed. And the coolie guards, with their
warlike posturing, and gongs and shrieking half the
night, saw to it that the barbarian enemy had plenty
of food and water.

But Steven Wu was not strictly Chinese, and she was beginning to lose faith in him.

"I think you're right." She turned slowly back to Matthew. "I think he's up to something. And I think it's going to be awful."

Fourteen

Gallagher was finding that he liked Hong Kong. He leaned back in the only chair in the small room that might have been called a parlor had it sported anything more elegant than packing crates for benches, a rough-hewn wooden table, and two wobbly three-legged stools. It was well into the night, but the raucous sounds of the new community, shouts and laughter and quarrels, drifted with the smells and dampness through the open window.

He liked the sheer rowdiness of what promised to be a rough-and-tumble town. The stodgy brick house of the traders, with their wood roofs and glass-paned windows, were nearing completion in Happy Valley, but a mile to the west, along the waterfront, the heart of the city pulsated with teaming activity.

Gallagher liked pushing his way through crowds of beggars and coolies and sedan chairs on streets still muddy from yesterday's downpour; he liked the constant din of saws and hammering, the pungent odor of mortar and raw lumber, and it amazed him each day to discover that a new block of warehouse had gone up, or a jail, an apothecary, a shoeshine stand, tea shops, taverns, hotels. He liked wandering through the vast tent cities, especially colorful at night, lanterns flickering through open flaps to reveal long tables of men in various stages of inebriation, whores calling out bawdy invitations that left nothing to the imagination. He even liked the shanty town that was spreading across the hillsides, fed by long lines of Chinese staggering under the weight of their possessions as they moved like perpetual columns of ants up from the harbor, claiming their part of this new territory from England, as the English had claimed it from them.

It was his sort of place, and he felt a dim sense of regret that he wasn't going to be able to stay and watch it grow. But Gallagher had never been much of a one for staying. And he did not regret the challenge that lay ahead.

He looked down at a sheet of white paper in front of him. A crude ship's lantern spat and smoked; the light it released was barely adequate, and he had to squint to read. Most of the traders had chosen to remain with their families aboard ships in the harbor, but Gallagher, having no fondness for the water—and having a good, glib gift for words—had managed to procure rooms in what would one day be a warehouse but was now serving as a makeshift hotel. And raking in more cash, he thought with a chuckle, then it would ever see again, even in the heyday of the China trade.

He ran his eye down the paper one last time and nodded, satisfied. His facility with words applied only to speech. It had taken a long time to compose even that brief note, but he was comfortable with it now. It sounded right, and he folded the paper over and fixed it with a seal.

The seal of Barron Shipping—which he had had made up by a very clever Chinaman, who had only charged a little extra because he knew his customer did not exactly have the finer points of the law in mind!

Gallagher grinned as he checked out the brief address scrawled on the front. He also had a facile gift for what he liked to think of as "calligraphy," though the authorities in Ireland had had a different name for it. He had learned the skill early on, in his native Dublin, and it had served him well, except perhaps once or twice, the last occasion resulting in his hasty departure for India. It was for him almost an art form, and he took a certain pride in it. He enjoyed holding his hand in a different way—moving the pen just a little differently—and watching a whole new handwriting come out.

Right now, he was looking at the handwriting of

Matthew Barron. Strong, clean, simple of stroke—a good masculine hand, and one that was wonderfully easy to imitate.

He had wanted to address it to "Damian Varnay," but he hadn't been able to find an example of a capital "V" in any of Matthew's writing. That was the kind of thing that tripped you up. A man might overlook little irregularities, but he knew the way his name ought to look, so Gallagher had penned instead: "To the First Mate of the *China Dawn*."

He slipped the note into a canvas pouch, and with it, his little bit of luck—the cufflink Matthew had dropped on the deck.

"So it's proof you're wantin', is it, me bucko?" he said, and chuckled again. Matthew's voice had carried all over the ship. *Next time Mr. Gallagher—or anyone—relays orders, you make damned sure he's got something to back them up!*

Well, it seemed to him a very distinctive cufflink that everyone knew belonged to the captain was more than ample to back up a missive in his own handwriting. Or so it would seem to Varnay, which was more to the point.

He picked up another note, already written, sealed, and addressed. The Barron seal again—a touch of impudence he hadn't been able to resist. Young Matthew had a sense of humor; it would be his saving grace in the end, when the raging and fuming died down. Gallagher propped it up against the wall, where it couldn't be missed, then added a third, open note—the one that had been hardest to write.

He had loved her, in his own selfish way. He supposed he always would. He had never thought there would be any place for a woman in his life, except, of course, in the usual transitory ways. He had certainly never thought he would be faithful, and yet for a year, more or less, he had. The bawdy-tents and whore-houses on the sidestreets and the flower boats in the harbor had been pleasurable enough diversions; he had enjoyed seeing and exploring them, but for the first time, he had not been tempted to linger.

Not when he knew how soon they were going to be saying goodbye, he and the beautiful woman who was curled up, all warm and unaware, in his bed.

"It's sorry I am, Shanti, love," he said under his breath. "Sorrier than ever a man the likes of me ought to be. But it's the end we've reached, and that's a fact."

Shanti was half-asleep, naked, as she knew her man preferred, but beneath a heap of blankets; the nights could still be crisp in March, and she was used to a warmer climate. Her body stirred instinctively as she felt him slide under the covers beside her.

"You were a very long time, Gallagher," she murmured reproachfully. "I could not stay awake waiting for you."

"An' meself thinkin' you were lyin' here breathless, impatient as a bride on her second night. A man's vanity could be mortal wounded under a blow like that. . . . I had a small bit o' business needed tendin', me dove. But it looks like you're wide awake now."

"I am always awake when you want me to be," she replied in her slow, sultry voice. "I should not be. It is wrong to spoil a man so much. But I am."

"It is not wrong to spoil me this night," he said, his mouth filled with the sweet-scented blackness of her hair. "Or to be lettin' me spoil you. . . . An' where are all these *blankets* comin' from? Three, four . . . no *five*! It's suffocatin' yourself you'll be—and Christy Gallagher with you!"

"I was cold. You weren't here."

'I'm here now, girl. . . . And it's not cold you'll be with me.''

And she was not, Shanti thought, the chill of the night lost in the heat of his body against and on top of hers, and her own body warming from the inside, spreading out until the blankets were kicked aside, unneeded and forgotten.

It had always been like that, from the beginning. She had never been cold or hungry or lonely in his arms. All the ugliness of the past wiped away, or nearly gone. Life could be cruel in the villages of India for a girl whose mother emptied the night-soil pots, especially a girl who was beautiful and memories came back sometimes, as now, even at the beginning of their lovemaking.

Harvest time. Shanti remembered every detail with sudden hideous clarity. Twilight approaching, and she had been walking back from the fields of white poppies, the cloying scent of the "tears," the sap, clinging to her hands, her clothing, her hair. The smell of opium had hung like a pall over the entire village, and all the villages nearby, for this was their cash crop, their only means of subsistence.

There had been a man, blocking her path. She had known instantly, even before he had ordered her to go with him into a clump of bushes, what was going to happen. And because he had been of a higher caste, and she an untouchable, she had not dared disobey.

It was the first time her body had been taken by a man, and the blood and pain had frightened her almost as much as the anger and disdain with which he had treated her afterwards. There had been no one she could go to. Her parents would have been shamed and afraid. They knew what happened to the families of young women who broke the rigid caste system and slept with men above them, whether by choice or not was hardly the question. Even the kind, well-intentioned priest wouldn't have understood that the disgrace—and the punishment—would have been hers if she had been forced to name her attacker.

There had been nothing she could do but walk the same path the next evening, and wonder if he would be waiting again.

He had been.

Shanti was shivering as she tried not to remember, and trying, remembered all the more. Gallagher, whose lips were rarely gentle, kissed her very gently on the cheeks and brow, and she knew that he, too, was thinking of that afternoon he had found her on the crowded streets of Calcutta.

She had thought, when she ran away from the village, everything would be all right. She had had no illusions about her ability to earn a living; there had been no romantic daydreams about a handsome man sweeping her off her feet and carrying her away. But as long as she was going to be used anyway, she had thought she might as well go to one of the brothels in the city and at least be paid for it.

Only the brothels had been filled with girls from the villages, some pretty, some not—it didn't seem to matter—and no one had paid any attention to her. She had been just one more wretched soul in a city of wretched souls, sleeping in the street like the beggars and the dogs who scavenged in the gutters for food.

It had been only her second afternoon there when a man had come out of one of the shops. A bestial man, flesh sagging off his bones, an obscene fatness in that city of hunger. He had stopped her, as the man had stopped her on the path in the village, and tried to push her into an empty doorway. This time Shanti had fought back, desperately and passionately, but he had been much stronger, and she had known with a terrible sense of despair that she was going to lose.

Then a hand had come out, and the man had been dragged off her and flung to the side. The hand had been attached to a barrel-bodied, broad-shouldered, ruddy-faced man with very black hair and green eyes simmering with fury.

The only thing that had saved her assailant was the fact that Christy Gallagher couldn't chase the son-of-a-bitch and take care of the girl who was cowering and crying in the doorway at the same time. He had chosen the girl.

Shanti let herself relax in her lover's arms. The memories from that point on were no longer painful. When he had taken her back to his hotel room, she had assumed that he meant the same thing as the man in the street, if in a somewhat gentler manner. But when she had started to undress, because that was what she thought he wanted, he had stopped her.

"You don't have to do this, girl," he had said, gruffly, as if embarrassed.

"But I want to," she had answered, and strangely,

it had been the truth. Not because she had yet learned passion, but because she was grateful, and because he was the first person who had ever touched her with kindness. It had not been unpleasant, feeling him inside her. He had not entered her roughly that time; he had been almost tender, as he was being tonight, and she had rather liked it. Or perhaps she had liked the warm room and the soft bed, and the encompassing sense of protectiveness his strong male body had given her even them.

"I will always be awake for you, Gallagher," she said. "Whenever you want me, I will always be here."

'I know, Shanti, girl," he replied. "I know."

Gallagher held her in his arms most of the night, looking down at her in the light that spilled through the open door from the other room and wondering why it was that the man who least deserved such a woman got her. Irish wit and dashing good looks, he supposed, but for once his little attempt at a joke did not amuse him.

He got up as he sensed the darkness beginning to ease. Dawn would be touching the horizon soon. He dressed hurriedly and, taking the rest of his clothes out into the other room, shut the door behind him and began to pack.

It was the coward's way out, saying goodbye without words, and he knew it. But being Gallagher, the thought of repentance did not cross his mind. He would have liked to bring her with him. He checked the valise one last time, making sure nothing had been left out, though most of his belongings were still stowed on the *China Dawn*. He might have brought her, if things had been different. But it could turn dangerous, what he had in mind. There was no place in such a scheme for a woman, even under ordinary circumstances. And he had not failed to notice the new curves in this woman's body, the swelling of her breasts and very rounded feminine hips.

He knew, as he sensed she did not yet, that she was pregnant. She had played her little tricks on him, and he had been aware of them—but he had been weak, and she had won. He was not angry with her for coercing him into unwilling fatherhood. He understood her hunger for a child, and he acknowledged her right to have one if she chose.

But Christy Gallagher was not a man for domesticity. He picked up his bag and started toward the door to the hallway. He could not imagine being trapped in a never-ending cycle of debts and responsibilities, with a wife and babe counting on him for everything, and not so much as a bit of room to breathe.

His life was free, by God—it always had been and it always would be. He came when he wanted, he left when he wanted; he answered to no one, and no one answered to him!

He paused for a moment in the doorway, his eye falling on the open sheet of paper on the table. She would sleep late in the morning. She always did. She had grown quite shamelessly lazy in her year with him, and he had wanted it for her. He would be nearly to the cove where the *China Dawn* lay at anchor by the time she found it.

Or would he be there already, hidden in his own small craft in a rocky niche, waiting for the response to the messenger who carried that other, devious missive? He tried not to think of the look on her face as she read it. Serene, of course-and tearless. He had never known her to complain, never seen her cry, except from terror that first afternoon on the street. And accepting. She always accepted everything from him.

Maybe he would come back for her. Not to stay. He could never be tied down—he would fail, miserably, if he tried. But at least he could see her through the birth. A woman should not be alone at a time like that.

If, of course, he was able to come back.

Gallagher smiled grimly to himself. The Yankee sea captain was going to be very angry when he found out what had happened to his ship. For all his youth and easygoing charm, Matthew Barron was a man to be reckoned with.

Well, either way, she would be provided for. Gallagher threw a last glance at the sealed envelope beside the note to Shanti. There was a little money set aside— not nearly enough, but a little—and the letter explained where it was and gave the youngest of the mighty Barron clan access to it.

Furious as Matthew was, he would never blame the woman for her lover's perfidy. And when he saw what a pittance had been left her . . .

Well, he could hardly let her starve, now could he?

Gallagher chuckled as he closed the door behind him and started down the hall. It was his last gift to the man he was about to betray, and it appealed to his sense of the outrageous. The chance to support Christy Gallagher's mistress and child for the rest of their natural lives.

And Matthew Barron was such a damned decent fool, he would do it!

Fifteen

I don't know why I let you talk me into this," Matthew grumbled. "I feel like a damned fool—my *ankles* are sticking out! How the devil am I supposed to pull this off?"

"You look lovely," Rachel said with a wan smile. The light of the lantern hanging on a peg in the front of the long factory passageway spilled on a lanky figure in dark-blue pants and quilted jacket, with crude sandals and a conical rattan hat tied securely under his chin. Face, hands, and protruding ankles were so smudged with dirt it was impossible to see the skin beneath. "But you're about as Chinese as your larcenous partner, Gallagher—even in that outfit. Really, Matt, it might be better if you stayed behind."

"And let you go out by yourself. Not a chance, tiger. I don't even like the idea of your going *with* me."

"I know, but we agreed on this," Rachel reminded him firmly. Like her husband, she was dressed as a typical Chinese peasant, a Hakka, in her case, which explained her large, unbound feet. And she had the added advantage of a concealing fringe of thin black fabric dangling from the broad brim of her hat. "We have to find out what's going on. You know that. And we have to find out before we meet Steven Wu at midnight, which is about four hours from now."

"*If* we meet Steven Wu. . . ."

"If," Rachel conceded. "But one way or another, there's going to be talk in the square. A little here, a little there—we ought to be able to piece together at least enough to figure out the general situation. And

I'm the one who understands Chinese. You could over-hear Steven's entire plot—in great detail—and you wouldn't even know it! Gallant as you're trying to be, my love, you need me for this.''

"Granted," he replied wryly. "But that doesn't mean I have to like it.''

"No, but you do have to play your part well. Otherwise, you're going to make things even worse for me. If you want to look Chinese, you have to *feel* Chinese. It's not the costume so much—a good disguise comes from the inside. You're a little too tall . . . you're going to stand out as it is. When eyes turn your direction, there can't be anything to make them pause.''

"And how in the name of all that's holy am I supposed to turn my *insides* Chinese?''

"This way.'' Even as she spoke, Rachel's shoulders were sloping, the angles of her body changing subtly, taking on a kind of ageless weariness. "I remember how my back feels when I bend to pull the weeds out of the rice paddies, again and again—and again. My legs are very strong. I have lots of muscles from squatting all the time because there are no chairs in my hut. And my feet are big and ugly, not like the golden lilies of a true lady. They hit the ground when I walk, flat—like this. *Splats-splat-splat.*''

She turned and waddled over to the door, strong legs spread a little apart, shoulders and torso taking on a demeanor Matthew had seen a thousand times in the street. It he hadn't known better, he would have sworn she was exactly what she seemed. It was a little disconcerting to realize that he wouldn't even recognize his own wife if he glimpsed her across the square.

"Hey, Hakka," he called out as she reached the door. "Your feet are a little dirty, but I think they're beautiful.''

"What do you know?'' she retorted. "You're only a barbarian.'' And clearing her throat with the most obscene sound he had ever heard, she spat on the ground and went out.

Matthew hesitated a second, then followed her, wishing fervently that his own bent back looked half as convincing, and knowing it didn't. She had been right. It would be better, and probably safer for her, if he remained behind. But how could a man let the woman he loved do something like this and not even *try* to protect her.

The night was almost oppressively dark; a scattering of clouds had drifted across the face of the moon, and the wind coming up from the river was cold and damp. For all her bravado of a moment before, Rachel felt a shiver run down her spine. This was her country. She had been raised here, nurtured on its culture and customs, and for the first time she was not comfortable walking out among the people she had always trusted and loved before.

The mood in the square seemed strangely intensified, almost surly, although there was nothing Rachel could put her finger on. The hawkers were out in their regular numbers; the clouds cleared momentarily, and moonlight dulled the yellow flicker of the lanterns that illuminated their wares. Torches shimmered in constant waves of motion as their bearers moved to and fro. The smell of duck and sausages rose from braziers, and flower-girls leaned out from their boats, calling to men as they passed, though half-heartedly, as if sensing there would be no customers tonight.

They almost seemed to be waiting, Rachel thought. Anticipating something, and she wondered if they even knew what it was. She slipped into the shadows near the cowyard. Matthew, a step behind, had a firm grip on her shoulders, and she wanted to tell him to let go. Chinese males didn't touch their woman in public. But she knew she would never persuade him, and it was a comfort, feeling him so close and strong behind her.

"Nothing *looks* different," she whispered. They were enough away from the crowd to risk a few words. "But it feels different. I have the strangest sense everyone's waiting for something."

"I know. I felt the same thing," Matthew agreed, his voice, like hers, low and tense. "Have you noticed there are more torches than usual? They seem to be concentrated in groups instead of scattered around the square.''

''No . . .'' Rachel hadn't noticed, but now that he called her attention to it, she sensed a pattern: three or four here, half a dozen there. ''It's almost as if there's some organization behind it.''

''As if someone is—*inciting* the crowd? Yes . . . it does seem that way, doesn't it?''

Someone? Steven Wu? Rachel left the unspoken question hanging as she scanned the square, looking futilely through the throng for any trace of him. Only she was not looking for the Steven she knew. She was looking for the furtive figure she had seen gliding from darkness to darkness the night before.

They did not have a chance to speak again, for the crowd seemed to be spreading out, and small clusters of excitedly chattering men passed within earshot. Matthew remained close beside her, one hand still firmly on her shoulder to keep her from stepping out and mingling with them, and Rachel had to strain to catch what they were saying.

A sudden spattering sound startled her, and she turned to see a man urinating on the wall beside her. She started to jump out of the way of the resulting spray, then remembered just in time that she was a Chinese peasant, not some prudish Western lady. It was fortunate the wind was blowing in the opposite direction!

The moment's distraction had been enough for everything to change. The atmosphere was shrill now, noise drowning out noise, and all Rachel could make out as she turned back toward the square were a few hoarse shouts above the general din.

''I think Ch'i Shan is being recalled,'' she told Matthew as they found themselves briefly alone again in their patch of shadow. ''Something about the Emperor . . . about sending him a letter. . . .''

''I'd heard that,'' Matthew admitted. ''Some of the other traders were talking about it this afternoon, but I thought it was only a rumor. The good commissioner

seems to be that rarity among Chinese bureaucrats—
an honest, courageous man. He had the effrontery to
tell His Imperial Holiness that the defenses of Canton
were hopelessly out-of-date and the men in charge
spineless and venal. I wonder what he'll get for his
candor.''

"Nothing good, I imagine,'' Rachel said. "The Son
of Heaven doesn't care much for earthly realities.
Don't hold me so close, Matthew,'' she hissed warn-
ingly. "Someone will notice. Well then, try getting a
glazed look on your face, as if you're dull-witted and
can't make out what's going on! It's all right if you're
holding onto me for security. Chinese men lean on
their wives. Especially big-footed Hakkas.''

"That won't be hard,'' he hissed back. "I'm feeling
a little dull-witted at the moment.''

"Shhh, something's happening,'' Rachel started to
say, but the words were drowned out by a sudden tumult of gongs and drums from the far end of the
square, between the customs house and the English
garden. As she watched, horrified and fascinated, a
procession moved slowly out into the large open space,
heading toward the docks. Bannermen in richly ornate
costumes—no common coolies here—bore torches and
waving standards, their way cleared by soldiers with
flails to drive back the crowds.

A moment later a man appeared, on foot among
them, weighed down by heavy chains. An iron collar,
a sign that his life was forfeit, hung around his neck.

"Oh, dear heaven, Matthew . . . that's Ch'i Shan.''

"I know, tiger,'' he said, not bothering to lower his
voice. The crowd was roaring, a great animal noise
that filled the square and drowned out everything else.
He noticed that she didn't object this time when he put
a hand on her waist and held her close. No one was
looking their way.

Ch'i Shan made a small, forlorn figure, all his former glory stripped away. No luxurious, fur-lined robes
guarded now against the winter chill; there was no
magnificent carved jade buckle at his well-fed waist,
no black satin boots with thick, soft soles on feet that

rarely touched the pavement. The button of his rank had been removed from his cap, and the peacock feather that flaunted imperial favor. He was just an old man in a humble gown, stooped under the cruel weight of his chains.

"So much for honesty," Matthew said dryly.

Rachel shivered. "What will happen to him, do you think? Will they really execute him?"

What, the good, kind, gentle Chinese? Matthew was tempted to say. Execute a man just because they don't like hearing the truth? But she had already been bitterly disillusioned as it was; he could sense the terrible pain in the trembling of that slim body beside him, and he couldn't bring himself to add to it.

"They'll probably commute the sentence. Send him to a military camp somewhere in the north. A bleak future, but no bleaker than being the only sane man in all this madness down here and not being able to do anything about it."

Some sort of proclamation was being issued. Rachel could hear the blare of the conch shells, and an occasional word floated across the square, but she couldn't make out enough to tell what was being said. Which is just as well, she thought. It would be more of the flowery, pompous, overblown rhetoric the Chinese were so good at when they wanted to sound important and official. And it would mean nothing, except that a decent man's life was about to be taken away, one way or the other, because he had tried to put an end to what Matthew called "this madness down here."

She watched, feeling sad and sick, as Ch'i Shan was dragged in his chains onto a waiting boat. The sound of the crowd was almost deafening now; they were trying to push forward, through the line of guards with their flails, toward the riverbank. Then the boat was pulling away, and a collective bellow seemed to rise out of them: a horrible bloodthirsty cry torn from the throat of every man at once.

They loved this! Rachel could have wept with despair. They *loved* it. This was not curiosity—the ghoulish urge to peer at something gruesome. They were getting an almost physical pleasure out of it. Reveling in the pain and humiliation of an innocent man!

"I believe they would have liked to see him flogged," she said bitterly.

"Or lynched. These are not men anymore, love. They've turned into a mob, and a mob has a character and personality all its own. They'll be ashamed tomorrow, some of them—and some will bluster and denounce the poor fellow to justify what they've done. But tonight they have no control over what they say or think . . . or feel. It happens like that with a mob."

"Yes, I know, but . . ."

But she had never thought it could happen here! These people were different—she had been so *sure* they were different. She had read their poetry and responded to the peaceful harmony of their paintings; she had thought she understood the soul of the civilization that created that body of art. But there was no goodness or peace or harmony in the mob that surged through the square tonight. There was only anger and cruelty, and a fierce, primitive hatred that seemed to come from somewhere deep within.

She started to turn to Matthew, then stopped as his head jerked suddenly toward the north edge of the square, near the factories. Glancing around, she saw a stealthy black-clad figure with shortish hair, just growing out.

Steven Wu. The anguish of the moment forgotten, she forced her mind brusquely back to the task that had brought her out in the first place. The potential for violence seemed to be growing every second; she could feel the incendiary tension of the mob around her, like a keg of powder waiting for the least little spark to ignite it.

Her eyes narrowed as she stared at Steven. He was speaking urgently to two other men, dressed and looking much like him except for the pigtails dangling down their backs, and she had a horrid feeling he was planning on being that little spark himself.

"I'm going to find out what he's up to," she said, impulsively.

"Don't be foolish, Rae," Matthew caught her arm before she could move. "You don't seriously think he'll confide in you. He's too sharp for that."

"I wasn't considering asking him. I thought I'd slither over and listen in on his conversation."

"And you don't think he'll get suspicious when he notices you?" Matthew's voice was dubious, but he had let go of her arm.

"Why should he?" Rachel replied reasonably. "He's never seen me dressed like this before. He won't even think about me. Steven's sharp, but he's arrogant. He thinks he's already outsmarted me. What does he have to fear from one big-footed Hakka cow-chillo? That's a Hakka female for those untutored in the subtleties of pidgin."

"All right," Matthew conceded reluctantly. "We do have to find out what he's planning. Quickly. And I know what a cow-chillo is. But there's going to be a straw-hatted Hakka husband standing next to this female."

"Not unless you want to ruin everything. You're conspicuous enough in the shadows, and one of them is carrying a torch. No, two—somebody else has joined them. We wouldn't stand a chance. I'm not going to be far away, Matthew. Just between New China Street and that little alley next to the Danish Factory. You could reach me in a minute if you had to."

"I don't like this, tiger—"

"Besides, what's Steven gong to do if he catches me? He'll think I'm pulling a prank, and he may be annoyed, but he won't risk antagonizing me. He still thinks he has the silly missionary's daughter in his pocket. And he still needs me for whatever he has in mind."

Without giving him a chance to think it over, Rachel darted out into the light of a passing torch. When she didn't feel a hand grabbing her back, she breathed a sigh of relief. He might not like it, but he knew she was right. Steven Wu would realize something was

wrong instantly if he spotted Matthew. And he would
be alarmed. He wasn't that arrogant.

She found a place to stand a few feet away, in a
shadowy corner near the Spanish Factory. Steven
glanced her way, his eye taking her in quickly, but the
hat obscured her features and her body was stooped
and middle-aged. She was only a Hakka woman; she
couldn't even understand his dialect, and he turned
back to the others, spelling out in low, very intense
tones exactly what they were going to do that night.

The color drained from Rachel's face as she listened. She felt so ill she had to reach out and steady
herself against the wall. Heaven help her if Steven
turned and caught her now! He would know she had
heard everything. And it was enough to prompt him
to kill her in cold blood!

Matthew had said what Steven was planning might
be evil. But it as more than evil—it was total insanity!
And it would hurt the very people he claimed he
wanted to save!

I have to get back to Matthew, she thought, but she
didn't dare move too quickly. The last thing she could
afford now was to alert Steven and his companions.
There were four of them, and only one of Matthew.
Even with the gun tucked into his belt, there wasn't
much he could do.

She had to tell him what she had just discovered.
Somehow, between them, they had to figure out a way
to stop it! And they had less than three hours to do it.

She started out from the protection of the wall, moving cautiously, taking care not to look at the small
group of men. She had just gotten past them when
suddenly all the pent-up tension seemed to erupt in
the square. She heard a loud shrill sound, like the cry
of a single conch shell, then bursts of motion flared,
almost simultaneously, in several places at once; everyone was moving, an undulating, swelling mass,
surging toward the streets that led out from the square.

Rachel saw Matthew start toward her, his instincts
faster than hers, but it was too late. The mob was no
longer a milling throng; they were stampeding like

wild animals, set off by something no one else could see. She had one last glimpse of him before bodies crushed around her, an overwhelming, terrifying force, and suddenly she was part of that great mindless current.

There was no way she could resist, nothing she could do but try desperately to keep her footing as she felt herself being swept around the corner and into New China Street. They were running now, not for any reason, just running—totally out of control. Rachel was aware of looters on both sides, smashing down the doors of the little shops that lined the street, but she couldn't have stopped them even had she dared. A clatter of metal and breaking porcelain mingled with hoarse shouts of triumph, and she could see priceless vases and lengths of shimmering silk being tossed out over the heads of the crowds, grabbed by greedy hands, then lost again in the tumult.

It was senseless and sickening. They weren't even getting things they wanted! They wouldn't be able to keep them, anyway—it would all be destroyed in the end, and for what? The chance to act like an animal for a night?

She tried to crane her neck, searching frantically for Matthew behind her. She thought she saw him once— he was tall enough to stand out—but it was hard to be sure, and she had to turn her eyes forward again. It was all she could do to keep her balance as elbows jammed into her ribs, boots and sandals scraped her bare heels.

A man stumbled just in front of her. Rachel watched, helpless with horror, as he fell and the mob trampled over him. She barely managed to swing to the side to keep from being taken down with him. He seemed to crawl out of the way, causing a tumble of bodies that at least slowed some of the momentum, but she had a vivid impression of blood and screaming, and her heart was beating wildly with fright.

It seemed forever, but finally they reached Thirteen Factory Street at the end of the lane. The crowd separated but did not slow. Like stampeding beasts, Rachel thought again—following their leader.

Only this time there seemed to be three leaders, for the crowd surged in three directions, some heading east, some west, others continuing straight, through the tangle of miserable little hovels that led to the gate of the inner city.

Rachel had been on the eastern edge, and she found herself pressed in that direction down Thirteen Factory Street. The road was wider here, the crowd less dense, and she was able to get over to the left, instinctively moving away from the settlement. Hoping desperately that Matthew was near enough to see, she managed to work one hand up in a frantic attempt at a wave. She was tall, too—and the Hakka hat with its distinctive black fringe ought to make her easy to spot.

Thank heaven she had had the sense to tie it tightly under her chin! She didn't dare think what would have happened if it had come off and red-blond hair tumbled out. With the savage mood of the mob tonight, she could well believe they might have beaten her to death.

She veered off to the left, north into Hog Lane as it rambled away form the factories. Others were coming that way, too, but aimlessly, almost as if they had somehow gotten off course. Rachel turned a corner and found herself alone in a narrow, shabby *hutung,* a foul-smelling alley littered with garbage. The moon was waning, but no clouds obscured it now, and the light was clear enough to see.

She was too frightened even to weep. She was safe for the moment, but the horror of what she had seen and experienced was still fresh, like a raw, gaping wound, and she was shaking so badly she could hardly stand. A low rock wall ran along one side, the last pathetic remnant of a house that had once been pleasant but long since fallen into decay, and she leaned weakly against it.

She had never been through anything so awful and mindless before. And never in her most terrible nightmares would she have imagined it could happen in her own beloved China.

Matthew was right, she thought bitterly. She had been foolish and naive. She loved these people, and *she* wanted peace and perfection, so naturally they wanted perfection, too. She had hungered so much for the beauty she had gleaned out of poetry and paintings; she had needed to trust and believe. She hadn't been willing to listen to anything negative, and now she was paying for it dearly.

There was a slight motion at the end of the street, and she looked up sharply. Matthew? But even in that first quick glance, she saw that the man was shorter and stockier. And while his clothes were the dark-blue of the lower classes, his pants were looser and longer, the jacket unquilted.

He did not look surprised to find her there, and Rachel realized with a rush of horror that he had seen her turn into the *hutung* and deliberately followed her. He wasted no time coming toward her, his intentions brutally clear. The violent frenzy of the crowd had translated into a different savagery centering in his loins. She was only an ugly, big-footed Hakka, but Hakkas had the same space between their legs as other woman, and he was going to relieve himself in her.

Rachel's first instinct was to scream. If Matthew was anywhere nearby, he would hear and come to her rescue. But if he wasn't, and someone else responded, she would just be faced with another man— or men. And she had no illusions about what kind of treatment she could expect from anyone in that mob tonight.

She raised her hands, trying to push him back, but he was too fast for her. He was already groping, one hand under her jacket, on her breast, the other trying to pull down the front of her pants. The wall behind her crumbled, and Rachel panicked, sure they were going to collapse in a heap, this crude, gross man on top of her. But it seemed to hold, only a couple of stones clattering down.

No, she started to cry out in English, but caught herself just in time. If he knew she was a foreigner, his thoughts would not stop with rape. She tried to get her knee up for one quick jab, but his body pushed menacingly against her. The smell of sweat and garlic was suffocating, and she wanted to retch. If she could get him back, just for a second.

"You're too rough," she whined in the dialect she thought he would understand. "I don't like it this way."

It seemed to have an effect, for he stopped, Whether because of the words or because he sensed something in her tone, she did not know. But she hastened to press on.

"I'll do it if you want. I don't mind. But we have to do it the way *I* like."

He hesitated, looking confused, but did not release his hold. A thin line of drool ran down his chin, and it occurred to Rachel that he hadn't *wanted* a consenting woman. He preferred the erotic appeal of force, but sex was sex, and he seemed to be thinking it over.

"Do you want to see my breasts?" she wheedled. Her hands were on her shirt, opening it. "I'll show them to you. See?"

That got him. He took a half step back, watching, hungry and fascinated, as moonlight played on firm young mounds of flesh. Rachel tried desperately to remember what the alley was like behind her, whether she could make it or not if she tried to run. But she didn't know where it led, and he looked strong enough to catch her.

There was only one thing to do. Her knee jerked up, finding its mark with precision. He let out a grunt of surprise and pain, and doubled over, but did not fall. He was still in front of her, still blocking her way to the relative safety of the busier street.

Rachel reached for the only thing at hand, one of the rocks that had come out the wall. Blinded with fear and anger, she brought it down on his head, hard. Damn him for what he had done to her. Damn him, *damn him*, for the degradation of his foul hands all over her body! She watched as he sank to the ground and hoped with all her heart he was dead!

She was still standing over him, still looking down at the rock by his motionless body, too confused even to try to sort out the conflicting feelings flooding over her, when she heard a sound at the end of the alley.

She cried out in alarm, but this time it *was* Matthew. He covered the few steps between them in a fraction of a second, his eyes taking in first the man on the ground, then the disarray of her clothing. Her jacket was still hanging open, her breasts exposed to the night.

"My God, Rachel! What happened?" He was clasping her to him, holding her fiercely, tightly. "He didn't . . . ?" he rasped hoarsely. "If he hurt you, that swine—if he did *anything* to you, I swear I'll—"

"No, no, I'm all right," she said shakily. He was holding her at arm's length now, studying her intently in the pale bluish light. "He tried to, but I gave him a knee where it would do him the most good. Then I hit him over the head." She saw the look on his face and attempted a weak smile. "Any girl with four brothers has been taught to defend herself. But, oh, Matthew . . . I think I killed him. I *wanted* to kill him."

She had started to cry. Matthew heard it in her voice before he saw it in her eyes, and he refrained from making a few choice remarks about the fate that suited that bastard on the ground. She had been through enough as it was. She didn't need a husband ranting and raving because he felt inadequate at not having been able to protect her. Dropping to one knee, he laid an efficient thumb on the man's neck and felt a not-totally-welcome pulse.

"Well, you didn't," he said as matter-of-factly as he could manage. "Though he'll be out for a while— which is fortunate for him, because *I* would have killed him. And I wouldn't have apologized to anyone for it. Not even my beautiful, compassionate wife."

Anger mingled with waves of helpless frustration as

he rose to his feet again. This animal had violated his wife—had tried to debase her in the most despicable way—and he couldn't do anything about it without hurting her more! He was very conscious of her eyes on him, and it was with considerable effort that he restrained himself from giving the wretch a swift kick in the head.

"I didn't know I *could* kill anyone," Rachel said softly. "I didn't know a lot of things before tonight. Those people out there in the square . . . they're people I loved. . . ."

"You still do, tiger. You just expected too much of them, that's all. Here, your hands are trembling. Let me help you with that." He tugged the edge of the jacket out of her fingers and began gently to fasten it up. "They can't help being human, with failings like the rest of us. You forgave my failings once, as I recall. I expect you'll forgive them, too. And anyone can kill, under the right circumstances. I think protecting yourself from an attack like that qualifies."

"I suppose so," Rachel replied wearily. "But it's not a lesson I wanted to learn. I wish I had listened when you tried to warn me."

"Come on, love." His arm was around her waist, and he was guiding her toward the end of the narrow *hutung.* "Let's go back to the factory. The crowd was already thinning by the time I got out of the square— I was toward the end. I could barely see you up ahead. I'm going to pack our things and get you out of here if I have to steal a boat! Whatever the problems on the river, they can't be as bad as this."

"But, Matthew—" Rachel pulled back, her eyes widening as she remembered suddenly what she had been intending to tell him when the rioting broke out. "We can't go. Not tonight! We're not finished here."

"Good God, Rachel! You're not still obsessed with that blasted opium?"

"It's not the opium. I don't care about the opium anymore. I was a fool to think we could get it in the first place. Steven talked me into it. But I know now why he wanted me there when he destroyed it!''

Matthew felt cold suddenly though the night was mild and his quilted jacket thick.

"You found out what he's planning to do?''

"He's going to set fire to the warehouse.''

Sixteen

He's going to—*what*?''

Matthew's face was ashen in the moonlight, but he didn't look surprised, and Rachel realized that this new aspect of Steven Wu's character was one he had already considered.

''He's going to set his torches to the warehouse. Everything inside will go up in flames. And every-*one*,'' she added with a shudder. ''All this rioting is just a diversion. He wants bands of men roving through the outskirts of town, even threatening the city gate itself. Whatever soldiers can be rounded up will be occupied elsewhere.''

''And at midnight . . .''

''At about twenty past, actually. The building belonging to the prosperous *hong* merchant Howqua on upper Hog Lane—where the opium that Captain Matthew Barron brought from India is stored—will be one great crackling blaze, to the lasting glory of Steven Wu and his gang!''

''Lord, Rachel . . .'' Matthew was shocked in spite of himself. ''Look around you. These hovels are packed together—blasted heaps of bamboo and rattan, one on top of the other. It's like a giant tinderbox . . . and the wind's rising! The fire will be all over the place in no time at all.''

''And hundreds—thousands—of people are going to die. Steven's own people.'' Rachel made no effort to hide the horror and sadness in her voice. ''He's beyond caring, Matthew. He's not a fanatic anymore—I could understand fanaticism! It's almost as if he's gone mad.

His hatred for opium is so consuming, he doesn't care *who* he has to hurt to destroy it.''

And his hatred of the foreigners, Matthew thought—and perhaps some of his own countrymen—although he stuck to the subject at hand.

"What's your place in all this, tiger?''

"What you guessed, I think. He wants me for my nationality and because I'm the daughter of a minister. It gives what he's planning a sort of ghoulish respectability, in his eyes at least. And in the eyes of the Chinese. They're very big on that sort of thing. They would think it gave him great "face." It would look as if God and the flowery-flag devils, the Americans, are on their side. A major symbolic victory for Steven Wu over the evil, greedy opium smugglers.''

"And the corrupt *hong* merchants who feed on them,'' Matthew agreed darkly. "But for that to work you'd have to be there. Physically. He didn't seriously think you were going to wander through the streets tonight in a long gown and flowery little bonnet?''

"I would have been all right. I know Steven. He would have had a cloak for me, or something like that. And the area would have been quiet. You notice none of the rioters were channeled in that direction. I might have been on my own *after* the fire, but he might have sent someone to see me safely back, too. I would have given him what he wanted, after all.''

Or he might have realized the angry denunciations she was going to heap publicly on his head the next day, Matthew thought grimly, and decided he didn't want to lose "face." Unpleasant accidents had a way of happening in the midst of unchecked rioting. A woman trampled to death? What a pity.

He noticed that nowhere in all that speculation had there been any mention of a certain Yankee sea captain. He had a feeling he knew only too well what Steven Wu had planned for him.

"We have to stop him, tiger,'' he said quietly.

"I know. We've got to warn Howqua. I hate it—but

if he has enough guards, he might be able to do something. It's our only chance.''

They paused at the corner where the small *hutung* ran into Hog Lane as if progressed north from the settlement with its waterfront and long row of foreign factories. Everything was almost unnaturally quiet. Only one man staggered past, and he smelled as if he had fallen into a tub of *samshun*. Somewhere in those drab anonymous buildings, Howqua's *hong,* or warehouse, was squeezed in with the others.

''It's the ultimate irony, isn't it?'' she said as they started slowly up the street. Her eyes, like Matthew's, darted continually to the shadows, though there seemed no immediate danger. ''To save the city from destruction, I have to save the opium, too. Because of me, Howqua is going to keep his supply intact.''

''Maybe not.'' He took her arm, then dropped it, remembering her admonition against touching in public. ''I have an idea. It's a long shot, but it might work. Of course, we're going to have to get in to see him, if he's even here. If I were Howqua, I think I might have arranged a nice little vacation in the country about now.''

''If you were the most powerful merchant in the *Cohong,*'' Rachel corrected, ''and all your wealth and reputation was tied up in your warehouse, you'd be where he is right now. Making sure it's safe.''

A number of doorways appeared at intervals in the high, drab walls, and as Rachel counted them under her breath—Howqua's would be the tenth on the right, she told him—Matthew reviewed in his mind what he knew about the man. He was not unique, but one in a long line of similar characters. There was always a Howqua, just as there would always be a Mowqua, in the *Co-hong,* the guild of ten merchants through whom all foreign business in China had to be transacted. If a trader wanted food, he contacted the *Co-hong;* if he wanted servants, the *Co-hong* again; if he needed a comprador to act as intermediary in his affairs, he had no choice but to turn to the *Co-hong* once more. And its most important member.

It was said that the current Howqua was particularly shrewd. It was also said that he liked dealing with Americans, whose freewheeling ways it pleased him to imitate, and Matthew devoutly hoped it was so.

He heard Rachel make a little sound and turned to see that she was shivering.

"You don't have to come with me, love. Howqua is used to traders. We can manage well enough with pidgin. I should have time to take you back first."

"What makes you think I'd be safer in the settlement?" she said in a thin, strained voice. "Anyhow, I'm not frightened. I . . . I was just thinking. All this is my fault, Matthew. if I hadn't been so stupidly naive, I would never have encouraged Steven. I went along with him step-by-step—so gullibly! I even pressed for more. It was *my* idea to go after the opium at Howqua's!"

"If it hadn't been that opium," Matthew reminded her, "he'd have found some other supply. You said it yourself—it's a symbolic gesture. And one symbol is as good as another."

"Still, if I'd been a little sharper . . ."

"If you'd been sharper, he'd have cut you out early on and taken a different tack. This madness in the guise of patriotism that has turned your old friend into a monster has nothing to do with you, love—or me. Or *both* our gullibilities. I've been far worse than you. I knew all along something was wrong, and I was too damned shortsighted to figure out what it was!"

They reached another doorway, slightly recessed, as dingy and unprepossessing as the ones that had come before it. The *hong* merchants did not advertise their wealth.

Rachel stopped. "Well, let's hope we can make up for it now," she said, and doubling her fists, began to pound loudly.

When Matthew saw the number of guards that appeared as the door swung open, he was impressed in spite of himself. He could make out perhaps fifteen or twenty, but the small lighted area at the front receded into deep black shadows, and he sensed more lurking there. And probably a good number crouched behind the large packing crates that were piled nearby to the ceiling in places, with narrow aisles between.

They were armed, he noticed, not with ancient jingals and muskets captured in wars long past, but modern, efficient weapons.

Rachel spoke rapidly to one of the guards, who seemed to be resisting her urgent pleas. But she pressed, and finally, after gesturing pointedly to his fellows to keep an eye on the intruders, he vanished somewhere in the back.

"He's going to see if Howqua will receive us," she explained in an undertone to Matthew. The other guards were just far enough away not to be able to hear what language they were speaking. "He didn't want to. But I told him I had important information, and there would be dire consequences if he didn't report immediately to his master."

"And he believed you? An ugly-footed Hakka woman?"

"This Hakka speaks better Cantonese than he does. That kind of thing makes people nervous. He was afraid to check, but he was more afraid not to."

Whatever the guard reported to his master seemed to have had an effect, for lights glowed suddenly at the rear of the drafty, cavernous room. A moment later, they were being escorted back, or rather prodded, for their escorts took care to remain behind them. Rats could be heard scurrying out of the way as they passed between high stacks of crates.

"We're to be received, but not trusted, apparently," Rachel said under her breath. "Howqua is supposed to have very luxurious chambers for himself somewhere upstairs. But it's easier for the guards to keep us covered here. I wouldn't make any sudden motions if I were you."

"I wasn't planning on it," Matthew replied earnestly.

Howqua was waiting for them in a brightly lighted space. Huge boxes around and behind cast ominous, angular shadows. He was an old man, with snow-white hair and a drooping moustache setting off dark eyes that sparkled with what looked distinctly like curiosity.

There could be no doubt either of his wealth or his importance. Even alone, not expecting visitors, Howqua was richly gowned in varying shades of blue satin that fell with luxurious fullness to his insteps. His cap was a matching color, accented by a vivid scarlet crown. Technically, the *hong* merchants were the ninth, or lowest, rank of mandarin, hence the *-qua* in their names; but some had managed to work their way up, and the button on the upturned brim was blue, signifying his importance.

The soles of his shoes were thick and soft. Not a sound could be heard as he took a step forward, then stopped, still a comfortable distance away. Those sharp eyes dismissed Matthew after the briefest of seconds, then came to rest with some interest on Rachel.

He listened quietly as she spoke, the look on his face changing subtly after the first few words.

"Cow-chillo not Chinese," he said as she finished. His sing-song tones were oddly out of keeping with the elegance of his appearance. "Look Chinese. Dress Chinese. Almost talk first-chop . . . but not Chinese."

"No." Rachel pulled off her hat with a graceful sweep and flipped her head defiantly, spilling a burst of color onto her shoulders. Her back was straight, as always; she was not bending to the enemy. "I am an American. And I am not your friend. You know me as Rachel Todd. My father is Gideon Todd, of the American Mission in Macao."

He nodded, seeming to understand, though Matthew noticed she had not spoken in the customary pidgin. If he resented her rudeness, it did not show as shrewd dark eyes came back to rest on Matthew again.

"Friend not look Chinese. Look plenty dumb. Dress werry bad, heya?" He ended with a sharp cackle that could have been either amusement or malice.

"Admittedly," Matthew agreed, doffing his own

hat, though not quite as facilely, for the ties got caught
under his chin. "Captain Matthew Barron at your service, sir. Of the trading house of Barron Shipping. Or
should I say, 'Turtledung trader man werry plenty glad
Howqua help-help can'? "

Crinkly lines deepened around the dark eyes as
Howqua held up one bejeweled hand with the long,
curving fingernails of his class. He was definitely
amused now.

"Howqua savvy plenty good, trader man. No talk.
Werry bad-bad. But savvy."

"Good, that makes things simpler," Matthew said,
taking care all the same to speak slowly and clearly.
"You know what is happening tonight? There are many
men out there. They are all over the city by now.
Breaking into buildings, stealing—doing many bad
things." He could see by that changeless expression
that he was not telling the old man anything new.
"Do you also know they are planning to burn your
hong? They will be here in less than an hour. With
many torches."

That brought a flicker of surprise, just for a second.

"You've got to stop them!" Rachel broke in urgently. "It's not just you. I wouldn't be here if it were
just you. You know that! The fire will spread all over
the city. Many people will be killed! If you put your
guards outside instead of in here, maybe it will help.
I don't know . . . but you have to *try*!"

She switched to Chinese, repeating what she had
said in case he hadn't understood, but he didn't seem
to be listening. He was looking at Matthew very intently.

"Of course, the men can always return," Matthew
said softly. "Even if the guards are strong enough to
chase them away. They can come back with more
men, more torches. Hundreds and hundreds. Your
guards cannot kill them all. They want the opium,
you see. Very badly. *My* opium. They want to destroy it."

"No trader man opium now. Opium my. Fast-talk,

redheaded, devil-rat partner sell Howqua.'' He was chuckling softly under his breath. ''Plenty good pricey.''

Matthew wondered which Gallagher would resent most. The allusion to him as British, or the slur on his ability at bargaining.

''The opium was mine once,'' he said. ''I want it back . . . and you want to give it to me.''

''Wantshee give you?'' Howqua ran the tip of one claw-like nail slowly down his moustache. ''*Wantshee*?''

''You give me the opium—I promise these men I will take care of it—and what reason do they have to burn your *hong*?'' He heard a sharp intake of breath from Rachel beside him and knew she had figured out what he was up to. ''They want to look like heroes. Very bold. There is much face in this for them. If they set fire to the warehouse for nothing, they will not look bold. They will look stupid.''

''Howqua, too,'' the old man said shrewdly. ''Werry plenty stupid. Big problem, trader man say Howqua. Fire burn *hong*, whole city—so solly, most sad. But give opium my, and trader man save. No fires. Everything quiet, yes? So Howqua werry grateful. But maybe everything quiet anyway, heya?''

''And maybe *give* was the wrong word.'' Matthew withdrew a folded sheet from his pocket and held it out. ''You understand English very well. Perhaps you also read it. This is a draft on my personal account at Barron Shipping.''

Howqua hesitated, then stepped forward and took the paper. His face betrayed no emotion, but Matthew sensed he could make out at least the figures. And he knew it was far more than he would get for his goods on the open market.

''Present that at our offices in Macao as soon as the chests are delivered downriver. Leave them with Olyphant and Company. That way there won't be any doubt. You've done business with us before. You know the draft will be honored.''

''You buy back own opium?''

He could not quite keep the incredulity out of his voice. "Why not?" Matthew said. Now he was the one who was amused. "I want the opium enough to pay for it. You want your warehouse to be standing tomorrow. And you want that very exorbitant bit of cash. Do we have a deal?"

The faintest touch of a smile played at the corners of Howqua's lips, the most he ever allowed himself with the devil barbarians.

"Deal, trader man."

He was still shaking his head minutes later, after the young couple had left and the lights were low again. The rats had come back out and were skittering over the floor. He had had many business affairs with these strange, brash Americans, and many had surprised him; but none had been as surprising as this. He was thinking that it was good, growing to such an old age, when there were so many wondrous things to see.

"You already knew what you were going to do!" Rachel tried to sound indignant, but she couldn't keep the admiration out of her voice. "You had everything planned, even before we went out tonight. That draft was in your pocket all the time, and you never said a word."

"I didn't *know* anything, tiger." Matthew touched her elbow lightly, steering her out into the center of Thirteen Factory Street, away from the refuse and offal in the gutter. There was almost no one visible, but a glow of torchlight showed over the rooftops in several directions, and the sporadic sound of shouting drifted to their ears. "I figured Steven was up to no good, and I thought we ought to have a plan of our own. I knew how disappointed you'd be if we didn't get the opium. I had given you that first batch as an early wedding present—I intended this as a late one. But I had no idea my little plan would come in quite *this* handy."

"Let's just pray it works. If there's a fire. . . . "

"It will work," he assured her, a little more confidently than he felt. "It has to. Look at it this way. If Steven didn't care about appearances, he wouldn't have made such an effort to bring you along. There's a great deal of face, as you pointed out, involved in this matter tonight. He thinks his country needs a revolution—"

"And maybe it does," Rachel cut in softly. "Things are awful, and getting worse. But—"

"But something like this would only add to the burden his people are already carrying." Matthew finished the sentence for her. "Unfortunately, revolutionaries don't think like that. Especially the ambitious ones, and I guarantee you, Steven Wu is a very ambitious young man. He not only wants a revolution, he wants to be one of its leaders. For that he needs to look very good tonight. And very heroic."

"By setting a fire? I can't imagine that revolutionaries inspire great loyalty burning out potential followers."

"Ah, but the fire would be an accident, of course. Steven would have boldly wrested the foul opium from the greedy merchant's *hong*—at the very risk of his own life! Could he help it if all that rabble running around with torches got out of hand? What did they have to do with him, or he with them?"

A sound, like a footfall, came from somewhere behind. They both turned, tensely, but it was only a hungry cur nosing through the shadows. A man appeared at the far end of the street, but he was moving slowly, reeling from side to side in a drunken manner. The taverns and brothels in Hog Lane must have been thoroughly depleted of their supply of *samshun* tonight, Matthew thought.

He stopped, catching Rachel by one arm and holding her for a moment before going on.

"Listen . . . is there any possibility—any at all—that your brother is mixed up in this?"

Rachel shook her head. "Sam is nowhere near as naive as I am. Steven wouldn't have let him catch a hint of what was going on. That raid on the junks was already getting too drastic for him. And he would never have allowed *me* to be involved."

No, Matthew thought, relieved as they started toward the end of the alley again. Sam Todd was extremely protective of his younger sister. His qualms about the raid probably stemmed from the guilty realization that she had come very close to getting hurt. He certainly wouldn't let her walk into what might well have been a death trap tonight.

The square was somewhat brighter when they reached it. The few scattered wisps of cloud were insignificant, and moonlight splashed almost dawn-bright across the broad expanse. The mob was gone, but a few torches remained, fixed in the ground by the docks or near the entrances to the factories. Shirt-sleeved men were scurrying back and forth, alone or in pairs, heaving what appeared to be luggage onto their shoulders and dragging crates on the ground between them.

The last of the traders loading their boats and getting out, Rachel thought. And no doubt with considerable wisdom.

Steven was nowhere to be seen, and she had a moment's panic as she stood in the light of one of the torches and no one approached her. She had no idea what time it was; Matthew had hardly tucked a watch and fob into his quilted Chinese jacket! What if it was past midnight, and Steven hadn't waited? But then she remembered he wasn't looking for a coolie and the big-footed Hakka woman he had not recognized before.

She scanned the shadows and spotted him immediately at a wall near the cowyard, almost where she and Matthew had been standing before.

"Hsst—Steven!" she called, and laughed at the look on his face when he spun around and saw her jerk off her hat. "Plenty good cow-chillo, heya?"

His expression darkened almost instantly. "I thought I told you to dress in proper clothes," he hissed, barely managing to control his rage as he approached. "Like a Western woman."

Matthew, who had stepped up protectively, could

feel Rachel shiver beside him, but she tilted her chin up gamely.

"But naturally, I just assumed that would be too dangerous." Big brown eyes widened ingenuously. "You couldn't have known when you told me what to wear how awful everything was going to turn out to-night. Besides, we figured out a much better way to get the opium, without any risk. Didn't we, dear?" She cast an adoring look at her husband, as if he were the cleverest man on earth.

"Money talks, my boy," Matthew said, taking his cue from her and making his voice as bluff and jovial as he could. "I thought, since all this trouble was my fault in the first place, I ought to be the one to fix it. No point rushing in—getting hurt, and all that. So I just bought the stuff back."

"You . . . *bought* it?"

"Blasted clever, don't you think? I ran into a couple of fellows from Jardine, Matheson on the way back, and, uh—" He glanced quickly around the square, catching sight of one of the directors of another trading house hurrying toward the docks with a stack of ledgers un-der his arm. "And good old Miller there, from D. M. Rudolph. They all think I'm a fool, of course, but it's a jolly good joke!"

"How convenient for you," Steven said very slowly, "that Mr. Miller is just leaving."

"That's why I told him," Matthew replied quietly. Then, lapsing again into heartier tones, he added: "He'll be the first one back, so he can spread the news right away. Everyone will know about it. Your bosses over at Olyphant will be thrilled! I'm giving you full credit—and Rachel here, of course—for talking me into it. The opium is going to be shipped to them. They'll know what to do with it."

"So you see," Rachel said softly. "There's no need to worry about it now. And really, our plan wouldn't have worked anyhow. You should see all the guards Howqua has at his *hong*. You might have been able to bribe a few, but there are dozens!"

"It would have cost a blasted fortune," Matthew cut

in. "Damn fool waste of money! Cheaper buying the
stuff. . . . Hey, Richardson!" He called out to a man
who was just heading up from the docks toward the
Chungho Factory. "You bailing out, too? Rats desert-
ing the sinking ship, eh?"

"I couldn't have put it better myself," the man said,
stepping over for a second. If he was taken aback by
the way Matthew and his pretty wife were dressed, he
was tactful enough not to mention it. "I trust you'll
be joining the rest of the rats."

Matthew nodded. "Stop by for a drink before you
go, why don't you? On Lippincott and Co. It'd be a
damned shame to leave all that good liquor behind.
Why don't you go on in with him, darling? I'll be right
along."

He watched until they were nearly to the door, then
turned to find Steven Wu regarding him with open hatred.

"You think this is going to stop here?" Fury flashed
like black fire in his eyes. "You think you have defeated me?"

"I know it," Matthew said evenly. "You want
something. You want it very badly. And you're not
going to get it if you can't point to a damned good
excuse for letting a few thousand innocent people burn
to death."

"What I want is freedom for my country," Steven
made no effort to hide the anger and passion in his
voice now that the others were gone. "From the British and our own short-sighted, tyrannical leaders. If a
few people die—if *many* die—that's the price of a revolution. One day we will be proud to look back on
this, our humble beginning! One day we will cast off
the yokes that enslave us!"

"And cast them onto others, is that it? Only this
time, *you* will be the master. . . . Never mind. Your
heart may be as pure as your mind is warped, but
I'll tell you one thing. Leave my wife out of it. You
mess with Rachel again—you so much as come *near*
her—and I will personally cut your heart out and

feed it to the coolies for breakfast! And that's a promise.''

They were packed in twenty minutes and out of the factory. Richardson had remained with Rachel only until Matthew got there, then declined the offer of a drink and went back to get the last of his own belongings. Things were tossed in bags with no attempt at order, and they were on the docks with the other traders, hastily negotiating for craft to carry them down the river.

Costs were high—the boatmen knew the value of their services that night—but no one was complaining, and Matthew managed to hire a filthy lorcha, about half as appealing as the one that had brought them there in the first place. Leaving Rachel with Miller on the dock beside a cluttered little sampan, he went off to confer with some of the other men.

It was quickly agreed that they would travel in convoy for safety, though there didn't seem to be any trouble on the water. Or anywhere else for that matter. Even the square was almost eerily quiet now that that sudden orgy of violence was over.

''It's the damndest thing I've ever seen,'' Richardson was saying as they walked back together. ''The whole blasted uproar came out of nowhere. It just *happened*! I thought for sure they were going to torch the settlement. And now look—!''

''They still might,'' Matthew said grimly. He glanced toward the dock where Rachel was speaking quietly with Miller. She was still wearing the Hakka pants and jacket, but her hair floated to her shoulders, shimmering in the light of the boats' lanterns. ''If not tonight, another time. Soon. I think the days of the settlement are numbered.''

''It's too hellish hard to protect,'' Richardson agreed. ''As soon as Elliot gives these heathens a little lesson in humility, we'll have to look around for something better. One of the islands with a little water around it, maybe.''

''It's a possibility,'' Matthew started to say, breaking off as he spotted a chop boat that had just angled into place among all the other vessels at the crowded dockside. As Richardson went on ahead, he stood and watched five men leap out.

Damian Varnay. And with him, the *China Dawn*'s carpenter—the best man Matthew knew to have on his side in a fight—and the three most trustworthy members of the crew.

What in God's name—?

Matthew raised one arm abruptly, a dramatic enough motion to catch their attention. Changing direction, they hurried toward him.

"We came as soon as we got your note, sir," Varnay called out as they approached. "I gather there's trouble. We had the devil's own time getting through. I've never seen a river so crowded—"

"What note?" Matthew asked abruptly.

Varnay faltered. He was looking into his captain's face and seeing much the same expression he had once before.

"The one that ordered us to Canton on the double. It was in your hand, sir. At least, it looked like your hand."

"I told you once before," Matthew said, his voice ominously even, "if you ever got orders from anyone again—*anyone*—there'd damn well better be something to back it up."

This time Varnay stood his ground. "It came with your cufflink. The one with the ruby that looks like the Barron flag. I've never seen another man with anything like it. Who else could have sent it but you?"

Who else, indeed? Matthew looked toward the river, calculating the time it had taken them to get up, the time it would take him to get down again. There was no point blaming his mate for this. He remembered only too well where he had lost the cufflink. And who had been there.

He also remembered the new crewmen he had noticed and dismissed at the time as the natural result of too long a stay in one port. And he knew why it had been so important for Gallagher to get rid of Damian Varnay and four thoroughly dependable men.

The son-of-a-bitch had stolen his ship!

PROMISES
OF SPRING

Hong Kong, late March 1841

Seventeen

Music floated down the hillside, shrill, but enthusiastic and eminently danceable. A tamped dirt path crisscrossed up the slope, its edges lined with glowing torches that sent a smoky odor into the night. A gala in progress, and a large one, judging by the lights and noise.

Matthew lingered for a moment at the base of the path, near the docks, and looked around him. The last thing he had expected to find when they had sailed into Hong Kong harbor at sunset was anything remotely resembling a city. But the waterfront area was already built up. Godowns and offices were in operation; he could see lights flickering in many of the windows, and families were starting to move into Happy Valley, a mile or so to the east.

He had spent the last two weeks in a desperate, often fruitless search for some trace of the ship that had been lost, the fabulous *China Dawn*, on which, as he was all too well aware, much of his family's reputation was staked. She had also been his own personal pride, and rage had mingled with bouts of despair as the days had passed and he had feared sometimes he would never find her.

He had turned in the lorcha at Whampoa for another, slightly more ample vessel of the same sort. Rachel had scrubbed it thoroughly, inside and out, applying her father's exacting standards, and it had almost been livable, or would have if he had not been so consumed with his mission. Every inlet, every river mouth, every bay for nearly a hundred miles up the coast had been thoroughly scoured. He hadn't even taken the time to shave. The beard that Rachel enjoyed teasing him about was back, itching abominably, and he promised himself it would go in the morning. At the moment, all he had been able to manage was to trim it somewhat before coming ashore.

He had finally succeeded in his quest. He had found the *China Dawn* anchored again in a small cove, not as well protected as the last time, for the shore, while rocky, was accessible, and assault was possible from that side. But her cannons were in working order, and the men Gallagher had hired doubtless well versed in their use. Guile would be required to take her without damage.

He had worked out a plan. Not foolproof, but close enough, and he needed only men and boats to execute it, which was what had brought him to Hong Kong. He had not been the least bit worried, as they had approached the new city, that Gallagher would move the *China* in the meantime. The location was too good; he was running a rousing smuggling operation. He would be there until the last of the opium was gone, and that would be some time.

"Now, if only I have a little luck," he had said as he had stood on the deck of the lorcha with Rachel and squinted into the glare of the dying sun. "Just a *little* luck."

But his luck had run out. Tall, sailless masts stood out in bold black silhouette against the shimmering horizon. Forty or fifty vessels at least, and Matthew caught sight of the Barron colors fluttering over the *Eliza Dawn*. That was to be expected. She was under the command of Aaron Rawlings, a cautious, conservative captain, who would not risk the Pearl River before he felt it was safe. And who would not want to miss the stirring music that was clamoring down the hillside now.

No *Scarlet Dawn* among the others. That was expected, too. Newcombe would already be at Whampoa, itching to get into Canton as soon as trading opened again. There was always a *Scarlet Dawn* in the Barron fleet, a reminder of the first ship that had started it all, and she was always a rickety old tub. But her captains were the best in the business.

Only one ship was unexpected, Or perhaps not *totally* unexpected, Matthew had to admit. A sleek-hulled, rake-masted, very arrogant-looking clipper.

"That's the *Shadow Dawn,*" he had said to Rachel. "About four months out of Boston, I'd guess. She was supposed to have been captained by Cousin Alex, but what do you want to bet my brother's taken over? Jared was never a man to ride patiently on someone else's ship. And he sure as hell isn't a man to stay calmly at home when he hears rumors about his baby brother and that obscene stuff you and he both abhor."

"And every other thinking man—or woman," she had reminded him gently.

"And a few of the light-headed ones," Matthew had agreed. "I've already admitted I was wrong. But I don't think, under the circumstances, that's going to carry much weight with my brother."

"You're so sure he's here?" she had asked. "Maybe the rumors didn't get to Boston—or at least not before *Shadow Dawn* sailed."

"I'm sure," Matthew had said quietly. "And I'm sure there's going to be the devil to pay. If there's anything that can make my brother angrier than daring to tarnish the Barron name, it's risking the flagship of the whole blasted Barron line! And Jared's temper is as legendary as our grandfather's."

The wind picked up. Matthew thrust his hands in his pockets and wished he had brought along a jacket as he stood on the path and looked up at sparks blowing from the torches into the darkness. Just for a moment, he felt again the same sick feeling that had knotted his stomach as he had stood on the deck of the lorcha and stared across the bay at the *Shadow Dawn*. It was almost as if he were a little boy again, knowing he had disappointed his brother. He always seemed to disappoint Jared, no matter how he tried. And he was waiting for that same terrible wrath to come down on his head.

Only he wasn't a little boy anymore. Squaring his

shoulders unconsciously, he started up the path, hands
out of his pockets now, hanging loosely at his sides.
He couldn't stand forever in awe of his brother; he
couldn't plan every act of his life around what Jared
would think, how Jared would feel, whether Jared
would admire him for this or that.

He had made a fool of himself; he would acknowledge it freely. But *he* would set things straight. He was
going to have to insist on that.

He wanted to be his brother's friend. He wanted
desperately to win his respect. But he wanted his self-
respect, too. And he had come to a point in his life
where he realized which was more important.

The music had changed, a waltz this time, tinny but
sweet, and a faint sound of laughter echoed down the
slope. The party, whatever it was, seemed to be in full
swing, and he had no doubt he would find his brother
there. Where there was music and dancing, there were
beautiful women—and Jared was far from immune to
the family weakness for beauty and charm.

He would meet his match one day. Matthew was
sure of that, and he wanted to be there when it happened, Lord knows. But in the meantime, Jared was
doing everything he could—which was considerable—
to uphold the rakish reputation of the Barron men.

Matthew thought briefly about going back and
changing. He had not realized the occasion would be
quite so grand. His trousers, though well tailored, were
hardly formal, and white shirtsleeves were fastened
with plain gold links since Varnay still had half of the
more elegant pair.

But for once he wasn't interested in clothes. If he
was going to be ill-bred enough to push his way in
without an invitation, he might as well do it improp-
erly attired.

He threw a quick look back over his shoulder at the
anonymous mass of small boats, in which he could no
longer pick out his own lorcha. Rachel had wanted to
come with him, and he had been sorely tempted, but
he had known that her presence would only put off the
inevitable.

"I have to settle things with my brother, tiger," he had said. "It's no good softening him up with a pretty young bride. The most I'd buy is a few minutes of pleasant chitchat. The explosion is still going to come in the end."

She had agreed, almost too easily—though there had been just a faint glint in her eye, which he had not paid any attention to at the time. Now, as he heard a noise behind him and turned, he knew he should have.

Rachel was standing in the middle of the path. Or rather, the Hakka woman that Rachel could be when she set her mind to it. Clearly, her mind was set now. A bulky black jacket hung over pants that had been rolled up almost to her knees. Her feet were bare, her hair covered with a large conical hat, every inch of her skin smudged beyond recognition.

And her eyes were dancing with delight.

"Cow-chillo plenty good-good, yes? Big brother *werry* impressed!"

Matthew tried very hard not to smile. "I told you, love—no wife tonight. At least not until Jared cools down. *If* Jared cools down."

"Where Supreme Lady?" She looked around with exaggerated twists of her head. "No Supreme Lady. Humble cow-chillo servant girl. How cow-chillo soften up big brother? . . . And besides," she added, her voice low and teasing, "what's wrong with a few minutes of pleasant chitchat? It could help ease the way."

Matthew hesitated, than gave up with a grin.

"Why not?" he said. "We might be able to use a little laughter tonight."

The gala was much more elaborate than Rachel had expected. Even the parties thrown by the great trading houses in Macao were nowhere near so sumptuously decorated. And there seemed to be two bands, the navy vying with the soldiers in their brilliant scarlet uniforms, so the music would never have to stop for more than a moment or two.

Everything was open-air and very enticing. A prettily carved railing surrounded the slightly raised, wide-

plank dance floor, giving it the look of a real ball-
room. Flowers seemed to be everywhere: wild myrtle
twining with orchids and sweet-scented camellias
around tall posts and swinging in great festoons over
the top. Vividly colored Chinese lanterns glittered like
jewels, casting circles of crimson and topaz, azure and
emerald, on the swirling pattern of dancers, and similarly lighted paths led to a number of blue-and-white
tents with refreshment tables and cloakrooms for the
ladies.

Rachel stood on the edge of the dance floor, gaping
openly as a Hakka cow-chillo would. It amused her to
pick out figures she recognized in the elaborate cotillion, and to know that not a one of them had recognized her. Most of the major traders were in
attendance, though she didn't see Robert Carpenter,
and she suspected he had made the tiring trip back to
Canton, or at least as far as Whampoa. The *Nemesis,*
with the other gunboats, had ventured upriver one
more time, crushing resistance as brutally as before,
and things seemed to be stabilizing at last.

Camilla was there, however, partnered gracefully by
Aaron Rawlings, captain of the *Eliza Dawn.* But she
was pouting—prettily, as only Cammie could—and
casting dagger-looks at a tall, extremely beautiful
woman with lush auburn hair who was standing on one
of the paths on the opposite side.

As Rachel's eyes moved from the woman to the man
beside her, she felt herself stiffen. He was a good two
or three inches taller than Matthew, his hair was
slightly darker. He was more powerfully built, with
muscles that strained the shoulders of his jacket. But
she would have known that profile anywhere: the high,
strong brow, the slightly hawkish nose, the jaw that
looked as if it had been set in stone.

He was not as handsome as Matthew, and he did not
have his easy, careless grace. But the arrogance she
had only sensed sometimes in her husband showed
clearly in those hard, Yankee features.

This was Jared Barron. And he did not look as if he
were disposed to be gentle.

Her heart seemed to stop for an instant, and she realized she had been half-hoping he wouldn't be here after all. That the meeting could be put off, for a little while at least.

But Matthew, who had spotted his brother at the same time, almost seemed relieved. He was laughing softly under his breath as he started out onto the dance floor. The band was still playing. Ladies in their gem-bright dresses and gentlemen in fine formal coats were still performing the rigidly patterned steps of the cotillion as he threaded his way among them, exaggerating the beat of the music, quickening it somewhat, to perform a little bobbing dance of his own.

The laughter was full and unforced by the time he reached his brother.

"Now, how did I know I was going to find you here?" he drawled. "Or more to the point, how did I know you'd be coming to this part of the world?" He extended his hand quite amiably, almost as if there were nothing between them, and Rachel, who had followed several paces behind, dared to breathe again as Jared reached out and accepted it. "Actually, I expected you much sooner. What took you so long?"

"I was delayed," Jared replied dryly. Rachel, listening, was struck by the similarity in the two men's voices. The timbre and expression were almost exactly the same, and she could swear she caught a trace of humor she had not expected.

She must have made some slight movement, for Matthew turned and saw her.

"This is . . . Chin-Chin," he said. His eyes met his brother's with a jesting challenge that did not go unnoticed. Jared's brow went up, pointedly, and he took a lingering look at the sooty-faced peasant in front of him.

"Werry plenty happy meet big brother," Rachel trilled obligingly in her most atrocious pidgin. "This piece cow-chillo hear plenty good big brother. Want-shee meet long time." She squatted on the ground in front of him and tilted her head back, beaming up in a most impudently inappropriate manner for a humble serving girl.

Jared seemed undaunted. "Werry plenty glad-glad meet cow-chillo, too," he replied, the wording correct, but with none of the sing-song tone that usually accompanied it. The same challenge she had seen in Matthew's eyes seemed to be echoed in his. They were a smokier color, Rachel noticed, halfway between blue and gray, and quite surprisingly pleasant.

"Jared . . . ?"

The auburn-haired woman laid a hand on his arm, and he turned with an almost dotingly fond smile. Now that Rachel could see her closer, she looked even lovelier, with a stately kind of elegance that hinted at character and good breeding. Not at all the sort she would have expected to find with a notorious womanizer like Jared Barron.

"I'm sorry, my dear. This, of course, is my brother, Matthew. And this is, uh . . . Chin-Chin. This is Mademoiselle Dominie d'Arielle."

Matthew allowed a faint smile to play with the corners of his lips. Obviously, his brother had taken a little time out for something other than trading on his voyage to the Orient. Hadn't he thought, just minutes before, that this was bound to happen sooner or later? And, judging by the absurd look on Jared's face, it had happened with more than the usual force.

"Mademoiselle? That means 'miss,' if I recall my French correctly. . . . " Which, being fluent in the language, he had no doubt he did. "And I don't see a ring on your finger, so I assume it would be premature to welcome you to the family—now. But I trust it won't be long."

Jared's head snapped back. "Now how the devil did you know that?"

"Easy. I know *you,* big brother. I knew the instant I saw the lady—even before you got around to acknowledging her—that this was it for you. And about time, I might add." He took a deep breath, then dropped his voice so the people who were beginning to gather curiously around wouldn't hear. "And you

know me, though you won't let yourself trust your
instincts. I am impulsive, I am foolish, I can be a
downright ass at times, but I am not a complete son-
of-a-bitch. I did pick up a shipload of opium in Calcutta, and I did think I was going to make my fortune
selling it in China. But I have long since changed my
mind. I destroyed some of it, as much as I could. And
when I get my hands on the rest, I'll destroy that,
too.''

He smiled suddenly, disarmingly.

"So you see, I have learned my lesson . . . even
without my big brother to spank some sense into me."

The silence that followed was long and strangely
ominous. Rachel was aware of eyes all around: Camilla's, sparkling and curious; she alone of all the
watchers had seen her friend's disguise before and
knew what was going on; the beautiful fiancée's green
eyes, looking somehow troubled; and beside her, gentle gray eyes belonging to a man with light brown hair
and somewhat softer features, but clearly the third of
the Baron trio. Alex.

If he can't accept even this—Rachel thought, her
heart in her throat as she watched Jared search his
brother's face, darkly, intently—what's going to happen when even more awful things have to be revealed?

"You give me your word," he said at last, "that
there is no opium on any of the Barron vessels?"

"Of course not. That's a preposterous question.
There is undoubtedly opium somewhere, in *somebody's* possession, on at least seven Barron ships. But
I can give you my word that there is none in my possession. I do not stand to make a profit from the sale
of any drug. Now or ever.''

Rachel had stepped up beside him, instinctively, for
support. "Little brother plenty good man," she said
softly. "Plenty stupid sometimes. Brain like miserable
good-for-nothing turtle, but heart first-chop. Werry
plenty good-good man."

"And this werry plenty good-good woman," Matthew said, making no effort to disguise the tenderness

in his voice. "No, better than good . . . She is the best."

He put an arm around her waist and drew her closer.

"Brother Jared, I'd like you to meet your new sister-in-law."

Not a sound could be heard when he finished. The band had paused briefly, and everything seemed to stop as all those eyes turned now to Jared. This time it was Rachel who was searching *his* face, waiting for some sign of the legendary temper. A Chinese bride? And a peasant? *That* would put a spot or two on the Barron reputation!

But he only ran his gaze very expertly from her hat down to her toes, and laughed.

"By God, Matt, you were always one for surprises! She looks like she'll wash up quite nicely. I congratulate you, brother. You seem to have beaten me to the altar."

Matthew grinned. "I've been waiting for years to do something better than you. Though perhaps 'better' isn't quite the word," he added with a playful glance at the fiancée, Dominie. "Equal, but first—for a change. Being seven years younger, I've always had to watch my brother do everything first. And do it so well I never measure up. It can be a strain."

Jared's manner was easy and surprisingly cordial as he turned back to Rachel.

"Now it's I who must welcome my brother's wife to the family. I'm not sure congratulations are in order—we're a most difficult family to put up with. But I expect you'll learn that as you go along, uh . . . Chin-Chin?"

The question lingered pointedly, brimming with suppressed laughter which Rachel found very hard to resist. "Wat for big brother no like 'Chin-Chin'? Werry plenty good name Chinee cow-chillo, heya?"

"Plenty good. For a Chinee cow-chillo. But I think it might be easier all around if I had your real name. And I am most curious to know what color hair is hiding under that enormous hat. I'm betting on red. Barron men have always had a weakness for red hair."

Rachel gave up with a laugh. "That's very unfair, Captain Barron. . . . Jared, if I may. And most unkind. I thought I was going to have at least a little fun with you. What gave me away?"

"Two things. In the first place, as my brother said, I *do* know him. He has always had an eye for lovely ladies. He's been looking them over quite expertly since he was twelve—"

"Eleven," Matthew protested.

"Eleven. And his taste has grown ever more discriminating. I knew that the lady he finally picked would be the loveliest of all."

"And you didn't think he would find a yellow-skinned woman lovely?" Rachel's chin went up, just a hint of defiance, which Jared either did not notice or chose to ignore.

"Quite the contrary. I wouldn't have been the least surprised if he'd shown up with a Chinese beauty—and I would have approved. But I did say there were *two* things." He ran a finger just lightly across the tips of his lashes. "Next time you might want to take a little more care with that stuff around your eyes. It's smudging—quite charmingly—and there's something lighter showing through. Yes, definitely red, I'd say."

The laughter that followed was easy and warm, and Rachel was surprised to find that the unexpected had happened. She actually liked Matthew's brother! There was about him none of the stiffness of bearing she had anticipated, nor the smug, judgmental superiority that had set her teeth on edge just thinking about it. He was strong, she sensed he could be stubborn—she had not forgotten that temper of legend—but she also sensed he was fair.

Perhaps his engagement to the beautiful French woman had mellowed him, Rachel thought. But the easy banter between the two brothers, the way each seemed to pick up instantly what the other was thinking, hinted at a longstanding affection that ran deeper than she suspected even Matthew himself knew.

And for all the drama of that one long silence, Jared *had* accepted Matthew's word about the opium.

He knew that there was something still unsaid. She could see it in the speculative looks he sent his brother's way. But he was apparently willing to wait and let Matthew bring it up in his own time.

Rachel spent the next few minutes getting to know her new family. The gray-eyed man was indeed Alex, and she found herself responding immediately to his kindness and thoughtful warmth. He seemed the quietest of the Barron men, or perhaps the most inward, and she detected just a hint of Southern softness in his speech. But beneath that somewhat gentler facade was the same strength of purpose, the same maddening iron will, and she sensed that this was a man who could be every bit as rigid as the others when it came to something he believed in.

He was going out of his way now to keep the conversation running smoothly, and Rachel fervently hoped he believed in his youngest cousin's cause. Matthew was going to need all the friends he could get when Jared found out what had happened to *China Dawn*.

It was Dominie, however, Jared's fiancée, who proved the pleasantest surprise. Not only was she delightfully charming, but she turned out to be a kindred spirit as well, for she had a much-loved brother who had also been a missionary in the Orient.

"In Vietnam. Indochina, some people call it," she said. "My brother was—is—a Jesuit."

Rachel caught a hint of defensiveness and, knowing the special bigotry that one church could reserve for another, hastened to explain that many of the black robes, as the Chinese called them, had stopped by to visit over the years. "Ours is primarily a medical mission. I've always admired the Jesuits greatly. They're men of dedication and self-sacrifice. You must be very proud of him."

"I am," Dominie replied simply, and Rachel sensed that with very little effort she had just made a friend.

She would like to have had more of a chance to speak with Dominie. She had not failed to notice that correction in tense when the young woman had spoken of her brother, nor the sadness that had come just for an instant into her face. She remembered suddenly the way Jared had sounded when he said they had been "delayed," and she had a feeling there was a good deal more of this unusual love story yet to be learned. But a crowded dance floor, with the band playing an energetic galop, hardly seemed the place.

Besides, Matthew, who had apparently changed his mind about the value of a little "pleasant chitchat," was impatient to get back to their small vessel and put on something a little more suitable.

"Darling as you look in trousers, my love," he teased, "I suspect you'd be more comfortable on the dance floor in something just a bit more graceful."

"If we get to dance," Rachel said, then caught herself with faint half-smile. "Never mind—I have a dress in my luggage that ought to do. It's not very elegant for evening wear, but I suppose everyone will forgive me. I packed rather hastily. Matthew, of course, never travels without a tailcoat and silk cravat. I think if we went to the jungles of deepest Africa, he'd tote along a full case of formal wear."

"You never know when a good party will come up," Matthew protested with the insouciance that Rachel sensed had served him well in the past. It seemed to work, for there was an almost festive air as they said goodbye, as if this were merely a happy reunion, and nothing loomed ahead to mar the rest of the evening.

Matthew turned serious only for a second as they were leaving.

"There is no more opium," he told his brother again. "We've still got a few little matters to discuss, but I can swear to that at least. There is no more opium, and there never will be again. Now, unless you want to be humiliated by a brother who looks like a beggar, I suggest you give us an hour or so to put on some fancier duds. You're looking like a fashion plate yourself."

"We Barron men have a reputation to uphold—don't we, Alex?" Jared's voice sounded guarded, but he had obviously decided not to press. "What do you say? Should we let them go get changed?"

"If we don't," Alex replied with a faint drawl, "we'll never see how much red is under that hat. Being a Barron man myself, I'm waiting with great anticipation."

Alex was still thinking of red hair as he stood alone at the edge of the dance floor, staring off in the direction where Matthew and Rachel had just disappeared. He had not failed to catch that hint of warning in his cousin's last words, but right now he was caught up in other feelings, other times.

Copper-colored hair floating on a rising wind. . . . Funny, how things could come back when you least expected them. The Barron men had always made fools of themselves over redheaded women. Old Gareth had started the tradition. One quick glimpse, and a heart lost forever. Though it looked like it might be turning out better for Jared and Matthew, at least.

"You do realize, don't you," a soft voice cooed in his ear, "that you are the last of the Barron bachelors? What a heavy burden of responsibility."

Alex looked down to see short-cropped black curls and coyly laughing violet eyes. Camilla Crale had been barely more than a child, though hardly childlike, a year ago on his last voyage East. Plump breasts pushed scandalously out of the neck of her dress, and sweetly sultry perfume exuded a raw sexuality which he recognized but had never found particularly appealing. He liked a little mystery in a woman.

"Cammie. You're all grown up, and very prettily, too. Are you still leaving a trail of broken hearts behind you?"

"I was born grown up," she said matter-of-factly. "And I do believe you're evading my question, Captain. You have to admit it's intriguing. Only *one* of you still available. . . . And talk about trails of broken hearts. . . . Or would tears be more appropriate? The Barron men are *very* popular with certain ladies, you know."

"I take it you number yourself among them. At least as far as my cousin Jared is concerned. Or do all those nasty looks at his future bride mean you're envious of her gown?"

"Her gown is atrocious," said Camilla, whose own ball dress combined silver and gold with several other colors in a most extraordinary manner. "But, yes, you might say I have rather a fancy for her fiancé. And the younger brother, too, of course. Jared has a certain, um—*basic* appeal, but Matthew is my favorite. Or *was*." She turned the full force of her eyes on his face. "Now there's only you left."

"Should I be worried?" Alex asked, amused in spite of himself. Camilla could be a catty little witch, but he rather enjoyed her prattle.

She was regarding him intently, a thing she rarely did.

"I think not. You're the handsomest of the Barron men—or Matthew, perhaps, in a different way. But when you look at me, I have a feeling sometimes you see all the way through to my soul. I don't think I want a man who can see my soul."

"Not me. I looked into a woman's soul once, and I didn't like what I saw. I don't believe I'll repeat the experience."

"So . . . you *have* been in love."

"I didn't say that." Alex picked up a cup of punch from the tray being circulated by a passing waiter and handed it to her. "Here. This will give those pretty lips something to do besides pout. I'm surprised you weren't glowering at the bride whose hair color we have yet to see under that hat. You did say Matthew was the best looking of us. Or don't you like good-looking men?"

"I *love* good-looking men." She curled her hands around the cup and lifted it almost to her mouth. "And I would have loved to have had that one. I might even have kept him. . . . But he belongs to Rachel."

"That's right. I had forgotten. I heard you were friends with the missionary's daughter." It was hard somehow, thinking of Camilla with a female friend, but she was reputed to be extremely loyal to her.

"Anyway, I had the first chance at him. Rachel gave it to me . . . for all the good it did. He turned me down—can you imagine?" Little unexpected lights of laughter showed in her eyes, no less so because the jest was on her. "Very nicely, mind you . . . *very* nicely. . . ." Her voice softened as she remembered the light touch of masculine lips on her breasts, a most unique goodbye kiss. "But very definitely. There are only two men who ever turned me down."

"And Jared was the other?" Alex guessed.

"I don't like being called a piranha. Now that I know what that is. One feels one ought to be able to return the favor." Her gaze lingered briefly on Jared Barron's beautiful fiancée across the dance floor. "Still . . . it's hard when the man doesn't care."

"And you do?"

"Oh—" She brightened, pink lips teasing as she took a sip of the punch. "I expect I've gotten over him by now. Be careful, Alex Barron. You're safe enough with me, but there are other piranhas out there. You're just the type they'd love to sink their teeth into. Such a good, decent man . . . and good, decent men get eaten alive."

She was laughing as she left. Alex didn't know if she had been having one of her rare serious moments or baiting him as usual to see his reaction. Nor did he have time to dwell on it, for the other traders were gathering around, enjoying the situation, as Camilla had, and ribbing him relentlessly about being the only Barron male yet unattached.

"*Someone* has to maintain sanity in the family," he protested with a grin. "Besides, we seem to be doing this in reverse order. Matthew is the youngest and he went first, then Jared. I, as eldest, naturally have had the sense to hold out longest."

Laughing, he extricated himself from the jovial, if overbearingly loud, bonhomie and asked Jared's fiancée if she would care to dance. She would, and the band struck up a waltz, always Alex's favorite. She was a good dancer, and so was he, and soon he had forgotten all about Camilla's dire predictions and the beautiful, man-eating piranhas waiting in his future.

Matthew and Rachel had their dance together, not under the colored lanterns with the rest of the celebrants, but outside, on the tamped-dirt path. Torchlight cast a flickering yellow glow on the same simple white dress that had seen so many of their important occasions: that first tempestuous meeting, their wedding day, and now the encounter between the two brothers that could change their lives forever.

It was a waltz again, and if the band was somewhat strident, at least the music was rhythmic and rousing, and it felt good to be in each other's arms. Rachel barely noticed the ground beneath her feet as they floated around and around, alone for the moment and completely happy. The world seemed a wonderful, magical place; even the unpleasantness that still lay ahead couldn't take that away, and the future was a dream about to come true.

This was their first waltz—their first dance—and a whole new life was dawning just over the horizon. All they had to do was conquer this one last obstacle. Then they could forget opium and stolen ships and raging brothers, and concentrate on the only thing that really mattered. Their love for each other.

She had seen a new side of her husband tonight. He had not tried to justify what he had done; he had been honest and forthright, but he had stood straight and proud before his brother. He had demanded, not asked, for his respect, and she sensed that he was ready to forfeit it if it could not be won honorably.

There was a strength in him now that had been latent before. She had felt but not seen it, and she knew that he had come to terms with his own private demons, as she had come to terms with her pain and disillusionment that night of the rioting in Canton.

"I love you very much," she said as the music stopped. "And I have never been prouder of you than I am tonight."

"Nor I of you, tiger," he said. They were still standing together, still touching in the silence. "It's not going to be easy when we go back in there."

"I know."

The music changed, a cotillion this time. One of the dances that could not be done by a couple alone.

"Do you suppose they're trying to tell us something?" Matthew teased. His hand was light on her back as guided her gently forward. "Tell me, love, have you ever watched a warehouse full of powder explode? I have. Flames and smoke everywhere. Great billows of both, spewing into the sky. It was something to see."

Eighteen

The legendary temper lived up to its reputation, though not quite in the colorfully explosive manner Matthew had predicted.

They had retired to one of the smaller tents, well in the rear, which they had for the moment to themselves, and the roar of rage Jared let out could have been heard all the way to the dance floor if the band had not been quite so boisterous. But no flames leaped into the air, no sparks came from his nostrils; there were no great billowing puffs of smoke, and the silence that followed that one brief outburst was more terrifying than all the shouting and recriminations Rachel had imagined.

Jared Barron simply stood there, jaws clenched, blue-gray eyes unblinking, as Matthew related everything that had transpired from the time he left the *China Dawn* in the small cove with his thieving Irish partner to the moment he saw Damian Varnay and four good men getting out of a chop boat on the docks at Canton.

"Gallagher had sent him a message," Matthew concluded. "In a blasted cunning imitation of my own handwriting! I still don't know why he did it. I suppose he must have heard of my marriage, though that wasn't general knowledge. But with all the rumors of Lord-knows-what going on in Canton, it wasn't unreasonable to believe that I might be in trouble. I can't fault Varnay for being duped. I don't hold him responsible for any of this."

"Nor do I," Jared replied in an ominously even voice. "But I do hold you responsible. That ship was under your command. You had no business leaving her with your so-called partner, even if you thought he wasn't going to pull any tricks. God only knows where she is now, or in what shape. Or how I'm supposed to get her back.''

"She's up the coast,'' Matthew said quietly. "About five or six days' journey if the wind is right, and in good shape so far. And *I* am going to get her back, without any damage. She is, as you pointed out, my command. You can help if you want, Jared. I'd be glad to have you with me—I can always use an extra man. But this is my operation. It's going to be handled my way.''

"The devil it is!'' Jared had begun to pace, back and forth, taut with anger that threatened to erupt at any moment. "I came here with our grandfather's authorization to act as his agent in *everything*! The orders come from me now. I can relieve you of your command any time I choose. And I will.''

Alex had taken a step forward, as if to intervene, but Matthew waved him back with an abrupt gesture.

"I don't give a damn what you do,'' he retorted, raising his voice for the first time. "Or what Grandfather says! I'm going after the *China Dawn*—with or without you. I have the men, and I have the boats. They were already waiting when I arrived in the harbor. We're going to be heading up the coast whether you like it or not. It'll be easier if we work together. We'll have a hell of a lot better chance of getting the *China* back intact. But that's up to you.''

"You sound like you have a plan,'' Alex interjected hastily, attempting to ease the potential quarrel into practical channels. "Based on fact, or wishful thinking?''

"A little of both,'' Matthew admitted, his sense of humor returning as he saw how close he had come to flying into a fury himself. It seemed there was no middle ground with him. Either he stood in helpless awe of his brother's superiority, or he had to try and match him in the famous Barron rages! "But mostly the former. I know Gallagher. I know what makes him tick.

And I know his weaknesses. Which aren't many, but they are glaring.''

"If you know him so well," Jared said, stopping his pacing long enough to glower at his brother, ''how the hell did you let him get your ship? If you had half a brain, you'd have stayed where you belonged and not gone—''

"If he had," Rachel broke in, completely forgetting that this wasn't her fight and she had vowed to let Matthew handle it in his own way, ''we would never have gone to Canton, and a good part of the city would have been destroyed. You may not like what he did— you may hate it—but thousands of people would have died if he hadn't figured out a way to thwart Steven Wu's plot. Maybe you think your ship is worth more than some yellow-skinned wretches living in squalor, but I don't. What Matthew did took more than 'half a brain,' and a lot of courage! And if you aren't proud of him, I am!''

There was a fraction of a second's silence, and Rachel had an awful feeling she had just made things a thousand times worse. Then, unexpectedly, Alex began to laugh.

"She has you there, Jared. Barron men not only have a weakness for red hair, they have a definite penchant for the spirit that goes with it. It may have been blind luck, but Matthew was in the right place at the right time. . . . And maybe that was the place he ought to have been. He was accountable for the opium he had brought into the country. And the risk to the *China* must have seemed slight.''

Jared did not reply immediately. His face was dark and brooding, and Rachel, watching, felt her heart sink again. The Barron pride, which she had only glimpsed occasionally in her husband, seemed to be a driving force in this man's character. And for the Barrons, pride was all wrapped up in the tall, swift ships that bore their banner. He would never forgive Matthew for losing the jewel of that arrogant fleet!

But his expression changed, subtly, and Rachel realized that, like his brother, Jared Barron had an in-

finite capacity for doing the unexpected. If that was
not exactly a smile playing at the corners of his mouth,
it was not a grimace, either.

"You said you had a plan?" He seated himself at a
round wooden table, still littered with ashes and drinks
from the gentlemen who had occupied it previously.

Matthew nodded. He wasted no time acknowledging that slight concession. "Gallagher was relieved of
a load of opium a while ago. It was his second try at
smuggling, and they made him look like a damned
fool." He and Alex took places beside Jared at the
table, while Rachel busied herself clearing away the
clutter. She didn't want to be tempted to break her
resolve again; she had gotten away with it once, but it
would be foolish to press her luck again. "Gallagher's
not the sort to give up gracefully. He's a vain popin-
jay—rather like the fellow who used to be his captain.
He doesn't like being bested. He's going to be waiting
for something of the same kind to be pulled on him
again."

"Which was . . . ?" Alex leaned forward, interested.

"As it was described to me, a group of sampans
threatened the bow of his vessel. About fifteen or
twenty, I'd guess. While he was busy 'swatting them
like gnats,' two war junks came up from the stern and
blew him out of the water. Probably literally, though
I notice he had time to lower a boat and get away."

"And you think he'll be expecting the same trick
again?" Alex said thoughtfully.

"I know it. Gallagher was mad. He tried to pretend
it didn't matter, but he was mad—and he'll be looking
for a chance to even the score. I thought I just might
arrange it for him. Rachel sent a message ahead to one
of her brothers to get us some boats with native crews.
We're a couple of days early; there are only ten sampans and not as many men as I hoped for, but we can
make do. I have one junk left from, uh—a previous
venture. And the lorcha I'm using now is junk-
rigged."

"So, when a group of sampans approach the bow of the *China Dawn*—"

"Gallagher's going to run hellbent for vengeance to the stern. And see a pair of junks bearing down on him! He's going to be so blasted eager to return the previous favor, he won't stop to think that he's leaving one section of the vessel extremely vulnerable."

"Midships seaward . . ." Now it was Jared who was leaning in.

"Landward," Matthew corrected. "The ship is anchored in a small inlet. The shore's rocky, but not inaccessible—Gallagher has to worry about an attack from that side. He's positioned the ship starboard out, so the lifeboats are more protected, facing the sea. A natural mistake, and Romack, the only mate left, isn't sharp enough to pick up on it. When the sampans appear on the horizon, men will gather fore and aft, with at least a couple in position to guard the lifeboats—that's the only means of escape if things get rough again. But there's not going to be anyone near the port side, toward land. All I have to do is get on the ship. The men know me. They're used to my command. Hell, they probably don't even know they've been pirated!"

"You might be able to keep them occupied," Jared admitted. "But they're still going to see a boat approaching. And don't count on every crewman being on your side. You'd make a damned inviting target."

"Yes, in a boat . . . but if there happened to be a rope dangling over the port side, down into the water, and if I happened to be a strong swimmer, which I am . . ."

Jared eyed him cautiously. "Just how would this rope *happen* to get there?"

"Any number of ways. The most obvious is probably the best. A party of natives clambering on board, selling fish or fresh vegetables, something like that . . . big eyed with curiosity and crawling all over everything. It happens all the time. And there are ropes coiled up in several places on deck."

Jared was quiet for a moment, seemingly mulling it

over. Then he leaned back in his chair and, very slowly, said:

"I'm a strong swimmer, too. And every one of those men is going to recognize Jared Barron. They'll follow me as readily as you."

"Or me," Alex cut in, heading off the volatile situation before it could get started. "I'm a better swimmer than either of you. It might as well be me—and in fact, it will probably be all three of us. I can think of three trouble spots that need to be controlled—fore, aft, and midships starboard—and it had better be done quickly or we're asking for trouble. It doesn't matter *who* climbs up that rope, or who's in charge. What's important is recapturing the *China Dawn*. At least, I thought it was."

Jared seemed to relax slightly.

"Point well taken." He gave Matthew a long, steady look. "All right, little brother. The plan is yours, and it looks like it has possibilities. We'll do it your way. . . . But God help you if it doesn't work."

The men split up hurriedly, wasting no time on unnecessary conversation as they left the tent and started separately down the paths. Jared, anxious to pick up detailed maps of the China coast that only he could locate, headed for the *Shadow Dawn* at the far end of the harbor, and it was left to Alex to make his brother's apologies to Dominie and see her safely back to their quarters. The two would meet later at the junk, which would be under their command, but would be crewed visibly by three of the fifteen Chinese at their disposal.

It worried Matthew a little as he and Rachel made their way back past the dance floor toward his own vessel that they were going to be so badly shorthanded. More men would almost certainly be arriving in the morning, and at least half a dozen sampans, but they couldn't afford to wait even one more day. There was always the chance that Gallagher would move the *China Dawn*, however unlikely it seemed. Or that his smuggling operations might be discovered and the war junks would decide to make an example of him.

"I wish your brother could have gotten here a little sooner," he said as they reached the dance floor and hesitated briefly at the edge. "We could use a man like Sam Todd, though maybe it's just as well. What I've got in mind could be risky. I'd hate to have to try to explain to your parents why I let anything happen to him."

"Almost as unpleasant as explaining to your brother what happened to the precious Barron flagship?" she teased. "Sam can take care of himself, and I don't think it's going to be all that dangerous. But he is good in a tight spot. I'd feel better myself if he were with us."

Matthew stopped to look at her. Gently swinging paper lanterns cast changing patterns of light and color on her face.

"Not us, tiger . . . me. I got myself into this mess. It's something I have to get myself out of. Alone. Whatever the risk, I'm not going to expose you to it, too."

"I thought you wanted to share your life with me." Rachel's head tilted back, a warning that came a second too late, and Matthew realized he should not have been quite so plain in his intentions. "Isn't that what marriage is all about? Sharing the difficult as well as the easy? Or do you just want to share your bed and have someone to act as hostess at your dinner table? Because if that's the kind of wife you had in mind, you picked the wrong woman. I want to be a partner in this marriage . . . or nothing at all!"

Matthew stared at the indignation that flashed out of her eyes and tried to imagine what he had done to deserve it. Surely she didn't think any man would allow his wife to become involved in something so reckless? And for no reason, except that she didn't want to be relegated to hostessing at dinner!

He started to put his foot down, firmly. Then, remembering what had happened earlier that evening when he tried to say no, he decided a different strategy might be in order.

"Very well," he said. "I don't have time to argue. I suppose it can't hurt anything. As you said, it probably won't be dangerous. But you've got to promise to stay out of the way and do what you're told."

"Oh . . . I think I can manage that," Rachel replied, smiling to herself. It would look like a very pleased smile to him—and in fact, it was. She knew her husband so much better than he knew her, and she knew that he had no intention of taking her with him. It did not suit his masculine image of himself to share anything like danger or trouble with his wife.

And it didn't suit her independent image of herself to be left behind like an excess piece of baggage!

She was still smiling a moment later when he left her with Camilla and went off for a chat with Captain Rawlings. "A little business that needs tending to while I'm gone," he explained. "I'll just be a minute."

"Men are so transparent, aren't they?" she said under her breath as she watched them move a discreet distance away and begin speaking earnestly. "And so foolish. . . . We always see through them."

Camilla looked amused. "I gather they're not discussing business?"

"They're discussing me, actually," Rachel told her. "I need your help, Cammie. Matthew is telling your handsome swain to keep me occupied for a couple of hours. Just long enough so he can get out of the harbor with his brother and cousin. No doubt, I'm supposed to be dumped with some safe chaperone who can watch me while he's gone."

"And you, of course, have no intention of letting him get away with that."

"Of course. I intend to be safely stowed away in one of the accompanying sampans until it's too late to send me back. But I have to throw my watchdog off the track first. Be a friend, Cammie—tell Captain Rawlings I'm going to be with you for a while. You could be showing me the new house in Happy Valley.

Is it ready yet? A carriage ride there, a tour of the grounds, and back again—that should be just about the right amount of time.''

Camilla's lower lip went out, an instinctive gesture which worked well with the opposite sex but had little effect on her friend. ''You know I love you dearly, Rae, but I did have more entertaining plans for the rest of the evening.''

''Oh, for heaven's sake, Cammie!'' Rachel retorted, exasperated. ''Can't you ever get your mind up from between your legs? I only need you for a couple of hours. Then you can go back to whatever you had planned with my blessing!''

She half expected Camilla to be annoyed, but the girl only laughed.

''I think you've been spending too much time with me. Your speech is really becoming quite vulgar. I'm sorry. Of course you're right. I'll let Aaron tell me all about your Matthew's plans, and then I'll volunteer to help him by taking you out to Happy Valley. I'm sure he can arrange to find us a coach.''

''You don't think he'll insist on escorting us?'' Rachel said, apprehensive.

''Not Aaron.'' The mischievous sparkle in Camilla's eyes was hard to resist. ''He'll be glad enough to be relieved of the burden your husband put on his shoulders, and female prattle would bore him to tears. Besides, I don't think he'll mind very much if I promise to drop you off wherever you're supposed to go an hour or two before I'm due to go back to my own rather lax chaperone.''

They were laughing quite merrily as the men came back. Rachel could almost see Matthew patting himself on the back at how well his clever scheme was going.

''Why don't you stay here for a while, love?'' he suggested magnanimously. ''It'll be dawn before we're ready to sail, maybe even later. It would be a shame for you to miss the rest of the party. I'm sure Rawlings here and Camilla will look after you.''

''What a lovely idea.'' Rachel put on her most in-

genuous look as she laid a hand lightly on his arm.
"And so thoughtful. I believe I will, at least for a
short time. I'll be along soon. . . . Don't leave without me."

"I wouldn't dream of it," he said.

Rachel managed to stay out of sight on one of the
sampans the following day. Matthew had forgotten that
the men Sam Todd would have recruited were men
who had also worked with her; some had even been in
her own group that night of the fateful raid on the
junk. They knew and liked her, better than they knew
and liked her husband, and it had not been difficult to
find one who would agree to keep her hidden in a pile
of old quilts and baskets in his small cabin.

The winds continued strong throughout the day, and
they made good time. Matthew's lorcha pulled even
with them occasionally, and while he was careful to
remain concealed from eyes that might be watching on
shore, she caught glimpses of him now and then. He
had shaved off his beard again, and she felt a little
pang as she remembered that she was the one who had
teased him to grow it back.

It was as if she were completely forgotten now that
he was back in the all-male world of Barron rivalries
and Barron pride. All he cared about was getting the
China Dawn back. No, she thought, not just getting it
back—getting it back *his* way! Being a hero in front
the others. Proving himself once and for all.

The winds died down by dusk, and unable to pro-
ceed any further, the men put into a shallow bay to
check their maps and get some sleep. Rachel waited
until Matthew had gone on board the junk to confer
with his brother and cousin, then transferred to the
lorcha and went into the cabin to wait a little nervously
for him to return.

Fortunately, her luggage was still there. Matthew
had neglected in his haste to put it off someplace where
it could be delivered to her. She pulled out the crimson
silk outfit he had always loved and slipped it on. Or
rather, she slipped on the shirt, fastening it with a

long, tasseled sash, and brushed her hair so it fell in a soft reddish-gold cloud to her shoulders.

He was going to be angry. She knew that, and she was already beginning to have qualms about the impulsive decision it was too late to undo. But he loved her enough to forgive her, no matter how outrageously she behaved. At least, she hoped he did.

Still . . . it wouldn't hurt to remind him that there were certain compensations for the nuisance of having to bring a wife along.

Her heart thumped in her chest when she heard his footsteps on the deck, and just for a second, her confidence left her. What if she had gone too far this time? What if he hated her for what she had done? This was Barron business; it was a Barron ship that had been lost, and there was no place on that arrogant Barron team for women and their foolishness. Jared's fiancée had been dumped as unceremoniously as she—even more so, for it was Alex who had been sent to say goodbye—and she hadn't made a fuss!

What if he was so furious he *never* forgave her?

But his eyes, in that first unguarded moment, held none of the anger Rachel had expected. Just a flicker of surprise, and before he brought it under control again, something very like pleasure.

He was glad to see her. Her heart soared, and it was all she could do to keep from laughing with sheer relief. The anger would come later. He would berate her. He would tell her that she had no business being there, that he didn't want her—but he would never make her believe it.

He *did* want her—as much as she wanted to be there with him—and she was not going to let him forget it.

"I told you not to go without me," she reminded him. "And you said you wouldn't dream of it."

His face darkened into the expression she had expected before.

"I'll have Rawlings' hide for this. . . ."

"No, you won't. Cammie told him I was going to be with her. She can be very persuasive when she wants. Captain Rawlings didn't stand a chance."

"I'll have her hide, too," he said, but the moment had passed, and a hint of humor was sneaking back into his voice.

"She'd *love* that," Rachel teased. "But I don't think I can allow it. Cammie's hide is much too pretty." She held out her hand and smiled as he came and sat beside her on the bed. "I know you're glad to see me. It's no use pretending. I saw the way you looked at me when you came in the door."

"I'm always glad to see you, tiger, even when I shouldn't be. And I don't pretend."

"You did last night, at the ball. When you said you weren't going to leave until dawn, and I could stay and have a pleasant chat with Cammie."

"I didn't *pretend*. I lied—something you do yourself with considerable aplomb when you believe the occasion warrants it. Unfortunately, I don't seem to be quite as good at it as you." He ran the side of his finger down her cheek, a surprisingly tender gesture, and one that hurt somehow, as if she had taken advantage of his love. "You're going back in the morning, Rae. I'm sorry, but you are. This isn't the time for games. There's too much at stake."

"I wasn't trying to play games," she protested somewhat guiltily. "I told you—I want to be a partner in this marriage. That means *equal*, Matthew. I don't want to be shut out. Besides, it's too late to turn back now. Even if the wind picks up again, you'd lose two days. And I doubt very much that you have enough confidence in any of the men to send me back with them."

"No, but I can take you myself," he said. "And I will. Jared and Alex can manage without me. You're the most precious thing in my life. I would never let anything happen to you. But dammit, Rae—it isn't fair! You *knew* how important this was to me."

There was enough anguish in his voice to make her feel even guiltier. Rachel longed to reach out and clasp his hands, as much to take as give comfort, but she wasn't sure her touch would be welcome. She was the most precious thing in his life, he had said. More precious even than that infuriating Barron pride.

But he was the most precious thing in her life, too, and she would hate herself forever if she hurt him so badly.

"Did you know," she said softly, "that the men Sam sent are all men he met while working with Steven Wu? In the early days, before the *tong* became so deadly. He must have been suspicious, even without hearing what happened in Canton, because the ones he chose are those with the loosest ties to their leader. But I think, in two cases, he made a mistake."

"No . . ." Matthew admitted slowly. "I didn't know."

"One of the two was probably with Steven in Canton. I didn't see him clearly, so I can't be sure. And I might be wrong about the other. He just makes me uncomfortable somehow. So you see, my love, I really can be helpful if you let me stay. I'll recognize things you won't. And I'm very good at picking up bits and pieces of other people's conversations in Chinese. If you need someone to spy on the crew—"

"Then I can enlist one of the more reliable men," Matthew reminded her. "Pidgin may be inexact, but I'll get across what I want to know. And he can communicate what he heard."

"Yes, but which one will you trust? The head of the two-man crew on your lorcha?" His reaction told Rachel she had guessed right. "But he's the man I just told you about. The one with Steven in Canton."

Matthew put one hand under her chin and tilted her face up. "You're not making this up, tiger? Or exaggerating to prove your point?"

"No." She was very conscious of his hand still touching her face. She longed to turn, just a little, and brush it with her lips, but she was afraid of pushing too hard. "And if that man's here, it means his leader might be somewhere nearby. You're going to need all the eyes and ears you can get. Steven Wu is an enemy much more to be reckoned with than your two-timing partner."

"All the more reason to get you back to Hong Kong," Matthew started to say. But this time she did take his hand, and was pressing it against her lips.

"You said before I was not being fair, and I wasn't. But you're not being fair, either. I'm much more capable than most of the men you brought with you. I can do my share, and then some. But because I'm a woman, you're not even going to allow me to try!"

"You're not just a woman, tiger . . . you're *my* woman. Do you have any idea how I would feel watching you put yourself into danger?"

"Do you have any idea how *I* feel when you do the same thing? Is my heart somehow immune to fear and the need to protect, just because I'm a woman? Or is it simply that it's a woman's place to wait and pray while her men go into battle, and if they don't come home again—well, that's the lot of women, after all?"

Matthew squirmed a little uneasily. "You're twisting things around . . ."

"I am not." Her voice was low in her throat, deliberately sultry. "I'm stating the truth. Very clearly. You just don't like it."

No, Matthew admitted to himself, he didn't. But he sensed she was right. He was the man—he wanted to make the decisions, take the risks. Just as he needed to compete with his brother to see who was going to be in charge. And he sensed both were equally pointless.

Marriage *was* a partnership. At least, any kind of marriage that would hold his interest for the rest of his life.

"I don't know . . ." he said. But he did, and they were both aware that she had won.

"I can stay, then?" She had moved closer, the supple softness of her body disturbingly tantalizing. Matthew appreciated her restraint in not using her sensuality before, when it would have been such a telling weapon.

"It's not my decision alone. I have a brother and a cousin who may be none too pleased to find you here. We'll see in the morning."

He was untying the long silken sash. The shirt come open, and she was arching toward him, all warmth and sweet, flowery perfume. Matthew was vaguely aware that he was not nearly as reluctant as he should have been at the thought of letting her stay.

Her lips parted; a pink, very provocative temptation.

"Have we just had our first quarrel, husband?"

"I think so," he admitted.

"Then . . ." Rachel ran her tongue lightly around the contours of his mouth, savoring the man-taste of him, "this is our first chance to make up."

She heard the sound of his laughter, very soft, as he surrendered.

"A most interesting opportunity. . . . We'll have to make the most of it."

Nineteen

Rachel met with surprisingly little resistance the next morning when she put on a pale blue dress with a demure neckline and prim, puffed sleeves and followed Matthew over to the junk, where his brother and cousin were already up and ready to sail. Alex balked briefly at the idea of allowing her to come along, but after a quick consideration of the alternatives, each of which seemed more unpalatable than the last, he gave in quite easily, almost with a twinkle in his eye.

"When I mentioned that Barron men are fond of the spirit that goes with red hair," he said, "I didn't expect it to be carried to this extreme. But I daresay it won't do any harm. We aren't expecting serious trouble, and the lady looks like she can take care of herself. What do you say, Jared?"

Rachel threw an anxious look at Matthew's unpredictable brother, but he only grinned.

"Why not? I'm used to strong-willed women by now. I ought to be, by God! And I have a feeling this one might actually come in handy. We could use someone who knows the country and speaks the language."

Alex had to agree. "Especially if you're right about this man, Wu," he said to Rachel. "We aren't anticipating trouble, as I said. Our main concern is to get the *China Dawn* back without damage. But it doesn't hurt to be prepared."

"I think," Matthew added unnecessarily, "that means we're all agreed. You can stay. But only if you promise to behave, tiger."

Rachel not only promised, she made very sure that she continued to behave primly and didn't raise any eyebrows throughout the long morning and afternoon that followed. The last thing she wanted was for them to change their minds and force Matthew to take her back to Hong Kong.

As it turned out, their main concern at that point seemed to be not the rescue operation itself, but the state of the wind, which alternated between calm and barely stirring. It was beginning to look, as Matthew pointed out to her, like they'd be lucky to make five or six miles by nightfall.

Restless as the men were becoming, however, Rachel found herself enjoying their leisurely pace. She spent part of the day on the lorcha with her husband, and part on the junk, getting better acquainted with Alex and Jared, particularly the latter, who was keeping a close eye on shore from the shadows in the stern while his cousin pored over maps in the cabin.

Jared proved an easy conversationalist, with a good gift for telling a story, and Rachel quickly learned why he was used to strong-willed women. He had met his fiancée off the coast of imperial Vietnam, and they had gone into the jungles together to search for her brother, who, as a foreigner and a priest, risked death every day he remained.

Rachel listened wide-eyed as Jared explained that the Emperor, the Vietnamese Son of Heaven, had turned against the very people who had helped to re-unify the north and south of his land after centuries of separation—the French priests—and had issued an edict outlawing them. He and Dominie had been terrifyingly aware that her brother would be captured and executed if they couldn't rescue him in time, and indeed it was only her knowledge of that country and its language that had enabled them to survive themselves.

Even for Rachel, who had always considered herself adventurous, it seemed an incredibly bold thing to do, and she marveled, not only at Dominie's courage and self-sacrifice, but the fact that Jared Barron, with all his fierce male pride, had not been afraid to fall in love with a woman whose mind and abilities clearly rivaled his own.

"Did you find him?" she asked quietly. "Dominie's brother?"

"Briefly," Jared replied. "But he was dedicated to his cause. He wouldn't have fled with us, even had he been able to. He's still there. Or was. In all probability, he's dead by now. I think Dominie knows that, but she can't bring herself to give up hope."

Rachel turned her head to stare at the water behind the silently gliding junk. So placid, it almost looked like glass, broken only by a pair of sampans dragging a fishing net between them. She remembered the sadness she had seen in the other woman's face, and she couldn't imagine what it would feel like if she had to accept the death of one of her own beloved brothers, or Cammie, who had been like a sister to her. Dominie's heart must feel as if it were being torn apart.

And Jared had just gone off and left her! He loved her, clearly, but he had left anyway, at a time when she had to be needing him desperately. What was it with these Barron men and their consuming need to stand taller and stronger than the rest of the world? They were so wrapped up in themselves, in their ships and their masculine passion for power, they lost sight of what was really important. Would they ever learn? she wondered. Or was it up to their wives and sweethearts to learn to live with their obsessions?

Her eyes picked out a man on one of the sampans, and she was startled by a brief flicker of recognition. He was clad in blue, like the others, with a large straw hat concealing his head, but something in his movements seemed vaguely familiar, though she wasn't quite sure what it was.

Then she realized, and in spite of herself, she started to laugh.

She had thought for one split second it was Steven Wu. Now, looking closer, she saw that he didn't have short hair at all, but a long queue down his back. And he wasn't moving like Steven any more. One similar gesture, that was all it had been, and even that was gone now. She had been letting her imagination run away with her.

She turned to find Jared watching her intently.

"You are welcome to stay, Rachel," he said. "More than welcome—we are pleased to have you with us. But you promised before that you would do what you were told. I hope you meant it. If Matt has to worry about you, he's not going to have his mind on what he's doing. And that could be disastrous. For him and for us."

"I know," Rachel admitted.

"You swear to it, then? You give your solemn oath that you will obey orders, whether you like them or not?"

Rachel hesitated. If she gave her word, she would have to keep it, and she sensed he knew that. But what he was asking was not unreasonable, after all. And she probably deserved that subtly implied rebuke.

"My solemn oath," she said.

They anchored that night in a shallow bay which looked to Rachel much like the place they had spent the night before. The wind was rising, but the coast would be treacherous for the next several miles, with unpredictable currents and outcroppings of rock, and they dared not travel with only a sliver of moon to light their way.

Most of the evening was spent on a short strip of beach. The sky seemed especially dark and brooding; the sea vanished away into nothingness, and there was a sinister sound to the howling of the wind and the hissing and crackling of a fire that was being allowed to die down to coals. Damian Varnay had joined them, and the ship's carpenter, Moody, a big brusque man with a bellowing voice, but the other crewmen and most of the Chinese were on their vessels. Matthew had apparently taken her warnings about Steven Wu seriously, for Rachel noticed that he posted sentries at several places on the rocks behind them.

She also noticed that one of the men was Li Shu, on whose sampan she had chosen to hide on that first day. Obviously, her husband trusted her judgment, she thought with a smile she took care to hide. She wasn't proving to be a *total* nuisance.

"We're agreed, then?" Matthew was saying in a low, steady voice. Rachel had been listening to the men go over their strategy step by step for the last two hours. Matthew, as commander of the lost ship, was still nominally in charge, but his brother was watching him closely, as if judging everything he did. "We make our move between three and three-thirty in the morning. Almost the end of the night watch. The men on duty will be getting drowsy—it's their least alert time—and everyone else will still be asleep. That should give us a few extra minutes."

Alex nodded. "The light will be perfect. There should be a little less than a quarter moon when we get there, if the wind keeps up like this. Just bright enough so the men on board will spot the sampans right away. But they won't be able to make out much in the shadowy parts of the deck."

"We're going to have to move fast," Jared warned. "At least some of the men are going to be armed. Probably Gallagher's hand-picked crew. We damned well better hope they're still in shock when we reach them if we want to get some weapons for ourselves."

"Once the alarm sounds," Alex agreed, "there are going to be guns all over the place. That doesn't give us much time."

"God help those poor devils in the sampans if we haven't got things under control before they can do any damage," Jared added grimly. "The junks are in better shape. They can fire back if they have to. But I sure as hell don't want to blast holes in the *China Dawn*!"

Matthew ran his hand unconsciously over his chin. It was the weakest part in the plan, and the one that worried him most. Swimming out to the ship meant they were going to be armed with just knives and fists. The only way to get a gun was to jump someone for it.

But two-man teams ought to give them an advantage,

he reminded himself. And surprise would be on their side.

"We should be able to swim out in about the time it takes the crew to pull on their trousers and get up on deck. The ship's anchored dangerously close to shore—I suppose to make smuggling easier—but it's going to prove a costly mistake for Gallagher. Add another minute or two to get up the rope—"

"And I'm the first," growled Damian Varnay. He wasn't usually so forward, but he was still angry. His pride had been wounded, and he was itching to vindicate himself. "When I get my hands on that smooth-talking Irish son-of-a-bitch snake, there won't be enough left of him to feed to the fish!"

Jared allowed himself a chuckle. He understood only too well how the first mate felt. "I don't blame you, but I'm first up, and Moody right behind me. We've got to take care of the gunners in the bow before anyone gets hurt. You and Matt are next—you'll have to fight *him* for position. I imagine he's as anxious as you to settle a few things with his former partner."

The men continued to talk, going over the plan again and again, making sure nothing had been left out. It should be a fairly simple operation; the risks were few, but they were there, and they had to be taken into consideration.

Only three trouble spots stood out, the three places where guns were likely to be a factor, and it was around these places that the plan centered. Two men would go immediately fore, two to the stern, where Gallagher was almost certain to be taking his stand against the oncoming junks, and two would see to the lifeboats on the starboard side. A seventh man, the lookout, would take his position high on the main mast.

It had not been easy finding seven men who could swim well enough to get out to the ship. Sailors were notorious for hating the water, and Damian Varnay, no exception, could barely paddle in a circle. But what he lacked in talent, he made up in sheer will—he had been so eager to go, he had thrown himself in the water fully clothed and splashed around for twenty minutes until the others agreed to take him.

The fifth man was Moody, who, fortunately, had grown up on a riverbank. For the other two, they had had to recruit the only Chinese among the party who admitted to knowing how to swim.

One was the man Rachel thought she had seen in Canton, though he would be in the least troublesome spot, with Alex, tending to the lifeboats on the starboard, seaward side. And the other, at least, was Li Shu, who, though he couldn't manage even the most rudimentary pidgin, knew quite a number of shrill, very distinct whistles, and would make an excellent lookout.

Rachel got up restlessly and, feeling strangely left out, wandered away from the firelight. The night seemed even darker, but it was almost warm, with promises of spring in the air. The men had been very cordial to her, when they thought about it, and unfailingly polite, but it was clear that she had no place in their plans.

There was a cluster of rocks a few yards away, blocking off the south end of the beach, and she took a few steps in that direction. Out of the firelight, it was barely visible, more like a deeper patch of shadow against the slightly more luminous tones of the sky.

She wasn't being altogether reasonable, she knew. Matthew, too, had made concessions that must have cut deeply. He had wanted very much to go on that rescue mission alone—he had argued long and hard that he could do it—but in the end, he had had to give in to the more cautious inclinations of the others.

Still, it *did* seem unfair. Rachel brushed back a wisp of hair that the wind had pulled out of its pins. She could swim better than either of the Chinese they had chosen, and she knew as many whistles as Li Shu, but they wouldn't even *consider* using her.

And she couldn't insist, because she had given Matthew's brother her solemn oath that she would obey orders and not create any problems!

A faint movement startled her, as if the rocks were

shifting, and Rachel had a sudden sense that someone was there, listening in on the conversation. She spun around and signaled swiftly to the men by the fire.

Jared was up almost instantly, followed by Moody, but by the time they reached the rocks, no one was there. Lanterns were fetched and the area searched thoroughly for some time before they finally gave up. Not a footprint had been discovered, and Rachel was beginning to feel more than a little foolish as she watched them douse the fire and prepare to head back to the ships.

No wonder they didn't take her seriously. They were being very kind about it. Jared in particular went out of his way to remind her that the ground was solid there—a man wouldn't necessarily leave traces if he was making an effort to be careful—but she knew they had to think she was imagining things.

And, in fact, she was beginning to think so herself. Just like she had let her imagination get wildly out of hand that afternoon. The south end of the beach was where Li Shu had been positioned as sentry. Li Shu was much too reliable to have dozed off and let someone slip through. And he was the one Chinese she was sure they could trust.

Rachel stood alone at the edge of the water, looking back at Jared and Matthew as they finished with the fire and came toward her, side-by-side. They were so alike, and yet so different. Both strong, both stubborn, both vulnerable, though they would never admit it, but they needed such opposing things from each other. Her heart ached suddenly, and she was very tired.

Would they ever settle matters between them? she wondered. It was hard to imagine, coming from a large, demonstrative family, where affection and laughter were a part of every day, that two brothers could have let such a wall come up between them.

Jared had shown restraint thus far. He had acknowledged Matthew's plan to be reasonable. He had let him take the lead for the time being. But she sensed a tenseness in his manner, in the way he could not keep from pacing sometimes, as if the tension inside was straining to come out. She was terribly afraid, when they came to the end and it was time to act, that he would reach out and grasp the authority again, if for no other reason than because he was used to having it.

And she was afraid that Matthew, for all the control he had shown so far, would react with anger and bitterness, and the rift between them deepen until it could never be healed.

The night remained dark. The fire was long dead, the beach a barely perceptible ribbon of sand outlined by the frothy edges of gently crashing waves.

The sentry Li Shu stepped out from behind the rocks. It was a forbidden act. He had been given strict orders to stay at his post, but no one was there to see his disobedience or punish him for it.

And what was the use of guarding the area behind when he knew what was there?

It was strange the way the *fan-quai*, the foreign devils, thought. If a man looked sharp, they watched him constantly, the way a hawk circled round and round, eying a lone rabbit on the ground. But if he looked amiable and dull-witted and smiled a big, gap-toothed grin, they thought he was a gentle soul and trusted without question.

Didn't it occur to them that it took more wits for a bright man to appear stupid than for a stupid one to pretend to be smart? That sort of thing happened every day.

But they were just turtledung barbarians. Li Shu spat between his missing teeth onto the ground. What could one expect from such miserable good-for-nothing lumps of dogmeat?

He heard a sound behind him. Half a whistle, half a hiss. It was the sound he had been expecting, and he turned just in time to see a shadowy figure emerge from the mass of darkness that was the rocks.

The conflict Rachel had imagined between the two brothers was not to materialize, and for a reason no one could possibly have anticipated. Word reached them the following evening that Jared's beautiful French fiancée had been abducted at the point of a gun.

The Chinese messenger who brought the news had traveled day and night, risking rocks and rough water to catch up with them, and he was exhausted almost to the point of collapse as he squatted beside a single lantern in the camp they had made on shore. He seemed to Rachel half paralyzed with fear; apparently he had heard of the famous Barron temper.

It did not show now. Jared said nothing, though his face was ashen as he hastily gathered together his belongings and prepared to transfer to the other man's vessel. Rachel, listening—and translating when the awkward attempts at pidgin failed—was relieved to realize that the situation was nowhere near as dire as it sounded.

It appeared that Dominie had been taken by a former fiancé, an elderly man who obviously doted on her. He had come halfway around the world because he feared for her safety when he heard of her frantic attempt to rescue her brother. Clearly, he meant her no harm. He probably thought Jared was some blackguard who had abducted her himself, and he was saving her from a fate worse than death.

Still, she had to be frightened and feeling desperately alone. Rachel's heart went out again to the young Frenchwoman so far from home. She had a man who loved her, deeply and passionately, as every woman longed to be loved. But heaven help her, he was a Barron man, which meant that his love was buried sometimes beneath an avalanche of pride and ships and family rivalries!

Only this time, it seemed that Jared was finally getting the point. He had learned the hard way, and the woman he loved was paying the price for it.

"I'm a damn fool, Alex. A damn fool! I had everything I wanted. Everything I've *ever* wanted, and I risked it all for . . . what? To show how rugged and forceful I am? To prove that Barron Shipping can't do without me?''

His cousin generously ignored the obvious reply—which hovered temptingly on the tip of Rachel's tongue—and did his best to reassure him, instead. They were alone for the moment with the Chinese boatman, the lantern casting garish yellow light up on faces that looked gaunt and eerily unreal. Matthew had gone to see to the vessel that would take them back down the coast and make sure it was stocked for the return voyage.

''She's a fighter, cousin,'' Alex reminded him. ''She's feisty and she's strong—a man would have to go some length to put anything over on her. Besides, you're forgetting, he took her back to the *Scarlet*,'' he added, alluding to the fact that Dominie and her captor had been seen boarding another of the Barron vessels, bound for the Hawaiian Islands. ''Newcombe is one of our best captains. He won't let anything happen to her.''

But Jared wasn't about to let himself off so easily, and it was all Rachel could do to keep from agreeing out loud. Dominie might not be in any physical danger. Alex seemed sure of it, and Jared probably was, too, for all his obvious concern. But she had been abandoned at a time when she needed her man beside her, and he had left for precious little reason.

''I *am* a fool,'' he muttered again. ''Barron Shipping could survive very nicely without me.''

''Not necessarily,'' Alex said calmly. ''But you're not the sole reason for the line's existence. You don't have to do everything all by yourself. It's a bitter way to learn a lesson, *younger* cousin, but there are some quite capable shoulders more than ready to share the burden.''

''Meaning, elder cousin,'' Jared replied with a faint touch of humor, ''I would have been better to leave this little task to you?''

''Considering the fact that you have a very beautiful young fiancée who could use some attention, and considering the fact that I can handle this as effectively and perhaps a bit more tactfully, yes, I think you should have left it to me.''

''And considering the fact that you have a younger brother,'' Rachel put in, ''who needs a chance to prove himself—and that Alex would be fairer—yes, you should have left it to him!'' She had held her peace as long as she could; it was impossible to keep her feelings inside any longer. ''It's just a ship, Jared. If it's lost, it's lost. I don't think it is, but does it matter so much?''

''It isn't 'just a ship,' '' Jared replied somewhat stiffly. ''It's the *China Dawn*. The largest, finest clipper the tea trade has ever seen. And the most expensive, I might add.''

''It's still just a ship!'' Rachel could feel her eyes flashing. She knew she was being much too bold, but she couldn't stop herself. ''Just wood and brass and canvas and rope. All you have at jeopardy is an economic investment, and maybe some family arrogance, of which there seems to be an abundant supply. Matthew is a living, breathing person, and the only brother you'll ever have. If you don't know which is more important, I think you need some basic lessons in the realities of life.''

The corners of Jared's mouth twisted slightly. From surprise or suppressed laughter, Rachel couldn't tell which.

''I know Matt is more important than a ship,'' he said gruffly. ''I never claimed he wasn't.''

''Didn't you? But you implied it. Matthew has always looked up to you. You were more than his big brother—you were his idol. All he ever wanted was to please you. And he always failed because you set exactly the same standards for him that you had for yourself. You wanted him to have the same aspirations, the same values, the same talents. Just like old Gareth. Only he was trying to make his grandson into the son he had lost . . . and you were trying to make him into a little image of Jared Barron! Why is it that no one ever wanted Matthew to be himself?''

''I can fight my own battles, tiger.''

Matthew had returned quietly when no one was looking. He stood now, just at the edge of the light, and thought of another flash of fire in those same beautiful brown eyes, a second before the contents of a glass of champagne had splattered in his face.

Lucky for his brother, he thought as his gaze shifted that way, he had returned when he did!

"Are we battling, Matt?" Jared asked.

"We are if you're going to try to pass judgement on me," Matthew said, and reminded his brother quietly that the opium in Howqua's *hong* in Canton had been there because of him. He didn't add that Rachel had been duped by Steven Wu into going after it personally, nor did he think that was relevant. The choice had been a simple one. Leave the *China Dawn* in Damian Varnay's capable hands, or let the opium go through. "Opium destroys lives," he said. "I didn't think there was really a decision. And I can't believe you would have wanted me to do anything else."

"I would have preferred you not to put yourself in the position where you had to make that kind of decision."

"Ah, well . . . I would have preferred that myself. What do you want me to say, Jared? That I was stupid? I was. I've never had any difficulty admitting my mistakes, unlike some people I could mention. But the young man who got himself into that predicament wasn't the same man who came to grips with it later. The opium was my responsibility. I decided to do something about it—and the devil take the wood and brass and canvas and rope!"

The corners of Jared's mouth were twitching noticeably now: definitely laughter. "You were listening a little longer than you let on."

Matthew grinned. "I may not need anyone to fight my battles, but I do like hearing a lovely lady stick up for me. I have a great deal of affection for you, big brother, though that may surprise you. And you have a great deal of affection for me, which may surprise you even more. If you tried trusting me for a change, you might not be disappointed. I *will* get the *China* back. Or die trying.''

''It seems I have no choice.'' Jared tried to smile, but he was tired and worried, and it didn't quite come off. ''Though I'd prefer you didn't go to such drastic extremes.''

He reached for the canvas bag that held some of his clothes and, heaving it on his shoulder, started down the path, his brother beside him, Alex and Rachel following a short distance behind with the lantern. The night had grown chilly. The spring-like warmth seemed to come and go, and there was an almost wintry bite to the breeze.

They paused for a moment awkwardly on the shore. Goodbyes were always clumsy occasions in a family where emotions were never openly displayed.

''She'll be all right, Jared,'' Matthew said quietly.

''I hope so,'' his brother responded. ''God, I hope so!''

''She will be.''

Matthew stood and watched as Jared tossed his bag to the boatman, who stowed it in the stern. The vessel wasn't much to look at, a lighter which had been fitted out with sampan rigging, but it had a sharp, well-shaped hull and oversized sails. It would get them swiftly down the coast to Hong Kong, where Jared could take over the *Shadow Dawn,* the fastest of the Barron ships still in port.

With the right winds, he might overtake the *Scarlet* somewhere in the mid-Pacific. And knowing Jared, Matthew thought, he would probably ram broadside into the other vessel and come leaping on board like a pirate. Thank God Newcombe was a prudent sort, and not the kind to set the ship's guns blazing before he had a good look at the situation.

''Do you remember that brothel?'' he asked impulsively. ''A really foul, disgusting place, when I was about seventeen? You came and dragged me out, kicking and bellowing like a wounded ox.''

Jared turned back with a vaguely surprised expression.

"It would be hard to forget."

"I was glad to see you. I would have died before I'd have admitted it, but I was never so relieved in my life."

"I know." Jared finally managed the smile he had been trying for before. "I felt the same way when our Uncle Garth extricated me from a similar situation."

"*You*? In a place like that? Did you kick and bellow, too?"

"And then some. My pride was at stake. . . . Uncle Garth was very tactful. He said he'd had to rescue Alex, too, a couple of years before, though naturally I didn't believe him. Alex is much too sensible to get himself into such a stupid fix."

"Would that it were so," his cousin said with a soft laugh as he and Rachel reached them. "I think it's a rite of masculine passage. Every young man feels he has to prove himself—and once there, he's too embarrassed to admit he's scared to death. If he's lucky, someone cares enough to come and get him out."

"She really *will* be all right," Matthew said quietly. "And look at it this way. You'll be headed for one of the most romantic spots on earth. The Hawaiian Islands. The perfect place for a honeymoon, wouldn't you say? I'll bring the *China Dawn* to you there, after I've recovered her with my masterly plan. Whole and unharmed."

"Meet me in Lahaina," Jared agreed. "And by all means, bring the *China* if you manage to get her back. But don't bring her to *me*. She's still your ship. Once she's in your hands again, you can do anything you want with her."

Matthew got a deliberately devilish look in his eye. "Anything?"

"You heard me, little brother. Anything. You're on your own now. Alex is here to back you up, but this is your command. You decide what's right for the *China*—and what isn't."

"And God help me if I don't get her back?"

Jared shook his head, almost imperceptibly. "God *keep* you, either way." He helped push the boat out and climbed on board, turning just as they caught the tide. "Oh, and Matt . . . don't die trying. It's just wood and brass and canvas."

And *rope,* Matthew thought as the boat drifted off past the crest of an incoming wave. Was that really his brother who had just disappeared into the darkness? Wood and brass and canvas and rope? One of the mighty Barron clippers?

Love had a way of changing a man, it was said. He of all people ought to know that. But it changed different men in different ways. Love had softened Jared Barron, gentled him, made him somehow more human. And Matthew Barron was feeling stronger and more resolute than he had ever been in his life.

He turned to Rachel, wanting to take her hand and walk side by side with her back up the path. But there was a strange, speculative look in her eye that drove everything else from his mind.

"This leaves you in rather a quandary, doesn't it?" she said softly.

"A . . . quandary?" He was aware that Alex was watching her, too, with the same uneasy curiosity.

"You're one man short now. And no one else knows how to swim. Which position can be spared? The lookout? But that could prove deadly."

Matthew felt his nervousness grow, like a knot in his stomach that kept expanding.

"What are you getting at, Rae?"

"Oh . . . I was just thinking. I'm a *very* good swimmer."

Twenty

Matthew had been tempted many times in the days that followed to call off the operation and head back to Hong Kong. Most of the opium had no doubt been distributed. They couldn't recover it, anyway, and Rachel had long since given up the idea of destroying every last chest he had brought from India. As for the *China Dawn* . . .

Matthew paused on the crest of the hill and looked down. He could just make out part of a tall mast through the trees. They had found the ship early that afternoon, exactly where he had expected, though things were strangely quiet, as if part of the crew had abandoned her. A thick fog was lifting, but wisps still blew in the wind here and there, and the sky was a heavy, impenetrable gray, though dusk was nearly three hours away.

The *China Dawn* was just wood and brass and canvas and rope. He let his eyes linger on the mast a moment longer. A very beautiful accumulation of those materials, to be sure, but still an object made by man that could be made again if necessary. And there were other ways to get her back, he reminded himself. Gallagher would have no use for her soon. It might appeal to his distorted sense of humor if Matthew were to offer to ransom her for an outrageous sum.

No amount of money was too much to protect the woman he cared for more than anything in the world!

His first reaction when Rachel had suggested herself as Jared's replacement had been an emphatic no. An attack on an armed clipper was no place for a woman, it would be much too risky—he couldn't allow her to take such foolish chances! But she had argued, calmly for once, and very reasonably, that this particular woman was a match for at least two of the men he would have with him. If he didn't want her on deck, where fighting might break out and strength would be an issue, then she could be the lookout.

She had made a valid point. Matthew didn't like it, but he had to admit they *did* need someone on the mast. The chances that anything would go wrong were slim, but if the unexpected occurred, advance warning might spell the difference between success and God knows what! He had tried desperately to find someone else for the job. He had even forced his own men into the water in an effort to teach them to swim, but it soon became apparent that if he was going to have a seventh "man," it would have to be his wife.

"I don't want her to do this," he had said to Alex, angrily, despising himself for the helplessness and frustration that made him feel like he had been backed into a corner. "Blast it, I don't want her anywhere near that ship when we go after it!"

"I don't either," Alex had agreed, "but maybe that's our male vanity. She's asking for respect, Matt, and she deserves it. She *is* as competent as a man, hard as that may be for us to admit. She would be a good lookout. And she *does* have experience in matters of this sort."

She did indeed. Matthew had half smiled in spite of himself as he recalled reaching out for a long black pigtail and having it snap off in his hand. "She'll probably do better than anyone and show us all up! But dammit, Alex, it turns my stomach just thinking about it. It truly does!"

In the end, however, he had had to agree. And, after all, he thought, consoling himself now, she was going to be high on the mast, well out of things. If there were any problems, it would be on deck. She would be safe enough, unless—

He shivered slightly. Unless something went wrong, he thought, and started as a hand touched his arm.

"You're so lost in thought," Rachel teased, "I believe you've forgotten I'm here."

He had in fact, just for a moment, but he decided it would be unchivalrous to admit it. Besides, he had only let his mind wander because he had been so absorbed in his concern for her.

"I never forget you," he said.

"Liar," she countered, but she was laughing as they strolled arm in arm down the slope toward the place where they had made their camp. The sky seemed even darker now. The fog was rising rapidly, but it still hung like a thick veil between the earth and the sun.

Matthew felt a little guilty as he remembered the way they had just spent the last hour, and why. That jesting accusation had been more apt than she realized. Rachel had been pressuring him to let her go with the men on the sampan when they peddled their vegetables to the *China Dawn* and set the requisite rope in place. It would seem more natural, she had insisted, if there were a woman with them. They would arouse less suspicions. Peasant women could be brash and very pushy—and she did a pushy peasant to perfection!

But this time, Matthew had said no and meant it. Wanting to avoid an argument, he had managed to take her mind off the matter in a way that had proved most diverting indeed. For him as well as her. His own mind had been on nothing more troublesome than the scratchy prickle of the grass against his naked limbs and torso for the pleasantest part of an hour, and he had not given a thought to the consequences that were sure to follow.

He had intended it as a distraction, not deceit, but he knew it was not going to look that way to her. As they came in sight of the camp and saw the sampan just dropping anchor, he was not the least surprised to hear a sharp intake of breath in his ear.

"So that's why you took me up the hill," she said. "You wanted to keep me away when the boat went out!"

"I took you up that hillside because I love you"—

Matthew's voice dropped low in his throat, and his breath tickled her neck, but for once she did not respond—"and I thought it was a much more interesting way to spend the afternoon. . . ."

"You did not," Rachel retorted, feeling hurt and somehow betrayed as she pulled away from him. "You took me up there because you knew I would insist on going with them."

"I had already told you I wouldn't permit it. We've been all over this, tiger. It would have been much too imprudent. Gallagher has seen you at least once, and he has a canny way of catching onto things. I wasn't going to change my mind. I just thought—truly—that there was a much more interesting way to spend the afternoon than quarreling over things that couldn't be changed."

Rachel bit her tongue, but she was nowhere near mollified as they went over to where the men were jumping out of the boat and wading excitedly ashore. She hadn't, in fact, been planning on arguing anymore. She had already decided he was right. Gallagher *was* canny, and if she got caught, that would just give him a hostage to hold over Matthew's head. She had been perfectly ready to give in.

But he hadn't given her a chance to say so! He had just *decided*—arbitrarily—and that was that. No more discussion.

And having made up his mind, he hadn't had the courage to be honest about it! He had *tricked* her, however appealing the guise. How was she supposed to trust him if she had to wonder all the time what was behind everything he did?

And trust, it seemed to Rachel, was every bit as important a part of marriage as passion.

The men were already ashore—there were four of them, including Li Shu—chattering and laughing as they disposed of the leftover fish and vegetables they had not induced Gallagher to buy. And no wonder, Rachel thought. They were the sorriest-looking specimens she had ever seen. She managed to push her annoyance with Matthew to the back of her mind, though it was still there as she listened curiously and translated what they said.

It had all gone exactly as planned. They had climbed over, around, and through everything on deck—there was no way the sailors could have watched all of them at once. The youngest and wiliest had managed to slip over to the other side. The coil of rope had been right where Matthew had said it would be, and he had tied the knot precisely as he had been taught. No one would see it unless he leaned far over the rail and deliberately looked down. And night was approaching.

Only one thing had been unexpected. Li Shu's normally placid eyes bulged; his voice was shrill, almost shouting, as he described it. An oddly shaped metal tub, whose dimensions it seemed to have occurred to him to gauge with some accuracy. It looked, he swore in very loud tones, just like the thing his cousin's wife's brother had seen on the deck of the ship that breathed smoke like a great iron dragon into the air.

"A Congreve rocket?" Matthew speculated in considerably quieter tones. "They had one on the *Nemesis*."

"It's smaller," Alex said thoughtfully. "Quite a bit. But it sounds like the same principle."

"He could have had it made up almost anywhere. The Chinese are devilish clever at imitating things, and it's just the sort of invention that would appeal to someone of Gallagher's reckless nature. If it's got local powder in it, I don't suppose it's much of a threat. Still . . ."

Still, he couldn't help worrying about it after Alex had gone to see the sampan tucked safely away with the others in a sheltered inlet several hundred yards down the coast. It was an unknown factor, one he hadn't taken into consideration. And he didn't like unknowns at this stage.

He also didn't like the way Li Shu's voice had risen when he talked about it. Matthew found his eyes scanning the trees behind him, fruitlessly, for nothing seemed wrong.

Rachel trusted the man. He knew that, but he himself was becoming increasingly wary. Li Shu was too bland, too obliging, too willing to play the foolish peasant all the time. It might not mean anything, but he would bear watching all the same.

"Matt—"

Rachel's voice broke into his thoughts. Matthew looked back, anticipating the reproach he was going to see in her face. He should perhaps have been more forthcoming, but she did make it difficult at times!

"I'm sorry, tiger. I probably ought to have told you what I had in mind. I just thought it would be pleasanter this way."

Her eyes were serious as she looked back at him. More hurt than angry, he thought uncomfortably.

"This is getting out of hand, Matthew. Games are one thing, but it's going way beyond teasing when you deliberately use lovemaking to keep something from me. Women have minds and feelings, too, just like men! You have to learn to be more honest with me. I suppose we have to learn to be more honest with each other."

"There have been lapses on both sides," he reminded her. "I seem to recall a certain cow-chillo following me up the path when she had promised to remain behind."

"That *was* teasing. And besides, you don't leave me much choice. You decide what we're going to do. You make up your mind, and you don't care to hear any arguments about it! I'm not your child and you my father. I've told you more than once—I want to be an equal partner in this marriage. I thought you understood I meant it."

Matthew was aware, as she turned and walked away, that she was still angry. It was the first time they had parted, even for a few minutes, with a quarrel still between them. Damn, he thought. He hated the nightmare this rescue operation was turning into. He hated the tension in the air that made him short-tempered and no doubt affected her, too. And he hated like hell putting Rachel in danger and feeling he didn't have any other way out!

He was half tempted to go back to the original plan, to just swim out there now and board the *China Dawn* alone. The more he watched, the surer he was that Gallagher was shorthanded. If there had been desertions, they were probably the newer hands. With any luck, it would be over in an hour—

But that would be foolhardy. It was not impossible, or even unlikely, but it wasn't the best plan. Without the distraction of the sampans ahead, the junks to the stern, he would be asking for trouble, and he might get it.

He just didn't want Rachel involved. Dammit, he didn't want her involved, just as he knew she was unhappy with his involvement. They worried about each other. That was a part of love. But it was harder for a man, who needed to feel he was taking care of his woman!

It was not until he had spotted Alex returning and started forward to meet him that Matthew remembered he had left his jacket on the hillside. He considered briefly going back for it, then dismissed the thought. Even with the fog, the day was warm, and muggy, and the night promised to continue much the same.

He would hardly be needing it. And it couldn't do any harm where it was.

The lack of sun made the transition from afternoon to twilight almost imperceptible. Gallagher felt rather than saw it as he stood on the deck of the *China Dawn* and stared absently out to sea.

There had been something strange about that group of Chinese who had clambered on board just as the day was easing itself toward an uneventful close. Nothing he could put a name to, but it hadn't seemed right somehow, and every Irish instinct in him quivered with foreboding.

They had been exuberant, the whole noisy lot of them, but that was the usual way with these peasants. And curious. That was usual, too. Nothing in their boisterous behavior or singsong pidgin had led him to think there was anything out of the way about them, but still he couldn't shake the nagging feeling in his bones.

Maybe it was that fellow climbing all over the rocket. A cheeky bucko, he'd been, even for a Chinese. Staring and pointing and burbling out all sorts of things Gallagher couldn't understand. Or the other fellow, the one who'd wandered off while nobody was looking and gotten all the way over on the other side of the ship.

Gallagher had had him searched when he came back, and they had found several nails in his pockets. Just the sort of thing they always stole, these people. Anything metal that wasn't bolted down.

But wasn't that what a clever man might do if he were up to something he didn't want go get caught at? Gallagher tried the thought out in his mind. Make himself look like a common thief, and that could be an end to it? And these people were clever. He had had more than one occasion to learn that. Nearly as much of his cargo had been stolen as sold, and he had no idea where or how any of it had gone.

They'd probably paid his crew more than he had, he thought wryly—and gotten more for their money! He'd already dismissed several of the men, his own primarily, leaving himself dangerously shorthanded, and still the pilfering continued. He'd be in a damned sight of trouble, that was for sure, if young Matt Barron picked now to come after his ship.

If . . .

He ran his eye along the empty horizon from one end to the other. Nothing there now, but in the fog an entire armada could have passed within half a mile and he wouldn't have seen it.

There was no reason to associate the Chinese this afternoon with the captain of the *China Dawn*, but there was no reason not to, either. Gallagher had searched the ship carefully after they had gone, and if there was anything missing save those few puny nails, he had seen no trace of it.

But then he wasn't much of a man to be paying heed

to a ship. He wouldn't notice a mite or two out of place.

And the fellow *had* seen the rocket. He turned back toward the bulky tub sitting on the deck. That was his secret card, the fifth ace up his sleeve, the one Matthew Barron would never guess he had . . . unless that little party today did have something to do with him.

Gallagher had no idea if the rocket actually worked. He had never tried it. But it appealed to his sense of adventure, and he had no desire to leave it vulnerable.

"Here, boy!" he called out to a passing sailor who was easily his own age. "Get one o' your buddies and trot on over here. I need t' be loadin' this thing onto a jolly boat."

He saw the look on the man's face and bellowed:

"Three or four, then, an' on the double if you value your hide! This'll be on the boat, nice and steady, within the hour—or it's swimmin' ashore you'll be with the anchor tied t' your left big toe!"

He watched the sailor scurry out of sight and grimaced with satisfaction. If young Matthew wasn't there—if the men today weren't reporting to him—there was no harm done.

But if he was, and they were, the rocket and all its fiery potential would be safely loaded on one of the boats, and the boat hoisted onto the davit, ready to be lowered at a moment's notice.

"Come on, me bucko," he chuckled, half under his breath. "If you be out there—and I think you be—then come on. And I'll give you the surprise o' your bloomin' life!"

Dusk had turned almost to night as Damian Varnay headed up the hillside on the narrow path which had been tamped down that afternoon by their own comings and goings. Beyond lay the beach, and over the next rise the spot where the junks were anchored on a much-too-exposed section of shore. It had been a risk, but a calculated one. And it had worked out well, for fog was easing into darkness and they hadn't been spotted.

He hesitated a moment near the crest to get his bearings. He could still see, but barely. He didn't want to have to venture too close to the water. The mist had lifted somewhat, more cloud than fog now, but it didn't look like there was going to be much moon showing.

That meant their plans would have to be changed. He didn't care for it any more than the captain, but there wasn't bloody much either one of them could do about it. That was where he was going now, to tell the men, though they weren't such fools that they wouldn't have figured it out well enough on their own.

Unless nature cooperated, they'd be attacking with first light, counting on the gray haze of predawn to accomplish much of what they had expected from the moonlight. But they'd have to do everything faster now. There would be only a little time before the sun became bright enough to be dangerous.

Something dark and rumpled stuck out from under a bush, and picking it up, Varnay recognized Matthew Barron's jacket. Being a man of some imagination, and having had quite a way with the ladies himself when he was younger, he had a good idea how it had gotten there. Though, of course, he would never be so forward as to mention it.

Draping it over his arm, he started on the downward trail toward the beach.

The men would chafe at the delay, he knew. He was chafing himself! But they would hold their tongues. They liked their young captain, and they knew he was doing the best he could. If the signal—a brief lantern flash on the opposite hill—came a few hours later, and if they didn't have any sleep before, at least it would give them time for a pleasant chat. And maybe a drop or two, though the Barrons ran tight ships, and God pity the man who showed up with liquor heavy on his breath.

He pushed his way through a thick patch of brush. A little off the path, but he was going the right direction. Varnay had been bitterly disappointed when he learned that he was to be cheated out of the satisfying confrontation he had been looking forward to ever since they began planning the assault. But with both the Barron men occupied elsewhere, he would be needed to help Moody take care of the gunners in the fore, who would almost certainly be under the command of the second mate, Romack.

He was still smarting with the injustice of it, but not too much. If he couldn't wring Gallagher's neck, at least he'd have a crack at Romack. He'd see the little weasel in chains—if he decided to be gentle!

The light seemed brighter when he reached the beach, though the sun had settled well below the horizon. Varnay noticed a faintly luminous glow where the moon ought to be. The clouds were clearing, then? Perhaps their plans wouldn't change after all.

He thought of turning back to check. But his orders had been clear, and Damian Varnay was a man to whom orders were almost a religion. He would have to be on his deathbed before he disobeyed. Perhaps not even then.

The jacket was growing heavier, and it occurred to him that it would be foolish to carry it all the way to the junks, then all the way back again. He would be meeting the others here, whether at three or just before dawn. It wouldn't be likely to get up and walk away in the meantime.

Varnay folded it neatly and set it just on the edge of the sand, where the vegetation ended. No chance he would forget it there. On impulse, he slipped his hand into his pants pocket and took out the cufflink he had found that afternoon in his hastily packed effects.

The letter from Gallagher had been left on the ship, but he had taken the cufflink with him when he went to meet its owner in Canton. The captain had believed him. Or said he did. But this was his only vindication—the only visible proof of the way he had been used—and he clung to it with the tenacity of a simple man whose honor had been called to question.

It would be a shame to let anything happen to it. He transferred it to the pocket of the jacket where it would be safe until they returned from their mission.

A faint sound startled him, and Varnay swiveled

abruptly. But it was only the wind rustling through the trees. A good wind, not too turbulent, not too calm. The junks and sampans would glide like wild ducks through the water.

Yes, he thought again as he started toward the shallow rise on the other side, he wouldn't mind the least if he was a little rough and Romack's neck got broken!

Steven Wu waited until Varnay was gone, then stepped quietly out of the trees onto the narrow strip of sand. He wasn't afraid of being seen if anyone was watching from the ship. The light was almost completely gone by now. As long as he didn't move too quickly, he would blend in with the shadows.

So . . . the first mate was going to speak to the men on the junks, was he? That meant they had almost certainly changed their plans. No surprises there. Steven had anticipated it earlier in the day when he had first spotted the fog rolling in. He knew the weather patterns in the area well enough to realize that there would be little moon that night.

He turned his eyes speculatively toward the *China Dawn,* still visible, though fast fading on the horizon. It had been interesting, that news about the rocket. Very interesting. He had heard that one had been ordered—he knew the craftsman who had fashioned it and respected him—but he had not heard for whom it was intended.

Very clever of Li Shu to recognize its importance and make sure his voice was shrill enough to carry. Steven's faith in him had been more than justified. A man could do much with a rocket like that, he thought—if he could get his hands on it.

A pity he had broken so completely with Matthew Barron. It had been foolish, showing his hand that night in Canton. He was not usually so careless, but he had been angry and bitterly disappointed.

If he had been just a little more cautious, he might have been part of that small group swimming out to the ship—when? With the first pale hints of dawn?

He could follow later, of course. Only a few minutes, but by then pandemonium would have broken out, and it would be much more difficult to reach the rocket. He would give a great deal to figure out a way to get Matthew Barron to have confidence in him again.

Or if not to have confidence, at least to accept him. A *great* deal.

The jacket was still lying where Varnay had left it. Steven dipped his hand into the pocket, curious to see what the other man had placed there. The light was barely a shimmer, only the faint haze of a partially obscured moon, and he had to hold the thing up and turn it first one way, then the other, to make it out what it was.

A cufflink!

He was contemptuous and not at all surprised. Typical of such men to worry about expensive baubles at a time like this! Neither the fate of the countless wretches who had been affected by their opium, nor the boatmen in the sampans who would soon face the gunners on their own ship bothered them in the least. But they took care to protect a piece of jewelry!

He tossed the cufflink scornfully on top of the jacket and strode to the water's edge, daring in the darkness to be bolder than he should. He was wearing white man's boots. His feet were large, like a white man's— a legacy from his father, he supposed—and he made no effort to brush away the tracks that would show clearly if the moon came out at last.

Let them think what they wanted when they saw that trail of footprints leading to the water. He waded through the surf to the spot where a cluster of rocks jutted out into the frothy waves. They were too stupid to make anything out of it anyway.

Men like that were swine! He thought of the cufflink, symbol of all those useless lives dissipated away in ballrooms and salons, and the anger crystallized inside him again. Unfit to walk the earth. They ought to be exterminated, right down to the last man!

And it might happen sooner than they thought.

By two o'clock, Matthew knew there was no hope of salvaging their original plan. The clouds had broken, but only occasionally, and the dim bluish light could not be counted on. He waited another half hour, then sent Moody to let Varnay and the others know what was going on, while Rachel informed the Chinese in the sampans.

It had made him vaguely uneasy, letting her go off by herself. But the way was safe enough, and she would be carrying a lantern, for that part of the coast was not visible from the ship. He could hardly have objected, but he couldn't quite feel comfortable about it, either.

Probably nerves, he thought. The tension of waiting—but he had an unpleasant feeling that something was about to go wrong.

A bit of Gallagher rubbing off, God help him? He was beginning to feel like he had that Irish ''gift'' of foreboding!

''I'm standing here wishing things were different,'' he said to Alex behind him. ''I know they can't be. I know we need a lookout, and Rachel's the only possible choice. But I keep wishing there were some way I could change things and she didn't have to go out to the *China Dawn* with us.''

''Unless Providence sends someone who speaks good enough English to understand your plan,'' his cousin reminded him, ''and has sharp enough eyes and wits to be a good lookout—and swims like a fish, to boot—I don't think it's likely.''

''I daresay.'' Matthew glanced back to see the other man seated on a log beside the one lantern they had dared to light. ''But I think I'd make a bargain with the devil himself to keep Rachel out of this.''

Alex inclined his head slightly, and Matthew sensed, for all the studied ease of his manner, a tautness coiling inside him, straining until he was ready to snap.

We're all tense, he thought. Just the waiting? Or was his normally unfanciful cousin having premonitions, too? Matthew stared briefly at the place where the ocean ought to be. But the moon had disappeared again, and there was nothing but a vast black void.

"It's hard to believe," he said quietly, "that this will all be over tomorrow. We'll have the *China* back—or we won't—and life will go on as before."

"Not quite 'as before.' " Alex had gotten up and, moving with the effortless grace that was characteristic of him, came to stand beside his cousin. "Jared will be living in Boston. Imagine, Jared giving up the sea! There'll be a bit of old Gareth there, I suspect. The lion trapped in a cage—though he'll have Dominie, and that will make a difference. And you'll be settling somewhere yourself. Hong Kong?"

Matthew saw what he was doing, but he welcomed the distraction. "Probably. I had thought originally I'd set up a branch of Barron Shipping in Macao, but it looks like everyone's moving to the new colony. Probably just as well. I'd never have been able to keep Rachel out of her parents' clinic. She works much too hard there—it tires her greatly. She's not as strong as she likes to pretend."

"And not as fragile as you fear," Alex said gently. "It will all be over, as you said, in a few short hours. It's the inactivity that's setting us on edge. The old family firm is getting quite cosmopolitan, isn't it? Headquarters in Boston, now a branch in the Orient. We'll have to change the name to Barron International. How do you think that will sit?"

Matthew allowed himself a faint chuckle. "About the way *you* think it will. I remember when the name was changed from G.C. Barron to Barron Shipping to emphasize the fact that we weren't just whalers and privateers. Though, in fact, at the time we mostly were."

"The world is changing." Alex seemed to relax somewhat. "Grandfather has never cared much for change. He roars and blusters at the mere impudent mention of such a thing! But I notice he always comes out a bit ahead of where he went in."

"What about you?" Matthew said curiously. "Jared and I are busy carving up the Barron empire, picking out the pieces each of us wants. Where do you see yourself in all this?"

"Ah, well . . ." Alex drawled, almost ironically, as if Matthew had inadvertently said something amusing. "I expect my place will be the same as it always has been: to see to the trouble spots. Whatever vessel needs a captain, whatever trading port is causing problems—Alex Barron to the rescue. A knight in somewhat tarnished armor off on nineteenth-century financial crusades."

His tone was not quite a match for the carelessness of his words, and it occurred to Matthew for the first time that Alex was the only one among them who had never made demands for himself.

"But if you could have anything you chose?" he persisted. "If Barron Shipping—or Barron International—were to offer you the one thing you really wanted, what would it be?"

Alex seemed to ponder the question. A faint hint of moonlight suffused the night again. Little ribbons of light danced on the waves, but it didn't look as if he saw them.

"Out," he said at last.

"I bet your pardon?" Matthew wasn't quite sure he had heard right.

"If I could have anything from the family firm—anything at all—I'd want out. You forget, the sea has never been the passion of my life. I wasn't born with salt water in my veins like Jared or old Gareth, or even you. I reserve my love for the land. To take a handful of moist, red earth—to smell the pungent richness in my nostrils and know that it belongs to me—is as close to a dream as I'll ever come. I should have been born into a long line of farmers instead of an international trading family."

"Perhaps you *will* have your dream," Matthew said, a little embarrassed. It was hard for him to imagine that the family business could be a family obligation. All he had ever wanted, as long as he could remember, was to be old enough to be taken seriously and have a place in it! "Maybe we should leave you off in Hawaii. I hear the soil is very rich there. Anything will grow in it, they say, and the winters are mild. After all these years sailing the southern seas, I can't picture you on a farm in Vermont or New Hampshire. Or even Virginia.''

Alex seemed to change subtly. He shook his head, a little sharply. "Not Hawaii. I never . . . I've never been partial to Hawaii. There are too many things there I don't care for. At least, not in Lahaina. An old whalers' port doesn't appeal to me.''

''Another island, perhaps? The South Pacific is full of possibilities.''

''Perhaps sometime. But most likely not. It does seem odd, doesn't it, that the one of us with no great love for the sea is the one who looks like he's going to end up on it?''

Something in his voice did not welcome further conversation, and Matthew, respecting his privacy, took a few steps away into the darkness. Strange how that closed look on Alex's face had appeared at the casual mention of Hawaii. But there was no point asking about it. Alex had always been like that. His feelings were his own, kept deep inside and never shared.

Matthew was just turning back toward the lantern when he saw a solitary figure dressed in black, halfway in the light, halfway in shadow. A slender hand partially covered the man's mouth, as if gesturing for silence. In spite of himself, Matthew choked back his exclamation of surprise.

Steven Wu stood absolutely motionless, but his entire body seemed to be charged with energy. Matthew was startled to realize suddenly why he had been growing his hair. So it would be long enough to attach a false pigtail! He remembered having seen someone like that among the boatmen on the sampans.

His *own* sampans. And the men who were supposedly in his hire!

One black-clad arm went up, beckoning him boldly into the darkness. With a quick glance at Alex, who was still looking the other way, Matthew followed, curiosity getting the better of caution. The young Chinese led him a short distance away, just far enough so their voices wouldn't be heard if they spoke quietly.

And Steven Wu took care to speak very quietly.

"You said you would make a bargain with the devil himself for a man with sharp eyes who can swim. I know how to swim . . . and my eyes are very sharp."

And your ears, Matthew thought, making an effort not to shudder visibly as he recalled all the times someone had seemed to be listening in.

"You want to come with us?" He strained to see the other man's face in the almost impenetrable shadows. "What makes you think I'd be willing to trust you?"

Steven Wu's expression did not change, but Matthew could have sworn he was smiling. "*Trust* is such a relative word. Let's just say, I think you might like to use me. And I you. You want to recapture the *China Dawn*. I want destroy the opium in its hold."

"And you'd just as soon set a torch to the ship to do it!"

"Perhaps sooner. . . . But there are four of you, and only three of us. What could we do? Isn't it worth the risk?"

The smile was open now. Cruel and almost childishly smug, as if he knew he had won. And, of course, Matthew thought, he had.

He would try to pull something. Matthew knew that. But they wouldn't be carrying torches this time. He could hope to keep an eye on them—and even if he didn't, as Wu had said himself, what could they do?

At any rate, it would keep Rachel out of it. That was worth whatever risk he had to take.

"I *did* say I would make a pact with the devil, didn't I?" he replied drily. "I rather suspect I just have."

Matthew was nowhere to be seen when Rachel returned to the camp. Alex appeared to be alone, but he was lost in thought, staring off in the direction of the sea, and he didn't see her as she started up the path that led to the beach where they would all be assembling in a short time.

She was much too restless to sit there, idle and fidgeting. And while she didn't like to admit it, butterflies were romping around in her stomach and she was finding it increasingly difficult to breathe.

It was silly. Rachel knew that. She had not been nearly this jittery the night of the raid on Matthew's junk, and their plans for the *China Dawn* had been much more carefully laid. Every contingency had been considered and prepared for. There was just something in the air, a kind of tension that almost seemed contagious, as if it had blown in on the wind.

Perhaps it was only that Matthew hadn't been in the camp when she had passed through. Rachel had expected to find him there, waiting anxiously for her return, and it had made her strangely nervous when he wasn't. Though of course, as the leader, he had other responsibilities to occupy him. He was probably on the beach already, checking things out one last time.

But the shallow strip of sand was empty when she reached it, and surprisingly bright. The moonlight was clear now, if only for the moment, and an underlying lightness presaged the coming of dawn. It was later, then, than she had realized.

Soon the others would be arriving. Any minute now, and it would be time to begin. . . .

It was then that she saw it. A dark bundle, crumpled and anonymous on the tawny brownish sand. It almost looked like a jacket. Matthew's? But how could it have gotten there? Rachel stooped to catch hold of it, and a bright object flew out.

She didn't even have to pick it up to examine it closer. She recognized her husband's cufflink, and in that same instant, her eyes followed a shadowy trail of bootprints to the water's edge.

"Oh, dear heaven!"

She understood immediately what had happened. Matthew had said often enough that he wanted to do this by himself. It was his plan—*he* would see it through—and she realized, sick with horror and fear, that that was exactly what he had done.

And, God help her, it was at least partly her fault!

Rachel could have wept with despair. Jared and Alex had talked him out of the idea once. It was much too dangerous, they had warned him. Too many things could go wrong. And he had listened and agreed.

But he had been worried about *her*! He hadn't wanted her to go. He had been so desperately afraid that something would happen to her, he had taken all the risks on his own shoulders. Now he was out there, alone, with no one to back him up. And all because of her!

She had to go to him.

It was not a conscious decision. Not something she thought about or reasoned out. It was just what she knew she had to do. She threw a quick glance back at the hillside, but there was no time to go for the others. Even if she ran all the way, it would take at least ten or fifteen minutes. Matthew must already be on the ship. There was no trace of him in the water.

Perhaps, if she was lucky, the others would not be too long. She was already slipping off her dress, wishing she had had the foresight to bring the clever bathing costume she had made—pants cut off below the knee and a sleeveless cotton jacket—but there was no time to go back for that, either. She would have to make do with what she had.

Rachel shivered for a moment, feeling almost naked in the moonlight. She couldn't go on a shipful of men clad only in drawers and a chemise! Even if she could endure the horrible embarrassment, she'd be asking for the worst kind of trouble.

But she could hardly swim with a long skirt twisting around her ankles, either.

Impulsively, she bundled her dress up, and using the fichu as a sash, tied it into a neat package on her back. She was going to feel a little foolish, like a turtle toting its shell through the water, but at least she'd have something to wear when she got there.

She took only a moment to scrawl out a quick message in the sand. Big, bold letters so they couldn't possibly miss it.

GONE AHEAD, she wrote, and wanted to add WITH MATTHEW, but she had started too close to

the water and there wasn't room. She could only hope
the tide didn't wash it away as it was.

Adding a last, large R, she threw one more glance
over her shoulder, but the hillside was silent and motionless.

Please let them be coming soon, she thought as she
turned resolutely back to the sea. And please, *please,*
let him be all right until we get there.

The water was cold against her ankles, then her shins
and thighs. Rachel shivered, but the feeling was almost welcome, for it took her mind off the fear and
the dread. Then she was swimming, surely, swiftly,
and after that one initial shock, the chill was gone,
and the warmth of exertion coursed through her veins.

Matthew needed her.

She wouldn't think of anything else. Nothing mattered except that, not even her own safety. Matthew
might be in trouble even at that moment. He had been
there when she needed him.

She had to be there now for him.

Twenty-One

The moonlight was unnervingly bright on the ship. The clouds were clearing alarmingly fast. Rachel pressed back against a wall, shoving herself as deeply as she could into the shadows.

The night was warm, but the wind had picked up, and her dress clung like a clammy second skin to her legs and body. She had wrung it out before putting it on, but it was still wet, and she was horribly conscious of the faint *drip-drip-drip* of water on the decking.

How she wished she knew more about clippers, and this one in particular. She tried to look around, but nothing made sense. Matthew had said Gallagher would head for the stern at the first sign of attack, and she had assumed, foolishly, that that was where she would find them. But the attack had not occurred yet! Gallagher would still be asleep in his cabin. If Matthew wanted to take him by surprise, surely that was where he would go.

And she hadn't the vaguest notion where the passenger cabin on the *China Dawn* might be.

Shivering a little in the wind, she stared down the long empty deck that curved just slightly from bow to stern. She had been on board for fully ten minutes—though it seemed like *hours*—and she had seen no one but the men on watch moving around. Wherever Matthew was, whatever he was up to, there ought to have been some sign of him. Unless—

Icy fingers of fear clutched her heart. Unless Gallagher had found out what he was doing and had already taken action. She had no way of knowing when

Matthew had boarded the ship. He could easily have been there the better part of an hour.

Even then, she thought, struggling to reassure herself, there should have been *something*. Angry shouting, a fight—even pistol shots, though that was what she dreaded most. It shouldn't have been so ominously quiet.

Rachel forced herself out of the shadows and started walking as stealthily as she could along the deck. "Quiet" wasn't exactly the word. She shivered again. Sounds and movement were everywhere. The masts groaned overhead, spars creaked in the wind, casting grotesquely swaying shadows, and a long rope had come loose, slapping sharply on the deck.

But there were no human sounds. No *human* motion. It was almost as if the vessel were deserted. She glanced nervously from side to side, but still there was nothing. A ghost ship in a haunted sea, inhabited only by the wraiths of men who had sailed her in years past. . . .

The eerie illusion was broken abruptly by the distant sound of very human footsteps behind her. Rachel barely had time to push herself back into the shadows. Not as good a hiding place as before, but she had no choice. It was almost the end of the wall, and the darkness was nowhere near as deep.

She stood as still as she could, not even daring to breathe, praying that whoever it was would turn and go the other way.

But the footsteps came on, and a second later a man appeared. Not Gallagher. Someone taller, thin and slightly stooped, and Rachel realized to her horror that she could see him clearly, from the buttons on his jacket to dark, protruding eyes to the coarse knit of the watch cap pulled down low on his forehead.

The moon was almost uncannily bright now. She had not known a quarter moon could give such light, and she was aware again with a terrible sinking feeling of the sound of water dripping from her dress.

If he noticed, if he grew curious—if he even turned his head idly—he would see her as clearly as she could see him. He stopped briefly, a terrifyingly long second, and stared out over the rail in the opposite direction. Then he was moving on again, down the deck and mercifully out of sight.

It was fully two minutes before Rachel dared to draw in a normal breath. What a fool she had been, thinking all she had to do was get on the ship and she would somehow be able to help Matthew! She had been so frantic to reach the top of that long, dangling rope, she hadn't stopped to wonder what would happen when she did.

She had no idea where Matthew was or what he was doing. She couldn't even begin to figure out where to look for him. Or what earthly use she would be if she somehow managed to stumble across him.

She took a last look down the deck in the direction the man had disappeared. Everything seemed still again, no traces of anyone visible. It was a bitter realization that these last minutes would have been far more productively spent on shore running for competent help.

But it was too late to worry about that now. Rachel squared her shoulders and tried not to think about things that couldn't be helped. She was on the ship, whether she belonged there or not. And she was going to have to stay. It would be much too dangerous to try and find her way back to the place where she had climbed up the rope, even if she remembered where it was.

She had better find Matthew now, she thought grimly, as much for her own sake as his. Or at least a place to hide. The sun would be peeking over the horizon soon, and heaven help her if she was still on deck when it did!

This time, she crept out of the shadows more cautiously, glancing back over her shoulder. The other men on watch might not tread quite so heavily. Matthew had said this was their least alert time, and while she fervently hoped so, she didn't dare count on it.

A second later, a door appeared in the shadows. It was getting much lighter. Rachel could make out every detail of the panels and hinges, and her hand rested tentatively for an instant on the knob. Cold. It felt so cold. Like the pit of her stomach. And she didn't know what lay beyond.

But if she didn't even try, she would only wander around and around on the deck until the sun came out!

She made her hand move, and the door slid soundlessly open. It was almost pitch-dark inside, but a smell of sawdust and grease told her she had happened upon the carpenter shop and probably the galley. Muted snores came from somewhere nearby. There must be a passage leading to the crew's quarters, she told herself, and closed the door as stealthily as she had opened it. Clearly, there was nothing for her here.

She had better luck at the next door, which had been propped or latched open. Moonlight spilled down a short flight of steps, and a faint yellowish glow at the bottom hinted at lamps left burning in the night.

Rachel stood at the top and listened tensely. She could hear nothing but the beating of her own heart, which seemed to be drumming wildly in her ears. Either no one was there, or someone was sleeping very quietly. She tiptoed down, carefully, one step at a time, the weight of her wet skirt making her unexpectedly clumsy.

There was another door at the bottom, not open, but ajar enough to give Rachel a clear view of a surprisingly luxurious cabin. Everything seemed to be green and deep red-brown, dark mahogany paneling setting off the plush richness of emerald velvet upholstery. A sitting room, apparently, for there was no bed, and a darkened doorway seemed to lead to another chamber beyond.

Not the captain's cabin. Matthew had described that to her in detail. The passenger's suite, then—where Gallagher was staying.

And obviously he was out. Rachel took a moment to scan the room again. If he were here, Matthew would be here, too. This was the first place he would have looked for him.

Rachel tried not to think about what they might be

doing, what might be happening elsewhere. Now was her chance to search the cabin, and she had to do it quickly. Gallagher almost certainly had a gun. If he had gone out hurriedly, perhaps on some routine chore, he could have left it behind.

And with a gun in her possession, she would not be quite so helpless after all if she found Matthew.

She slipped inside and began to throw open the drawers. She was moving as silently as she could, not wanting the sound to carry through the walls, but haste was more important than stealth. The first drawers held a rainbow of shimmering silk garments, heavily scented with sultry perfume. Rachel was vaguely surprised. She hadn't thought Gallagher would be sentimental enough to keep a woman's garments, but she didn't have time to dwell on it now.

She didn't even bother to close any of the drawers behind her. She just went on to the next, and on the fourth or fifth try, she found it. All by itself in a bottom drawer. She had to bend down to get it.

Relief was flooding through her, a welcome sense that somehow, against all odds, she had finally made it, when hands gripped her shoulders, jerking her up and thrusting her roughly against the wall.

A very red face with tousled black hair appeared in the lamplight. Rachel did not even have a chance to cry out in fear. Gallagher *had* been in his cabin, in the darkness of his bedroom! And he must have been expecting trouble, for he had been sleeping fully dressed.

His eyes were almost startlingly green. Dancing not with the anger she might have expected but something hideously like amusement.

"An' what have we here? By God and the seven saints, I do believe it's the missionary's pretty daughter. An' herself out takin' a most peculiar midnight swim."

He had grabbed both her wrists in one hand and was reaching with the other for the gun, which he tucked deftly into his belt. "Let me go—" Rachel started to protest, but he tightened his hold painfully, forcing her to stop.

"It's sorry I am, lass," he said, and almost sounded as if he meant it. "I take no pleasure in hurtin' a woman, and that's the truth. But there's a fine bit o' help you're goin' t' be givin' me now."

The laughter in his eyes was even bolder, and Rachel realized to her horror that she had just delivered into his hands the one thing that would put Matthew Barron completely in his power.

Her absence had been noted the minute Matthew got back to camp. Alex couldn't tell him anything, but the two Chinese who were set to go with them later, including Li Shu, had been loitering around the area. It was an odd bit of behavior which would ordinarily have given Matthew pause, but one of them had noticed Rachel on the path heading for the beach, and he forgot everything else as he started after her, half running in his haste.

He could hear Alex's footsteps behind him and the oddly stealthy patter of Chinese canvas shoes. Throwing a hurried glance back over his shoulder, he saw that Steven Wu had joined the others, but he didn't have time to worry about him now, or explain his presence to Alex.

He knew he was probably making an ass of himself. There was no reasonable cause for concern. Typical of Rachel, she had probably just gotten bored and gone on ahead. But the same premonitions he had been fighting all night were still there, even more persistent now, and he had a terrible, illogical feeling that something *had* gone wrong.

Alex felt it, too. Matthew could see the concern in his cousin's face as he pulled up beside him on the beach, and he knew they were both thinking the same thing. Too much that was unexpected had happened. This wasn't going according to plan. And now Rachel . . .

He ran his eyes along the beach. Empty, he thought with a terrible, wrenching feeling in his gut, and the first dark sense of what had happened gnawed at his consciousness. It was a second before he saw the note

in the sand, half washed away as Rachel had feared.
But enough was left to make it excruciatingly clear.

GONE AHEAD—R.

Matthew stood and stared for a moment in rage and
desperation.

She had learned what he was up to!

Matthew cursed himself for his carelessness. That
was the only possible explanation: she must have come
up in the dark and overheard him talking to Steven
Wu.

She hadn't wanted to be left behind. She had made
that clear all along. An equal partnership was all she
would accept—and the equality had to be on *her* terms!
She had been furious with him for the way he tricked
her the afternoon before. Now she was getting even,
and then some. She had turned the tables and pulled
the same kind of trick on him, only this one could get
her killed.

Going as a lookout with the rest of them would have
been dangerous enough; trying to make her way alone
around an unfamiliar ship was the worst kind of folly.

The moment of inertia broke abruptly. Anger mingled with blinding fear as Matthew kicked aside his
boots and plunged into the water, not even bothering
to rip off his shirt. He barely took a moment to call
out to one of the Chinese, telling him to go and alert
the others. The assault on the *China Dawn* would begin immediately! Then he was swimming toward the
ship, Alex a stroke behind him all the way, though
ordinarily his cousin was a much stronger swimmer.

Steven Wu stood on the beach with Li Shu beside
him and stared after them for several seconds. He had
not failed to notice that Matthew had chosen the other
man to deliver that vitally important message. Not that
it would have mattered. Either of them would have
gone quite willingly. They were going to need one of
the sampans later themselves to make their own escape.

Still . . . it *was* interesting. Steven watched the
splashing in the water that marked their progress. The
Yankee captain seemed to have grown suspicious of Li

Shu's wide eyes and vapid grin. He was more intelligent than he appeared. It would not do to underestimate him, though fortunately that was not going to be a concern now.

He took his time slipping out of baggy clothes, leaving himself only in a snugger pair of trousers and sleeveless tunic. It would be better if the others were up the rope and out of sight by the time he arrived. How considerate of Captain Barron to instinctively select the man he could spare the most. He would want Li Shu himself for what he had in mind.

And, Steven Wu thought, as he slipped noiselessly into the water, everything was going to be so much easier now.

Rachel gasped as Gallagher jerked her up the narrow steps to the deck. One large, strong hand was like a vise around her wrists, iron-hard and impossible to break. The other hovered menacingly near the gun at his belt.

Somehow she had to get away from him. She was bitterly conscious of that, but the harder she struggled, the tighter his grip became, bringing tears of pain to her eyes. She couldn't even get her knee up to give him a sharp jab, as she had with that disgusting animal in the *hutung* in Canton.

He seemed almost to be anticipating it. Rachel struggled against the fear and despair that threatened to overwhelm her. As if he could see what she was thinking! Every time she tried to wriggle around to get herself in position, he would give her wrists an extra tug that drove everything else out of her mind.

The night wind gusted in her face as they reached the top of the steps and made their way out into the open. Only it wasn't night anymore, she realized suddenly. Dawn was almost there. If Matthew hadn't called off the attack, the sampans would be visible soon on the horizon.

Hope caught her heart, just for an instant, followed by a sudden, terrible wave of dread. The sampans would be a distraction, and the junks bearing down from the rear, but there was no telling how Gallagher would react.

The junks had made a fool of him before, Matthew had said, and he hadn't liked it. His grip was already cruel enough, despite the regrets he had expressed before about hurting a woman. What was he going to do if something made him really angry?

Rachel craned her neck, desperately searching for some trace of Matthew. Where could he be? He had to have gotten to the ship before her, but he hadn't been in Gallagher's cabin. Surely that was where he would have gone first—unless something had happened to him.

Gallagher seemed to sense what she was doing and tightened his hold, but just briefly, for a sudden commotion broke out somewhere beyond the range of their sight, startling him as much as her. Footsteps clattered sharply across the deck, and men were running and shouting—a confused medley of conflicting sounds. Then a voice sounded clearly above the general din, barking out an unmistakable order.

Rachel could not make out what was being said—the words were muffled by distance and barriers between—but she recognized Alex Barron's voice.

They had arrived! The attack was already beginning. They must have found her message in the sand and come before the boats.

The brief moment of relief she felt was short-lived. Even if they managed to subdue the resistance and make order out of the chaos on deck, Rachel thought miserably, it wouldn't do any good. Heaven help her, *nothing* would do any good as long as Gallagher still held her hostage.

She could almost picture that ugly scene. The men rushing in, Gallagher pulling out his gun and holding it to the side of her head. No one would stop him then. Not Alex or Varnay or even Moody would dare to make a move. He could have anything he wanted.

She *had* to get away! Rachel was furious with herself and even more frantic now. This was all her fault. If only she hadn't been so stupid! She had to do something, and quickly. In the panic of the moment, the only thing she could think of was the most obvious.

Looking over his shoulder, she put a startled expression on her face. "Who's there?" she cried, and heard him laugh.

"That's an old trick, girl. Not much of a one at that. An' you're not after doin' it very well."

Rachel felt herself giggling helplessly, an idiotic, nervous reaction, but it seemed to catch him off balance. She hastened impetuously to press her advantage. "He doesn't believe me," she said to that same vacant spot behind his left ear, and miraculously, this time he fell for it.

It was only for a second, but his grip loosened, and Rachel tugged her arms free. She didn't know where she was going. She only knew that she had to put space between them, and she spun urgently and began to run.

She tried to go forward. At least she thought it was forward. She had gotten all turned around in the darkness. But there was some large obstruction looming in front of her—she wished again she knew *something* about ships—and she veered around it, aiming toward the other side. Port?

Rachel could just see a section of railing through the tangle of masts and ropes, and she changed direction slightly, running blindly toward it.

She almost made it. She had always been able to keep up with her brothers, and fear lent swiftness to her feet. But her skirt was still wet, clinging and catching, and she stumbled awkwardly, losing her momentum. Gallagher caught the back of her dress—she heard it ripping as she struggled to pull free—and suddenly she was falling.

Every muscle strained and ached. She seemed to be bruised all over, but she rolled instinctively, somehow getting to her feet again. Now the rail was closer. She was almost there.

Rachel recognized the place where she had come onto the ship. Full circle, then; back where she started.

Just beside a mounted cannon, which partially obscured the rope.

If she couldn't find Alex—if none of the men were here—she would have to leap over the side into the water. A desperate move. Much too dangerous. But at least Gallagher couldn't get his hands on her there!

She made it to the railing without being caught again and managed to climb up. A quick glance back told her that Gallagher had tripped on a coil of rope—she had no idea there were so many things all over a ship's deck!—but he would recover in a second. And there was no sign of Alex or anyone else.

She *was* going to have to jump.

Rachel looked down, dizzyingly. The water seemed so far below, and she felt herself panicking again. What if she were hurt when she landed? And she was still wearing her dress. She couldn't swim like that.

But she couldn't stay where she was, either. Maybe if I catch the rope when I fall, she thought, her mind reeling frantically. Gallagher didn't know it was there. He would assume she had gone into the ocean and not come after her.

At least it was chance. A slim one, but she didn't have time to come up with anything better.

Taking a deep breath, Rachel hurtled herself over the rail and grabbed for the rope.

His timing had been perfect.

Steven Wu congratulated himself as he slipped into the waning shadows by the main mast. A whirlwind of desperation and reddish golden hair had just enveloped that same space at the railing where he had come up only seconds before. A little less luck, and he would have been embroiled in the kind of chaos he didn't need right now.

He took a quick look in the direction of the lifeboats. Everything seemed quiet. What commotion there was appeared to be centered around the bow, and even that was fading fast. The eldest of the Barron men, Alex, was proving to be unfortunately competent.

He would have four minutes, Steven judged. Maybe five. But four or five minutes would be more than enough. Raising his arm, he beckoned to Li Shu, who was hovering stealthily near the hatch.

They already knew what they were going to do. Every detail had been worked out, nothing left to chance. They advanced now in the prearranged pattern, Li Shu slipping around the forward end of the nearest boat, Steven dropping to his belly and crawling underneath toward the stern.

There were two guards, he saw as he peeked cautiously out. Good. That was what he had guessed. They looked nervous, but they were holding their ground.

Too bad, he thought—for them.

Li Shu showed himself first. The guards still hadn't seen him. He crept silently, like a cat, toward the closest one. The other guard finally spotted him, but before he could react, Steven was on his feet, blade ready, and the man's throat had been neatly cut. His companion was similarly disposed of, equally efficiently, without a sound or single excess motion, by Li Shu.

Steven did not waste time dragging the bodies out of the way or attempting to hide them. He had an unpleasant shock when he turned his attention to the rocket and found it not on deck, as Li Shu had described, but in one of the lifeboats which had been hoisted onto the davit.

His brow clouded for a moment. Apparently the Irishman had arranged a quick getaway for himself. So that little group yesterday with the fish and rotting vegetables had not been quite as convincing as they thought. Fortunately, it looked as if the early assault had thwarted Gallagher's plan. At least, Steven hoped so. What he had in mind would hardly have the same effect farther out to sea.

Still, there was no point worrying about it. Only a very stupid man expended energy on something he could not change, and Steven Wu was far from stupid.

He climbed into the jolly boat and gave the makeshift rocket a cursory examination.

It was exactly what he had expected, and he knew just what to do. Precisely four minutes after the first guard dropped to the deck, Steven was climbing out again, and he and Li Shu were diving, almost in unison, from the railing into the water.

The sampans were already approaching, a little earlier than planned. But the clouds were gone, the fading moon combined with the first faint hint of morning light, and it was clear enough to see even in the distance.

One of them drifted a little apart from the others, angling slightly out to sea, and Steven set his course for it. In a few minutes, they would be on deck. And a few minutes after that . . .

He forced his mind back to the rhythmic motion of his arms and legs, and concentrated on the current and the waves. There would be time enough to savor his victory when it came.

Rachel clung desperately to the rope and prayed that Gallagher had been fooled. She had fallen perhaps six feet before she managed to stop herself, twisting clumsily in the process, and the stout cord had coiled itself tightly around one ankle.

Like a noose, she thought grimly. But at least it helped her keep her grip, for it took some of the pressure off her hands. If only Gallagher hadn't noticed that there was no splash when she went over the railing. If only the commotion on deck was loud enough . . .

But even as she dared to hope, there was a sudden tug on the rope, and Rachel felt herself being drawn upward. He hadn't been fooled, of course. It had been the wildest gamble, and she had lost. A few seconds, and he would have her.

You have to let go! she told herself with a gasp of fright. It was the water now, or she was sure to be captured. Quickly, not giving herself time to think, she kicked her leg out, trying to work her ankle loose.

But the harder she struggled, the more it seemed to tighten.

His arms were so strong! Rachel refused to give up, but there was nothing she could do. She was flopping and fighting for all she was worth, and he just kept pulling her up.

She felt the chill of metal against her hands and knew they had struck the rail. He was already reaching for her. Rachel could see his face, wine red with rage, glowering down at her. How reluctant would he be to hurt a woman now?

One hand was on her forearm, the other clutching her shoulder. She was almost even with the railing when her eyes fell on the gun at his belt, and she reached out instinctively, grabbing for it.

Gallagher saw what she was doing, but too late. She had the gun; her finger was just finding the trigger when a massive fist closed over her hand. Rachel fought him as hard as she could, but it was no use. He was already bending her arm back. Only sheer will kept the gun in her grasp as she jerked her hand up, frantically trying to break his hold.

The sudden explosion startled her, almost deafening her ears. She had not even felt her finger squeeze the trigger. He recoiled back, grunting, and Rachel felt a searing pain jolt through her chest, as if the bullet had gone straight to her heart.

Then she saw the red stain spreading on the shoulder of Gallagher's immaculate white shirt, and she knew it had been a jolt of fear. With a cry of horror, she pitched the gun, which was now in her sole possession, into the sea.

Matthew stopped abruptly when he heard the loud report. He had just spotted Gallagher leaning over the railing, pushing—or pulling—something in the vicinity of the rope, and he had lunged forward, every instinct telling him speed was vital. Then the shot had come, and he had felt a split second of sheer terror. Like someone had kicked him in the gut.

But Gallagher was staggering back almost immediately. Matthew saw the blood on his shoulder, and his heart started beating again. The two men almost brushed against each other as the Irishman hurtled by in an effort to flee. Matthew paid no attention to him. Completely forgotten now were all the things he had been planning to say and do to his conniving partner. Gallagher didn't exist for him anymore.

All he wanted was to get to the rail and see what was hidden behind that bulky cannon. And if it was Rachel, pray God there had been only that one shot and she was all right!

His heart stopped again when he looked down and saw her. She was hanging several feet below the railing, her body twisted in a strangely unnatural position. Then he realized that her foot was caught and she was trying to work it free. He reached down and grabbed the rope, tugging with all his might. Rachel saw him, and suddenly she was helping, pulling herself up hand over hand.

All the emotions Matthew had been holding back came out in one swift rush. Relief mingled with anger and love and the most incredible frustration he had ever felt.

"Why the devil did you do it?" he called down to her. "It was insane, coming here alone!"

"I had to," she shouted back. "When I found out you were all by yourself, I couldn't just stay on shore."

"I don't know what you're talking about," he said, but it didn't matter anymore. He had her over the railing now and on the deck. The rope untangled easily from around her leg, and she was in his arms and he was holding her tight.

They were in each other's arms, holding each other. They had been so frightened in their own separate ways; they were joined now in gratitude to the kindly fate that had brought them safely together again. All they could do—all they *wanted* to do—was cling and clasp and feel the nurturing strength of their love. Matthew was aware of the sound of the davit creaking loudly and urgently on the far side of the deck, and he knew Gallagher was lowering the boat for his escape, but he didn't care.

He could have his freedom and welcome. And if he managed to carry some of his ill-gotten cash off with him, he was welcome to that, too! There was no room in Matthew Barron's heart for malice or vengeance. He had found Rachel; she was in his arms again, and he couldn't think of anything else.

She was the most maddening woman he had ever known. She drove him crazy sometimes, and he sensed she always would. There was no point imagining that she would become docile and easier to handle as the years went by. But he loved her to distraction. *Beyond* distraction. She was his wife, his joy, his very life, and he trembled, visibly and unashamedly, as he realized how close he had come to losing her.

They were a little more composed when Alex found them a few minutes later. The takeover had been accomplished smoothly. Only Romack had resisted, and then only briefly; Alex had left him tied to the foremast, with two men to stand guard. The rest of the crew had rallied immediately, relieved to have clear and consistent orders to follow again. The strange goings-on of the past few weeks had made them increasingly nervous.

"I did tell you," Matthew said, feeling almost giddy now that it was over and everything had gone so well, "that all the men had to do was see me and they'd snap to attention."

"Or me, little cousin," Alex replied with a wry twist to his mouth.

"Or maybe even Varnay." Matthew threw an amused look over the rail at the first mate, who was still flailing and splashing in the water. He was going to be mad as hell when he got there and found out that everything was over. Moody, a faster swimmer, was just reaching the top of the rope, and they sent him forward to provide Romack with a proper escort to the brig. "I run a tight Barron ship. The men are used to authority. They respect it. I knew they'd come through for me."

Alex nodded. "It looks like your pal Gallagher is getting away." He pointed toward the stern where a boat was bobbing on the water. The irrepressible Irishman didn't have much experience with oars, and his shoulder had to be giving him trouble, but he had managed to put considerable distance between himself and the *China Dawn*. "We could drop a couple of boats and try to go after him . . . ?"

Alex left the question dangling, and Matthew knew his cousin understood. He strolled toward the rear of the vessel, slowly, Rachel clinging a little to his arm, but remarkably recovered after her ordeal. Gallagher was still close enough to be clearly visible. He had apparently spotted them, for he was putting the oars aside and standing up.

"No, let him go," Matthew said. "Lord knows he's a scoundrel. The world would be better off if he were locked up forever. But I've grown rather fond of him."

Almost as if he heard, Gallagher raised his arm, halfway between a salute and an obscene gesture. So exactly like him, Matthew thought, and tried without success to be annoyed. Thumbing his nose at the very fate that had just defeated him.

He started to lift his own arm, offering back what he had just received, when he saw to his surprise that Gallagher had struck a light. A bright yellow glint seemed to reflect the rising sun, and Matthew noticed for the first time the cumbersome object in the boat with him. The thing that Li Shu had described, which looked like a Congreve rocket.

Alex had also spotted it. "The damned fool! What does he think he's doing?"

But that was exactly like Gallagher, too. Matthew felt a grudging admiration, even through his mounting horror. No slithering off into the shadows for him, like a beaten cur with his tail between his legs. He was going to send back one last flare of defiance!

Matthew could almost see the thoughts spinning around in Gallagher's head. If it hit the ship, fine. That would be something to remember. If it didn't, at least for one brief moment it would rival the sun.

He tightened his arm around Rachel, holding her closer. There was no point trying to run. Rockets were notoriously inaccurate, even when they had been made by professionals. It was impossible to guess where this one would hit, or even if it would. One place was as good as another.

He heard Rachel gasp as Gallagher tossed the light in a graceful arc into the tub, and he knew she had figured out what he was up to. Nothing happened for an instant. They could only stand there and watch, not even knowing what to pray for. Then, suddenly, there was a loud burst of sound, and a solid sheet of flame blazed up straight into the air. A second later, the small boat was engulfed.

None of them said a word. They just stared as the fire surged again, briefly and dramatically, then slowly died down. Matthew thought for a moment that Gallagher might have been thrown free by the explosion. But flames were spreading over the water, as if there had been oil on the boat, and it occurred to him that it would not be a kindness to hope he was still alive. Only a very strong swimmer could possibly survive something like that. And Christy Gallagher hated the water.

One last burst of flame shot up abruptly. Bold, as Gallagher had always been. Defiant, even in death, and determined to have the last jest.

"My God," Matthew said. It was not blasphemy.

Steven Wu watched expressionlessly from the deck of the sampan as the fire burned and disintegrated into black ashes floating on the water.

Too bad, he thought. It would have been so much more effective it if had occurred on the *China Dawn*. Now *that* would have been a blaze.

Well . . . never mind. He turned back toward the tall, proud masts, standing out against the lush green velvet of the hillside behind them. There would be another time. Another chance.

We will meet again, Captain Matthew Barron, he

vowed silently to himself. Sometime. Someplace. And you will not always come out ahead.

Things settled down within the hour. Alex Barron took a quick tour around the deck and was relieved to find no serious damage, though there was much to be done. Gallagher had not kept up the rigid discipline, and conditions had disintegrated disgracefully. The men were already grumbling about all the holystoning and brass polishing that would be expected of them, but Alex sensed they were secretly embarrassed at the way the ship looked and anxious to be getting back to honest work.

He had not recognized the two dead men who had been found on the starboard side near the boat davit. Obviously part of the crew Gallagher had signed on, though how and why they had been killed would probably always be a mystery. Of the three remaining men loyal to Gallagher, two had leaped overboard, one apparently making it to shore, though it looked as if the other had drowned.

The third had stayed on board, deciding to brazen it out. He had had no idea what was going on, he claimed. He had been as amazed as anyone to discover they had been pirated. And because he had seen which way the wind was going early on and had given up without a fight, Alex sensed he would get away with it.

At least Romack was in the brig. Alex took a certain satisfaction in that as he went down the short flight of steps to the passenger cabin in search of some help for his wardrobe. No one on board was as tall—he would have to let his pants dry on him in the sunlight—but there was no point suffering in a soggy shirt. Poor Damian Varnay, he thought. He had been bitterly disappointed when he had finally made his way up the rope and found the second mate already subdued and being led away.

And just as well, Alex thought, as he reached the door to the small outer salon. He had no fondness for

Romack, heaven knows, but another corpse would have been difficult to explain.

He was surprised to step inside and see the open drawers with their colorful array of gold-edged silk which he recognized as Indian saris. He had not been aware that Gallagher had a woman, and he wondered if Matthew knew her. She would have to be located, he supposed, and told.

He felt suddenly very tired. Whoever she was, Gallagher's woman, he hoped she hadn't cared that much. Love was hard enough under the best of circumstances. Love and loss could be unendurable.

Alex found a shirt in one of the drawers, and peeling off his own, put it on. It was not a perfect fit, but Gallagher's shoulders had been broad enough, and at least he didn't feel cramped.

Matthew and Rachel. . . . His thoughts drifted to his cousin and the slim young woman who had managed to look winsome even with red-gold hair plastered wet against her head. They would be fine now. Jared and Dominie, too. For all that initial alarm, Alex was sure she was all right and they would be happily reunited soon.

Two Barron bachelors, safe on the tempestuous shores of love. And with the redheaded women who had always been the family weakness.

It didn't have to turn out badly, as it had for his grandfather all those years ago. Alex found himself wondering if the old tyrant ever thought about her now, the legendary Dawn, and if he missed her still. He had not failed to catch the subtle cruelty in christening all the Barron ships after the false-hearted Jezebel who had gotten away. But he couldn't have hated her so much, if the love and hurt weren't somewhere still within him. Even years of a good and probably passionate marriage hadn't completely washed it away.

She had been his first love, and a man did not forget his first love. At least not a Barron man.

That seemed a family weakness, too. Alex finished buttoning the shirt and tucked it into his still-damp trousers. Loving once and for always—and at first sight. Matthew spotting Rachel across a sea of other faces in a festive garden. Jared and Dominie on the decks of adjacent ships in the harbor at Ceylon. And he . . .

Alex tried not to remember, but trying only made it all the clearer. Red hair and meltingly soft blue eyes. So hard to forget. Sweetly rounded, very sensual, treacherous, lying lips. Why was it that the dreams and the longing always seemed to come back, and not the ugly way it had soured in the end? *If you could have anything you chose. . . . If Barron Shipping were to offer you the one thing you really wanted, what would it be?*

Alex stepped over to the narrow window and glanced out. The sun was up, but it was still low in the sky, and a golden shimmer glistened across the water. Out, he had said, and he had meant it. But he sensed now, as he had then, that "out" was something he would never have.

It seemed the ultimate irony. The one Barron who least enjoyed being a bachelor was the one who was likely to remain so to the end of his days. And the one with the least feeling for the sea was the one who would never leave it.

He caught himself and smiled unconsciously. What a morbid picture he was painting. He was just tired—he had been up all night—and perhaps, though it was not usually part of his makeup, just a little jealous at the happiness his cousins had found. There were worse things than being the captain of your own ship and having a wealthy family behind you.

He closed the drawers with their sad assortment of prettily hued silk and went back up on deck to begin putting the *China Dawn* in order.

Rachel and Matthew remained for some time alone in the captain's cabin. The questions had all been asked, explanations made as they had changed into dry clothes, Rachel in man-tailored trousers and shirt again, and huddled together, both shivering now, on the narrow bunk. All the coincidences and misunderstandings had been sorted out. The jacket on the beach—Matthew still couldn't figure out how it had gotten there. The cufflink, which it had never occurred to him to mention he had lost. The footprints leading to the water's edge.

This time it was Rachel who comforted her husband. She held him in her arms, not speaking, not even wanting to make love, simply knowing that he needed to feel her closeness and support. He was blaming himself, wrongly but inevitably, for the awful tragedy that had occurred. Wishing somehow he could go back and relive these last days and weeks. Futile, but understandable, and Rachel cradled him wordlessly closer.

It was that first night in Canton all over again, only in reverse, after the horrible carnage of that voyage up the river past the ravaged Bogue forts. She had needed him then, desperately. Now he needed her.

She would not let him down, as she hoped she never would. The strength of a marriage was based on the strength a man and woman drew from each other.

"It was Gallagher's own fault, you know," she said after a while. "He pirated the *China Dawn*. He had to have known it could be dangerous. He brought that makeshift rocket on board—and he chose to set a light to it. He has only himself to blame."

"True." Matthew leaned back against the wall of the bunk, looking wearier than Rachel had ever seen him. "In a way. He did take the ship, and he was responsible for the rocket. . . . But all the blame can't be laid solely on his shoulders. This started when I decided to pick up some opium in Calcutta—to make a profit and prove to my big brother how bold and clever I was!"

"And it was Gallagher who persuaded you to purchase it," Rachel reminded him.

"Granted, but every man has to be accountable for his own actions, regardless of who put the idea in his head. I started the chain of events that led to a man's death this morning. There's no getting around that. If

I hadn't been so intent on my own selfish ends, none of this would have happened.''

"And if I hadn't been so naive, Steven Wu wouldn't have threatened to burn down half of Canton to destroy a few chests of opium. Do you remember what you said when I told you that? You said, if it hadn't been *that* opium, Steven would have found some other supply. Or another way to carry out his evil schemes.''

"And so he would,'' Matthew replied. It occurred to him, irrelevantly, that he hadn't seen the young Chinese since he'd left him behind on the shore. No doubt the quick recovery of the *China Dawn* had thwarted whatever plot he'd had in mind. "A man with evil in his heart is not a man who lets go so easily.''

"Or a man bent on larceny,'' Rachel said. "Gallagher would have found some other opium, too. Or another unscrupulous way to make a dollar. I daresay, the end would have been much the same. He died quickly, Matthew. And probably with little pain. The people who got the opium he managed to distribute will not find their deaths quite so easy.''

Matthew glanced over at the window. Sunlight was spilling in, a warm, welcome sight, and Rachel sensed that the terrible vision of flames on the water was finally fading from his eyes. It would haunt his dreams for some time, as the charred and battered forts on the river haunted hers. But it would ease slowly into a less painful part of his memory.

"It was the death Gallagher would have chosen,'' he admitted. "Swift and spectacular. How he would have loved to be there, watching us all stand around with big eyes and open, gaping mouths.''

"Perhaps he was,'' Rachel said softly. Her heart ached at the stoic acceptance she saw in his face. Why was it that men always felt they had to be brave and never cry, even when tears would help them heal? They were so much more fragile than women, who allowed themselves the solace of their emotions, bending more easily so they would not break.

She would have to take care of him, Rachel thought. They had both made terrible mistakes; they had both learned the hard way, and both had been hurt, but his were the wounds that cut deepest. She would have to soothe and pamper him, let him know he was loved and needed, so he would feel whole and strong again.

But right now, being a man, what he needed most was a sense of purpose and self-importance.

"Don't you have a ship to run, Captain?" she teased.

He turned back to her, looking faintly surprised, and more like himself than he had for days.

"By God," he said, "I believe I do!"

Twenty-two

It was dawn when they sailed into Hong Kong harbor, not on a humble lorcha this time, but on the mighty flagship of the Barron fleet. Rachel, standing beside Matthew at the wheel, could not help recalling their last entrance into that broad, sheltered bay. The sun had been setting then, darkness closing in, and a sound of music drifted down the hillside.

From dusk to morning. . . . It seemed to Rachel an especially appropriate passage. A symbol of the dark night through which they had come safely to a perfect dawn, the beginning of the rest of their lives together.

The sun was barely peeking over the horizon; streaks of color lit up the clouds and splashed boldly across the sky: deep rich red, like the veins of brightness that occurred sometimes in rare old pieces of jade, exquisite and breathtakingly pure. The water was still, highlighted with glittering reflections, a natural mirror catching the beauty of the heavens and holding it on earth.

"Jade dawn," she said softly. "That would make a good name for a ship. Especially in the China trade. I think I shall always remember this morning. When everything was new, and the whole world still lay ahead of us."

"The *Jade Dawn* it is," Matthew agreed. "The next Barron clipper to be christened will carry that name. But I have to warn you—one day it will turn into a tired old tub, and you may be sorry."

"I shall never be sorry for anything that reminds me of this morning." Her eyes were bright as she looked back at him. "We really can be happy now, can't we? For always."

"That's what I was rather hoping, love," Matthew teased, and turned his attention to the wheel as the *China Dawn* glided gracefully and haughtily into the newly constructed pier.

The colony of Hong Kong had grown even in the short time they had been away. It would continue to spread out and up, along the coast and high into the hills, but the central city had already been built and was occupied. Warehouses lined the shore near the docks, offices and shops and taverns were humming with activity, and a pair of newly opened hotels vied with each other for business. And were doing quite well, for newcomers arrived every day and space was at a premium.

They were surprised to discover that Jared, for all his frantic concern over his fiancée, had given a moment's thought to their comfort, and a pair of suites had been reserved in the Barron name. Alex had declined his, preferring to stay on board, which turned out to be just as well, for there were several small incidents. Nothing serious, but they might have been if he hadn't kept a close eye on the ship. The war continued to drag on, though the outcome was painfully apparent, and traders' vessels, especially those that had carried opium, frequently found themselves the target of petty violence and retribution.

But Matthew and Rachel, who were still on their honeymoon, settled gracefully into an unexpectedly well-appointed suite. Hong Kong might be new, but it was setting out to show the world that it was ready to compete on a grand scale. It was going to be an exhilarating place to live, and while Rachel knew she would miss the graceful esplanades and stately old buildings of Macao, she was looking forward to returning and making a home there.

The last loose ends of their adventure were quickly tied up. The opium that still remained on board, a surprising amount—Gallagher had not been quite so good at smuggling as he had expected—had been disposed of, and Romack turned over to the authorities. Matthew had declined to press charges of piracy, so he would not hang, as he doubtless deserved, but he would be spending a good long time as a guest of the Queen in less than sumptuous quarters.

Steven Wu, it seemed, had disappeared, but there was talk of a particularly violent *tong* in the vicinity of Canton with a reckless and fiery new leader who was already making quite a reputation for himself.

There was just one last, sad bit of business to be attended to, and Matthew and Alex went together to call on Gallagher's woman and inform her of his death. She took it well, they said afterwards. Her eyes had blazed with the most horrible anguish they had ever seen, but she had not wept or bemoaned her fate. Or even seemed truly surprised.

It was almost as if she had expected the news. Perhaps she had simply dreaded it for so long, it was actually a relief when it came. But she was pregnant and practically penniless—as a note that had been slyly left for Matthew took pains to explain—and the two men had decided together it would not be feasible to leave her alone. The Reverend Gideon Todd's charity and Christian tolerance were about to be put to the test again.

Rachel agreed wholeheartedly when Matthew came back and put the suggestion to her. She loathed what Gallagher had done, but her heart was too generous to blame his mistress for it. She would not have felt good sailing off and leaving her behind friendless. At least at the mission, the woman would have a chance to build a decent life for herself and her child.

Camilla came to say goodbye on their last afternoon, her arms full of flowers, as they so often were when she was looking for an especially romantic gesture. Rachel couldn't help remembering that dawn she had shown up at the China Gate after a most eventful evening—how different things would be now if Matthew had been just a little weaker—and she knew Cammie had to be thinking about it, too.

''I *did* tell you,'' Camilla quipped, ''that he was a

very nice man. I expect you've finally discovered that. I wonder why it took you so long to believe me.''

''There are some things,'' Rachel replied, ''one has to learn for oneself. And I do think he's a little more than 'nice,' Cammie.''

''I said he was handsome as well.'' Camilla's eyes danced with merriment. ''And *extremely* dashing. I do want you to be happy, Rachel. I don't say it very often. It always seems so embarrassing to be *sincere*. But you are my best friend, and I love you very much.''

Rachel was touched, and illogically saddened. ''Perhaps you should try matrimony yourself. The suitors your uncle keeps finding for you aren't *all* bad.''

''Actually, I proposed to Captain Rawlings.'' Camilla's face puckered in the impish way that always made onlookers wonder if she was making up another of her fabulous stories. ''But he, clever man, had the good sense to turn me down. And really, I don't think I *want* to be married in Hong Kong. It's going to be exciting, living here. The house in Happy Valley is finished, you know. We move in day after tomorrow.''

''Your uncle doesn't still consider it a stinking, fever-ridden swamp?'' Matthew put in. ''Unfit for human habitation?''

''Of *course* he does. Once Uncle Robert makes up his mind, it's made up forever. But his business is here, and besides, he knows I *adore* it. He blusters a lot, poor dear, but he really hasn't learned properly how to say no.''

They were still laughing after she left, but gently. She had come like a maelstrom of color and motion in one of her more astonishing gowns, and departed in much the same way.

''Do you suppose she really proposed to Aaron Rawlings?'' Matthew asked.

''Who knows,'' Rachel replied with a bemused look. ''Probably. . . . But she probably didn't mean it.''

''It might not be such a bad thing,'' he ventured.

"Not Rawlings. I can't see him settling down. But if she had *someone* who could handle her . . ."

"Unfortunately, Cammie's always had a preference for Barron men . . . and now two of you are taken. Maybe we should match her up with Alex."

"Lord, Rachel!" Matthew stared at her. Even for a joke that was going too far. "She has a better heart than you'd imagine, and I do truly admire her spirit. But I can't picture her with my cousin."

"I know. Alex is so—proper. It's impossible to imagine Cammie with a proper man." She wandered over to a table by the window and stared down at bits and pieces Matthew had emptied from his pocket the night before. "It was really hard saying goodbye to her. I don't know why. It's only for a little while."

"Three or four months," he promised her. "Maybe five. Think of all the gossip you'll have to catch up on when you get back. And Cammie will have every last little bit of it."

"I'm sure she will." Rachel tried to smile, but she was feeling strangely sad again. "It's just . . . I almost felt like I was saying goodbye to her for the last time. As if I'd never see her again. I suppose it's because so many things in my life are changing. Everything keeps getting left behind, and we'll be so far away."

Matthew was watching her closely, his expression troubled, and Rachel regretted the moment of foolishness that had already nearly passed. "We don't have to go, tiger," he said. "It's not important. Alex can deliver the *China Dawn* to Lahaina as well as I."

"Of course it's important!" she replied indignantly. "This is the last time you'll ever sail your own ship as captain. How can you say that's not important? And it might be years before you see your brother again. Besides, you forget, I used to live in the Hawaiian Islands. I have friends there. I wonder if Polly will even recognize me."

"Polly?" It was a name Matthew had not heard before, and he was a little surprised to realize that there was still much he didn't know about this woman he had married. "I don't think you've ever mentioned anyone named Polly."

"Maria, actually. They called her Polly when she was a little girl. Maria McClintock. She used to be my best friend, though I'm not sure I was hers. She was five years older and had the most glorious red hair I've ever seen. What a terrible nuisance I must have been, tagging after her all the time!"

"A redhead, eh?" Matthew raised a wicked brow. 'Maybe we should match Alex up with *her.* You do know about the Barron men and redheaded ladies."

Rachel laughed. "I do indeed." Her eye picked out the wooden gaming piece among the other objects on the table, and she found herself recalling quite vividly how it had all begun between them. "But I don't think this would be the appropriate redhead. She was married several years ago to a handsome, very wealthy man. Somehow that doesn't seem Alex's style."

"No," Matthew agreed. "If there's one thing on this earth I'm sure of, it's that my cousin would never have anything to do with a married woman. *I,* on the other hand, have been known on occasion . . ."

His eyes slid rakishly down her body, lingering here and there with deliberate emphasis, leaving no doubt as to which particular married woman he had in mind. Rachel thought how fortunate it was that she happened to be wearing the same white dress she had had on that first afternoon. With the same lacy fichu tucked into her neck.

She closed her fingers around the gaming piece and picked it up.

"You played a most unfair trick on me," she said, her voice light but provocative as she flipped it over, pointedly, on her palm. "I think it's my turn now. Shall we make a little wager?"

"A kiss against another donation to your father's mission? I'm afraid I'm a little low on funds right now. That fiasco with the opium was expensive."

"It wasn't cash I had in mind." Rachel's eyes sparkled with teasing challenge. "I thought we might make it a little more, uh . . . *interesting.*" She twisted the wooden circlet coyly between her thumb and middle finger. "Besides, I never make the same wager twice. You, of course, are free to demand a kiss . . . if you win."

Matthew laughed, very softly, enjoying the game. Her lips puckered almost unconsciously when she mentioned the kiss, and he knew she was remembering every sensuous detail of that other, most pleasurable occasion. He hoped she had something similar in mind now, though she was capable of toying with him quite mercilessly. As he had toyed with her, in truth, at that first meeting.

"I think there's no point demanding anything," he said, "since we both know I'm not going to win. The coin is in your control. The outcome is hardly in doubt."

"But it wasn't in doubt that other time. You were absolutely certain what was going to happen." Her tongue darted across her lips, an invitation not quite offered. Matthew ached to hold and caress her. And she knew it, the minx! "The kiss was definitely yours, but you tossed the coin anyway . . . and made me play my part. Now it's you who must play."

"And what shall I wager?" he asked, knowing already what he wanted and thinking, perhaps, after he lost, he might still be able to persuade her.

"Whatever you wish. . . . Just don't tell me. And I won't tell you what I've selected. It will be a surprise." She smiled, a strangely secretive look. "Assuming, of course, I win. Do you have your bet?"

"I have," Matthew said, and thought how desirable she was at that moment and how much he would like to have been holding the two-sectioned piece in his own hand. He would give her whatever she wanted, and gladly. Plainly she had something sly up her sleeve, and no doubt he deserved it. She'd waited long enough to pay him back for this. But the way she looked in simple white, that frothy thing fondling her bosom, as he longed to do . . . "Toss the coin," he said.

"Call it."

Matthew shrugged. "Tails. Why not?"

Looking down at the carved bit of wood in her hand, Rachel made no effort to be subtle as she worked the two sides apart and examined them intently. "Heads for me, then," she said, and flipped one piece in the air.

It landed with a soft thud on the carpet. Matthew stared in faint surprise at the clearly visible curve of a dragon's tail.

"That's not the way it's supposed to work, tiger. You're supposed to pick the section of the coin that *you* bet on."

"I know," she said softly, "but I had a feeling I'd like your wager more."

Her lips parted, an invitation at last, and Matthew found himself remembering how defiant she had looked that earlier afternoon. And frightened. Unable to admit even to herself the intensity of her desire for him.

"I have a feeling you will, too. . . . " His hands were gentle as he laid them on her shoulders, drawing her closer. "What do you think it will be?"

Rachel felt the passion beneath his tenderness. Just like that first time, she thought, and she could almost feel his mouth on hers again, his fingers pulling the fichu away, shocking and exciting her breasts.

"The same kiss as before?"

"No," Matthew said, struggling to keep his passion under control and barely succeeding. "I want what would have happened *after* that kiss. If I hadn't been so blasted scrupulous."

"Ah . . . I thought that might be it."

He was touching the side of her face, exactly as he had that other afternoon, and Rachel shivered with delight. Her eyes closed, but not to mask her emotions this time. To hold them hungrily, tantalizing inside.

She had forgotten how soft his mouth had felt, how sweet and compelling, and just for a second, it was their first kiss again, and he had never touched her before.

Rachel's own mouth was responding, the same in-

stincts now as then, and she was longing for him. Her
body seemed to melt into the hard, provocative
strength of his. Matthew, feeling her urgency, did not
hold back. His tongue turned bold, a challenge and a
torment both as he thrust it demandingly into her. His
hands had found her breasts at last, and he was claiming them roughly, ravishingly.

Only this time he would not pull away. This time
there would be no stopping what had begun so many
months ago. Rachel felt him lifting her into his arms,
felt him carrying her to the couch, too eager even to
take the few extra steps into the bedroom, and she
knew that destiny had finally brought them full circle.
From the dawn of that first desire through all the trials
and misunderstandings to the complete fulfillment of
a love that would last the rest of their lives.

Then he was entering her, and she forgot everything
else but the sheer joy of being with him again.

Twenty-three

The newly christened *Jade Dawn* glided majestically out of Hong Kong harbor, silhouetted against the splendor of a rising sun. Rachel, standing at the rail with a shawl around her shoulders against the early morning chill, smiled as she thought about how surprised she had been the night before when they had boarded the *China* by lanternlight and she had looked up and seen a new name painted on the hull.

"I wanted to call her the *Tiger Dawn*," Matthew had explained. "But I wasn't sure you'd appreciate having a ship named after you."

Rachel had laughed, not ungratefully. The way the Barrons felt about their fleet, she knew it was the highest compliment. But sleek though the most extravagant of the *Dawns* may have been, a ship was nonetheless an extremely bulky object. She wasn't at all sure she'd enjoy the comparison as the years passed and they both became "old tubs."

"I like this much better," she had assured him. "Now the ship is named for both of us. For the special dawn that brought such hope and beauty and reminded us how lucky we were to be alive and have each other."

"And for all the dawns to come," he had promised her, teasing, but with deep affection in his tone. "May every one be more beautiful than the last."

Rachel smiled again, thinking back on the moment. The wind was strong and surging. Her hair had long since come loose from its pins and was blowing back from her face; the rigging flapped and groaned noisily overhead. Just for a second, the power and excitement,

the sheer force of the weather and the sails, gave her
a glimpse of the passion that men felt sometimes for
the sea.

"Are you sure your grandfather isn't going to object?" she said to Matthew who had lingered at the
rail beside her to watch the city disappear from view.
"When he finds out you've renamed his prize vessel?"

"I'm sure he *is*. Grandfather likes things to stay the
way they are. Anything new or different makes him
exceedingly uncomfortable, but he did authorize Jared
to take charge here. And Jared did tell me to do whatever I wanted."

Rachel caught a glint of humor in his eyes. "You
don't think Jared will be surprised when he sees the
Jade Dawn sailing into port at Lahaina?"

"I think Jared will be much too involved with the
lovely Dominie to even wonder about it. Or care. I
had the hold swabbed down. The smell of opium is
gone, but there's still a taint in the name. She's a good
ship. She deserves a new beginning."

"A dawn for her, as well," Rachel said softly.
"How very appropriate. I do agree."

Her eyes drifted back toward the shore, which was
already evaporating into the last glowing reflection of
sunrise. She had only been on the open sea once, when
she was a little girl. She had not realized how swiftly
a ship could sail, and she felt a little pang as everything she had known and loved most of her life faded
from sight.

Matthew slipped an arm around her waist. "No regrets, love? It isn't too late to turn back. It would only
cost a day, and Alex can deliver the ship to Lahaina."

"No regrets," she insisted, lying, but only partly.
"I was just thinking how beautiful it is, the outline of
the buildings against the sky. Hong Kong is going to
be one of the great cities of the world someday. But I
can wait a while to see it again, and I really am looking forward to our time on Maui." She paused, glancing over at him, his silhouette strong against the clear
blue of the morning sky, and she remembered again

that he was, above all, a Barron. "And you?" she asked quietly. "What about you?"

They began strolling along the rail toward the bow of the ship, taking their time. Matthew was officially captain, but he and his cousin were sharing the actual duties, and Alex was at the wheel now.

"I always look forward to Hawaii," Matthew started to say, but she cut him off.

"I didn't mean that. I meant, do you have any regrets? Forsaking the sea? Your home in Boston? Hong Kong isn't that different for me, but it will be a drastic change for you. Will you look back, I wonder, and regret what you've given up?"

She was relieved to hear him laugh, softly but very definitely. "I thrive on change, tiger. Haven't you figured that out yet? The whole world is changing, and I *want* to change with it. Trade is the business of the future. Countries are opening up, goods moving back and forth, especially in the Orient. If Barron Shipping is truly going to be Barron International, we have to meet the challenge boldly. And there's nothing I like better than a challenge."

The corners of Rachel's mouth turned up faintly, "Perhaps . . . that's why you married me?"

"Perhaps," he agreed, and they leaned against the railing, looking not back or forward, but at each other. They were both recalling an afternoon in a crowded garden, and the wondrous, complex tangle of emotion and events that had begun most unpromisingly with a glass of champagne.

Still, Rachel thought happily, it was just as well they hadn't served red wine!

Alex, at the helm, turned his head for a moment to watch them. The sun was bright on Matthew's fair hair, the golden-red warmth of Rachel's, and he smiled a little at the love he saw in their faces as they gazed at each other. It was a fine day; the wind was brisk, the air was balmy, and it felt good to be alive.

He turned the wheel, angling slightly south. Around

Formosa, just ahead, then north toward the islands that made up the kingdom of Hawaii.

Perhaps, after all, Matthew had been right. Alex squinted into the glare of the light on the water. He had been tired that morning they had retaken the ship, and unusually discouraged. But a man owed it to himself to pursue his dreams, and with both his cousins proving so capable, Barron Shipping—Barron *International*—did not need him any more.

He might just find an island someplace and stake out a bit of land, where his heart would be happy and his soul could find some peace.

Not Hawaii, of course. His jaw tightened unconsciously at the thought of the brief sojourn he had been dreading in Lahaina. But another island, another potential paradise, drenched in the tropical sun, cooled by the breezes of the Pacific. There he could find a good, gentle, loving woman and give up the nomadic ways of the sea at last.

A woman with black hair and lustrous jet-black eyes. Alex laughed aloud at the thought. That was what his problem was! He kept trying to live up to the famous Barron reputation for becoming enamored of fiery redheads. He had forgotten that he had as much of his mother's blood in his veins as his father's.

Good, rich earth—that was what he needed. A warm climate, a home he could call his own, and a pure-hearted woman to bring stability and serenity into his life.

He looked back at Matthew and Rachel, holding hands now, utterly oblivious to anything else in the world. Jared and Dominie, too, would be together by now, looking excitedly toward the future. A future with all sorts of possibilities opening up.

It was a new era for the Barron men. And, his optimism returned, Alex Barron was eager to be a part of it.

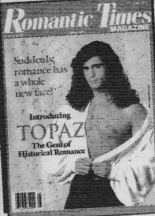